CORPSE WHISPERER
THE SERIES

H.R. BOLDWOOD

OLIVERHEBERBOOKS

Cover art by Dar Albert at Wicked Smart Designs

Published by Oliver-Heber Books

This title was previously published.

0 9 8 7 6 5 4 3 2 1

PRAISE FOR H.R. BOLDWOOD

"Anita Blake and October Daye, scoot over to make room for Allie Nighthawk, the fiercest and funniest heroine to hit the streets since Buffy first quipped while laying the undead to rest. *The Corpse Whisperer* is smart, witty, and so much fun you may just start it again as soon as you finish it."

— LISA MORTON, SIX-TIME BRAM STOKER
AWARD-WINNING AUTHOR AND CO-EDITOR
OF HAUNTED NIGHTS

"If Anita Blake and Stephanie Plum had a lovechild, it would be Allie Nighthawk. One of the funniest and freshest takes on the zombie genre I've read, with genuine heart at the core of the humor and gore."

— DANA FREDSTI, AUTHOR OF THE *SPAWN
OF LILITH* SERIES

"If you like flawed heroes, badass female characters, and biting prose (pun intended), get yourself some Allie Nighthawk."

— TOM DEADY, BRAM STOKER AWARD-
WINNING AUTHOR

CONTENTS

DISCLAIMER

This work of fiction includes information about Cincinnati's historic subway and brewing tunnels. While these magnificent tunnels exist, the author has taken literary license in regard to their location and size. Additionally, Cincinnati's *Flying Pig Marathon* is held annually on the first Sunday in May. However, in 2021, the race was held on Halloween due to the pandemic.

DEDICATION

This book is affectionately dedicated to Lisa Morton, friend and mentor. Without her unfailing support and encouragement The Corpse Whisperer series would not exist. Thanks for believing in me and cheering me on.

It's also dedicated to Joseph Daniel Back, my spouse, whose eagle-eye and tireless logic reign in my ridiculously right-sided brain when it wanders off. Thanks for understanding and for reading these chapters so many times you could probably recite them by heart.

Last, but not least, it's dedicated to the memory of two of Allie Nighthawk's biggest fans: Rick Burdick, who faithfully served as my law enforcement and weaponry expert, and Barbara Kuroff, a wonderfully gifted writer and delightful friend. I wish both of you were here to read the rest of the series as it unfolds. But I know you're up there smiling.

1

STOP THE WORLD

Just after sunrise, I jumped on my Harley and hurtled toward Templeman's Funeral Home, packing Hawk, my custom 9mm, a backup Glock, and a seven-inch Ka-Bar knife—the standard-issue zombie-hunter's tool kit.

Not that I'm standard-issue, by any stretch. I was born with the ability to raise the dead. It's a genetic thing. Don't ask me how it works. I didn't write the playbook. I'm just living the dream. But I'm living it in a world we humans share with zombies and the Z-virus. From one day to the next, I get paid for raising 'em up, or putting 'em down. On a good day, both.

According to dispatch, this morning's target was a newly turned rotter, more commonly known as a freshie—dangerous, quick, and totally unpredictable. I got to wondering, as I tore across the highway, what the world would be like if I weren't here to save it.

Not just any old schmo can do this job.

Exterminating the undead takes a steady hand, nerves of steel and a cast iron stomach. It also helps to be an emotionally stunted badass. At least, it helps me, anyway.

The one thing zombie hunting is not, is rocket science. Think simplified. Think Wile E. Coyote.

Step One: Lure deadhead.

Step Two: Drop deadhead.

What happens in-between is highly fluid from one case to the next, so strategizing ahead of time never works. I prefer the balls-to-the-wall, go-with-the-flow methodology. And any zombie hunter worth her salt knows that the best way to lure a freshie is with a bag of Doritos, like the one I'd tucked inside my duster before I left my house.

Newbie biters will eat anything from tar paper to aluminum siding, but they'll chew off their own body parts if they're fried in vegetable oil. Supposedly, grease stimulates their appetite for flesh.

Cheesy, delicious Doritos never missed the mark.

I pulled into Templeman's lot and parked around back, beneath the covered portico where caskets are loaded into the hearse. I shut down the lowrider and listened. No screams. That was either a very good sign or a very, very bad sign.

A quick walk around the building yielded nothing, so I circled back to the main entrance. When I reached for the doorknob, some not-so-pleasant memories of my last visit to Templeman's clawed to the surface. It wasn't so much a visit, as a B&E. And that was just the icing on the rotter cake.

I pushed the memories aside with a wince, and thought of something I'd picked up not long ago from a task force psychologist:

According to Barbara 'Psycho Babs' McMillen: "Bad memories are often tainted with exaggeration. If a person revisits an event factually, they'll usually find its reality far less distressing."

So I followed her advice, closed my eyes, and put her theory to the test.

Nope. That entire night was still as ugly as a three-dollar whore.

What the hell did Babs know, anyway?

But, I reasoned, as I entered the funeral home, at least, nobody had died that night—nobody that wasn't already supposed to be dead, anyway. And besides, that cringe-worthy episode had happened many months ago. Surely, the old fart who owned the joint would have forgiven me by now, or better yet, forgotten all about it.

———

"Mr. Templeman?" I called, easing into the foyer. "Mr. Templeman, it's Allie Nighthawk."

His voice echoed from the hallway ahead. "What are you doing here? I called the police."

"The police sent me. They tell me you've got a zombie problem."

Sounds of mayhem drifted out from deeper in the building.

"You're not allowed in here," he shouted, as he reached the foyer. "I have a restraining order against you."

"Mr. Templeman, that was a simple misundersta—"

"You broke in here in the middle of the night and raised a corpse!"

Damn it. "Well...I...I put it down when I was finished with it."

"For that, you want a cookie?"

"How about we table this topic for now, so I can solve your problem?"

"Ah, why not? No one else is lining up for the job."

I followed Templeman as he waddled back down the hall, tossing his hands in the air. "What is it with you and these... these...abominations?"

Something crashed against a door marked Prep Room.

"I locked it in there," he whispered. "That *thing's* wrecking the place. It's unnatural, I tell you. Unnatural."

"What happened?"

"A body came in. Like any other body that ends up here. I was about to start working on it, when it sprung off the table and came after me! I thought someone was playing a nasty trick at first. But that...that thing snapped its teeth and growled, like it wanted to eat me!"

"Did you see any bite wounds or injection sites on its skin?"

"Like I got close enough to look? I shoved the thing over the mortuary table, then ran out into the hallway, and locked the door behind me." His face blazed magenta. "*Oy gevalt!* There are other bodies in there—paying customers."

I closed my eyes and groaned. "Are they out in the open or in the cold storage unit?"

"Two, out on the floor. On adjacent tables."

Crap on a cracker. Why is it every time I get a call from Doc Blanchard's morgue or some podunk funeral home, there are always other bodies lying around? Give me a break. How many people have to die at the same time?

The truth is, you break a few eggs in the business of zombie hunting. And by breaking eggs, I mean scrambling gray matter. That's just the way it is. With all the damn bodies lying around, I'm forever having to worry about cross-contamination. But that's where my job ends. I only handle the extermination process. I don't do windows. I don't do bathrooms. And I don't do brain pulp clean-up in aisle three.

I took the old man by the arm, led him back through the foyer and opened the front door. "Why don't you go across the street to the Sunoco and wait for me there? I'll come get you when I'm finished."

"And leave you alone in *my* funeral parlor? The only reason you aren't in jail is because your partner talked me out of filing charges, you weirdo!"

4

"Have it your way," I said, stepping across the threshold and out onto the sidewalk. "I'll wait here while you call 911 again."

The prep room door exploded off its hinges and thundered to the hardwood floor.

"Change your mind yet, Mr. T?"

The crabby old coot screamed and flew past me like he had a rocket strapped to his ass.

"Hey," I hollered. "What's this corpse's name?"

"Paul Messmer. He was released by the ME's office. Heart attack at work, no autopsy. COD confirmed by the attending."

I pulled Hawk, stepped back inside, then closed the door and locked it behind me. A small, blender-like appliance sailed out of the prep room and smashed against the hallway wall, bursting into pieces. I mentally reassembled the pile of rubble into an embalming machine.

"Mr. Messmer?" I called, from the doorway. "You're behaving badly, sir. C'mon out, huh? Be a good biter. I haven't even had my first cup of coffee."

Growls and grunts burst out of the room, followed by a deafening crash.

"You're going to make me come in there, aren't you, Mr. Messmer?"

I slid into the room, holding Hawk at high ready and quickly sliced the pie. A tall metal shelving unit lay on its side along the back wall. Open cardboard cartons, resting upside-down on the floor, had spilled dozens of plastic bottles across the tile. Some of their lids had popped open and fluid was seeping across the floor. Several file cabinets had been over-turned, as well as the two occupied gurneys.

My bogey, crouched behind the toppled shelving unit, hadn't noticed me yet. He was too busy munching the bicep of one of the cadavers.

Toppled gurneys meant that we were already in the cross-contamination zone. No matter how quickly I wrapped this up, the funeral home was going to need biohazard remediation services.

Templeman was going to have a meltdown.

The shelf's support brackets crisscrossed in front of Messmer's head, obscuring my line of sight. I shifted my feet and accidentally kicked one of the plastic bottles. It skittered across the tile floor, bowling into other bottles along the way.

Messmer snapped his head up and snarled at me.

I centered Hawk on his forehead with my left hand, then used my right hand to pull out the Doritos. After ripping open the bag with my teeth, I held it out to him. "Look what I've got!"

With a gentle squeeze to the bottom of the bag, I nudged a chip out onto the floor. "That's for you, dude. Go on, take it. You know you want it."

Messmer scrambled to his feet, sniffed the air, and did the one thing I hoped he wouldn't do. He twitched.

Why do I always get the twitchers?

The rotter grabbed hold of a toppled cabinet, pivoted toward me, and brought it high above his head. I stepped back to brace myself, but my foot landed on one of the plastic bottles and I fell just as I squeezed the trigger.

My first bullet went high.

My next bullet went wide.

The third hit him right between the eyes.

Target acquired.

It hadn't been pretty. And it certainly hadn't been clean, considering the ceiling slathered in zombie blood and brain sushi (known as *zushi*, in my trade). But, at least, the job was over, right?

I'd almost made it to my feet when a brilliant flash blinded me, and the entire world went black.

I OPENED my eyes and found myself back out in the hallway, smashed up against the wall. I leaned forward with a moan and pulled my head from its skull-shaped crater in the drywall.

What the hell?

I pulled myself up along the sheetrock and surveyed what was left of Templeman's Funeral Home. The back half of the prep room, and whatever had been behind it, was completely gone. Police and fire trucks were arriving at the scene.

I wobbled through the carnage toward daylight, replaying the events as best I could, and made my way to the gaping hole in the building. Climbing over the crumbled brick and out onto lawn, I came face-to-face with Mr. Templeman.

The old buzzard was pointing at my gun and stomping his feet, but the gist of what he said was overridden by the ringing in my ears.

"Don't worry. I'm fine," I yelled, shaking drywall dust from my hair. Slowly, the haze in my brain began to lift. The noise-induced hearing loss faded and the sequence of events took shape in my aching head.

I'd fired three shots. The first had hit the ceiling. The second had gone wide, to the right of Messmer. The third had hit his forehead. The shot that went wide wouldn't have stopped until it hit the wall. For all I knew, it could have even gone through the wall and into the next room. If memory served, that had been a storage room.

I glanced at the pile of rubble and winced. "Mr. Templeman, were there chemicals in your storage room?"

"It's a freaking funeral home! I had thirty cases of formaldehyde in there."

Oh, shit. Shit, shit, shit. "Is that...flammable?"

His eyes blazed as he swept his arm toward the pile of pulverized building materials behind us. "What do you think, Einstein? I'm not paying for this. My insurance isn't paying for this. You're going to pay—"

"Hold that thought." I reached into my pocket and pulled out my vibrating phone. The name on the display made me groan out loud. "Hi Cap. Yes, I'm fi— No...ah...uh-huh...uh-huh... Well, I... Stop yelling! Hey, send Doc Blanchard over here. He needs to examine the biter I put down. Of course, I put it down. I always get my deadhead. No. I have no idea why it turned. That's why Doc needs to check for bite wounds or needle marks. I know. Yes, sir...yes, sir. I've got another call coming in. Okay... Bye-bye now."

I took a deep breath and answered the other line. "Nonnie, can I call you back? I'm kinda bus—. What?"

The more Nonnie explained, the wider my eyes grew. It seemed a biter call had come in after I'd left the house. My apprentice, Vinny Abruzzi, thought he could handle the situation on his own. Nonnie did a ride-along to supervise. God help him. But he'd gotten in over his head and now he needed me to bail him out. If Nonnie's assessment of the situation was accurate, that little shit's screwup would make the noon news. That was the last thing I needed after my own ~~debacle~~ ~~mishap~~ unfortunate incident at Templeman's.

"Where is he?" I asked. "Got it. Kleinfeld burial plot. Section 32. Elysian Fields Cemetery. Be there in ten." After a look at the tangle of fire trucks and police cruisers surrounding the building, I corrected myself. "Make that fifteen."

I ended the call and stole a glance at Mr. Templeman. "Good seeing you again, sir. Gotta run. We'll chat again soon."

"You come back here, you...you...whack job! This isn't over! You blew up my funer—" His rants followed me around the building and through the jumble of emergency vehicles as I climbed onto my Harley.

"Damn it, Vinny," I mumbled, threading my way out of the parking lot. "Of all the days for you to pick to fly solo."

2

BITER BLOWOUT

The trip across the interstate gave me time to kick myself for bringing Vinny on in the first place. A while back, after I'd returned from a case in New Orleans, Nonnie dreamed up this get-rich-quick scheme for a company named American Corpse Management Executives (ACME, Inc.). Up until then, most of my cases had come from the Cincinnati Police Department or the FBI's Z-virus task force.

The ACME business model allowed me to cut out the middleman by taking cases from the private sector. Which meant I made more money. I could make a living doing what I do best, downing deadheads—a skill I'd honed over the years.

We had become entrepreneurs: Me, the best of the badass zombie hunters, CEO and president of our wishful windfall scheme, Nonnie Nussbaum (aka Nonnie the Nose) my fossilized neighbor/corporate office manager, and last but not least, Vinny Abruzzi, my agent-in-training who, as of this morning, had apparently promoted himself to Field Investigator. Vinny is the son of a former 'client' of mine, a murdered mob accountant whose wit and wisdom had grown on me—albeit like a fungus.

ACME was what you might call a unique...what the hell, a freakishly bizarre niche company:

ACME, Inc. offers state-of-the-art corpse management services to the public at large. Whether you're putting down a wayward rotter, or raising the dead for unfinished business, ACME is your first and only stop.

At least, that's what our marketing brochure said.

While I'd been working on CPD's case at Templeman's this morning, Vinny had taken a call from Elysian Fields Cemetery, asking ACME to quietly resolve a 'green burial' gone wrong. Whatever that was.

Vinny, a shitstorm of arrogance, attitude and self-assurance, was truly his father's son. The kid had a knack for landing us both in hot water. I pulled into the cemetery, annoyed that he'd jumped the gun. He hadn't been ready to head out on his own. My mind drifted to the unpaid bill for ACME's liability insurance shoved into a mound of other unpaid bills, in the middle of my kitchen table. A chill slithered up my spine.

Don't be silly, I chided myself. *We're in a cemetery. How much damage could he do?*

Little Allie, the judgmental diva who squats in the back of my brain, heckled me about past cemetery-related damages of my own that had totaled in excess of $13,000. *Remember the backhoe incident at Rose Hill Cemetery? The Kapiniski mausoleum...*

I shut her down in mid-snipe. The little bitch spouts like a geyser until I actually need advice. What good is a voice in your head if it never has your back?

The murmur of distant screams caught my ear. I reached the top of the slope in Section 32, slipped in my ear buds, and checked my mic. Nonnie and a small group of mourners, voices shrill and hands flailing, were gathered below what I presumed was the Kleinfeld burial plot—the empty Kleinfeld burial plot.

They turned to me in unison and pointed across the cemetery to points unseen.

The hair on the back of my neck stood up. Vinny was pursuing a runaway rotter. My self-anointed field agent was about to get a baptism by fire.

The mourner's shrieks faded in the crisp October breeze, but I was willing to bet the blood-soaked body sprawled on the freshly manicured grass beside the grave was at least one cause for their hysteria. An empty, obliterated casket rested on the straps of a lowering device over Kleinfeld's freshly-dug grave.

Biter blowout, I deduced, trotting toward the site. Blowouts happen from time to time, when uncooperative corpses refuse to play nice.

A gunshot popped in the distance and I breathed a sigh of relief. Crisis averted. Vinny had gotten his bogey, after all.

I reached the blazer-clad body lying prone in the grass, swiped my finger across a bloody name tag pinned to its chest, and ID'd our vic: Fred Winston, a funeral director with Templeman's Funeral Home. What was left of his throat had been shredded to the consistency of coleslaw. The jagged edges of the wounds were rife with tooth marks. Classic biter attack.

Nonnie, who'd finally caught up with me, spit three times, shot Dead Fred the Italian horned-hand, and snarled. "*Oh, cazzo!*"

"Stop it," I hissed, smacking her outstretched hand.

She wilted under the glare of my stink-eye and took a step back.

We were supposed to be professionals, for God's sake. At least, I was. Nonnie, the Sicilian-born widow of a Jewish mobster had always been, and would forever be, a riddle wrapped in a mystery, inside of an enigma.

Shards of some ultra-thin, faux-wood material littered the grave site. Cardboard, maybe. The concept of a green burial instantly clarified. Ira's casket had been biodegradable. Efficient, economical and eco-friendly. Utterly useless for containment of the living dead.

I turned to the mourners. "Which one of you is the next of kin?"

"None of us," answered a tiny prune-faced woman. "He never married and he didn't have any children. He was all alone, except for a few of us from the nursing home."

"Does anyone know how Mr. Kleinfeld died?"

The group exchanged glances and offered a collective shrug.

"Was he, by any chance, infected with the Z-virus?"

Still nothing. I tried again.

"Was he attacked by a rotter—an oozing, festering, walking-dead zombie?"

One of the geezers cocked his ear. "What about Romney?"

"No," snapped the woman on his arm. "Abercrombie."

"Like the finch store?"

"Fitch," I said, rolling my eyes. "Abercrombie and Fitch."

"What's a fitch?"

Holy Hannah. I moved closer and yelled, "How did Ira die?"

The geezer nodded. "Heart attack."

"Pneumonia," insisted the woman.

"He was ninety-two," barked a voice from the back of the pack. "Isn't that enough?"

A pocket-sized biddy jostled to the front. "Mrs. Shumacher said he died of a stroke. She was his assisted living aide."

"We're from the senior center," bellowed a codger, as if that clarified everything.

Dead Fred the Funeral Director would have known the answer to my question. But he wasn't talking. I debated raising him to ask about the cause of Ira's death, but Fred had only been dead a few minutes. The ability to raise the dead was a gift from God, but it hadn't come with an instruction manual. I had learned the hard way that controlling freshies, corpses that had been dead for less than seven days, was like herding cats—viral-infected, batshit crazy cats. Hell to the nope. I could check Ira's COD in the coroner's records. Problem solved.

A shot rang out, followed closely by another. I closed my eyes and sighed. *Come on, Vinny. Ice the thing, already.*

Random bursts of gunfire echoed from beyond the rise, and my stomach bottomed out. Panic fire, damn it. Case number ACME-0010 had gone sideways.

I grabbed Nonnie's arm. "Get these people into the chapel and lock the door. Don't open it until I tell you it's safe."

How many shots had Vinny fired? I wondered. *And how many did he have left?* I pulled out my mental abacus, carried the one, and groaned.

Vinny packed a Glock 17, loaded with 18 rounds of 9mm hollow-points. Between the isolated rounds and panic fire, I had counted seventeen shots, give or take.

I unsnapped my shoulder holster, drew Hawk, and sprinted after my fledgling field investigator. "Vinny," I screamed into my mic. "Vinny, come in. What's your sitrep?"

My earbuds crackled. "Son of a bitch! Situation FUBAR, Nighthawk! Repeat, situation FUBAR! Backup requested."

I topped the next slope on a dead run, cursing ACME, Inc., our harebrained, high-risk goat rodeo—a boneheaded idea from the start. But I'd needed money more than air. I was always broke. I could have been rolling in dough, but I'd made a point early on of not raising every Tom, Dick, and deadhead just so clients could figure out where their late Aunt Sophie had stashed her millions.

I'd needed boundaries, a guiding set of principles, so I created my own moral code. My own set of rules.

Rule Number One: Never raise the dead to lessen the grief of the living. It's selfish. And trust me, the dead never come back the way you remember them.

Rule Number Two: Any corpse I raise, I put back down. The dead deserve our respect.

It's a helluva way to make a living, but even a corpse whisperer needs to eat. I've got other mouths to feed too. A kinetically-challenged bulldog, a sassy African Grey Parrot, and an as yet unproven business asset, Vinny Abruzzi. Not to mention I have operating expenses. Small arms ammo and napalm don't come cheap. And thanks to a huge misunderstanding on the Hamilton County Treasurer's part, I was on the hook for $12,850 in back property taxes.

So, despite my reservations, ACME, Inc. had oozed to life, dragging me along, kicking and screaming. Fair enough. I'd made my own bed. But Vinny had followed me in, hook, line and sinker. And I'd let him.

The deeper into the cemetery I ran, the clearer it became that Vinny hadn't been ready to handle this call on his own. His marksmanship sucked. Concrete angels were missing noses. Monuments had been strafed. And courtesy of one unfortunate confluence of bullets, the surname on one tombstone had been changed from *Tucker* to *Fucker*.

I sprinted past the carnage, totaling the damages in my head. By the time I caught up to Vinny, my brain had run out of zeroes.

Worst of all, Ira Kleinfeld was nowhere in sight.

Slowing to a stop, I bent over and put my hands on my knees to catch my breath.

"Where's your target?" I finally huffed.

Vinny, plopped on the ground, slouched wearily against a tombstone with his head down and legs splayed out, looking like a big, dumb Raggedy Andy doll.

He shrugged, tossed up his hands, and mumbled, "Gone."

This couldn't be happening. I scanned the grounds from left to right and peered into the distance. Not a rotter in sight. But that didn't mean our rotter wasn't there. The grounds were filled with towering monuments, mausoleums, and ornamental landscaping—places that could shield a biter from view. I kicked Vinny's outstretched feet and wapped him across the top of his head.

"How do you know he's gone? Get off your whiny ass and hunt down your bogey, damn it!"

"He's gone," Vinny said softly as he climbed to his feet. "Just...gone."

"He was ninety-two and dead, you loser! How fast could he be?"

Vinny massaged his lower left leg. "I had him in my sights, but I tripped over a sprinkler head, rolled my ankle, and fell. The bastard got a lead on me. Once I got back up, I watched him stumble over that broken wall and disappear into the trees."

He pointed toward to a pile of crumbled stone. On the far side of that wall lay Sharon Woods Park.

I glanced at my watch. "How long ago?"

"Five, ten minutes, tops."

Shit, shit, shitty shit, shit. Eleven a.m. and our deadhead du jour, Ira Kleinfeld, was in the wind. I kicked at the ground and glowered at Vinny. "Good job, kid. It doesn't get any worse than this."

Vinny looked beyond me and winced. "Wanna bet?"

I spun on my heel and stifled a curse. Less than thirty-feet away, Channel Ten media maven Jade Chen and her pet rock cameraman Rip Saccha were closing in for the kill.

3

THIS WAS SO NOT MY FAULT

"Let me handle this," I whispered to Vinny. "Not one word. You hear me?"

Gel-Boy nodded and began primping for his thirty-seconds of infamy. He straightened his tie, ran his hand through his product-infused hair, and shot a winning smile at Jade.

The ninety-pound collection of silicone, hairspray and makeup bore down on him like a heat-seeking missile. He took a half-step back and tripped over a grave marker, landing on his bad ankle with a grimace. He managed a quick recovery but not quick enough. The Chanel Ten News camera was already rolling. Jade pounced, barreling past me, mic in hand, and thrust it in Vinny's face.

The freaking jackal. How had she gotten here so fast?

She swept her long black hair from her shoulders, flashed a predatory smile, and nodded to her loyal fans. "Good afternoon, Cincinnati. I'm Jade Chen, for ABC News Affiliate, Channel Ten, reporting to you live from Elysian Fields Cemetery. We're following a breaking story concerning a gruesome graveside murder, as well as the mid-burial disappearance of a corpse."

I barged between them and fixed Jade in a stony stare. "Later. We're a little busy right now."

I shoved the mic away and gave her my shoulder, but Nancy Newshound wasn't about to back off.

"Ms. Nighthawk, where is the missing corpse?"

"Out for a stroll."

Her eyes blazed. "You have no idea where it is, do you?"

"I said *later*."

"The story's breaking now," she snapped. "I'm a journalist. Like it or not, covering news is what we do."

I wheeled around, grabbed her mic, and mugged for the camera. "Maybe someday you'll learn how to do that. Don't feel bad, Ms. Chen. It's not your fault. I blame the cloud of Aqua Net around your head."

"Cut!" Jade snatched the microphone from my hand and sidestepped me to get to Vinny, but I blocked her.

She stomped her prissy little Louboutin in the grass. "You may not have time to chat, but I'm sure your associate does."

"Not today, he doesn't. Besides, I'm the P.R. officer for ACME, Inc. You want quotes? You come to me."

"Ha! Those should be priceless." She cocked her head and pursed her lips. "Fine. I didn't want to go here, but you've left me no choice: New Orleans."

"What about it?"

"You owe me. I nearly died because of you."

"Technically, you were only a little...zombified. Or corpsified. Potato, po*tah*to."

"You'd have shot out my brain stem if I'd turned, wouldn't you?"

"Without hesitation."

"You're a piece of work, Allie."

"I'm a corpse whisperer, Jade. Like it or not, putting down deadheads is what I do."

That shit she'd dug up and thrown in my face had

happened months earlier and the whiny hose-bag was still bent out of shape. She also had her facts ass-backwards. No way I was going to let her off the hook.

"Actually," I said, "Toussaint injected you with the Z-virus because *you* stuck your face where it didn't belong. *I* saved your life. *I* kept you from turning. And *I* make the meds that continue to keep you from turning every single day. A simple 'thank you' would suffice."

Jade tossed her head. "I wouldn't have chased you to New Orleans in the first place if you had helped me with my exposé, instead of fighting me at every turn."

She jutted her chin and waited for my response. Fat chance. She could have waited until the rapture and I wouldn't have given her that satisfaction.

She finally got tired of waiting, and sighed. "Just...help me now. Give me a sound bite...something...anything."

The clock was ticking. I didn't have time to argue. "Fine. One quick comment. Then, once I've wrapped up the case in a pretty pink bow, I'll give you an exclusive. Agreed?"

Jade motioned for Rip to start filming and beamed her blinding-white caps at the camera. "We're here with Allie Nighthawk, Cincinnati's premier zombie hunter. Ms. Nighthawk, what can you tell us about the mutilated body found at Elysian Fields Cemetery early this morning? And where is the missing corpse that was scheduled for burial today?"

I ran my tongue over my teeth to make sure I didn't have food stuck in them, and struck a thoughtful, talking-head pose.

"Unfortunately, since a crime has been committed, the scene will be part of an ongoing investigation and therefore, I am not at liberty to discuss the details at this time. Regrettably, I am also unable to release the name of the victim found slain here on the cemetery grounds until the next of kin has been notified. But rest assured, Ms. Chen," I leaned toward the camera, "ACME, Inc., that's American Corpse Management Executives, your first and only stop for all your corpse management needs, is actively engaged in the pursuit of Mr. Kleinfeld."

ONCE JADE HAD GOTTEN her sound bite, and the Channel Ten News Crew had left, I laid into Vinny. "Guess what we have to do now, hotshot?"

His eyes widened as I pulled out my phone. "Who're you calling?"

"There's a freshie on the loose. Who do you think I'm calling?" I hit Captain Dorsey's number and glared at Vinny. "I ought to make you call this in."

Captain Dorsey, better known as Cap, runs Cincinnati's 51st Precinct. He also heads up the Paranormal Crimes Unit, the biggest end user of my...unique skills. The cheap bastards won't hire me full time, so I have to subcontract my services and take direction from Cap (since it's city business). I get paid by the case, so money is tight.

If it wasn't for Nonnie, my diet would consist of dog biscuits, ketchup soup, Doritos, and Jack Daniel's. Pissing off Cap was the last thing I wanted to do. I broke the news, then held out my phone and shared Cap's conniption fit with Vinny. The kid turned sixteen shades of gray.

I managed to work a couple of 'uh-huhs' and 'buts' into the conversation between Cap's rants, but he was on a roll. At some point, he ran out of breath and the line went dead.

Vinny trailed me in silence as we trudged back toward section thirty-two where the nightmare had begun. Sirens whirring in the distance grew louder as we approached the Kleinfeld burial plot and the ravaged corpse of Fred, the Funeral Director. Fred's death posed more than one problem. We didn't need a second rotter on the run.

I nodded toward Vinny's gun, tucked neatly back in his shoulder holster. "Clean up your mess."

He took a deep breath, pulled his Glock, aimed it at Fred's head and squeezed the trigger. *Zippo. Zilch. Nada.* The slide was locked. The damn thing was out of ammo. Of course, it was. He'd single-handedly remodeled the cemetery using rapid-fire rounds of ballistic therapy.

I shot him a side-eye, also known as my Allie-eye. "You should always know how many rounds you have left."

Tough talk and it sounded good. Technically, it is true, but I've been in his position a time or two myself. It's easy to lose count in the heat of battle. Gel-boy didn't need to know that, though. Let him stew. I wasn't finished torturing him yet.

Vinny nodded, cast his eyes to the ground, and blushed like a school girl as he slipped in a new mag, took aim, and killed Fred so he wouldn't turn rotter. The sirens had stopped.

I glanced up to see a ripped, tall, hot guy strolling our way across the grounds, and stifled a groan. Rico De Palma, my paranormal crimes unit liaison with CPD. (As if our partnership wasn't complicated enough, he was also shtupping Jade Chen, the botoxed bitchelante).

I steeled myself for the crow Rico would shove down my throat. The last thing I needed was for Vinny to see me get dressed down, so I sent him to the chapel to give Nonnie and the mourners the all-clear.

Rico sauntered up beside me, shoved his Oakley's on top of his wavy black hair, and squatted beside Dead Fred to get a closer look.

"Nasty," he said, nodding in cop-like appreciation. "You want to tell me what happened?"

"Not really."

"Come on. I need a good laugh."

"It was Vinny's case. This mess is his fault."

"Of course, it is."

The smirk on my partner's face made me want to slap the crap out of him. He can be a sarcastic prick sometimes. I gave him a...somewhat skewed...version of the events, that focused on Vinny's mistakes and left out any mention of my run-in with Jade.

Rico pulled out his phone and called in a BOLO on the not-nearly-as-dead-as-he-should-have-been Ira Kleinfeld. Situation addressed and handled. Time to move on. But I just couldn't let things be.

"Vinny wasn't ready to handle a case on his own."

"Water under the bridge, now." Rico shrugged. "We'll get your deadhead. It's not the end of the world."

What the fu... "Wait a minute. Since Vinny ran the case, you're just going to let him skate? If this had been my screw up—"

"Oh, it's totally your screw up." Rico's eyes twinkled. "But I know you. And you're kicking yourself enough for the both of us."

He straightened up, flipped down his Oakleys, then walked toward Vinny and Nonnie and the mourners as they exited the chapel. Rico chatted with them all at length, no doubt getting their take on the graveside attack and the ensuing Operation FUBAR. Once their conversations ended, the mourners went their separate ways, and my partner headed for his car.

But he stopped short and turned, calling over his shoulder, "Better your ass than mine, Nighthawk. Meet you in Cap's office in an hour. Oh, I almost forgot. He also wants to talk to you about the Templeman's job, from, uh...earlier."

What a surprise.

4

THE FRAT BOYS

Getting reamed by Cap would cost me more than pride. Time is money. Before all hell had broken loose, I'd planned to spend the rest of the day working two biter cases Cap had assigned to me a couple of days earlier. I'd been slammed with ACME work and hadn't even opened Cap's files yet. Clearly, they'd have to wait until he'd carved his pound of flesh off my ass. And wasn't it the perfect time for the additional complication of a runaway rotter?

I followed Vinny and Nonnie back to my house, where Nonnie would spend the rest of her day tending to ACME business and running herd over the oddball assortment of critters I'd accumulated in the last year. Headbutt, my biter-sniffing bulldog, Kulu, a mouthy African Grey feather duster, and her squawky baby Hyrum.

I zipped into the driveway behind Nonnie's wood-paneled, '72 Pinto Wagon, climbed off my lowrider, and stuck my finger in Vinny's face when he got out of the car. "Your case, your problem. Don't come back until you find that geriatric meatbag."

Nonnie shook her head, *tsk-tsking*, as she disappeared into my house.

"I...I'm sorry," Vinnie mumbled, gimping around to the driver's side of the car. "I'll fix this. You'll see."

He packed his stocky body into the Pinto, then backed out onto the street and rumbled away. Part of me felt sorry for him. But most of me still wanted to wring his neck. He needed to take responsibility for losing control of the situation, just like I had to take responsibility for letting him think he could decide when he was street-ready. Adulting sucks. Life lessons suck harder.

Nonnie constantly nags me about all the *vroom-vrooming*, so I walked the Harley back down the driveway to start it on the street. My phone rang. I scanned the call display and smiled. It was Sean Ferris, an FBI agent assigned to the federal Z-virus task force. We'd worked together on the Abruzzi case, and then again in New Orleans, and somewhere along the way, we'd become friends with benefits. He had been holding out hope for more, but that was about as much commitment as I could handle.

"Allie Girl! What's shakin'?"

"Same old, same old. On my way to get reamed by Cap."

"What'd you do this time?"

I told him, and he groaned. "Poor kid. Did you rip off his balls and shove them down his throat?"

"I would have, but then I'd have to hunt the damn thing down myself."

Ferris laughed. "Ready for a five-miler tonight?"

We'd been training for the twenty-six-mile Flying Pig Marathon that was only two days away. I wasn't optimistic about finishing the race and needed all the help I could get.

"Sure," I said. "How about six o'clock, Eden Park?"

"I'll pick you up."

"It's easier to meet there."

He paused. "Sure. See you then."

The disappointment in his voice was hard to miss. I started the Harley and took off, pondering our relationship.

I'd gotten pretty banged up on that New Orleans case and had stayed behind when the rest of the team went their separate ways. I'd needed time to heal, to rest, and to rethink my life —figure out what I wanted, and who I wanted it from.

On paper, Ferris was the perfect guy for me. He didn't flinch at what came out of my mouth. He didn't care that I wore zombie-stomping boots and ratty T-shirts stained with rotter guts. We took dancing lessons. He even let me lead. Once.

He likes me for who I am, and that makes me feel...weirdly pretty.

He's in love with me. And I should be in love with him. But every time it feels like I'm about to take that leap, I skitter away from the edge. I don't know why. Maybe it's because the people in my life tend to drop like flies. My mother, my father, Leo, and Harry. Maybe it's because I don't want Ferris to get hurt or become a statistic.

I know it isn't fair to lead him on when we both know he wants more. But we're really attracted to each other, and we get along so well. It's a strange dance.

I pulled into a parking space at the 51st, turned off my bike and figured, *whatever*. Maybe badass zombie hunters don't deserve to have love stories. Maybe all we're allowed to get out of life is an occasional late night booty call. Damn, that would suck.

WHISTLES, cheers, and applause greeted me as I entered the precinct. Someone had stapled a cartoon zombie head on an old wanted poster and taped it to a pillar in the center of the bullpen.

Wycowski, one of the old fart gumshoes, wobbled out and handed me a catcher's mask clipped to the end of a dog leash. He'd attached a note that read: *zombie containment system.*

The room exploded.

"Save it for your wife," I quipped, tossing it back.

Nicely played, I thought.

Wycowski: *One.*

Nighthawk: *One.*

But clearly, my missing meatbag and I were the joke of the day, courtesy of one blabber-mouthed Rico De Palma. My partner was a dead man.

Heat seared my cheeks as I stomped down the aisle toward Cap's office. I glanced at what was once the psychotically clean and strategically ordered desk of Miriam Miller, Cap's secretary for more than twenty-five years—until she was murdered in connection with Leo Abruzzi's case. She'd been injected with a synthetic version of the Z-virus, and turned full-on zombie. She even trashed the morgue. Two guesses who had to put her down. That hadn't exactly endeared me to Cap or the ME.

Since then, Miriam's chair has been filled with an endless string of bobble-headed bimhos who couldn't find their asses with their hands tied behind their backs. Today's temp glanced repeatedly from the stack of papers in her hand, to the fax machine, and back again. She looked up and grinned as I stomped by.

Rookie mistake.

"Excuse me, Ma'am." She giggled and held up her documents. "Do I put the papers on the glass face up or face down?"

"You can put your *ass* on the glass, for all I care," I said, never breaking stride. "The frat boys up front would love it."

Barbie could bite me. Today, I wasn't the answer to anyone's problem. I raised my hand and knocked on Cap's door, wishing I was anywhere but here.

5

EARTH TO NIGHTHAWK

To my surprise, the door swung open and Rico was on the other side. He winked playfully and pulled out one of Cap's raggedy-ass chairs for me. When I flopped into the seat, a whoosh of air exploded from the cushion. Stuffing farted through the cracked red vinyl upholstery and fluttered to the floor like foamy bits of yellow snow.

Cap had yet to say a word.

I plucked at the loose stuffing, stared at the picture of his late wife on the corner of his desk, and waited. And waited. Then waited some more.

He leaned back and settled into his chair, cast his eyes to the floor, and began twirling a pencil over his lip like a handlebar mustache. The second hand on his wall clock ticked like a time bomb waiting to explode at T-minus meltdown. My mouth went dry.

"Where's Numbnuts?" he finally asked.

"Vinny?"

Cap nodded.

"Chasing down Ira Kleinfeld. Why?"

"I understand this debacle was mostly his doing. Why isn't he here to answer for it?"

"Because he works for ACME, Cap. Not you. He answers to me."

Rico threw me a warning stare.

Cap's voice grew cold. "This crapfest might have started as an ACME job, but I assure you, once that rotter took off that job became a matter of public safety. It's my business now."

Rico leaned forward. "I interviewed Vinny at the cemetery, Cap. And Nonnie. And the mourn—"

"Stop," I said. The word had come out more sharply than I'd intended. "I don't need you to fight my battles for me."

Despite any reservations Rico may have had about that statement, he settled back with a sigh.

To hell with this. I jutted my chin at Cap. "Let ACME finish the job. I always get my rotter. You know that."

Cap dropped his moustache pencil, steepled his fingers beneath his chin and stared into space. I wasn't about to give up.

"Have I ever let you down?"

Time stood still. Invisible tumbleweeds drifted through his office while I waited for his response. I couldn't read his eyes, so I pushed again.

"Ever. Even once, have I *ever* let you down?"

"I'm sure I'll live to regret this," he said, shaking his shiny bald head. "But all right. Finish your job. Just do it quick. We don't need more bad PR. And the local press," he said, side-eyeing Rico, "has a field day every time you so much as scratch your ass."

Rico's face blazed with the heat of a thousand suns. "Message received."

Good, I thought. Maybe Rico will pry his mutant pit bull girlfriend off my leg and buy me some space.

"Moving on." Cap pulled a file from the mountain of manila

folders on his desk. "Or should I say moving back to your first case of the day. The CPD case at Templeman's Funeral Home."

Peachy. I shifted and crossed my legs. "Well..."

"Let me save you the trouble. Mr. Templeman called. He's going to sue you for destroying his building. Don't worry. You're not alone. He's suing CPD too because our pockets are deeper."

"Cap, I—"

"You didn't know formaldehyde was flammable."

"I had no idea. I never would have taken a shot if I'd known."

"Nighthawk?"

"Yes, Cap?"

"It's totally fucking flammable."

"Copy that," I said, sinking into my chair.

"We'll circle back to this later. What can you tell me about the biter?"

"Templeman said he'd just gotten the body from the ME's office and hadn't had a chance to work on it yet. The guy, this Paul Messmer, died of a heart attack at work. His attending signed off on the COD."

Cap nodded. "Doc's at the scene now, taking a look at what's left of Mr. Messmer. Once the prelim exam is finished, Doc will have the body transferred back to the morgue to run some tests."

I mined more stuffing from the arm of my chair. "For what it's worth, Messmer's body got thrown clear in the explosion. I didn't see any bite marks on him, but there had to be at least one. Or an injection site. After all, that's how the virus is transmitted, right?"

Yet even as I said that, I realized how naïve that statement sounded.

The room got hot and began to spin. Rico mentioned something about getting the basics on Messmer, but I missed most of it.

The next thing I knew, Cap was waving his hand in front of my face. "Hello? Earth to Nighthawk. Are we boring you?"

"Sorry," I said, shaking my head. "Just...thinking about the case."

"Why don't you and Rico go think about it together and come up with a game plan? The mayor and the press will want answers. I'd like to be able to provide them with those answers."

Cap's phone buzzed and he checked the display. "Hold on," he said, motioning us to stay put. "It's Doc."

Their conversation was short, and when Cap ended the call he looked like he'd aged ten years. "Doc's taking the body back for blood work. But his prelim didn't find any evidence of bite wounds or injection sites."

I stood up and rested my hand on the back of my chair to steady myself. "I'll call Dr. Christian at the European CDPC to see if there have been any reported cases of the Z-virus that weren't transmitted through either bites or injections."

The words that had just tumbled from my mouth were the words of a nightmare. God help us all if the synthetic virus had somehow mutated. I fought the urge to vomit and reminded myself that organic viruses mutate all the time. Maybe synthetic viruses could mutate on their own without chemical intervention too.

But maybe they couldn't.

And if they couldn't, that meant someone was manually changing the properties of the virus. Someone other than Toussaint Le Clerc.

Because Toussaint is dead, I reminded myself. *Dead and gone for months. You shot him in the head. You saw his body drop. Ferris saw his corpse lying there on the flagstones of New Orleans' Congo Square. He even felt for Toussaint's pulse. Ferris told you that. And Ferris wouldn't lie.*

Little Allie argued that I had blacked out after I shot Toussaint and had no way of knowing what really happened, other than what others told me after I woke up in the hospital. She reminded me of another thing that I'd buried in some cobwebbed corner of my mind. When the federal backup team had arrived to investigate the scene at Congo Square, Toussaint's body was gone.

6

WELCOME TO THE SHIT SHOW

Rico let me have my space as we left Cap's office and walked to his desk in the bullpen. Thankfully, the frat boys had disbanded, and the few remaining detectives were immersed in actual police business. It was nearly two o'clock here, making it eight p.m. at the European Centre for Disease Prevention and Control in Stockholm. Chances were slim that I'd reach Dr. Christian, but I had to try. He was the world's premier authority on carovescology, the study of the Z-virus. If anyone would know about similar cases, he would.

Since Rico was going to interview Messmer's spouse, he offered me the use of his desk for the international phone call.

"Just text when you're ready to join me," he said, shoving a stack of files aside to give me space. "You can meet me in progress."

I settled into his well-worn chair, mentally crossed my fingers, and placed the call. Ilse, Dr. Christian's secretary, quickly came on the line. It was good to hear her voice. She and I had bonded over the death of Dr. Christian's predecessor, Sandoval Latka, a brilliant scientist and close friend. I was relieved when she told me Christian was still there, so I stayed on the line and chatted with her for a bit.

Once she transferred me, Dr. Christian picked up on the first ring. Hearing his voice gave me hope. Whatever we were dealing with, he would be by my side. "Allie! So good to hear from you, my friend. How can I help you?"

"It's great to talk to you again, too. I know you're busy, but I have what I hope is a silly question." I sucked in a breath and felt my chest tighten. "Can the synthetic strain of the Z-virus organically mutate once it's introduced into the body?"

He paused, then said, "Yes, but that's far more likely to occur with an RNA-based virus."

"But it *is* possible?"

"Yes, it's possible."

"Have you seen any cases with transmission sources other than bites or injection?"

"No, why?" The lightness in his tone disappeared. "Allie, what's this about?"

"We have a case where the virus wasn't transmitted by bite or by injection."

Christian paused. "If the infection was the product of a new organic mutation of the disease, I think you'd be seeing the number of cases growing exponentially as the new variant spreads. It seems more likely that you're dealing with a new means of transmission—a new delivery system for the disease, if you will."

My mind reeled. The possibility of a new delivery system for the virus was every bit as frightening as the potential for a new variant. I needed to talk to Rico. And Ferris. Maybe Cap. Screw Dickhead, aka FBI Director Horton. If he caught wind of this, he'd be up my ass sideways.

"Thank you so much, Dr. Christian. You and Sandy have always had the answers. I'd be lost without you."

"Take care out there, my dear. And stay in touch. I'll be on the lookout for cases with negative contact tracing."

"Will do," I said. "Thanks again." I ended the call, feeling almost numb. Where to begin? Who would intentionally create a new delivery system for a virus that could destroy mankind? And why? The list of known viable candidates with that kind of brain power was short.

My stomach growled and I realized I hadn't eaten anything since breakfast and it was practically mid-afternoon. I'd join Rico later, after a couple of slices of Ricardo's meat-lovers pizza. Extra cheese, light sauce.

Wycowski hollered something as I walked past his desk and slipped out the precinct door. I neither knew nor cared what he'd said. So far, Dr. Christian's hypothesis was the cherry on top of my turd-encrusted day. And it was only the middle of the afternoon.

I'M GUESSING the walls inside Ricardo's Pizzeria must have been beige at one time. Over the years, they'd morphed into a Jackson Pollock painting, tastefully splattered in greasy marinara-red. The worn hardwood floors sloped like a carnival funhouse.

The guy making my pizza, Toby Arata, started there as a delivery guy and worked his way into management. He didn't just make the best pizza this side of the Ohio River, he also knew everyone, and had his eyes open and his ears to the ground. Nothing got past Toby. Plus, he was the only pizza guy who would still deliver to my house, what with all the (true) rumors of the zombie-related goings on there. Toby had helped me out big time on the Abruzzi case. I owed him. But by the time I get around to paying him back, he'd probably own Ricardo's.

I slid into a lumpy vinyl booth, more rips than vinyl, and pulled out my phone while I waited for my pizza. A text message from Nonnie showed up:

> NEW ACME CLIENT! CALL AT ONCE!!
> ROWING MERLOT.

Typed in all caps because Nonnie can't see lower case. No phone number. Who the hell was Rowing Merlot? A second text appeared, containing the phone number. Score one for the blue-haired fossil.

I typed in the number and waited. It rang a few times and an answering machine came on. "You have reached the Marlowe Agency, home of Mystic County's finest private detectives. Please leave your name and number at the sound of the tone. Your call will be returned by our president and founder, Rowan Marlowe."

Ah. *Rowing Merlot.* Close but no cigar. I hate leaving messages and almost hung up, but a breathless voice came on the line.

"Hello? Hello? Are you still there?"

"For the moment."

"This is Rowan Marlowe. How may I help you?"

"Allie Nighthawk. You called me."

"Yes! Yes, of course! Thanks for returning my call. I'm wondering if you'd have time to meet with me this afternoon. I think I have a job that's right up your alley."

"Do tell." *Let me guess,* I thought, *somebody wants to raise a stiff to find a hidden pot of gold.*

"I'd rather not discuss this over the phone, Ms. Nighthawk. Can you meet with me this afternoon? It's...private and rather urgent. I came to Cincinnati specifically to meet with you."

Too bad, so sad, sister. "Sorry, I'm awfully busy, saving the world from the zombie apocalypse and all."

I slid my finger across the screen to tap *end call* but stopped when I heard the magic words.

"I'll pay you for your time."

"How much?"

"A hundred dollars. For fifteen minutes of your time."

I looked at my watch. What the hell. Rico had been working crimes for years before he met me, and he was probably half-finished with the interviews already. Quick in, quick out. A hundred bucks in my pocket? Sold.

"Where would you like to meet?"

"You pick."

"Okay. Meet me in an hour at The Blue Note Lounge on Liberty Street."

"See you there."

The call disconnected and I smiled for the first time that day. Found money for a job I'd never take. Things were looking up. I texted Rico to tell him something had come up and I wouldn't be joining him. He could catch me up later.

Toby set my piping hot pie in front of me, then slid into the opposite side of my booth. He swiped his curls from his face and gawked at me over the top of his glasses. "What's shaking, Allie? Haven't seen you in a while."

"The money tree, baby. The money tree."

We chatted for a bit, but a customer came in and Toby had to scoot. Feeling generous after devouring his tasty, gooey pie, I left him a sizeable tip. Sizeable for me, anyway. I headed through the door, climbed onto my lowrider, and headed to the Blue Note to hear out Ms. Rowan Marlowe before turning her down cold.

7

SMURFETTE VS. GODZILLA

My wannabe client had caught me off guard asking for a face-to-face. Most of my jobs are on an emergency basis, if you get my drift. I suggested The Blue Note because it was the first place that sprang to mind. I'd worked there for a few months, as a waitress, bartender, bouncer, and anything else that Dallas, the owner needed, after I moved back home from St. Louis. All I'd brought with me was forty bucks, a half-pint of Jack, and a couple packs of Ramen Noodles.

That seemed like forever ago.

I pictured Dallas in my mind as I tore across Columbia Parkway. Seventy, if he was a day, with long gray hair and a scraggly beard that swallowed his face. He'd been in the bar business since Moses was a child. To say he was kind was an understatement. He'd taught me how to tend bar, slipped me money here and there, and kept me on when I gave him multiple reasons to let me go. But before long, he closed the bar and left town for Florida. He never sold the place, though. I had heard through the grapevine that he'd moved back and reopened the bar. I could have called to let him know I was coming, but why ruin the surprise?

I veered onto Liberty and two blocks later slipped into the bar's driveway as quietly as my Harley allowed. The parking lot was empty. But it was still early, when it came to bar time. Come happy hour, with any luck, that story would change.

The front door pulled open with a creak. I stepped inside and was instantly enveloped in darkness. My eyes adjusted and the flickering neon beer signs registered. Phantom wisps of old cigarette smoke filled my nose. Nothing had changed. From the beautiful burled walnut bar top to the dilapidated vinyl booths held together with duct tape. I'd hadn't realized how much I missed that stinky godforsaken hole in the wall.

Dallas's voice caught my ear. "Come on in. Have a seat. What can I get you?"

"Can you make a Jack Daniel's slushie?"

"Allie Cat?" He peered through his wire-rims and grinned. "By God, it is you. Welcome back!"

Dallas was the only human on earth who could get away with calling me Allie Cat.

He scuttled from behind the bar, crossed the room, and crushed me in a bear hug. Apparently, he'd forgotten that I'm not a touchy-feely kind of gal. I hugged him for point two milliseconds and extricated myself.

"Looking good, old man. How's business?"

"You job hunting?"

"Hell, no."

"Good, 'cause business sucks. But I just reopened a couple of weeks back. Things will pick up. One high-octane slushie coming up."

"Thanks, but I'm here on business. Hit me up later."

I instinctively headed to my regular stool—the second from the end of the bar. The stool at the end of the bar belonged to Harry Delk, my former partner. God rest his soul. "I'm turning down a potential client. She should be here any minute."

"Business must be good if you're turning it away. You still doing that...voodoo, hoodoo—"

The door opened and a woman, tall enough to swat helicopters from the sky, strolled across the bar and took a seat on Harry's stool. The moment she sat in that stool, a translucent image of Harry appeared behind her, hovering inches above the floor.

I blinked. Once. Twice. Three times. Still there.

Sure, I raised the dead but I didn't often see them wafting through the air like Macy's parade balloons—a pissed-off looking balloon to be exact.

Dallas, who apparently hadn't noticed Harry's presence, smiled at his new customer. "Welcome to The Blue Note. I'm Dallas, the owner of this joint. What can I get you?"

"Rowan Marlowe. Double Grey Goose, neat," she said, holding out her hand, palm down, like maybe he was supposed to kiss her ring.

Her voice was low and smokey. Her hair was flaming red. And her Amazonian ass was in the wrong damn stool.

"Nighthawk," I said, drawing her eyes to me. With a nod to the barstool on my left, I added, "You mind? That's somebody's seat."

Gigantor glanced around the empty bar, then pursed her lips and gave me the hairy eye. "Really?"

Harry smiled and shot me a thumbs up.

Free-form Harry had never visited me before, but the original Harry had loved this place. For all I knew, this was his version of heaven. It would be nice, if a little freaky, to hang with him again.

My soon to-to-be-leaving non-client moved to the other stool. I got the sense that she hadn't wanted to, but since she needed my help, she was humoring me.

Dallas placed her double on a napkin in front of her. She took a sip, then dove right into her pitch.

"I've heard a lot about you, Ms. Nighthawk. You come highly recommended in your field. We're very particular at the Marlowe Agency. Our clientele demands excellence. Rest assured, I wouldn't be here if your references hadn't passed muster. Outside subcontractors are thoroughly vetted to—"

I pointed at the wall clock above the bar. "You're down to fourteen minutes, Ms. Marlowe."

Her polished demeanor faded. She took a deep breath, then tossed back her double and looked me in the eye. "You got it, slick. I've been hired to find the last will and testament of my client's deceased husband. We've looked all over the damn place and can't find it. We need you to raise the old fart to find the will."

Ha! Nailed it. Only three minutes into her spiel and I could already run her out the door. But first, because I'm generally nosy, I had to ask. "Who's the stiff you want me to raise?"

"His name is Ira Kleinfeld."

"I'm sorry. Say that again?"

"Ira Kleinfeld."

No fucking way! De Palma was such an ass to pull this shit on me after the morning I'd had.

"Where is he?" I snapped and spun on my stool, scanning the room. "Where is that pinheaded son-of-a-bitch?"

Marlowe looked confused. "He was buried this morning at Elysian Fields Cemetery."

"Not the stiff, damn it! Where's De Palma!"

"De...who?"

I shook my head and pointed to the TV above the bar. "I'm guessing you haven't watched the news today."

Channel Ten's replay of my sound bite with Jade Chen filled the sixty-inch screen. Rowan Marlowe watched wide-eyed. Harry hovered beside me, glaring at her and shaking his head.

I had to agree with Harry. Something wasn't right with this scenario.

Marlowe smirked. "Let me get this straight. Kleinfeld's already above ground. So I don't need you to raise him. I just need to find him before you do, and get what I need before you put him down."

She grabbed her purse, threw ten bucks on the bar and broke for the door.

That's when it came to me.

"Wait just a damn minute!" I dove across the room and blocked her exit. "Ira Kleinfeld wasn't married. What's the real reason you want him raised?"

"None of your business, Smurfette." Marlowe bowled me over like a linebacker and raced out the door.

I reached the parking lot just in time to see her drive off. "Hey! Come back here, Godzilla. You owe me a hundred bucks!"

She laughed and flipped me the bird.

I thought about chasing the heifer down. The money wasn't worth it but my pride was. Dallas pulled me back inside before I could do anything rash (which, let's be honest, is the only kind of thing I would have done). I told him if I ever caught the bitch, I'd rip out her lying tongue and staple it to her forehead. I hadn't been shafted like that in very long time. The worst of it was that snarky, smart-mouthed biatch reminded me of someone. I just couldn't figure out who.

Spewing newly invented curse words, I returned to my seat and told Dallas to bring me a Jack Daniel's slushie, after all. Why the hell not? My day was so deep in the crapper, even Roto Rooter couldn't save it. And it wasn't close to over. Rico texted, asking if I was free yet. Cap wanted us to stop by with a quick update. And by 'wanted' he meant ordered. Cap was getting pressured from all sides for movement on the new cases.

Dallas looked disappointed that I had to leave, but said to come back soon, and that my slushie would be waiting for me, on the house. I waved goodbye, then turned to Harry's stool, halfway expecting his essence to be gone. I wondered if, in this setting that held so many memories, my mind had simply manufactured him. But the ghost of the best partner I'd ever had remained. Perching on his stool now, he smiled and waved goodbye. My heart tugged. I missed him. I hoped he'd still be there the next time I dropped in.

I climbed on my Harley and headed for the precinct, for another fun-filled meeting with Cap. Fingers crossed, I'd fare better than I had in our earlier meeting. But we're talking about me, folks. Custer had better odds.

8

THAT WENT WELL

Cap's latest secretary glanced up as I strolled past the bullpen and quickly buried her head in a file. She wasn't about to engage me, let alone challenge me for access to Cap's office. A small victory in my otherwise craptacular day. It's a sickness, this need I have to dominate. Truth be told, life in the 51st wasn't nearly as much fun with Miriam gone.

I knocked and entered without waiting for a response. Rico was already there. He and Cap stopped speaking when I walked in. The hair on the back of my neck raised.

"Let's make this quick," Cap said. "I have to meet my personal trainer at five."

I didn't dare look at Rico. Some low hanging fruit, no matter how tempting, was off limits. The aging, chrome-domed captain, rounder than he was tall, had high blood pressure and bad knees. When he really got upset, spit flew from his mouth and a big purple vein pulsed Morse code from his right temple. I'd seen that vein ready to blow more than most. If Cap was working with a personal trainer, it was likely under duress.

Rico glanced down at his notes. "I interviewed Messmer's wife. She wasn't able to tell me much, but she confirmed that he had coronary artery disease. She has no idea where he came into contact with the Z-virus. He worked for Phoenix Innovations on Fifth Street. That's our next stop."

Cap darted his eyes to me. "Your turn. Give me good news, hotshot."

Once again, I would disappoint.

"Other than our case, Dr. Christian hasn't seen any reports of Z-virus infection with unknown contact tracing. All the cases, up 'til now, have been transmitted either through bite or injection. Based on the minimal crime scene details I was able to provide, he believes it's possible we're not dealing with a new strain of the virus. A new strain would result in more than a single case. He thinks what we might be seeing is a new delivery system."

Rico frowned. "So the virus is being introduced into the body some other way?"

Cap tilted his head back and closed his eyes. "Sweet Jesus."

"But," I added, "Christian could be wrong."

They stared at me in silence.

"I'm not saying he *is* wrong. I'm just saying he's giving us his best hypothesis based on a very small amount of data. I think we need to be open to both possibilities."

Cap drummed his fingers on his desk. "So, where do we go from here, boys and girls?"

Rico rose from his chair and began to pace. "Delivery systems into the body...so what did Messmer eat? What did he drink? What form does the virus take? Maybe it's saturated on paper and absorbed. Or maybe it's ingested from blotters, like acid dots. What about medication? For all we know, it could be pumped into the body via asthma inhalers."

Rico was spinning out of control.

"How about this?' I said. "We can have the task force forensics team check out Messmer's home, but since his wife wasn't infected, I like De Palma's idea of checking out his workplace next."

"Great. Get on it." Cap glanced at his watch and pushed away from his desk. "I'm outta here. Stay on top of this and keep me posted. And for God's sake, if the press pushes you for leads," Cap glared at Rico and mimed twisting a key by his mouth, "tick a freaking lock."

We followed Cap out of his office, but I intentionally hung back a bit. Rico glanced over his shoulder when he'd noticed I'd stopped.

He back-pedaled a couple of steps and asked, "What's up?"

"I've got somewhere to be tonight. But I was thinking, before we call in the task force, we should reach out to Philippe Boucher."

Rico paused. "Who?"

"My dark web contact—the guy who led us to duat.com when we were working Leo's case. I'd like to see if he's heard rumblings of new viral strains or delivery systems—more importantly, does he know of any new players who might have crawled out of the woodwork."

"Let's do it." His eyes twinkled. "We'll hit him up first thing in the morning. Whatcha got going tonight?"

I'd hoped he wouldn't ask. Rico, Ferris and I worked great together as a team, but I sensed unspoken tension between them when it came to me.

"Just training for the Flying Pig."

"Oh, that's right, you're running. Good luck. Jade will be at the finish line. She's covering it for Chanel Ten."

Of course, she was...damn it.

After Rico and I exchanged *good nights* and went our separate ways, I headed for Casa de la Nighthawk to change into my running clothes and catch up on the daily damage report relative to Headbutt, Kulu and Baby Hyrum, also known as the Terrible Trio.

NORMALLY THE RUMBLE of my Harley announced my arrival and the menagerie went berserk. But that night Headbutt, locked securely behind the backyard fence, was otherwise engaged, whizzing through the chain-link on the Winstel's Wisteria. I parked the lowrider and shut it off, then strolled toward my kitchen door, noticing for the first time that the wisteria vine had wilted and turned brown. There was a definite cause and effect at play.

When I first brought Headbutt home, he took to peeing through the fence on the opposite side of the yard, dousing Nonnie's rose bushes. She broke him of that habit by spraying him with her hose.

One problem solved; another problem created.

Verdi's "Rigoletto" blasted me as I walked through the door. Kulu and baby Hyrum, both obnoxiously tone-deaf, whistled and screeched to the music, adding to the hellacious din.

Nonnie glanced up hopefully from the laundry she'd been folding at the kitchen table. "So we have new client, now. Yes? This Rowing Merlot?"

"No," I said, with a hangdog look. "But on the bright side, I made a new mortal enemy."

"Another one?" Nonnie rolled her eyes.

I grabbed a freshly-washed pair of sweats from the laundry basket, and glanced over at Hyrum as I hurried to the bedroom to change. Inquiring minds wanted to know, mine included, how that five-month-old fledgling had come to exist.

According to Nonnie, our newest feathered friend had been the product of the immaculate conception, part deux. Just like in the typical knock-em-up-and-run, no baby-daddy birdie had stepped up to offer support. Nonnie volunteered to raise Hyrum at her house, but she was at my place all day long running the business, so it made more sense to keep him here with Kulu.

On my way out the door, I thanked Nonnie for holding down the fort, then nuzzled my flocksters and gave them dog biscuits—liver flavored. The chicken treats are for me. I tossed two into my pocket, then headed out the door. Headbutt trotted over and snuffled, zeroing in on my pocket. I gave the best zombie-hunting dog a corpse whisperer could want a kiss on his head and handed him the treats.

As I walked my Harley to the street, I grabbed a folded piece of paper crammed into my mail box. It hadn't been there when I'd arrived twenty minutes earlier. *Oh, how sweet*, I thought when I read the note. It was a love letter from the Winstel's, complaining about their half-dead, pee-soaked wisteria vine. They wanted a hundred bucks to replace it.

Hey, I wanted the hundred bucks Rowan Marlowe owed me. But life's tough. The words *pound salt, you shit gibbons* sprang to mind.

They're afraid of me, you know. My neighbors. In their defense, some freaky shit's gone down at my house over the years. Half of the nosy nellies hate me, the other half fears me, and the HOA's main objective is to exile me. Apparently, they're too dense to realize that I'm broke and stuck here like toilet paper on the bottom of a shoe. I'm not going anywhere, so they might as well get their panties un-bunched.

I glanced over at the Winstel's house and saw the living room curtains flutter. With a black heart and a big smile, I started my bike, revved the engine in front of their driveway as loud as possible, and tore up the road to Eden Park.

FERRIS WAS WAITING for me at Mirror Lake. Handsome, loyal, sweet Ferris, with his hair slightly ruffled and his skin sheening with sweat from having warmed up before I got there. Everything a girl could want in a guy. So what was my problem?

"Hey," he said, bussing the top of my head with a kiss. "How was your day?"

"Making friends and influencing people, as usual."

"Jesus. What'd you do now?"

I rehashed Vinny's escaped rotter (leaving out any mention of mega-bitch Rowan Marlowe.) Then we discussed the new Z-virus cases with negative contact tracing, which were slowly becoming the talk of the town. I started my warmup, complaining about ACME and what a crazy idea the whole thing had been from the start.

Ferris nodded sympathetically, even though he'd heard it all a thousand times. There wasn't much about my life he didn't know, including my finances and the back taxes I owed.

Ferris lowered his voice. "I told you I'd give you the $13,000. No strings attached."

That was out of the question. I could never accept his money, especially considering my doubts about our relationship. For some reason, his keen, sapphire eyes that never missed a clue at a crime scene, simply couldn't see that.

"If you're uneasy taking the money," he said, "consider it a loan."

"A loan we both know I'll never be able to pay back."

The weight of his stare made me uncomfortable, so I trotted out to the running path that bordered Mirror Lake and took off. He followed and paced me at my side. Once we fell into an easy rhythm, I raised an even more awkward issue.

"There's something else I want to ask you."

Ferris cocked his brow.

"That day in New Orleans, when I shot Toussaint. You told me he was dead and that you felt his pulse to be sure. You're absolutely, one-hundred percent certain he was dead?"

I felt his body tense beside me, but he stayed in step. We

veered onto a wooded path that fringed Krohn Conservatory and started up a steep hill.

"Why would you even ask that?" He lengthened his stride to get in front of me. A few yards later, he stopped, turned around and squared his shoulders. "Are you accusing me of lying?"

"No." Yet, even as I answered, I knew that's what it had sounded like.

I motioned him to keep going and sprinted on. Again, he met my pace.

"I spoke to Dr. Christian today about these new cases. He said the virus wasn't likely mutating, organically or synthetically. That there'd be more cases if it was spreading. He thinks there could be a new delivery mechanism."

Ferris stayed silent.

We continued up the hill, muscles aching, lungs burning, before cresting at the top. The Ohio River lay before us, long and wide, as we huffed and puffed, bent over, hands on knees, gasping for air.

"If Toussaint isn't behind this," I finally said. "Then who is?"

"So I lied. That's your conclusion."

He turned and sprinted back down the hill, setting a pace I couldn't match. By the time I made it back to Mirror Lake, he was already in his car, sulking, judging by the way he refused to make eye contact with me.

The engine of his Miata roared to life.

"Hey," I yelled through his half-opened window. "One more run tomorrow? Before the race?"

"I think we've had our run. Don't you?" The window rolled shut, and he peeled off into the night.

That went well.

I took my time driving home, second-guessing the way I'd handled our discussion. But as I pulled into the driveway and parked, I concluded the problem wasn't me. Ferris had been acting like a twit and he would have to get over his sensitive-girl self. When it came to Toussaint, no questions should ever be off the table. His powers had seemed boundless, and the stakes were too high.

The back door opened with a soft creak. Headbutt was nowhere to be seen. Probably snoozing on my bed. The birds were covered and mercifully quiet. It was Friday night. I poured myself a double Jack slushie, then poured another shot in a coffee cup, and plopped on the couch with a sigh.

Slipping my hand beneath my shirt, I lifted the small gris-gris bag Mama Femi had given me over my head and placed it in the coffee cup. According to Mama, weekly Friday night soakings in Jack Daniel's would keep its magic strong. And Mama never lied.

After finishing my slushie, I plodded down the dark hallway and rapped on Vinny's bedroom door. No answer. I wasn't surprised. Nonnie's car hadn't been parked in her driveway, so he was still out with it. That was a good sign. He hadn't given up and come back to ask for my help with finding Ira Kleinfeld. Thank God. Even corpse whisperers need a night off every once in a while.

9

FOR THE LOVE OF GOD, DON'T SHOOT!

After a bad night's sleep worrying about Vinny, I rose at the butt crack of dawn and checked his room again. Gel Boy still wasn't home. I texted, asking him to check in, then showered and dressed, throwing on my *Zombie Hunter: Licensed to Kill* T-shirt and a fresh pair of black jeans. Then I slipped my gris-gris bag back over my head. I never went anywhere without it.

My freshly washed hair needed a containment system, so I gathered it in a scrunchy and threaded it through my *ACME, Inc.* ball cap. Since the morning was frosty, after I pulled on my zombie-stomping boots, I slipped into my leather duster.

Item number one on my daily *To Do* list completed: Fully clothed and ready to rock.

After downing a cup of high-octane coffee, I left Nonnie a note, asking her to gather cyber intel on both The Marlowe Agency and Ira Kleinfeld. I needed to know everything about them. Nonnie may be old and set in her ways, and her English may be a bit challenging, but she had taken to the internet like a zombie to Doritos. She knew how to work the web way better than I did.

A sleepy Headbutt wandered into the kitchen and padded to the back door, ready for his morning constitutional. I shook my finger in his face and warned him about whizzing on the Winstel's ugly-ass vine. Then I wrapped up a couple of slices of Nonnie's homemade rugelach and shoved them into my pocket. Headbutt could stay in the fenced yard until Nonnie arrived a few minutes later. I uncovered the birds, checked their food and water, and reached for the door knob.

"Bye-bye, birdies," I said, slipping outside.

As the door closed behind me, Kulu screeched, "Get outta here, ya loser!"

I couldn't help but wonder, as I pushed my lowrider to the street: Where do these foul-mouthed peckerheads pick this shit up?

Rico walked through the door of the 51st and found me seated in the chair beside his desk. A piece of Nonnie's rugelach, elegantly centered on a cheap paper plate, topped the mound of files that spilled across his desktop.

Rico's eyes lit up. "Wow. What did I do to deserve this?"

"You don't hate me."

"It's early," he said, cramming a chunk of home-baked crack into his mouth. "Give it time."

I grabbed us both some coffee from the kitchenette while he fired up his computer. When I got back to his desk, he was already googling search words like Z-virus and viral transmission. Most of the articles were months old. I read the ones with merit; there weren't many. Name the malady or the disease, there was a wealth of website misinformation to be found, and sadly, believed.

Rico and I had crapped out, like I'd thought we would. So I took a deep breath and messaged Philippe, the black-market mercenary who had a creepy way of knowing things before they happened. He responded instantly.

> I thought you might be in touch.

Rico and I exchanged glances.

"Don't share too much," Rico whispered. "His loyalty goes to the highest bidder."

I thought for a moment, then typed:

> Do tell...

Rico slurped his coffee. "That's playing it tight to the vest." Philippe's response popped.

> I have some intel you'll be interested in.

> Like what?

> Not so fast. You owe me. Remember?

Crap. I'd seen this coming. Time to ante up.

"What exactly do you owe him?" Rico asked.

"We never settled on that."

> I remember. What do you want?

> Many things. The question is, what have you got?

> Heartache and acid reflux, dude. Just tell me what you want.

Rico laughed out loud and pounded his desk. "This is better than watching CSI!"

Philippe took his time responding. When his message finally appeared, my eyes flew wide open.

I want to meet. In person.

Rico howled, then rolled out of his chair, onto the floor, laughing. Thank God it was early and the place was still empty,

"Get the hell up before somebody sees you," I said, darting my eyes back to the keyboard.

When and where?

Eddie Merlot's. Dinner and drinks tonight. Seven o'clock.

Ha! I can't even afford their napkin lint. Second choice?

My treat. Wear something sexy.

Rico climbed back into his chair and read the messages he'd missed. "What are you doing? The guy's dangerous. You said so yourself."

I shot him the Allie-eye and typed:

If I meet you, we're square?

Yes.

How do I know you have what, I backspaced, feeling heat rise in my cheeks as Rico hovered over me, reading the exchange. I retyped my sentence.

How do I know you have the intel I need?

Philippe's response, slow to arrive, included two images: an API photo of a zombie biting its victim, and a medical advertisement featuring a syringe. Beneath the images, he'd typed the words:

Silly girl, I always have what you need.

Rico moaned and shot the bird at his computer screen. "Freaking sleazebag."

"No," I said, grabbing his arm. "Don't you get it? He's telling me he has information about a new transmission source for the virus. We know about bite transmission," I said, pointing to the API photo. Then I slid my finger to the medical ad, "And we know about transmission by injection."

My fingers flew across the keyboard before Rico had a chance to reply.

See you there.

"No way!" Rico gawked at me. "This guy would cut your throat as soon as look at you."

"Don't be so melodramatic. He might be a mercenary, but at least he's honest about it. And he's always been straight with me."

"Sure. Right up to the time somebody pays him to gut you like a fish. I'm working backup for you tonight. Don't even try to talk me out of it."

"Suit yourself."

"Sometimes, even people we trust can chew us up and sp —" Rico's cell phone rang. He stopped mid-rant and checked the display.

"It's Jade," he mouthed and wandered off to take the call.

Talk about chewing people up and spitting them out. The irony was delicious.

Nonnie called while I was waiting on Rico. "Miss Allie, I finish searches for you. Something not on the up and down with this Mrs. Merlot. Article say they in business since 2010, but I check them on Domain Age Checker. It say company name created a month ago, same time as domain."

"Ha! I knew they were sleazebags. What about Kleinfeld?"

"So much dirts on this...this...stinker!"

I stifled a laugh. "And what did our stinker do?"

"News say he interesting person wanted for embezzles of 1.8 millions from Elite Trust Bank Corporations. But he never arrested. No sufficient proof. Bank offering ten percent reward for recovery of monies."

So that sketchy, red-headed stork was after the reward money!

"Nonnie, send your intel to Rico's e-mail address. And include some pics of our stinker."

"Sure. But what we do now, Miss Allie?"

"We beat her to the money. Then we shove it up her—Hold on. Vinny's calling in."

"Vinny, glad you call—"

"I got him cornered! Just wanted you to hear the shot when I put him down."

"Don't shoot! Don't shoot! For the love of God, don't shoot!"

"Whaddya you mean, don't shoot? I've been chasing this meatbag for two days! I'm hungry and tired, and I —"

"Vinny, don't! He's worth $180,000 without a bullet in his head."

"Say *what*?"

"Where are you?"

"The abandoned church on Freeman. Near Hulbert."

"I'm on my way. I'll explain when I get there. Just keep him cornered. And whatever you do, don't let him get away!" I ended the call and nearly forgot to pick Nonnie up on the other line. "Nonnie, I gotta go. Vinny found our stinker."

I didn't even know if she was still holding. I hit *end*, jammed the phone in my pocket, then scrawled a note to Rico.

> *Outta here. Located Kleinfeld. TTYL. Print out Nonnie's e-mail to you*
> *—A.*

10

VINNY VS. BIG BIRD: ROUND ONE

My Harley and I tore up the road on our way to Freeman Avenue. The church in question had been abandoned for years. It should have been razed long ago and the city safety council knew it.

Vacant buildings are hotspots for drug users and zombies. Living on the streets, the homeless are easy pickings for them both. Biters can't see in the sunlight, so they shelter during the day and prowl at night. At least the good, old-fashioned kind do. But the newer, zombie 2.0 models, products of the synthetic virus, aren't sunblind. They still hang in the shadows though, waiting for their next meal to wander by. Vinny had been smart to check out the church. Maybe there was hope for him yet.

That hope was instantly dashed when I pulled to the curb in front of the church. Vinny and Rowan Marlowe burst through the weather-worn cathedral door and sailed through the air, their arms and legs entwined in a death grip.

They rolled across the blacktop, over and over, swearing and beating the crap out of each other. Vinny wouldn't last long. That Marlowe chick was a beast.

I jumped from my lowrider and joined the fray, trying to

separate them. They were like two mammoths, horns hopelessly locked in combat. Neither one of them was giving up. Enough was enough.

"Vinny, let go," I yelled, wrapping my fingers around Marlowe's ear and yanking her head to the side. She rolled off Vinny with a grunt.

"Damn it, that hurt!"

She threw a hook kick but I blocked it, then grabbed her ear again. "Don't even try it, sister. Sit your ass on the ground, or I'll rip off this ear and shove it up your nose."

Exhausted, she raised her hands in silent surrender and I let go of her ear. Vinny wasn't doing much better and he was probably twenty years her junior.

I nearly burned a hole through his head with my stare. "What the hell's going on here, Vinny? And where's Kleinfeld?"

Marlowe started to speak, but I smashed her lips with my finger. "Was I talking to you?"

Gel Boy sat up with a groan. "I had him, Nighthawk. Right there, in the nave of the church. He wasn't going anywhere. Then this...this," he pointed to Marlowe, "*redwood tree* showed up outta nowhere and shoved a gun in my back."

"That was my finger, Einstein."

"How was I supposed to know that!" Vinny swiped his hair out of his sweaty face. "Next thing I know, she's smarting off, saying, *'Beat it, Pinhead'* and *'I'll take it from here.'* I tell her, 'The hell, you will' and spin around to grab her gun. Then she clocks me in the jaw and tackles me."

He ran his fingers over the blooming purple bruise she'd left behind and winced. "Nice shot, by the way."

Marlowe nodded. "You gave as good as you got."

"Make nice on your own time," I said, scowling at them both. "Where the hell is Kleinfeld?"

Vinny moaned and flopped back on the pavement.

Marlowe grimaced and dusted herself off. "The geezer took a hike while Pinhead and I were...negotiating."

"Are you freaking kidding me?!" I kicked at the ground. "That's two times in twenty-four hours this geriatric deadhead's given Vinny the slip. And this time," I said, standing toe-to-toe with Marlowe, "you're responsible. You tailed Vinny to find Kleinfeld. And I know why too—that ten percent reward Elite Trust is offering. Didn't think I'd find that out, did you? Ha!"

Marlowe spit out a tooth fragment. "I was hoping you wouldn't."

"That's the first honest thing you've said since we met."

She gimped away, glancing over her shoulder. "This ain't over 'til it's over, Nighthawk. That hundred-and-eighty-grand's as good as mine."

"In your dreams, Big Bird."

A block or so north, she darted down an alley, massaging her hamstring, and disappeared.

Vinny hauled his ass up off the ground and glued his eyes to the asphalt.

I was beside myself.

"What the... How could..." There were so many things I wanted to say, I got tongue-tied. "Really? You couldn't take a girl?"

"She's like nine feet tall!" He let out a long, drawn-out sigh, then lowered his voice, "I'll get this meatbag if it's the last thing I do. But first, I need some sleep—and some food."

"Go home. Grab a sandwich and get some shut eye. I don't need you falling asleep at the wheel and wrecking Nonnie's car."

His eye was already swelling.

"And put some ice on that shiner."

Vinny eased himself into the Pinto and puttered up the road. Backfire belched from its prehistoric tailpipe. I climbed on my lowrider, pulled out my phone, and speed-dialed Rico. He answered on the first ring.

"Wow, that was quick. Where are you? I'll send the meat wagon."

"Don't bother. Kleinfeld's still MIA."

"What the hell?" Rico's voice sounded like he'd caught his balls in his zipper. "He's a ninety-year-old zombie!"

"Tell me about it."

"Cap's gonna be pissed."

"Ya think?"

"Speaking of Cap," he said, lowering his voice, "I kind of... jumped the gun after I read your note. He asked me where you were, and I told him you had Kleinfeld in the bag."

"What the hell did you do that for?"

"I...this... *Jesus*, Nighthawk, you always get your rotter."

Perfect. For the third time in two days, Cap would want my head impaled on a pike high above the precinct. That was a record, even for me.

"Way to go, Chatty Cathy. You might as well set him straight. I'm on my way."

Rico sputtered something, but I hung up before he finished and jammed the phone into my back pocket. After taking a long, cleansing breath, I started the Harley and silently swore to rip the lips off Rowan Marlowe's face, if it was the last thing I ever did.

———

CAP'S TWAT-WAFFLE secretary had returned for her second day at the 51st. When Rico and I passed her in the hallway, she gave him a flirtatious smile, then saw me and wildly darted her eyes, as if looking for an escape. Apparently, I'd broken her. A small triumph, but at that point, I'd take anything.

Once again, I trudged into Cap's empty office and sank into

my usual chair, where I waited for him to return. Rico leaned against a filing cabinet, studying the case files he'd brought to discuss.

I caught myself mining the chair's ripped upholstery in search of stuffing. There was none to be found. Over the last two days, I'd put that chair, and Cap, through the wringer. I wasn't sure how much more either one of them could take.

Cap strode in quietly and stood behind his desk. He eased into his chair, pushed it back to a forty-five-degree angle, and clasped his hands beneath his chin. His face was pale; his eyes, the color of pitch. I'd often laughed about the vein in his head exploding, but the truth was every day brought him new challenges and stressors. I hated my place at the top of that list.

"From the beginning," he said, nodding at me. "And don't leave anything out. I hate surprises."

I thought about lying, maybe leaving out the part about Marlowe and the reward money. But the damned brain bitch threw a hissy and refused to cooperate, so I sat tall and threw myself on Cap's mercy.

"Vinny said he had Kleinfeld trapped in the old church on Freeman. I told him to keep his bogey cornered until I could get there."

"Why didn't Vinny just shoot Kleinfeld and be done with it?"

"I told him not to."

"Why?"

"I'm getting to that part."

"For the love of God, get there quick, please."

"I pulled up to the church and found Vinny, and this Nancy Drew wannabe, rolling around in the dirt, trading punches."

Cap rolled his finger through the air, silently urging me on.

"Her name is Rowan Marlowe. She's the P.I. who runs the Marlowe Agency in Mystic County—wherever the hell that is."

"And how does she figure into all this?"

"Although it was never proven, Kleinfeld, a longtime employee of Elite Trust, was the prime suspect in the embezzlement of $1.8 million in bank funds. In fact, he was the *only* suspect ever named. The bank has a ten percent bounty posted for recovery of the missing funds."

Cap leaned over his desk. "So Marlowe wanted to question Kleinfeld before you took him out—so she could collect the bounty."

"You got it!"

"That bounty's not our concern."

I bolted upright, knocking my chair to the floor. "It might not be your concern, but it's sure as hell mine! I need that money, Cap. I'm practically living on dog biscuits."

Rico groaned.

Cap rose to his feet and shoved his finger in my face. "I don't give a rat's ass about that money. You begged me to let you fix this—to put Kleinfeld down on your own without interference. And I did, despite the heat I took. But when you had the chance, you muffed it because you saw dollar signs."

His voice rose a couple of decibels. "Do you realize tomorrow is not only the Flying Pig Marathon, it's Halloween? What do you see happening when little kids go trick-or-treating in the dark with an escaped rotter on the loose? I want that deadhead decommissioned *now*! I'm issuing a BOLO on Kleinfeld. I don't care who takes him out, as long as someone does."

Cap was right. Thanks to the pandemic, the marathon had been postponed from its usual May date until the end of October.

He took a long, deep breath, returned to his seat, and then swiveled toward Rico. "Where are we on the Messmer case?"

"Phoenix Innovations is gathering their vendor contacts and shipping manifests for the last six months. They'll e-mail them to me ASAP. In the meantime, I'm reviewing their security tapes for any suspicious tampering or drug activity."

"Good," Cap said. "You can work on that 'til the records come in."

"Tomorrow's Sunday," Rico continued. "I was just about to call Director Horton to get a team here bright and early in the morning, so they can conduct some discreet environmental testing at Messmer's place—just to rule out any in-house contamination. It's unlikely, but better safe than sorry."

Cap swept his hand toward the door, inviting us to leave. "Not much more we can do for now, except find that stinking meatbag. I've called in additional street patrol from six to eight tomorrow for Trick-or-Treat, and even more for additional security at the Flying Pig. Keep me posted."

Per our last conversation, Ferris and I were supposed to be running that marathon. But now, I wasn't sure he'd show. All because I'd hurt his pansy-ass feelings, asking questions I had every right to ask. Well, he'd either be at the starting line or he wouldn't. We'd trained hard for this race—even put our dance lessons on pause to make time for it. I was going to run, with or without him.

My stomach bottomed out as Rico and I left Cap's office. It suddenly hit me that I might have actually lost my dance partner and my best friend, all rolled into one.

I snagged a bag of Doritos from the vending machine in the kitchenette, then joined Rico at his desk to help him review endless hours of security footage from Phoenix Innovations.

In my experience, the lion's share of police work involved turning old and gray while hovering over a computer monitor, evaluating facts and evidence. By the end of the day, Rico would have to tie me to a chair to keep me from poking my eyes out with a straw.

11

ALLIES AND ENEMIES

I volunteered to call Director Dickhead, so he could coordinate a team for the following morning's site eval at Messmer's place. He and I go together like matches and dynamite. Normally, I avoided him at all costs, but I'd do anything to avoid staring at security tapes until my eyeballs bled.

It was Saturday. I wasn't surprised that I got his voice mail. But he called back within the hour and said that he and his team would meet Rico at Messmer's house at 0900. It occurred to me, as I ended the call, that Ferris was a part of Dickhead's team. While my presence wasn't required for the site eval, Horton might pull Ferris in, just because he'd been a member of the task force and knew the Z-virus history by rote. If that was the case, I'd be running the Flying Pig by myself.

After downing a quick four-way onion at Skyline Chili, (spaghetti topped with chili, onions and shredded cheddar), we dug into the tapes—hours of corporate office and parking lot footage. Ten minutes after we started, my ADD kicked in. I couldn't sit still, and when I finally forced myself to glue my eyes to the screen, I got drowsy. Rico had to kick my foot a few times during the afternoon to wake me up. After the third kick, I got grouchy.

"You're not going to find anything on these tapes of open-access areas. You want to find evidence of dealing or suspicious behavior, you need to surveil the bathrooms."

Rico snickered. "You know that's illegal, right?"

I did not. Nor did I care. I spent an entire week watching film that afternoon. But as luck would have it, I had an ace in the hole. Since Flying Pig participants had to pick up their registration packets at Duke Energy before the end of the day, I had a built-in excuse to leave at four. Among other goodies, that packet contained the racing bib I needed to compete in the morning.

Rico followed me out of the precinct, promising to arrive at Eddie Merlot's slightly after seven and take a nearby table that was out of Philippe's line of sight. Before I'd made it to my Harley, he'd browbeaten me into wearing a mic and insisted on wearing his earbuds.

Battle plan secured; watches synchronized. Operation Dangerous Dinner Date was set to commence at 1900 hours.

I swung by the Duke Energy building and waited in a queue with other runners for my packet. Upon reaching the registration table, I showed my ID and was handed my packet. I spun to leave, but curiosity got the better of me.

"Sorry," I said, circling back to the volunteer. "Has Sean Ferris picked up his packet yet?"

She scrolled through the registration records on her laptop, then shook her head. "Not yet, I'm afraid."

I thanked her for checking, and tried to ignore the emptiness in my gut. I didn't have time for it. Once I arrived home, I'd have an hour and a half to sandblast my body, throw on some makeup, and dress *sexy*. Philippe's word, not mine. The odds were not in my favor. I started my Harley, threw it into gear, and lit out of Duke Energy like my hair was on fire.

NONNIE'S CAR was parked in her driveway, which meant that Vinny had made it home. I burst through my kitchen door and Headbutt jumped up to greet me, wearing a pair of toddler-sized track shorts and matching tee with the words *Team Nighthawk* silk-screened across the front. The back of the shirt read *Sponsored by ACME, Inc.: Corpse Management Services.* The material featured tiny, bright-colored zombies romping across a solid purple background.

"You like?" Nonnie asked, gleaming with pride. "Is Halloween costume for Headbutt. I take him watch the Flying Pigs tomorrow. We cheer for you and Mister Ferris."

"Wow," I said, for lack of a better response. "Just like the outfit you made me."

"Yes! You wear them for race. Be twins!"

Sweet Baby Jebus.

"That's so sweet of you," I said, hopping out of my dirty clothes and tossing them on the hardwood floor as I raced to my bedroom. "I have to get ready to leave. I have a...dinner engagement."

"Mister Ferris is such nice mens."

"It's not with Ferris," I yelled from the bedroom.

"*WHAT?*" Nonnie's orthopedic shoes thundered down the hallway.

I darted into my bathroom, naked, and slammed the door.

She pounded it with her fist. "Miss Allie! This very, very bad! Only a *tsatskeleh* two-times her mens. You no *tsatskeleh*."

"I'll take your word on that."

"But Mister Ferris!"

"It's for work, Nonnie. Relax! And get away from my bathroom door. This is...weird."

I showered and shaved my legs for the first time in...ever. After blow-drying my hair, I stood in front of the mirror, trying to remember how Psycho Babs (the profiler from the FBI task force) had styled it the night Ferris and I had attended the political fundraiser in New Orleans. She'd taken charge of my hair after my own attempt produced a creation she compared to a coon-skin cap.

"Gather, twist, pull up, and pin," I mumbled, mimicking her steps three times. The last effort produced something akin to an updo, and I pronounced it finished.

Next stop: Makeup. A little foundation and a hint of blush, a rose-colored shadow and a smidgen of liner, and...*voilà*!

Last stop: Wardrobe. It's not like I had a lot of options. I only owned one dress—the fringy, fire-engine red salsa dress I'd worn to dance class with Ferris. Thank God, Nonnie had picked it out. Someone like me, who spent her days elbow-deep in zushi, had the fashion sense of a lint ball. I slipped into my canary yellow dance shoes—the heels Leo bought me before he died.

A certified fashionista might have questioned the color coordination of that ensemble. But my feet would be under the table anyway. Name one guy who's ever noticed a woman's feet. Okay...one *normal* guy.

My heart sank as I checked for a text from Ferris and didn't find one. After a last glance into the mirror, I clomped out to the kitchen, practicing for a night on those bright yellow heels. No slips, trips or problems—other than Nonnie.

"For work, eh?" She said, casting my outfit the evil-eye. "I no believe you."

"I'm meeting one of my contacts, a guy from the internet who usually feeds me intel. Except tonight, he's feeding me dinner. Okay? Since Vinny is resting, may I please borrow your keys? I can't exactly take the Harley in this getup. If he wakes up, tell him I'll have the car back by eleven."

She snarled and tossed me her keys. "Bah! Have good time, you...you *tsatskeleh*."

Someday, I'd have to find out what that word meant.

I wangled into Nonnie's Pinto, blue book value negative $200, then puttered toward Eddie Merlot's in a $300 red dress and bitchin' yellow heels. That look had Allie Nighthawk written all over it. Screw the fashionistas. Those haute couture ho-bags wouldn't know style if it bit them in the ass.

I ARRIVED at the restaurant ten minutes early. Philippe had made reservations, so the maître d' escorted me to a cozy table for two and pulled out a chair for me. The chair faced the door. Once he'd wandered off, I moved to the opposite side of the table. I wanted Philippe to face the door. That way, Rico could request a table behind us, making surveillance more discreet. As I waited for my mercenary date, I couldn't help but wonder if he'd be a paunchy, balding man in his sixties, or a skinny computer nerd sporting a bow tie and pocket protector.

I needn't have worried. A tall, well-muscled man entered the dining room, nodded to the maître d', and instantly locked eyes with me as he sauntered toward the table. His eyes were almond-shaped. As he drew closer, I noticed they shone a silvery-grey, like the color of rough seas. His chiseled cheekbones angled to a square jaw that was perfectly shadowed with designer stubble. He wore a slightly amused smile and an exquisitely tailored gray suit that complemented his eyes.

The man was prettier than I ever hoped to be.

When he reached the table, he gazed down, raised my hand to his lips, and kissed it.

"*Enchanté*, Allie. My, my," he whispered, "but you look amazing." His voice was silky smooth and tinged with a French accent. He took his seat without another word and continued to openly ogle me. There was danger in those gorgeous eyes of his, and I wasn't entirely sure it was the good, fun kind of danger.

Determined to hold my own, I matched his silence and casually gazed around the room. Rico had just been seated at a table behind us and to the right, not thirty-feet away, facing the back of Philippe's head. The perfect position for audio/visual surveillance.

Philippe summoned the sommelier and asked for a bottle of Dom Perignon. The only reason I knew the word sommelier is because earlier in the day, when I'd had a free moment, I'd googled *eating in a high-class restaurant.*

I realized with a pang that my rules had doomed me long ago to an entirely different tax bracket than Philippe. But sitting there, across from him, he didn't look like the kind of mercenary who paid taxes anyway, so the point was moot.

Why was I so nervous?

I felt sweat beading on my upper lip. If I didn't say something soon, he'd think I was mute.

"It's nice. Meeting you," I blurted. "You know, putting a face to a message. Thank you for dinner, by the way, and the champagne. This place is...swanky. Bet even the leftovers taste good."

Good Lord, Little Allie moaned. *What the hell is wrong with you?*

Philippe's eyes lit up. "You're everything I thought you'd be."

"And yet, you're still here," I said, wanting to melt into the floor.

"There is no place else I'd rather be, *ma chérie.*"

I shifted my gaze a few degrees toward Rico. He'd leaned his head into his hand, obscuring his face, but from the way he was shaking, he was clearly busting a gut. The bastard actually snorted, but smothered it with a cough.

"Is it warm in here?" I asked, dabbing my face with a napkin.

The waiter arrived with our champagne and made a show of pouring it.

Philippe lifted his crystal flute and purred, "To new beginnings."

I clinked my glass against his and countered his toast with my own. "To learning that little tidbit of intel you promised me."

Philippe chuckled. "You are direct, aren't you?"

"Always."

"We could mix business with pleasure, no?"

Ferris's face popped into my head. I shifted in my chair. "I'm flattered. Really. But we'd be smart to keep things...simple."

Philippe sighed. "If we must. So, tell me then, how's business in this godforsaken burb?"

The conversation relaxed and grew more comfortable, for me anyway. We ordered and ate our dinner, chatting the time way, talking shop, namely weapons, tactics, and the location of hot spots we'd noted. I'd already pressed him once for the intel that he'd promised, so I played it cool, and waited for him to offer it when he was ready. Pleasant as the evening had been, I passed on dessert, and pushed the dinner to a close.

"More champagne?" he asked, moving the bottle toward my glass.

I waved it off with a rueful smile. "It's getting late. It's been a lovely night, but I really should be leaving."

Philippe leaned back in his chair and paused. "I quite enjoyed our time together. Maybe we will break bread together again someday. Perhaps then you will let me see that cautious heart of yours."

"It's just tha—"

He held up his hands. "It's quite all right, *ma chérie*. You are worth the wait."

He slid his fingers across the table until they gently covered mine, and slipped me a small scrap of paper.

Then he rose to leave, bringing my hand to his lips and brushed it with a kiss. "Until we meet again, Allie Nighthawk."

I sighed and watched Philippe walk away, thinking every girl needs a night like this to remember. Once he'd left the building, I opened my hand and unfurled the note.

I've heard rumors of an unnamed player experimenting with viral transmission modes, both indirect and vector related. If this is true, the entire world is in clear and present danger. I will be in your corner.

—P.

I wasn't sure of the scientific definitions of 'indirect' and 'vector' related, nor what they implied, but I knew for a fact, Philippe, a hardened mercenary with powers and resources of his own, understood the meaning of clear and present danger.

Rico was suddenly at my table, reaching for my hand. "What's wrong? You're shaking. Did he say something your mic didn't pick up?" His eyes snapped toward the window and he peered out into the night. "Did he threaten you?"

I handed him the scrap of paper and watched his face fall as he read the note.

"Jesus."

Jesus, indeed.

Out of an abundance of caution, Rico walked me to the Pinto. I started to get in when I noticed something stuck beneath one of the wiper blades.

A single black rose.

Rico and I glanced around at the other cars in the lot. None of them had received flowers, let alone the black rose of death.

Rico bit his lip. "Making new friends wherever you go, huh?"

He insisted on following me home, even though I said I was

all right. Because he knew I wasn't. Partners, good partners at least, always seem to sense those things. He parked at the curb in front of my house and waited while I pulled Nonnie's Pinto into her driveway and walked through the lawn, in the dark, to my side porch. As I unlocked the door and stepped inside, a double tap of his horn sounded good night.

The house was quiet. Nonnie had covered the birds and Headbutt lay sleeping on his favorite register vent. I kicked off my heels and padded down the hall, then knocked on Vinny's door to tell him it was time to get his raggedy ass out of bed and hit the streets. I shuffled to my room and slipped out of my dress, with a yawn. The Flying Pig would go off at six. That meant I'd have to get up at 4:30 to beat the crowd into town.

I sighed and set the alarm, wondering what in the world had made me think I could run this race. The answer came quickly. It had been Ferris. I grabbed my phone, hoping for a text or voicemail from him. Still nothing.

Headbutt trotted down the hallway and jumped into my bed, circling a couple of times before snuggling down beside me. His soft, rhythmic snoring had a way of lulling me to sleep. But not that night. My dreams were haunted with visions of black roses and the voice of the man I'd shot and killed in Congo Square.

12

AND THEY'RE OFF!

Whoever invented 4:30 a.m. needed to be slathered with honey and strapped naked on an ant hill. My phone app bellowed "WAKE UP!" from the top of the nightstand, scaring me shitless. I lay back down and closed my eyes, hoping to fall back to sleep, and then remembered it was race day. Bleary-eyed, I glanced at the phone. Still no message from Ferris.

Damn it.

For two-cents, I'd have slept in and said screw it. But he was already pissed at me. At least, if I showed up for the race and he didn't, I could be pissed at him. We'd put in too many training hours for him to blow this off. Surely, he would be there.

After a quick shower, I threw on my *Team Nighthawk/ACME Inc.* outfit and official running bib, then looked in the mirror and cringed, silently apologizing to Headbutt for having to share the same embarrassing fate. I munched on a chicken-flavored dog biscuit and threw more into my pocket for the ride downtown. Carbs are important on race day.

Nonnie would be at my house in a couple of hours, but I uncovered Kulu and topped off Headbutt's bowls, anyway.

Tossing my phone and some earbuds into my fanny pack, I grabbed a cheap fleece sweatshirt, ran out the door, and pushed the Harley to the street for a quiet start.

I cranked it up and checked my phone one last time before taking off. Still no word from Ferris. It wouldn't feel right, running without him. It wouldn't be as fun, if you call pushing yourself to the brink of death, fighting off cramps, and ignoring your body's pleas for mercy, fun. I pulled away from the curb, hoping that he'd show at the last minute, and not entirely sure what I would do if he didn't. With a parting glance at Nonnie's driveway, I noticed the Pinto was gone. Vinny was back on the job. That warmed the cockles of my heart. Misery loves company.

Even at that ungodly hour, traffic into town was slow, and the ride was frigid. But Ferris had warned me not wear my leather duster, asking me what I'd do with it while I ran. He'd said that by mile three, I'd be peeling off excess layers of clothing and tossing them to the side of the course. After the race, any unclaimed, discarded clothing would be collected and donated to Goodwill. Much as I love a good charity, I wasn't ready to part with my duster.

The Flying Pig, a qualifier for the following year's Boston Marathon, featured three days of racing, including a full and half-marathon, drawing tens of thousands of volunteers, runners, and "Street Squealers." The full-marathon alone could have up to 5,000 participants. Parking close to the river would be hellacious.

I zipped into an uptown lot, then threaded through a sea of faces toward Freedom Way, scanning the crowd for Ferris. I figured that even if I didn't see him, he might spot my ACME shirt. But the streets were clogged with a multitude of vampires, ghosts, werewolves, mermaids, and power rangers. Spectators and participants alike, showing off their Halloween-best, taking full advantage of the event being rescheduled this year, from

May to Halloween. Embarrassing as my shirt was, it hardly stood out in the mix.

At the starting line, runners trickled into their allotted corrals based on their anticipated finish time. Competitive athletes filled out corrals A and B. According to my bib, I'd been relegated to corral E. Ferris, faster than me, would be starting closer to the front. If he would have called me, I'd have known what corral he'd been assigned to or if he had been pulled into Dickhead's site eval at Messmer's place, and was skipping it altogether. If he was here, finding him in that mob during the pre-dawn darkness was going to be like looking for a needle in a haystack.

I thought about giving up and going home. The only reason I got into this mess in the first place was because Ferris wanted to run. As far as I was concerned, the words run and fun had no business in the same sentence. The yutz had left me hanging, but given the way he'd lit out after our last run, and his subsequent radio silence, how shocked could I really be?

Screw it, I thought, filtering into my corral. *I'm here. I'm running. Maybe he'll turn up somewhere in the next twenty-six miles, so I can beat the snot out of him.*

The opening ceremonies began at 6:00 a.m., followed by the start of the wheel chair race. I glanced at the runners around me, chomping at the bit, chattering in excitement. The best I could manage was a yawn. I wanted my coffee. I wanted my dog. But mostly, I wanted my bed.

At 6:30 a.m, the airhorn sounded, and the Flying Pig Marathon began. The first corral opened, releasing its runners, and then the second, and so on. *Oh, hell no,* I thought, as my corral opened and the tsunami of runners converged. *There are way too many people breathing my air.*

THE FIRST COUPLE of miles took us to the Ohio river and across the Southgate Bridge into Newport, Kentucky. After a quick jaunt through Covington, we veered back into Ohio over the Clay Wade Bailey Bridge. Packed like sardines when we'd burst from the corrals, after the second mile or so, we began to settle into our own individual paces. The next few miles were flat. Then came the three-hundred-foot incline up Gilbert Avenue through Eden Park (where Ferris and I trained) and on to DeSales Corner—miles six through nine.

Some runners called that stretch of the course hard. Ferris called it fun. I called it a murderous bitch, and by the time I hit DeSales Corner, seven words raced through my mind: *what the hell had I been thinking?*

Half-marathoners split off at St. Francis DeSales Church, leaving me and the other twenty-six milers to dry-heave our way to the finish line.

Water stations dotted every mile. Spectators packed the street corners, jostling for a glimpse, and cheering us on, tossing us Vaseline, Twizzlers, Swedish Fish, and Dixie cups of beer for added fuel. Screw the candy, folks. I'm a Jack Daniel's girl, but beer was close enough. I grabbed every cup of suds I saw.

If Ferris was participating and I'd simply missed him, he'd be miles in front of me. But I kept an eye out for him anyway. Scanning the crowd helped me focus on something other than pain as I put the next leg of the race behind me.

Near Erie Avenue, a tall female spectator stepped from the curb a few yards ahead of me and blocked my path. She stared at me with the most radiant green eyes I'd ever seen, raised her hand, and shoved a big red popsicle at my face. I pushed her hand away and sidestepped to keep from running her over, accidently jostling the runner beside me, a middle-aged woman wearing a pink tutu and a flying pig hat with wings.

"Sorry," I muttered, glancing back over my shoulder, hoping

to spot the pushy spectator and tell her off, but she was gone, hopefully off the street, hiding among the crowd. The freaking nimrod. She could have caused a pileup. Besides, I've got spatial issues. Nobody shoves a hand in my face. If I would have found her, I'd have crushed that hand into a bone-shard jigsaw puzzle. I might have gotten arrested, but at least I wouldn't have had to run the rest of the race.

Around mile fourteen, beginning the third leg of the race, my legs turned to silly putty and I got a stitch in my left side. After slowing to a walk, I took some deep breaths, raised my right arm over my head and bent into the stitch. Still there, but slightly better. Straightening up, I stopped and gazed absently at the single-lane traffic snaking through the intersection of Erie and Bramble.

Squinting into the early morning sun, I noticed a man dressed in a suit climb into the back of a black SUV at the corner. It was only a split-second glance, and a silhouette view at that, but I could have sworn it was Ferris. I jogged across the street as the SUV turned the corner and sped away on Bramble. I'd only caught the first three digits of the plate: PHO. By the time I reached the corner, the SUV was taking a right onto Settle Street.

As if I wasn't distracted enough, the theme song from Dragnet blasted from my fanny pack. *What the hell is Cap doing, calling me now?* I wondered. He knew I was running the marathon. Secretly thankful for the momentary break, I pulled out the phone and raised it to my ear.

"Wassup?" I asked.

"Where are you?"

"Mile fourteen-ish, at the corner of Bramble and Settle. Why?"

"A marathoner dropped-dead just ahead of you on Miami Road across from the medical tent. The EMTs watching the race said the guy grabbed his left arm and went face-first to the pavement. Classic heart attack. They got to him within seconds, applied CPR, and used the defibrillator but couldn't get his heart started. They even called time of death. But then the runner opened his eyes, twitched like a pithed frog, and tried to take a chunk out of an EMT's neck. Next thing they knew, the dead guy scrambled to his feet and disappeared into the crowd."

I frowned. "Any bite wounds?"

"Negatory, per the EMTs."

"Impossible. Infected zombies don't turn instantly."

"Tell that to the dead guy."

"Was that a joke?"

"Nighthawk, have you ever known me to joke?"

Cap disconnected, and I let out a groan. A freshie loose in a crowd of thousands. *Holy hell,* I thought. *It's anyone's guess how many spectators and locals are dressed like deadheads for Halloween.* Just what I needed. A ginormous game of zombie tag.

MY THOUGHTS SWIRLED as I sprinted the next mile to Miami Road. Somehow, in a matter of three days, the rules of carovescitis had changed. When I raised a corpse, the body instantly reanimated. But when corpses went rogue due to infection, the lag time between physical death and reanimation varied based on the amount of toxin released into the victim's system. Zombies had been known to turn in as little as fifteen minutes, but only in bite attacks where massive doses of the toxin had been systemically delivered in the attack.

Messmer, the corpse at the funeral home, had supposedly died of a heart attack too. Neither of these guys had been bitten. So why had they turned? And how had the dead runner reanimated so quickly? The more I thought about it, the more I believed Dr. Christian's theory held water. People were being infected in such a way as to enhance the metabolic rate of the virus.

But how?

The road crested and the intersection at Miami came into view. Patrol officers had cleared the junction and contained the crowd behind crime scene tape. A group of EMTs huddled in front of the medical tent, shaking their heads and gesturing in animated conversation. I slowed to a jog, suddenly realizing that I was the only marathoner left on the street. Strange as that seemed, it made perfect sense. CPD had obviously diverted the runners behind me. The last thing the investigation needed was thousands of feet trampling the scene.

One of the EMTs broke from the huddle and trotted toward me, wearing a vacant stare. I'd seen that hollow look too many times before to not recognize it. Poor guy. After what he'd just witnessed, handing out band aids and ice packs to runners probably seemed surreal.

"Hi, ma'am." His voice sounded distant, and his words fell flat. "What can we help you with? Pulled muscles? Blisters? Cramps?"

"Just zombies, today."

He darted his eyes back to my running bib and then paused. "Nighthawk. I know that name. You're that...the...ah... that cadaver diver chick who's always in the news."

"The correct term is corpse whisperer. And stop watching Channel Ten. Their field reporter has it in for me."

"Yeah," he shrugged. "But she's hot."

"Sure, if you like tiny, shiny and whiny. Just tell me about the biter."

"What can I say? The corpse started twitching and sprang back to life. It jumped up and went for my neck, so I doused it with pepper spray."

Crap.

"So it actually saw you—it went directly toward your neck before you sprayed it?"

"Yeah. Then I gave it a blast of chemicals. It ran in circles a few times and then took off through the crowd." He pointed west toward Elder Street.

Pepper spray! I thought. *Good choice.* That explained why no one in the crowd ended up as the main course. The damned thing wouldn't be able to see or smell after a faceful of pepper spray. But the bad news was that it would be temporary. This breed of biter was able to see in the daylight, so when the spray wore off, the crowd of spectators would be a giant buffet.

I called Cap to let him know my sitrep and where I was headed next.

"Rico's enroute," Cap said. "I'll give him your twenty. We've got choppers in the air, searching for your biter. Out of an abundance of caution, we've shut down the marathon, but clearing the crowd will take time. Be careful. And catch that biter pronto, before the chemical spray wears off and that damned deadhead eats its way across the city."

Like he'd needed to tell me that. He disconnected before I could ask him if he thought I'd been planning to stop for a latte along the way.

I shoved my phone back into my pack wondering why everyone else could stop running except me. Then I asked the EMT for some cold water and a towel. After a few gulps and a quick toweling off, I cut across the grass and sprinted toward Elder Street. No sign of the biter there. In fact, the police had already dispersed the crowd. The intersection looked deserted. The choppers were making wide sweeping loops as opposed to hovering in any particular area. Clearly, we were both flying blind.

On a hunch, I headed toward Eastern Avenue, which ran along the Ohio River. I figured once the chemicals wore off, the biter might instinctively head for the shadows of the tree-lined bank.

Not far up Eastern, I spotted something lying in the road ahead. Something long and thin that stretched across the pavement. Something body-shaped. The hair on the back of my neck prickled. I picked up my pace. The closer I got, the further away I wished I'd been.

A police officer's body lay crumpled on the ground, wallowing in a pool of blood. He'd been gutted and gnawed on at length. His Glock lay on the asphalt, inches away from his outstretched arm. I called the location in to Rico, knowing he was already on his way.

A distant scream pricked my ear from somewhere ahead. I grabbed the dead officer's Glock and sighed. These rotters were turning too quickly. I couldn't leave him lie. I said a silent prayer and put a 9mm slug in his brain, and then sprinted (as fast as I could after having run twenty miles) in the direction of the scream.

Two bends in the road later, I found a teenaged girl stranded on top of the roof of a Ford-F450, kicking at a biter that was trying to pull her down. The rotter was wearing running shorts, and a Flying Pig marathon bib. His chest was covered with electrodes.

Target acquired.

One round of ballistic therapy later, that target was neutralized. But the girl screamed again. I spun to find a corpsicle, the oldest, most decayed and smelliest kind of zombie, had wandered out from the tree line. I let it shamble close, then calmly squeezed the trigger.

Nothing happened.

No more bullets. No extra mags. And no other weapon. Crap on a cracker, I hate when that happens. I ripped the radio antenna off the girl's truck, held it in front of me like a foil, and yelled, "*En Garde*, motherfucker!"

The moldering meatbag growled and lunged for my arm, but I sidestepped and pivoted, ramming the antenna straight through its eye socket into its brain.

Allie: Two. *Biters:* Zero.

Booyah, baby. That's how it's done.

Rico's Mustang screeched to a halt behind me, as the girl scampered down from the roof of the truck and stared wide-eyed at the rotter. "Holy crap! What did you do to my antenna! My parents are going to be so pissed."

"Really?" I said, sliding into the passenger seat of the Mustang. "Why don't you walk your snapchatting, tic-tok-loving-ass over to that biter, pull your precious antenna out of its eyeball, and shove it—"

"Nighthawk!" Rico hissed under his breath.

"A little gratitude might be nice," I yelled, as Rico peeled away.

"Too much caffeine?" he asked.

"Not nearly enough. That's the problem with the world today, you know. Nobody appreciates anything anymore. I kept her from getting corpsified, and all she cares about is that broken antenna."

I kicked off my shoes and massaged my aching feet. "For future reference, don't fuck with me after I've run twenty-something miles, downed a couple of deadheads, and saved your ass from the horde. I'll get miffed. You wouldn't like me when I'm miffed."

"Roger that, Nighthawk."

13

IT'S LIKE I DON'T EVEN KNOW MYSELF

Rico glanced over at me as he circled back to the uptown lot where I'd parked. "I thought Ferris was running with you."

"So did I. He never showed." An unsettling vision replayed in my head as I shoved my aching feet back into my shoes. "I could swear I saw him climbing into the back of a black SUV at Bramble Avenue. Maybe he was working."

Or maybe not.

"Surely, he would have let you know if he'd been called in."

"You'd think." On the snippy meter, my response had measured an eight. I stared out the passenger window and noticed the nearly deserted streets. "I'm not the fastest runner in the world, but I'm not the slowest, either. Where are all the other runners?"

"The streets emptied pretty quick once the news about the biter attack spread." He shook his head and let out a soft whistle. "Can you imagine the chaos if there'd been even more rotters on the course?"

"A freshie that rose within moments of death *and* a stinking corpsicle that appeared from out of nowhere? That was no coincidence. That was a message."

"It's almost eleven," Rico said, as he pulled into the parking lot and stopped next to my Harley. "They're conducting the environmental sweep at Messmer's house now. We need to meet with Cap, Horton, and his team after they finish up."

Rico took an exaggerated sniff and wrinkled his nose. "That gives you enough time to go back to the house and shower."

———

THE RIDE back home gave me time to mull over all the strange happenings of the last few days: the seemingly unprovoked rising of two corpses, my surreal dinner with Philippe, and Ferris's knee-jerk reaction to ghost me—not to mention Vinny's boneheaded performance at the cemetery. But just because the ride gave me time to ponder the many shitstorms of my life didn't mean I'd made headway sorting them out. By the time I pulled into the driveway, I felt like a lost ball in high grass.

The moment I stepped through the back door and heard Headbutt growling low and long, my radar went off. Nonnie was stirring a pot of marinara sauce on the stove like she didn't have a care in the world. I should have been inhaling the scrumptious scent of tomatoes, garlic and herbs. Instead, the cloying stink of decomp filled my nose.

"Everything okay in here?" I asked, peering through the archway into the rest of the house. A horrible thought crossed my mind. "Headbutt, tell me you didn't disembowel the Winstel's cat in my living room."

Nonnie looked at me like I'd lost my mind.

"It smells like zushi in here!"

"Bah." Nonnie waved me off. "Is not one of your zumbas or neighbor's cat. You got delivery."

"Was it a corpsicle?"

She rolled her eyes.

"I wasn't expecting anything."

Maybe it's some kind of F-U gift from Ferris, I thought. But it didn't take long to kick that notion to the curb. No matter how miffed he might have been, sending me a mound of decomp wasn't his style.

Nonnie shrugged. "It stink, so I drag it to backyard. But smell still here." Before I could stop her, she grabbed a can of Lysol from the counter and doused the room.

The only stench on Earth worse than *eau de deadhead* is the eye-burning reek of Lysol-scented decomp. Headbutt and I gagged in unison. I opened the back door for some fresh air and decided it was the perfect time to examine my delivery. Headbutt raced outside ahead of me. The only time that dog races anywhere is when he's hot on the trail of a biter.

I followed him around the corner of the house and into the backyard. He launched himself through the air and landed at the foot of my delivery. I grabbed his collar and ordered him to sit and stay. He obeyed, but issued a spate of non-stop whines, howls and growls. I forced myself to tune him out and focus on the stinky, ten-feet-tall abomination that stood before me: The fugliest plant I'd ever seen. It smelled of death.

About halfway up the stalk, its chlorophyll-colored bloom had begun to open, revealing a burgundy lining on the interior of the blossom. Up from the center of the bloom thrust what could best be described as an erect five-foot-tall...dong.

What the actual fuck?

A card dangled from a thin black cord that encircled the tip of the dong. I gently lifted the card over the top of the plant and scanned the message:

Through death are we reborn

Chills snaked up my spine.

The cord was actually a strip of leather. Attached to the leather was a small piece of black obsidian carved into the shape of a bird. A nighthawk to be exact. I fingered the small gris-gris bag that hung around my neck and bit my lip. The obsidian necklace had been a gift that my mentor, Mama Femi, had given me long ago, on the day I'd left her to make my way in the world.

The last time I'd seen that necklace was the night Toussaint Le Clerc had stolen it from me, using his magick. That'd been months ago in New Orleans. I replayed the scene in my mind. Toussaint had died during our shootout. Ferris told me he had taken Toussaint's pulse. Ferris swore to me that the necromancer was dead. Twice. Once while I was in the hospital recovering from broken ribs, a crushed hand, and a concussion, and again only days ago, while we were training for the marathon.

The surgical pins in my left hand still ached, but not nearly as bad as the hole my heart. Ferris wouldn't have, *couldn't* have, lied about that. And yet…

Darth Vader's Theme blared from my phone in the runner's pack still strapped to my waist. Director Dickhead's ring. Perfect. Just the person I wanted to chat with in the middle of an existential crisis.

"Nighthawk," I barked, bringing the phone to my ear.

"I can't reach Ferris. He's supposed to be here at Messmer's house for the environmental sweep. Is he there with you? I need to speak with him."

My stomach lurched.

"No. He was signed up to run the marathon with me, but he didn't show. I thought I saw him climbing into a black SUV, so I figured you'd summoned him."

"Did he look like he was under duress?"

"I don't know. It was a split-second glance."

"Did you get the plate number?"

"Just the first three digits. PHO something. I was on the other side of the street, and the car rounded the corner before I got a good look at it."

"It's not like Ferris to disappear."

I didn't want to share the news about my delivery with Dickhead, but given the situation, I didn't have a choice. "This may or may not be related, but a big ugly plant that smells like a corpsicle was delivered to my house this morning. The card attached read: *Through death are we reborn.*"

"Cryptic."

"Isn't it, though. There's more. The necklace Le Clerc took from me at Congo Square was attached to the plant. Director, I don't know how, but I think Toussaint is back."

"From the dead? Not likely. But something's up. I'll put a BOLO out on Ferris. We're finishing up at Messmer's house. I'll bring the team to analyze your...delivery. In the meantime, don't get near it. It could be booby-trapped."

A day late and a dollar short. Typical Dickhead.

I disconnected the call, then led the half-crazed Headbutt back into the house so the task force team would have a plant left to analyze.

The situation called for clear heads and calm hearts. But the more I tried to compose myself, the more my heart thundered against my ribcage. *Steady,* I chided myself. *Now's the time for logic and deductive reasoning.*

Like that's ever worked for me.

The brain bitch, tired of my delusional attempts at self-soothing, clawed to the forefront and repeated the same two questions over and over again: *Could Toussaint really be alive? And where the hell was Ferris?*

14

BOLOS OUT THE YIN-YANG

As the convoy of government-issued SUVs paraded down Pitty Pat Lane and parked in front of my house, I walked out my kitchen door and wondered what my neighbors must have thought. But that ship had sailed long ago. The multitude of eye-popping things that had transpired at my house had given the 'hood enough gossip for a lifetime. The pitchfork-toting, binocular-wearing members of the neighborhood watch, who surveilled me from behind closed curtains, had given up trying to figure me out long ago.

Frankly, I liked it that way. A little mystery kept them at bay.

An unmarked white van, with its back-up beeper blaring, snaked up my driveway and stopped just short of my garage. Four dudes dressed in HAZMAT suits shot out of the back of the van, lugging instruments and an assortment of sinister-looking gear. They hovered at the rear of the van, waiting for their leader.

I nodded at Dickhead as he emerged from the first SUV. Quickly following him out the door was a familiar face. An impeccably dressed pelican wearing a trench coat, with her hair pulled back in a bun that squatted on her head like a dead ferret. I'd have known that topknot anywhere.

"Babs," I murmured, curious as to why Dickhead had called a profiler into the investigation so soon. We didn't even have a person of interest yet, unless you counted the reportedly dead Toussaint Le Clerc. As Babs trudged up the driveway, I found myself smiling at the assortment of memories we'd managed to create during our case in New Orleans.

Agent Barbara McMillen was a tightly-wrapped whack job, one of the smartest people on Earth, and had been a friend when I'd needed one. Or maybe a frenemy. Ours was a complex relationship based on thermostat control and her incessant need to psychoanalyze me.

She crushed me in a brief but awkward embrace.

"Good to see you, Babs," I said, gently freeing myself. "Surprising, but good."

"A bit unexpected," she said, with a nod. "But given the alarming change in the metabolic rate of the Z-virus, Director Horton thought it prudent that the entire team be on site and available for immediate response as needed."

She waved at one of the guys wearing a HAZMAT suit. "You remember, Dr. Eli Stanton, our bio-terrorism specialist from the task force meeting in New Orleans."

Eli, deep in discussion with Dickhead who had wandered to the rear of the van, raised a white-gloved hand in reply. The name Eli Stanton sounded vaguely familiar, but he'd only been a medical consultant on our case. I'd never gotten to know him.

Babs' eyes sparkled. "So where is this mystery delivery of yours? Eli and I are dying to get a peek at it."

"It's around back."

Rico's red Mustang roared up the street and screeched to a stop at the end of my driveway. He trotted across the lawn and joined the group as we trudged toward the most offensive plant in the history of plantdom.

Rico angled toward me through the cluster of agents, then leaned in close, and whispered, "Has Ferris turned up yet?"

"No."

"I can't believe Horton put a BOLO out on him already. If your boyfriend turns up safe and sound, Horton's going to kill him."

"The line forms in the rear, pal."

"By the way, I ran your partial plate from the race."

"And?"

"Nothing turned up."

I didn't share the growing sense of dread inside me. Putting that emotion out into the universe seemed like bad juju.

Babs gasped at the hideous growth looming behind my house. "Simply magnificent!"

Eli Stanton, still shrouded in his HAZMAT suit, nodded. "Amorphophallus titanium. Loosely translated as Giant Misshapen Dick."

Ha! I knew it looked like a dong.

Babs circled the plant slowly, the smile never leaving her face. "Allie, this is a Corpse Flower—aptly named for its carrion-like stench. It's extraordinarily rare! They're native to the rainforests of western Sumata, but they're cultivated by private collectors around the world. Someone has loved it and cared for it, and nurtured it into this glorious specimen you see before you."

"Amazing," Eli whispered, shaking his head. "This species has the largest unbranched inflorescence in the world."

"Sumat...glorious...inflor..." I mumbled, trying to appreciate my delivery in a new light. Trying to see its rareness—it's beauty.

It wasn't working for me.

"Get this giant stinky dick out of my yard."

Eli extended his gloved hand to the plant but stopped short of touching it. "Self-pollination was thought to be impossible.

But in 1999, botanists hand-pollinated a plant with its own pollen from ground-up male flowers."

"And look," he said, pointing to the two large petals near its base, "This spathe is already open! It can take up to ten years for these plants to flower. But here in the northern hemisphere, they bloom in the spring, not October. This bloom's been forced."

That sounded vaguely illegal, not to mention immoral.

Babs planted her feet and stood, arms akimbo. "That bloom won't last long. Twenty-four hours maybe, if we're lucky. It must be moved indoors as soon as possible and preserved."

"By all means!" I gestured to the big white van. "Load it up and haul it away. Consider it my gift to the city."

Dickhead strolled over and sneered down his nose at me. "You mentioned that a necklace and a card were attached. They need to be processed for prints and DNA."

I pulled them from my pocket with a scowl and placed them in his outstretched hand. "Obviously, you'll find my genetic profile too."

Damn it. I'd missed that necklace more than anyone could know. It hurt to part with it again.

"Make sure I get this back. As soon as possible. In one piece. Well, two. The cord and the bird."

Dickhead ignored me and focused his eyes on the troops. "That's enough show-and-tell for one day, boys and girls. Let's get to work."

Babs and Eli supervised the transfer of the giant stinky johnson into the van. The rest of the agents drifted toward their SUVs, and the shit show on Pitty Pat Lane came to an anticlimactic close. But I wasn't finished yet. I stood my ground under Horton's nose.

"What about Ferris?"

"A BOLO's been issued. That's sufficient for now."

"But you know he would never just ghost—"

"Hence the BOLO. For now, you and De Palma follow me back to the 51st. Agents McMillen, Stanton and I need to be briefed on your progress on the viral metabolic issue."

Progress? That wouldn't take long.

CAP'S OFFICE was a bit small for the task force meeting, so he booked us a conference room. Dickhead sat at one end of the rectangular table while Cap claimed the other. Rico and I grabbed the closest chairs. The nerd posse: Babs, cyber-specialist Kelvin Thomas, and Eli (now dressed in civilian clothes) sat directly across from us. Eli was on the far side of fifty, with a grey buzz cut and a geeky bow tie. If memory served me, it was the same one he'd worn to the task force meeting in New Orleans. Lanky, carrot-topped Kelvin Thomas looked like the poster boy for a sunscreen commercial. Of the three specialists, I'd only gotten to know Babs, which was all it took for me to realize that I had a one geek limit.

Dickhead called the meeting to order and quickly set about eviscerating me. "Nighthawk, why don't you start us off by filling us in on the incident at Templeman's Funeral Home?"

Let's not and say we did.

"The corpse of a Mr. Paul Messmer turned rotter in said funeral home and attacked the owner of the establishment. Examination of the body found no bite marks or injection sites, which are the known means of the virus transmission. Dr. Christian at the European CDPC is looking into it, sir."

Dickhead frowned. "I thought there was an explosion. Was there enough of the body left to conduct a proper forensic examination?"

"Yes, sir. The body was thrown clear in the blast."

"What caused the explosion?"

I squirmed. "That's not really relevant. The salient point

here is that we have no explanation as to why Mr. Messmer turned."

Dickhead's face blazed as he grabbed the sides of the conference table and leaned forward. "I beg to differ. It seems that Mr. Templeman's attorney has enjoined the FBI in their suit for damages connected to the blast."

"Wow! You guys too, huh?"

"The bureau will ask to be dismissed as you were clearly on CPD business at the time of the incident and weren't under the direction of the FBI. But the net result will be a tremendous amount of wasted time, energy, and money spent on defense."

I felt Cap's eyes burning a hole through me.

Dickhead took a breath and settled back in his chair. "Templeman claims that you caused the explosion by firing into a large supply of formaldehyde. Is that true?"

"Not exactly. The bullet from my gun went through the wall and into another room, where it may or may not have come into contact with formaldehyde."

"Oh. Was there a grassy knoll and a second gunman? Or an alternative cause for the explosion that we're not aware of? Other than the bullet from the gun you fired?"

Somebody get me the fuck out of here.

"No, sir."

"Let's circle back to this another time. In an unrelated matter, I understand that two days ago, while furthering the interests of your privately-held company, ACME, Inc., an associate of yours lost a biter, and that said biter is still AWOL. Is that true?"

"Yes, sir. But said associate is hot on the trail of said biter and will not quit until said biter has been permanently decommissioned. Sir."

A red-faced Cap chimed in. "Rest assured, Director, we have a BOLO out on him. The force is all over this."

"They damn well better be."

I couldn't blame Cap for a little CYA. I was pleasantly surprised he didn't rat me out over the reward money. But Vinny? Vinny was a dead man.

Horton glanced at his notes and then back to Cap. "Last, but not least, we have today's incident involving the instantaneous reanimation of a marathoner who appears to have died of a heart attack mid-race. Let me guess. We have a BOLO out for him too?"

Cap sat tall. "No, sir. Nighthawk put him down inside of an hour. Case closed."

"Good. Then I'm sure you won't object if she and De Palma join the task force investigation of Messmer's workplace first thing tomorrow morning."

"Anything we can do to help, Director."

"Noted. Meeting dismissed. Let's wrap things up quick before they spiral further out of control."

"What a dick way to end the meeting," I whispered to Rico as we stood to leave.

"Nighthawk, sit back down," Horton called. "We need to have a chat. She'll join you momentarily, Detective De Palma."

Rico cast me a worried glance, then left the room. I figured that my day had nowhere to go but up.

Fat fucking chance.

Dickhead kicked back in his chair and stretched, wearing a smug look. "Agent Ferris was supposed to run that marathon with you, correct?"

"Yes, but you assigned him to the environmental sweep at Messmer's."

"Is that the only reason he didn't join you that day?"

"Anything else is personal and none of your business. I'd rather discuss what you're doing to find him."

Horton's eyes flashed, but his tone remained even. "What's the last thing you remember before you collapsed in Congo Square?"

"Pulling the trigger on Toussaint. Why?"

"And it was Agent Ferris who verified Toussaint's death? Even took his pulse, just to be sure?"

"Yes."

Dickhead gathered his file and left the table in silence. He pivoted on his heel, turning back when he reached the door. "You, suddenly receiving gifts and cards from Toussaint, and Ferris, nowhere to be found. Doesn't that strike you as a teensy bit coincidental?"

"You arrogant fuck stick."

Thank God, the jackass had already tuned me out and started down the hall. I'm not sure whether those words had exploded from Little Allie or from me. It didn't matter. At least she and I finally agreed on something.

15

SO, SHOOT ME. I LIED

Rico glanced at his watch as we left the 51st. "Want to grab a beer on the way home?"

It had been one of the longest, shittiest days ever. My muscles hurt, my brain was in overdrive, and my ego was in the toilet.

"Thanks," I said. "But a long hot bath and sleep are all I want right now."

"You sure?"

"Yeah. I'm beat."

He stared into my eyes. "We'll find Ferris. You can bet on it."

"I won't stop until we do."

"Neither will I. Now, go home, grab that bath, and get ready for those Trick-or-Treaters."

"Screw the little beggars. I don't have enough dog treats as it is."

I climbed into the passenger side of the Mustang and buckled up. The next thing I knew, he was waking me up in my driveway. He told me he'd pick me up at 8:30 in the morning for the environmental sweep at Phoenix Innovations. When I crawled out of his car, he backed out, and left me with a beep.

I WALKED through the door and found Walter Adelman sitting at my kitchen table, smoking a cigar. Walter was Nonnie's boyfriend. They'd been dating the last six months or so. He'd been spending a lot of time at my house. A rumpled looking guy, mid-seventies, with long gray hair and jowly cheeks. He reminded me of Walter Matthau.

The guy had a tendency to wander in my door at will. He treated my place like he owned it. If that wasn't bad enough, his cigars smelled like dirty feet.

"Hello, Walter." I grabbed his stinky stogy, stubbed it out in the sink, and beelined for the living room before he had a chance to respond. It was a futile form of protest. No matter how many times I destroyed his cigar, another one appeared.

Taking a quick glance down the hall, I caught sight of Nonnie primping in my bathroom for their big night out. We had several discussions about her owning the house next door, and that she could entertain Walter there. But as time went on, more and more of her belongings were showing up at my house, things like a hair dryer, cosmetics and clothes. If I hadn't known better, I'd have sworn she was moving in.

"Nonnie, have you heard anything from Vinny?" I asked.

She stuck her head out in the hallway. "No, he still looking for that Zumba."

I flopped on the couch, put my feet on the coffee table, and checked my phone. No texts from either Vinny or Ferris.

Crap.

Headbutt ambled by and plopped next to me on the couch.

Kulu, hanging upside down from her perch, eyed him with contempt, and screeched, "Troublemaker!"

Baby Hyrum, busy devouring seed, couldn't have cared less about any of us.

Nonnie strolled by. She wore a low-cut black dress that

showed a little leg. She's got good fashion sense, better than me, at least.

"So where are you off to?" I asked, trailing her into the kitchen.

"Walter taking me to Golden Corral for dinner and then to play Bingos."

The tightwad needed to stick a crowbar in his wallet. But at least they'd be out of my hair for the night.

Walter had lit another cigar. I grabbed it and headed for the sink.

"Oh no, you don't." He wrenched it back and made for the door. "I'll finish it outside. Anyone ever tell you you're a control freak?"

"Anyone ever tell you your cigars smell like used butt wipes?" I closed the door behind them and wondered what Nonnie saw in him, but stopped wondering once disturbing visuals surfaced.

The two of them walked to Nonnie's house to pick up Walter's rust-bucket, a maroon '88 Grand Marquis with what was left of the hardtop. The cheapskate had snarfed down half a bag of my Doritos and left it laying open on the kitchen table.

No way I was going to eat them now, after he'd rubbed his stinky stogey fingers all over them. I dumped them into a bowl and threw it on my porch for the trick-or-treaters with a note:

Take one piece only or I'll shoot you.

Parents don't want kids reaching into a bowl of unwrapped food. Even a bowl of Doritos. If I played my cards right, maybe the little ankle biters wouldn't show up next year.

Before I settled in for the night, I needed to check in with Vinny. He answered on the first ring.

"Go for the Vin-meister."

"Don't ever call yourself that again."

"Sorry. Wassup?"

"Your lifespan if you don't bring Kleinfeld back—alive. Well, as alive as a zombie is, anyway. Cap's put a BOLO out on your bogey, and that Marlowe chick is after him, too. You need to find him first. We need that 180 grand."

"I've looked in every abandoned building, every back alley, and under every overpass in a five-mile radius of the church. I'm out of ideas. I did, however, find a different deadhead. Blew out his apricot. One up, one down, score one for the Vin-meis —. Oh, sorry. The coroner's office picked up the corpse an hour ago."

At least the day hadn't been a total waste. ACME could bill CPD for the kill.

"Look," Vinny said. "I know I screwed up. And I know you're pissed. But I need food, a shower and some sleep."

He wasn't the only one.

"Okay, you can come home, but only if you bring a Ricardo's Pizza. Make that two. Extra Cheese and pepperoni. One for me and one for you. Tomorrow morning, you head back out at first light and expand your perimeter. Who knows? Maybe Ira dove into the back of a garbage truck for a snack and got relocated."

That was a long shot. But until I could get Horton off my back, Vinny would have to think outside the box and solve his own clusterfuck.

"Extra cheese and pepperoni. Got that?" I said, hanging up. Another compulsive look at my phone confirmed there were still no texts from Ferris. This supremely craptacular day called for a Jack Daniel's slushie. A double, of course.

I stretched out on the couch and scanned the channel guide for a good horror flick. *Night of the Living Dead* popped up. Ha! Welcome to my world. No, thanks. Eventually, I came across *The Lost Boys*. Winner winner, chicken dinner. A half-hour into my favorite horror movie of all time, the doorbell rang.

Fuck balls.

It was too soon for Vinny to be back with the pizzas. And if the Doritos were gone, tough shit. No way I was handing out my dog biscuits. I had too many mouths to feed.

The bell rang a second time, so I cursed and paused the movie, then stomped to the door and thew it back. There before me stood the bitchiest she-demon of all time, Jade Chen.

"Go away," I shouted, pushing the door closed.

"Ah, ah, ah." She stopped it with her shoulder. "You forgot to give Rico my medicine."

Double fuck-balls.

"You know," she said, easing into the house. "You could just teach me to make the stuff myself. That way I wouldn't have to bother you every month. How hard can it be?"

"It's harder than you think, Princess. And last I checked, you didn't know shit about conjuring. Wait here," I said, padding through the living room and down the hallway.

Mama had taught me how to make Jade's tonic, but it was a time-consuming process—a process that had pushed my conjuring skills to their limits. I'd started ordering the pre-mixed potion from Mama months ago and had her ship it to me. But Rico and Jade didn't know that. Let them think I slaved over it twelve times a year. A little goodwill in my back pocket could come in handy someday.

I pulled the FedEx box out of the linen closet and peered inside. Two vials left. If I played it smart, that two months could parlay into two months of peace. I ripped the shipping label off the box and carried it into the living room. Jade had wandered in from the doorway and was rifling through a stack of bills and papers on my coffee table.

"May I help you?"

"What's in the box?" she asked, ignoring my question.

I shoved it at her and ushered her back to the door. "I was in a conjuring mood and made an extra batch. Merry Christmas."

So I lied. Shoot me. Bitchzilla deserved it.

Despite my invitation to leave, she anchored herself in the doorway. "Allie, is the Z-virus mutating? Why did Messmer and that runner turn so quickly?"

So that's what she'd been looking for on my coffee table. A scoop.

"Goodbye, now," I said, closing the door in her face.

"But, Allie—"

Vinny's voice drifted in from the porch. "Hi, Jade. What are you doing here?"

I threw open the door, dragged him inside, and slammed it shut again.

"What took you so long?" I asked, snatching a pizza from his hands.

"There's plenty of pizza. We should ask Jade to join us. I'll go—"

"No."

"But she's hot."

"She's Rico's girl."

"She's still hot. Hey, *The Lost Boys!*" he said, settling onto the couch. "Best movie ever."

"You can watch it with me, but only if you zip it, and take Headbutt out for his pee. Then get your ass back out there first thing in the morning and bring me back the only biter on earth worth $180,000 dollars."

"Got it, boss."

WHEN THE MOVIE WAS OVER, and Vinny had brought Headbutt back from his nightly constitutional, I sipped the last of my watered down slushie and locked up the house. Gel Boy ran his hands through his hair and yawned, then headed down the hallway to his bedroom.

I gave Kulu a nuzzle and covered her cage. Headbutt followed me to my room, hopped up on the bed beside me, and burrowed under the covers. The moment I closed my eyes, the scene at Congo Square looped through my brain, over and over again, those last few moments before I passed out. The pain. The fear. The anguish.

Sleep wouldn't come quickly and it wouldn't be sound.

I opened my eyes and stared into the darkness. "That was months ago," I whispered. "You're stronger now."

Little Allie reminded me that corpse whispering isn't for the weak and I needed to buck up. I hate when she's right. I rolled onto my side and hurtled an unspoken message into the cosmos.

Ferris, where the hell are you?

16

HOLY SHIT!

I awoke to the sound of my kitchen door opening and glanced at the clock. It was seven-thirty. Nonnie was here to start her workday at my kitchen table. Rico would be picking me up in an hour.

After a quick shower, I donned a pair of black jeans and my old *Zom-B-Gone* T-shirt. I looked down the hallway and found Vinny's bedroom door open.

"Good mornings," Nonnie called, as I strolled into the kitchen. "Vinny already gone. I making bacons and eggs for you. Coffee finished. Childrens have been fed," she said, scritching Headbutt behind his ears.

By the time I would make it home tonight, my laundry would be done and the house would be clean.

Everyone should have a Nonnie.

Kulu fluttered across her cage and flapped her wings, screaming, "Kulu treat."

I fed her a dog biscuit through the bars of her cage and stroked her feathers. Baby Hyrum screeched in protest, so I tossed the tiny terror a biscuit to shut him up.

RICO PULLED into the driveway at eight-thirty on the dot. We headed south on I-71 and joined the rest of the task force onsite at Phoenix Innovations. Apparently, Dickhead had other places to be and other underlings to torture, so Babs, Rico and I coordinated the sweep.

Messmer's employer had agreed to cooperate and to send us the requested documentation and security footage, but as of that morning, it had yet to materialize.

We entered the two-story River Road building just after nine. A security guard bolted from his corner chair as the HAZMAT TEAM filed in behind us.

The wide-eyed receptionist stiffened her back. "May I help you?"

Rico took the lead. "I'd like to speak with a senior executive, please."

"May I ask what this is in regard to?"

"Police business," he said, flashing his badge.

Randy—that was her name, according to her employee badge—punched an extension into her phone.

"Local law enforcement is in the lobby requesting the senior executive on duty." She paused. "No. They wouldn't say."

After a few nods, she ended the conversation and directed us toward a couch across the room. "Our Public Relations Officer, Blake Devlin, will see you shortly."

The clacking of heels on tile echoed from the second-floor balcony. A tall, willowy woman with long, wavy brown hair spread her hands on the railing and flashed a dazzling smile. "This way, please."

Leaving the tech agents huddled in the lobby, the three of us climbed a winding staircase and followed the woman into a corner office. She motioned us toward a set of chairs, then took her seat behind a large mahogany desk.

"I'm Blake Devlin, Public Relations Office for Phoenix Innovations. How may I help you?" Her voice sounded polished and sultry. She was cordial, but the practiced smile she wore stopped short of her dazzling green eyes.

Contact lenses, Little Allie hissed.

"Would you care for some Svabaldi?"

Rico arched a brow. "Excuse me?"

"Water," she said haughtily. "Bottled in Norway, made from the purest icebergs in Kongsfjordan."

"No thanks. We're in a bit of a rush."

Why does she look so familiar? I wondered.

After a round of introductions, Rico rose to his feet and squared himself in front of her desk. "We'd like to conduct a forensic search of the building in connection to the death of one of your employees, a Mr. Paul Messmer."

"And since we're already here," I added, "We'd be happy to take possession of the documents and security videos you agreed to supply."

Devlin's eyes narrowed. "I assume you have the requisite warrants for both the search and the items?"

Rico's eyes clouded. "Do we need warrants?"

"I'm afraid so. Legalities and all. You understand."

Like hell, you bitch.

I rose from my chair and stood shoulder-to-shoulder with Rico. "But you've already agreed to turn over the data. Don't you want to know what happened to your employee?"

Devlin pushed back her chair and crossed her long legs. "I'm very sorry, but if someone agreed to turn over information, the decision wasn't cleared through me. Should you produce the warrants, Phoenix Innovations will be happy to comply. Please convey our sympathies to Paul's family. He was much loved here."

Nothing about this woman sat well with me. And I knew I'd seen her before.

I dragged a fingertip across the top of her pristine desk, leaving a smudge. "What exactly does Phoenix Innovations do here, Ms. Devlin?"

"Research and development."

"Of what?"

"A myriad of products."

"Such as?"

"Chemicals, compounds. Polymers and the like."

Babs raised a hand. "Pharmaceutical research, by any chance?"

Devlin's smile faded. "On occasion. Why?"

"Just curious. Compounds are used in many industries."

"So they are."

Babs tossed her an enigmatic smile. "We'll be back with those warrants, Ms. Devlin."

"Of course."

Devlin turned and offered me her hand. "It's been a pleasure meeting you, Ms. Nighthawk."

I left her hand hanging.

It's her eyes, I thought. *I've seen those eyes before.*

"Have we met? We have, haven't we?' I said, finally remembering. "You stepped off the curb at the Flying Pig and shoved a popsicle in my face."

"Really? Well, isn't that a coincidence?" she simpered. "Phoenix Innovations is a good corporate citizen and a proud first-year sponsor of the race. I so enjoyed manning our water station."

She withdrew her hand and fixed me in her cold green gaze. "I heard about that poor runner, dropping dead, and turning into one of those zombie creatures. I hope you're close to finding out why."

"I believe we are," I said, burning a hole through her bougie-green contacts. "It's only a matter of time."

Babs grabbed my arm as we left the building. "Be careful with her. She's lying. Director Horton will be none too happy when he hears that we were refused access for the sweep."

"No kidding," I said. "Not to mention the physical evidence they're suddenly withholding."

"Wish me luck," she said, with a quick wave. "I'm headed to the local office to meet with him now."

Better her than me, I thought. I'd already decided to let Rico deliver the bad news to Cap. In the last few days, I'd given him enough agita to last a lifetime.

Rico and I returned to the Mustang. By the time I'd ducked into the passenger seat, I was struck with inspiration. "Before we go the precinct, let's stop at Ferris's place."

"Why?"

"I want to go over it with a fine-toothed comb."

"Horton already did that. They didn't find anything."

"Yeah, but the E-techs who swept his place don't know Ferris like we do. I have a key."

"I'm in," Rico said, peeling out of the parking lot.

Ferris's condo was roughly fifteen-minutes away on the west side of town. He turned into the residential development and headed for the only unit roped off with crime-scene tape.

I slipped my key in the lock and slowly turned the knob. The door creaked open and we were met with an eerie silence. The place was immaculate. Exactly the way neat-freak Ferris would have left it. The forensics team had even cleaned up after themselves. The condo felt cold and impersonal. Almost... empty. Everything Ferris was not.

I had no idea what we were looking for, but with any luck, we'd know it when we found it. The problem was, other than Ferris being missing, nothing stood out.

Rico checked the kitchen, bathroom and patio, leaving me with the living room and the bedroom (probably by design).

Ferris's desk was so neatly organized that Babs, the OCD Queen, would have been proud of him. Feeling like a voyeur, I opened a side-drawer in the Oak rolltop and rummaged through a stack of chronologically ordered bills, greeting cards, and correspondence. This was a serious invasion of his privacy, but it couldn't be helped.

A small straw basket was wedged in the left rear corner of the desk. I opened it and found dozens of business cards from auto body shops, insurance agents, dry cleaners, tailors, gun smiths, barber shops, other agents, law enforcement officers, and even his cable company. I made a mental note of the names, but nothing unusual stuck out.

In the opposite corner rested a small bag. I pulled it out and reached inside, finding a tiny velvet box.

Must be a tie tac, I figured. *Or a service pin from the FBI.*

I opened the lid and found a simple white-gold band with small channel-set diamonds. Pulling it out of the box, I held it up to the light of the window and read the engraved message inside the band:

To Allie Girl, my partner in life and love. Forever, Sean.

"Holy fucking shit!" I yelled, nearly dropping it on the floor.

"Wow," Rico whispered, peering over my shoulder. "I knew you guys were dating, but I had no idea you were that close."

That made two of us.

17

THE ICING ON MY SHIT CAKE

I repackaged the ring and returned it to its nook on the desk. Other than that unexpected bombshell, we hadn't found anything in Ferris's condo. Rico was subdued for the first few minutes on the ride back to the precinct. But soon, his questions began to fly.

"Did you know about the ring?"

No response.

"Are you guys really that close?"

No response.

"When's the big day?"

Sweet Baby Jebus. "I don't want to talk about it. Okay?"

Rico pulled to the curb in front of the precinct and I shot from the car like a cannon ball. By the time he'd taken off his seat belt and climbed out, I was at the curb waiting for him.

"Listen," I said, poking him in the chest. "Not one word about this to *anyone*. Especially your botoxed, blabber-mouthed girlfriend. That ring does not exist. You hear me? It doesn't exist."

"Copy that."

We walked into the station with the intention of updating

Cap on the Messmer investigation. But he crossed the aisle in front of us, along with the Chief of Police, the Mayor, and a bunch of nerdy civil service types carrying laptops and reports. They ducked into a conference room and closed the door behind them.

"Uh, oh." Rico winced. "First of the month. Budget meeting. Are your ears burning?"

That bean-counting bowl of assholes loved to run my 'expense' (i.e., damage) report up the flagpole and wave it around like a freaking red card at a soccer game. My damages had become the yardstick by which all other expenditures were measured. Cap told me once they even had a name for when a department's budget crashed and burned. They called it: *Pulling a Nighthawk.*

There it was. The icing on my shit cake. And it wasn't even noon yet.

SINCE CAP WAS OTHERWISE ENGAGED, Rico and I settled in at his desk to call Doc Blanchard to see if he had any updates on the Messmer case. It occurred to me, as Rico thumbed through his phone for Doc's number, that the ME might have been in that same budget meeting. Then I remembered the ME's office had its own budget. Not that it mattered. Doc had his own budgetary issues with me. A few raisings turned sideways in his morgue over the past year had cost him time and money on cleanup.

Whatever.

You bag biters, you make zushi. It's that simple. And she who bags the biter doesn't do the cleanup. Rule number eight in zombie hunting.

Doc answered after a few rings, and Rico put him on

speaker phone. "Hey, Doc. Hoping you have an update for us on the Messmer case."

"As a matter of fact, I got your vic's tox screen back this morning." Doc paused. "If I'd run it through normal channels, you'd have been waiting a while. But since Messmer's reanimation was so high-profile, what with the explosion and all, I asked a friend to bump it to the top of the list."

My cheeks blazed. "Thanks, Doc."

"Before we get started, you should know that I got two more bodies in my morgue last night. Both ran the marathon yesterday, and both appeared to die of heart attacks shortly thereafter." He paused before adding, "And both turned rotter. CPD had to put them down on the street."

My stomach sank, but I wasn't surprised. Whoever was behind this wouldn't have settled for one victim. I shuddered at the potential spike in deadheads if we didn't act quickly.

Rico sighed. "Just what we needed. A higher body count."

"Sorry to be the bearer of bad news. As for the tox screen results, we were looking for two determinants: Cause of death and identification of the applicable Z-virus strain—organic or synthetic. The typical tox screen is too limited to pick up the Z-virus, so we ran it through a mass spectrometer."

"And the findings?"

"He was system-present for aconite and the synthetic virus."

Rico frowned. "What's aconite?"

"It's a plant that, when ingested, produces high levels of both cardiotoxins and neurotoxins."

Rico rubbed his eyes. "Bottom line, Doc. What was his COD?"

"Refractory ventricular arrhythmia."

I wanted to grab the phone and pummel him with it. "In English, Doc."

"Loosely defined, it's an electrical storm in the heart."

"Wait a minute. Messmer had heart disease. That's why an

initial autopsy wasn't conducted. Are you saying he died of natural causes?"

"Mesmer suffered from heart disease. But I don't think he died of natural causes. Aconite poisoning would cause an arrhythmia in anyone. The presence of poison in his system suggests that his death was either homicide or suicide-related. He died at work in front of a multitude of witnesses. It certainly wasn't suicide. I'm ruling his death a homicide."

Rico scooted closer to the phone. "What are the symptoms of aconite poisoning?"

"Similar to those of a heart attack or stroke. Chest pain, numbness, weakness, gastrointestinal discomfort. At first blush, without extensive testing, it's hard to distinguish many poisoning deaths from cardiac or neurological episodes."

"What about the other marathon runners who dropped?" I asked.

"Evan Miller, who you put down, Elizabeth Warner and Thomas Grant. I sent their samples out about an hour ago. Once I saw Messer's results, I requested the same mass spec testing."

Rico eyes lit up. "Have Messmer's personal effects been released yet?"

"No. I have them here. Why?"

"Just a hunch. We'll be over later this afternoon to have a look-see."

"One more thing," I said. "Can you check your records and tell me Ira Kleinfeld's cause of death?"

"Sure." I heard his fingers clacking against a keyboard. "Well, what do you know? Refractory ventricular arrhythmia."

A chill raced up my spine. "If Vinny ever catches that gum-grinding rotter, I'll bet we find aconite and the synthetic virus in him too."

By the time Rico and I got back from an early lunch, Cap was at his desk. As much as I hated to voluntarily put myself in his line of sight on budget-meeting day, he'd want to know the latest on our investigation.

Rico rapped on Cap's open door and waited for a response before charging in. Cap lifted his bloodshot eyes from a file. He pinched the bridge of his nose and let out a long sigh. "I got my ass handed to me this morning...again. Give me good news."

Rico and I took our customary seats in front of his desk. We'd sat in those chairs so often that our butt shapes were molded into what was left of the leather. I gripped the shredded arms of my chair and braced for the worst. These update meetings always ended badly for at least one of us—usually me.

Rico cut to the chase. "Phoenix Innovations refused us access to conduct the environmental sweep. They also rescinded their agreement to provide the requested documents and security footage."

"I said to give me good news, De Palma. That isn't good news."

"No, sir. Agent McMillen is requesting a federal warrant even as we speak."

"Bah," he said, shaking his head. "That gives them time to destroy evidence."

That was technically true, but I had the feeling Blake Devlin wasn't too worried about our warrant. Someone as slick as she was would have buried her skeletons deep.

Rico sucked in a breath. "There's more. Doc got two more bodies at the morgue last night. Both runners, both suspected heart-attack victims, that turned and had to be put down."

Cap ran his hand over his bald head. "Jesus. What the hell's going on? We need to find out why Messmer and the runners were targeted—what they had in common."

I leaned forward and planted my elbows on Cap's desk.

"We're making headway," Rico said. "Messmer's tox screen results came back. Doc ruled his death a homicide caused by aconite poisoning. The presentation is similar to that of a heart attack. Doc's asking that the runner's samples be run through the same battery of tests as Messmer's to look for the poison."

Cap nodded. "That's a start. What about Kleinfeld?"

I chimed in. "I had Doc check his COD in his records. He died of that arrhythmia condition, same as Messmer. So we need to see what Kleinfeld had in common with Messmer and the runners. What ties them all together."

"That's a solid plan. Run with it."

Rico rose from his chair. "We're on our way now to the ME's office to go through Messmer's effects. Maybe we'll get lucky."

"Pretty Boy Swag" blared from my phone. Vinny was calling. Whatever he wanted would have to wait. I fished my cell out of my pocket, put it to my mouth, and didn't give him an opening.

"Vinny, let me call you back. I'm in a—"

"I've got Kleinfeld pinned down! What should I—"

The line went dead.

"Hello...Vinny? Vinny, where are you?"

Dead air screamed from the other end.

"Answer me, damn it!" The display screen faded, and the call disappeared.

Dollar signs flashed before my eyes.

"Rico, pull up Vinny's cell on your tracker app," I said, scrambling out of my chair. "Sorry, Cap, gotta run. We were pretty much done here, right?"

18

I JUST NEED TO BREATHE

Rico punched Vinny's cell number into the tracker app and smiled. "Bingo. He's at the old Hoffbauer Building in Over-The-Rhine."

My thoughts raced as Rico navigated the Mustang through traffic. I had way too many balls in the air. Vinny, Ferris, and Ira Kleinfeld—not to mention poisoned corpses that were reanimating at breakneck speed. And a cryptic message from the deceased Toussaint Le Clerc. Who else would have sent that stinky plant, with my necklace hanging from the tip of its dong.

I needed to breathe.

But how could I?

Vinny wasn't ready to be on his own, and Ferris was ominously AWOL. The last time I'd seen him was in Eden Park after our run, when he'd driven off in a huff. Yet, today I'd found a wedding band inscribed to me squirreled away on his desk. Did he love me or hate me? And where the hell was he?

What if he's already dead? Little Allie whispered.

He can't be, I reasoned. *If he were, I'd know it. I'd feel it.*

When all this was over, there would come a day when I'd

have to ask myself if I loved him—with a marrying kind of love. But that wouldn't be today.

"There!" Rico shouted, pointing to Nonnie's Pinto parked in front of our destination. He screeched to a halt behind it and we bailed out, guns drawn.

The two-story, red-brick building had seen better days. Crumbled concrete steps led to an arched entryway. Broken and missing windowpanes dotted the exterior. The cracked and weathered door, tagged with graffiti, hung ajar.

Rico trotted up the steps, put his ear to the door, and listened. "It's quiet as the dead in there."

He tapped the toe of his boot against the bottom of the battered door. It swung open with a low groan. On the count of three, we entered. He broke left; I broke right.

Afternoon sun streamed through the jagged windows and showcased the swirling dust inside. Splintered floorboards sagged beneath our feet. We'd entered into a large open area that looked like a foyer. Several closed doorways lined the crumbling plaster walls to the left. A winding staircase branched off to the right. We cleared the floor one room at a time, picking our way through yellowed newspapers, empty bottles, and garbage. Dead varmints, tangled wiring, and cobwebs galore. But no Vinny.

"Where the hell are you, Vinny?" I yelled.

"Up here!" he called over a wooden railing on the second floor.

Rico and I took the steps two at a time. When we reached the top, I shoved my finger in Gel Boy's face. "Why did you hang up on me?"

"My battery died."

That could've happened to anyone. But I should've known it would happen to him. Growls and bangs exploded behind a door to our right.

"Ira?" I asked.

"In the flesh." Vinny grinned. "Got your questions ready?"

Rico and I followed him into the room and instantly trained our guns on our runaway rotter. Vinny had managed to wall him in behind a mountain of antique furniture. The thing gnashed its teeth and swatted at us, but I had to give credit where it was due, it was properly secured.

"Good thinking, Kid," Rico said. "Next time, remember to bring your phone charger with you."

I studied his bogey and sniffed the air. "Vinny, did you have your eyes closed when you chased Kleinfeld through the cemetery?"

"Of course not. Why?"

"Do you need glasses?"

"C'mon, Nighthawk. What the hell?"

"How tall would you say Kleinfeld was when you were running after him?"

"I don't know. Six-feet, maybe."

"Six-one according to the intel Nonnie dug up. And how tall is the meatbag pinned behind that furniture?"

"Ah." Vinny cleared his throat. "Five-eight, five-nine."

"Notice anything else?"

"Like wh...what?"

"How long had Ira been dead when you started chasing him four days ago?"

"A couple of days, tops."

"A freshie, right. You smell anything odd in here?"

Vinny sniffed the air and dropped his chin to his chest. "Oh, no. Oh, shit, Nighthawk. I..."

He swept his hand through his hair and turned away.

Rico's eyes widened. "That's a corpsicle, isn't it?"

I nodded.

"Holy shit," Rico muttered. "He's got the wrong rotter."

"Gimme a break!" Vinny spread his arms and pleaded his case. "How was I supposed to know? He's a gum-grinding, gray-haired rotter wearing a charcoal-colored suit like Kleinfeld had on. How many of them can there be wandering around?"

"One too many, Gel Boy. One too fucking many."

Freaking Vinny. We would have to talk about this later.

"Say goodnight, Gracie," I said, squeezing Hawk's trigger.

Our mystery corpsicle hit the floor like a two-hundred-pound sack of zushi.

Vinny couldn't look me in the eyes.

I pointed to the lumpy puddle of chum, oozing out from behind the furniture. "Scrape, sweep or suck that shit up, then call the coroner. Don't forget to invoice Cap. And one more thing," I growled. "Bring me Ira Kleinfeld *now*, or I'll rip off your arm, beat you over the head with it, and then make you eat it, so you can shit it out and eat it again."

———

Rico and I left the Hoffbauer Building a little after three and headed for the ME's office. My usual light and cheery mood had soured. I'd promised Leo long ago that I would take care of Vinny, and I intended to honor that promise, assuming that I didn't kill the little dipshit first.

The moment we climbed into the Mustang, Rico started in on me. "You were a little rough on Vinny back there."

"Excuse me?"

"You've had a few clusterfucks of your own, you know."

"Like when?"

"Like the time you broke into Templeman's and raised the wrong corpse."

My cheeks burned. "Hey, that one was on Nonnie. She broke in. I just did the raising. I told her it was a bad idea."

"If I hadn't gotten Templeman to drop the charges, they'd have locked you up."

"That was so not my fault!"

"What about the time—"

"Just get to the point."

"He's young, Nighthawk. Give the kid some time. He'll come around."

I huffed and stared out the passenger window. "This may have escaped you, De Palma, but I am not a patient person."

I caught him smirking from the corner of my eye. The rat bastard.

———

DOC BUZZED us into the morgue and retrieved Messmer's effects from a locker. He'd already processed them for trace, so he gave us the bag and then showed us to a small conference room, where we could examine them privately.

The bag contained the usual fare: clothes, jacket, underwear, shoes, socks, watch and wallet. Messmer had a briefcase as well. I wasn't exactly sure what we were looking for, but I was hoping that I'd know it when I saw it.

We'd gone through most of it, when I picked up Messmer's jacket and rummaged through the pockets. They contained some spare change, an employee badge, a box of Tic-Tacs, and a popsicle stick. I picked up the stick, and held it to the light, wondering why he would have hung onto it.

Messmer had died at work. Maybe he'd decided to suck on a popsicle while he went for a walk on his break. And maybe he couldn't find a trash can. Maybe.

The stick was covered with a dried red residue.

A red popsicle.

Just like the one Blake Devlin had tried to force-feed me at the marathon.

I don't much believe in coincidence, and judging by the Head Hag's hissy fit, neither did she.

Rico glanced up from the shirt he'd been examining. "You expecting that thing to grow wings or what?"

"Huh?"

"That stick. You've been staring at it for a while."

I reminded him of my conversation with Devlin about our run-in at the marathon.

Rico wrinkled his nose. "So you think she wasn't just being obnoxious. You think she was trying to poison you with a popsicle."

"Yeah... I do."

"That's thin, Nighthawk. Sometimes a popsicle is just a popsicle."

"And sometimes, popsicle sticks need to be tested. That hoebag's hiding something. Messmer worked at Phoenix. *And* he died of a heart attack, right there in the office."

It seemed like we might be putting the puzzle pieces together. But were we?

19

IN VINO VERITAS

B y the time we finished pleading our case to Doc, it was
nearly five o'clock (a.k.a., beer-thirty.) Doc said he'd ask to
have the test expedited, but that we shouldn't expect miracles.

He needn't have worried. I don't believe in coincidence *or*
miracles. But I do believe in a good, strong Jack Daniel's slushie.
I suggested to Rico that we stop by The Blue Note. He said he'd
never been there, and that was all it took. After a quick call to
Nonnie, I was good to go.

The last time I'd been in The Blue Note was for that shitty
meeting with Maleficent Marlowe. Truth be told, I was curious
if Harry's ghost was still hanging out there. I hadn't told Rico
about 'virtual' Harry. Mostly because the two of them had
never even met in life. But also, because when De Palma and I
had first partnered up, it'd taken him way too long to come to
grips with what he called *my freaky voodoo shit*. Trying to get
him to believe in spirits from the great beyond seemed like a
bridge too far.

The joint was almost empty when Rico and I walked in. But
it was Monday night, and as I recalled, Mondays had always
been slow. After introducing Dallas and Rico, I took my usual

place at the bar. Rico sat beside me on my right. Harry instantly materialized, perched on his favorite stool, to my left. He raised his boilermaker with a broad smile and tossed it back. He was sitting directly in Rico's line of sight, but Rico was clearly oblivious to his presence. For a crackerjack cop, Rico could be oblivious about a lot of things.

We were two drinks deep when Rowan Marlowe strolled in the door.

I growled softly and slid from my stool.

"Friend of yours?" Rico murmured.

"Mortal enemy."

"*Another* one?"

Harry chuckled, crossed his arms, and leaned back to watch the show.

Dallas didn't want any part of it. "Welcome back, Ms. Marlowe. Be advised: The first person who throws a punch gets barred."

Rowan raised her hands. "Relax. I come in peace. In fact, I'll even buy the first round."

I stood her nose to nose, minus six inches, give or take. "I've got a better idea, Red. Why don't you march your butt back the way you came, and toss me the hundred bucks you owe me on your way out."

Marlowe snorted. "That's chicken feed. I'm here to talk about how we can get our hands on that hundred and eighty grand."

"We—as in you and me?"

"Yeah. We could...you know... throw in together."

Harry smacked his forehead.

"Fifty-fifty," she added.

Why was she suddenly so willing to cut me in?

"Three days ago, you wanted the money all to yourself."

"It's simple mathematics. I'm eliminating the competition

and upping my odds of recovery. Half of a hundred and eighty grand is better than none of it."

"You've got one problem," I said, rolling my eyes. "I can ask questions and I can shoot. What the hell do I need you for?"

"Intel, direct from the client. Intel you don't have."

"Such as?"

"Access to Kleinfeld's old work e-mails, business contacts, expense reports, etc. Look, I can ask the old geezer where the money is, but I don't have much experience in the deadhead department. That's where you come in."

"Sorry. Not interested."

"Why not?"

"I don't do partners."

Rico and Harry burst out laughing.

"Fine. Sixty-forty," she said. "That comes to 108 K. You can't turn down that kind of dough."

"I said no."

"This job would be a walk in the park for you. It's easy mon—"

I pulled Baby, my backup piece, from my ankle holster and fixed it between her eyes. "Get the hell out of here before I decide to explain *no*."

"Jesus!" Dallas scrambled from behind the bar. "Put that thing away before somebody gets hurt!"

"Careful, now," Rico said, rising from his stool.

Marlowe held her ground. "You wouldn't dare."

"Don't bet on it." I snarled, motioning Dallas to stand down. "Lady, you've fucked me over twice. If there's a third time, it will be your last."

"Have it your way, Half-Pint," Marlowe said, as she sauntered toward the exit.

When she reached the doorway, she turned and winked. "One way or another, I'll find that money."

"Over my dead body, you freakin' flamingo."

She flipped me the bird. "At least we agree on something."

The door swung closed behind her, and the room went still. I tucked Baby back in her holster and proceeded to eat a ration of shit from Dallas about pulling on Marlowe in his bar. Eventually, after he'd run out of cuss words, he settled down and let loose a snicker.

"Does that Marlowe woman remind you of anybody, Allie Cat?"

Rico snorted his drink through his nose. Harry rocked back and forth on his stool, laughing. Me? I failed to see the humor in any of it.

Two drinks later (maybe it was three), Dallas, Rico, Harry and I owned the joint. Dallas left us at the bar and returned to the kitchen to do the prep work I used to do. Rico smiled more than I'd seen in ages. His tone was lighter, his laugh quicker, and his words less guarded. The conversation ebbed and flowed. During one of the lulls, my thoughts drifted.

"Do you love him?" Rico murmured, snapping me back to reality.

"Love who?" I wasn't being obtuse. It was pure panic. Buying time to pull an answer out of my ass.

"Ferris," Rico said, with a hint of annoyance. "You know, the guy who bought you the wedding band. Had your name inscribed—"

"He's my partner...my friend. Of course, I love him."

"But do you *love* him."

If I couldn't answer that question for myself, I had no hope of answering it for Rico. After a long sip of my slushie, I blurted the only response that came to mind. "He loves me."

Rico picked up his glass of Johnny Walker and swirled it. "But do you love *him*?"

A tear welled in my eye. *Where the hell was Rico going with this?*

"What about you?" I asked, turning the tables. "Do you *love* your prissy little porcelain doll?"

A sad smile crossed his face. "I thought I did. Really. But when she wanted to get married and have kids, and a house, and a minivan..."

"It was the minivan, wasn't it?"

Rico nearly snorted his drink out on the table. But then he paused, like he might be carefully choosing his words. "When Jade wanted all that, I realized she could never be the mother of my kids. She's beautiful, fun and sexy as hell. She's a lot of things, but she isn't *the one*. It wasn't right to lead her on, knowing she wanted more. I moved out a couple of days ago."

"God. I'm...sorry, Rico."

It seemed like the right thing to say, even if it was a big fat lie.

"She took it well. A little too well, I think. Maybe, deep inside, she knew it was over too."

"Partner," I said, throwing my arm around his shoulder. "There aren't many good guys left in this world. But you're one of 'em. The girl that lands you is damn lucky."

Harry, who'd obviously been listening in, tried to goad me into Rico's arms by puckering his lips and making disturbing kissy-faces.

Some things never changed. Even from the grave, Harry thought he knew what was best for me.

I pulled my arm away from Rico's neck and motioned Dallas to bring us another round.

"Let's drink to Harry," I said, side-eyeing my ghostly mentor. "Great cop. Hella zombie hunter, nerves of steel. The real deal. But he had this annoying way about him. Coming off like a know-it-all buttinsky. Especially on things that didn't concern him."

Rico nodded. "Sounds like a dick."

Harry sniggered, then raised his boilermaker to me in a spectral salute.

Whether he was simply bored or had finished all his chores, Dallas returned from the kitchen and flipped through the TV remote. "You know...Rico is it? Allie Cat used to tend bar here. Best bartender-slash-bouncer I ever had. When she wasn't being arrested, stuck in jail, going on trial, or out hunting biters, that is."

Rico's eyes sparkled. "Do tell, Allie Cat."

I kicked him beneath the bar. "Nobody calls me that but Dallas."

"Well, I'll be damned!" Dallas shouted.

Harry pointed to the TV screen then slapped his hand on the bar.

I couldn't believe my eyes. "Holy shit! That's Tiffany Swarovski! Turn it up."

"Tiffany who?" Rico asked.

"A bimho buddy of mine who helped me solve a case once upon a time."

The massive ex-prostitute turned female-wrestler filled Dallas's sixty-inch flatscreen with spandex-compressed curves, poufy purple hair, and badger-length fingernails.

"Hey, babies, it's me, The Polynesian Punisher. Tune in to WWE Raw Monday at eight p.m. and watch me annihilate Becky 'The Buzzsaw' Buttafuoco. Best do as I say and tune in now, folks. Don't make me come punish you." She hissed and clawed at the air.

"Wow," Rico marveled. "I miss all the good stuff."

Eleven o'clock had arrived, and we'd had all the fun we could stand for one day. God knew we would regret it in the morning. Rico paid our tab and voluntarily surrendered his keys to Dallas. After that, he ordered an Uber for each of us and paid for that too.

What a day. And what a night. Thank God we'd gotten past all that touchy-feely, mumbo-jumbo crap about feelings. There's only so much of that shit I can take.

20

THE GAMES ARE AFOOT

I awoke to the sound of pummeling on my bedroom door.

"Miss Allie?" Nonnie called. "Miss Allie! Mr. Rico here."

"Wh...what?"

I glanced through slitted eyes at my phone on the bedtable. 7:30 a.m.

Snippets of the night before danced through my mind: *Rowan Marlowe, Harry, and wait...was Tiffany Swaorvoski there?*

I rolled over and my stomach flip-flopped.

Oh, yeah. There'd been whiskey. Way too much whiskey. And an Uber ride home.

"Tell him I'll be out in a minute."

I sat up with a wince, then powered to the dresser, and grabbed some fresh clothes. After inching the bedroom door open, and confirming the coast was clear, I darted barefoot down the hall into the bathroom and locked the door behind me.

Taking a shower may have been a bit optimistic on my part. The water felt like tiny knives slicing into my aching head. But the pain brought clarity.

Rico and I had had a conversation, most of which was still

shrouded in brain fog, but I remembered him having told me that he'd broken up with Jade a couple of days earlier. That would have been Saturday.

Funny, I thought. *Jade had been at my house asking for her meds on Sunday, and she never mentioned it.*

But then, why would she? I'd never made a secret of the way I felt about her. She was vain and opportunistic, and had played Rico for a fool. But trying to get him to accept that had gotten me nowhere. For his sake, and the sake of our partnership, I'd had to let that go. I was glad he'd finally come to his senses, but I had to wonder why. And why now? What had changed?

Something else nagged me too, as I toweled off and slid into my clothes. It seemed like there had been more to our conversation. Something...awkward, maybe. The thought tiptoed at the edge of my memory, taunting me, and leaving me feeling vaguely unsettled.

Whatever awkwardness there might have been would have to stay shelved for the time being. Rico was seated at my kitchen table, waiting to take my hungover ass to work.

"Morning," I said, making a beeline for the coffee pot.

Nonnie handed me a plate of rugelach as I slid into the open chair between them. I grimaced and eased the plate toward the center of the table. No food just yet.

"Is Vinny up and gone already?" I asked.

Nonnie's face tightened. "I no think he comes home last night. His bed still made."

Rico glowered at me, a silent reminder that I'd been too hard on Gel Boy.

Strike one for my judgmental partner. Time to turn the tables.

"How'd you get here?" I asked. "You gave your keys to Dallas."

"Spare set," he said, reaching for my pastry.

Strike two, dude. I snatched the rugelach from his grubby fingers.

"You pushed it away. Why can't I have it?"

"I changed my mind."

Nonnie rose from her chair with a scowl. She grabbed another pastry from the counter and handed it to Rico. "I made. I say who gets. Is his."

She wagged her finger in my face, hurled some gnarly combination of consonants that was clearly meant to offend me, and left the kitchen in a huff.

"Some night, huh?" Rico said, cramming the bonus rugelach into his mouth.

Do not make eye contact. Repeat. Do not make eye contact.

"Really?" I asked, dabbing up the pastry crumbs with my finger. "How so?"

My response had been meant to convey innocence, or at least plausible deniability. But the cat-being-strangled-with-piano-wire pitch of my voice might have given me away.

"C'mon," Rico said, jumping to his feet and wriggling into his jacket. "We're running late. Cap's going to be pissed."

Oh, my God! I thought. *Is he embarrassed? Upset? Or both? What the hell happened last night?*

I slurped down the rest of my coffee and burned my tongue in the process. "So, like, what part of the night made it so memorable? For you, I mean."

Rico was already headed toward the door. "It's just that you had a lot to say, is all."

For crap's sake, was he going to make me beg?

"Like...what?"

His eyes lit up. "You don't remember, do you?"

It's not often that words fail me, folks. Even bad ones. Especially bad ones. Of all the ways I could have reacted, I pretended I hadn't heard him. As if sticking my head in the sand would have made the moment any less awkward.

"Don't worry," he said, with an over-the-top wink. "Your secret's safe with me."

Chills slithered up my spine. *Is he just messing with me? Or did I actually say something stupid...or worse?*

With my mouth, it was a crapshoot at best.

Not knowing what I'd said was pure torture. He could pull this mystery out at will and hold it over my head forever. And I had handed him the ammo. What a stupid game.

Well played, partner. You ass-munch.

THE 51ST WAS in full swing by the time we walked through the door. Rico took his sweet time kibitzing with his frat pack around the coffee pot, so I made myself at home behind his desk. The morning had gotten off to such a lousy start, I'd forgotten to check my messages. It seemed ridiculous, hoping to hear from Ferris after all this time, but checking for his texts had become a superstitious habit. As if that somehow kept him alive and safe.

Of course, there was nothing from him. And just like every other day I'd checked, the hole in my heart grew a little bigger.

I logged into Rico's computer and scanned the web for surges in biter activity and rumblings of weird transmission anomalies. Nothing out of the ordinary popped up. But I did have a new message from Philippe.

Your old foe is alive and well.

Given recent events, the news shouldn't have come as a shock, and yet, dread seeped through every cell of my body. Needing to know, but fearing his response, I poised my fingers over the keyboard and reluctantly typed:

Do you have proof of life?

Seconds seemed like hours as I willed the screen to move. Eventually, a pixilated image appeared, modifying and recalibrating itself, before settling into a familiar shape that stirred the pit of my stomach: *Toussaint Le Clerc*. Very much alive, wearing a brittle smile meant only for me, as he posed beneath this year's Flying Pig banner.

Philippe signed off with words of advice:

The game is afoot. Be careful, ma chérie.

21

A LITTLE INTERFERENCE, PLEASE?

Rico hovered behind me, silently staring at the computer screen. He pursed his lips and darted his eyes to me, then back to the screen again.

"That...that's not possible," he murmured. "Le Clerc's dead."

"According to Ferris, anyway," I said, sick with disbelief. "But he's nowhere to be found. So...here we are."

"Maybe it's photoshopped."

"It came from Philippe."

Rico snorted. "Well, if it came from a mercenary who works for the highest bidder, then it must be true."

A fair point. I desperately wanted to believe that the image was a fake. And no one wanted to believe that Toussaint was dead more than I did. The problem was that his being alive was the only thing that made sense. And where the hell *was* Ferris in all this? If he hadn't been lying, why wasn't he here, working the case with us? Sure as shit, I'd seen him climb into that SUV during the marathon. I'd stake my life on it.

Had Toussaint somehow lured him to the dark side? Was that even possible? Or had he been forcibly taken? We were no closer to finding Ferris now than we were the day he disappeared. I kicked the corner of Rico's desk and then retreated into my shell.

Rico straddled the visitor's chair beside his desk and sighed. "Nighthawk, if I'd been in Congo Square with you that day, I'd vouch for what happened myself. But Ferris's official statement is the only game in town. For the record, I believed him then. And I still do."

True enough. Rico hadn't been there that day. He'd been in the hospital nursing a bruised kidney, courtesy of a beating by Toussaint. Everyone close to me had suffered at that bastard's hand in one way or another. Like it or not, I was the lightning rod to his fury.

"We'll find Ferris," Rico said, patting my hand. "And we'll get to the bottom of this, the same way we always do. By following clues."

His phone beeped with a text notification. He read the message and slapped his hand on his desk. "Agent McMillen got our warrant. Let's go find those clues."

RICO PARKED his Mustang around the corner from Phoenix Innovations, where we joined the rest of the task force, preparing to descend on Blake Devlin like the plague.

The November wind bit through my jacket as we hunkered at the back of an unmarked white van, while the HAZMAT team readied itself. Rico turned his collar to the cold and rubbed his hands.

"McMillen said she asked for a no-knock warrant. The judge turned her down flat. But that doesn't mean we can't surprise the shit out of Ms. Devlin."

I admired Babs' chutzpah, thinking she could burst through

the doors like a modern-day Elliot Ness, but we'd already attempted the sweep a full day earlier. Devlin had plenty of notice to ditch anything that might raise a red flag.

Babs took lead, and the rest of the team filed in behind her, as we barged into the lobby. She showed the receptionist our warrant and motioned the team up the staircase to the second floor.

"Randy, isn't it?" Babs said, double-checking the woman's name tag. "Please inform Ms. Devlin that we're on our way to her office."

Only yesterday, Randy Receptionist had reacted to our presence like a confused, frightened rabbit. Today, she already had the phone in hand before Babs had finished relaying her request. Phoenix Innovations had begun circling its wagons.

The willowy green-eyed monster met us outside her office door. She snatched the warrant from Babs' hand and scrutinized its contents.

"Everything seems to be in order. The documents, data and security tapes will be provided before you leave the premises today. Your team is free to proceed."

"Thank you," Babs said, flashing a steely smile. "But I don't recall asking your permission."

Eli Stanton directed the facility sweep under Babs' supervision. This was the second time Dickhead had put the op in her hands. That spoke highly of her. He may have been a blithering idiot who couldn't find his ass with a headlamp and barbecue tongs, but I couldn't fault his decision to let her run the case. If we were lucky, she'd keep him from jumping in with both feet and fucking the whole thing up.

Don't get me wrong. Psycho Babs was certifiable and could

make my eye twitch like nobody else on earth, but the chick was a walking encyclopedia with some crazy-mad analytical skills. As far as I was concerned, she'd earned her shot.

Rico and I trailed the team as they dusted, probed and sampled even the most innocuous places. We took our time, observing and absorbing everything around us. Neither of us were trained in biotechnology, but I'd have stacked us up against the best when it came to investigating. We focused on Messmer's work station and the breakroom, since he'd had a popsicle stick shoved in his pocket when he died. But not knowing what we were looking for made it hard to assign value to anything we found.

We chatted up employees and snapped pictures of Messmer's desk and inventoried his cubicle, even though Devlin--or one of her minions--had likely sanitized his work station before we arrived. We followed the same process in the storage, break and vending rooms, including the trash and recycling bins, but countless people had contaminated those common areas since Messmer's death.

I reminded myself that none of that mattered. If there was anything relevant to be found, we'd have a record of it. And as the investigation took shape, recognizing the right clue at the right time would break the case wide open. Without fail, that's the way the process worked.

But something nagged at me—my earlier conversation with Rico about that night in Congo Square. As we neared the end of the sweep, I told him that I wanted to check in with the biotech team up ahead and that I'd meet him out front. I needed a moment alone with Babs.

Rico hadn't been at Congo Square, but she had. It was a long shot—her remembering anything that didn't fit the accepted version of the events that had unfolded that night. We'd never even discussed the matter. We'd never needed to. Toussaint was gone from sight and mind, and as the months passed, I'd let him slide into an obscure and distant fog. It's funny how easily, how eagerly, I'd let that happen. Then again, nobody wants to believe in the bogeyman. Not even a corpse whisperer.

I CAUGHT up to Babs as the team was filtering into the lobby from the second-floor staircase. Devlin had already handed her the data, records and video that had been listed on the warrant. Babs hung back with me, out of earshot of the others, and listened patiently while I asked for her recollections of that night.

"Yes, Allie. I was there. But by the time I reached you, Toussaint was already down, and Ferris was at his side, checking for a pulse. He said Toussaint was gone and radioed in our position. Then he scooped you into his arms and drove you to the hospital, with me in the backseat, holding your hand and making sure your airway remained open."

Another dead end.

The only eyewitness on the scene who could have rebutted Ferris's story had nothing to offer, nothing that suggested he'd been lying. All I had left now was the same tired question no one could answer. Where was Ferris? Dead? Wounded? Or worse?

And where was I? I thought bitterly. *Instead of actively searching for Ferris, I was at Phoenix Innovations second-guessing the forensics team, hoping against all hope that he'd miraculously reappear on his own.*

I didn't want to hear platitudes. I didn't want to hear that I should keep my head in the game, and I sure as hell didn't want to hear that Dickhead had the situation under control.

Rico's footsteps echoed on the tile behind us. Babs seemed to sense that I needed a moment to regroup.

She slid her arm around my shoulder and guided me toward the staircase, calling over her shoulder, "Rico, Allie and I have so much catching-up to do. We'll meet you back at the 51st in a few."

Score one for Psycho Babs. Sometimes, we all need a frenemy to run interference.

22

THE LESSER OF TWO EVILS

"Thanks for that," I said, staring out the tinted window of Babs' SUV. "I'm not sure what happened back there. I'm not usually so...wimpy."

Wimpy. God, that word scraped like a pinecone rolling off my tongue. Especially since I'd used it in describing myself. Weakness and vulnerability had never been part of my wheelhouse.

I'm nobody's victim. I played this gig alone long before I ever took a partner. I'd never needed anyone, and I never would. Wimpy, my ass.

Little Allie snapped me back from the edge of the black hole I was about to fall in. *Don't make me implode your brain. I can do it, you know.*

Babs clucked her tongue. "It's no sin to be human, Allie."

"Ah, bite me."

She frowned but fought the urge to lecture.

We continued the drive in silence, which gave me time to collect my thoughts. Just when it seemed she'd given up psychoanalyzing me, she blurted, "Despite your delusions of grandeur, a superhero you are not."

"Delusions o—really? When's the last time you saved the world from the horde?"

"Careful, dear. Your narcissism is showing." She gripped the steering wheel and took a long, slow breath. "I shouldn't share this with you, and if Director Horton finds out that I have, we'll both pay the price. But I am in a position to know that he has launched a full-scale investigation into Sean's disappearance."

"Well, this is the first I've heard of it."

"The Director is keeping you at arm's length because he knows that you and Sean are involved. He also knows how... emotional...you can get when you're agitated."

"So now I'm wimpy *and* emotional. Just shoot me."

"You said wimpy. I said human. Horton said emotional."

"Whatever."

Babs cut to the chase. "Horton's pulled Sean's credit card statement and phone bill, as well as his GPS and banking data. Agents have canvassed Sean's neighbors and obtained the security video from his condo as well as other cameras in the vicinity. They're combing through all of it. So far, they haven't caught a break. But don't think for a minute that Horton's sitting on his hands."

"Let me help. No one knows Ferris like I do."

"That's not my call," Babs said, as she pulled into the 51st. "You'll have to discuss it with the Director. Some words of advice, though. Don't bring my name into it. Dial it back. And whatever you do, don't call him Dickhead."

THE TASK FORCE gathered in one of the conference rooms bordering the bullpen. My mind wandered as Babs doled out analytical responsibilities for the data we'd procured. Thankfully, I wasn't near the top of that list. She and I both knew that asking me to sit still and analyze anything was like asking a toddler to watch an episode of *Meet the Press*.

I caught a glimpse of Dickhead strolling into Cap's office and excused myself, ostensibly to use the head, then barreled across the bullpen to have my say.

Cap's door was closed, as if that had ever stopped me. I grabbed the knob, put my shoulder to the door, and then stopped, recalling Babs' words of wisdom. After a deep cleansing breath, I rapped on the door, and waited for Cap's response.

It wasn't natural, I tell you. It was like funneling a tornado through a straw. *Screw it*, I thought. *Something has to give or I'll explode.* I reached for the knob, but the door opened from the inside. Cap looked surprised.

"Nighthawk. I don't think you've ever knocked before."

"Don't underestimate me, sir. I'll do anything it takes to get in there. Even knock."

He opened the door with a sigh and motioned me inside.

I perched on the corner of his desk, but thought twice about it, then took the visitor's chair beside Dickhead instead. I locked eyes with him and his face clouded.

"I'm sure you're busy, Director. Running things and all."

Dial it back.

"I'd like to offer my help in finding Ferris."

"Not necessary, Nighthawk. We've got the situation under control."

"But I know him better than anyone. I could be useful...sir."

His eyes narrowed.

If nothing else, my diplomatic happy-crap had thrown both my bosses off guard. But Horton recovered quickly and dismissed my suggestion with a wave of his hand.

"I've got plenty of agents searching for Ferris. I need your help on the Z-virus investigation. Any other burning issues on your mind?"

"No, sir," I said, rising to my feet. "Nothing other than Agent Ferris being found. In case you missed it, his disappearance is connected to everything, from runners dropping dead at the marathon to the re-emergence of Toussaint. Let me know when you have a brain fart and clear the shit out from between your ears. Until then...Dickhead."

I pivoted on my heel, keenly aware that I'd tossed Babs' insight out the window.

Horton jumped from his chair. "You can't talk to me that way! You pre-pubescent paranor—"

I tuned him out and stomped toward the door, turning back only when I heard Cap sigh.

"And you," I said, pointing at my fearless leader. "Be on notice. I will no longer announce my presence by knocking on your door."

"I knew it was too good to last. Bye-bye now."

Dickhead's invectives followed me down the hallway and into the bullpen. His tirades had become more colorful over time. I'd like to think that I had something to do with that.

The flying monkey theme from *The Wizard of Oz* blared from the pocket of my jeans. I pulled out my phone and frowned at the display. *Jade Chen. What the hell could she want?*

I had two choices. I could either drum up excuses as to why I shouldn't have to lend a hand with data analysis or pick up her call. I chose the lesser of two evils.

"Wat up, Bimho?"

"I have some intel for you."

"Regarding?"

"Your case. I don't want to get into specifics on the phone."

Ugh, Jade and her Pulizter Prize-winning biter exposé... again.

"It's crazy busy here," I said. "I'm going to need more than that."

"It's *huge*, Allie."

The phone line echoed and whirred.

"Jade, where are you calling fro—."

"I gotta go," she whispered. "Meet me at Combs BBQ at one-thirty."

"But—"

The call dropped, and I had a decision to make.

Jade's lure of *huge* intel wasn't as compelling as you'd think. Odds were, any info she'd stumbled across was staler than leftover sushi. But the prospect of sweet, tangy BBQ sauce and some homemade sweet tea was hard to pass up.

Mind-numbing data analysis or Combs slow-smoked brisket? In what world would that choice require thought?

I stuck my head in the conference room and asked Rico if I could borrow his Mustang to follow up a lead in Middletown (totally leaving out that the tipster had been Jade). He hemmed and hawed, only surrendering his keys after I promised to drive carefully and bring him back a half rack and some jalapeño cornbread.

I'm a decent driver. It was crisp clear day and a straight shot up I-75, for some iffy intel and a five-star lunch. What could possibly go wrong?

23

SOME KIND OF HORNET'S NEST

I parked street-side across from the canary-colored building at the corner of Central and McKinley, home of Combs BBQ. The November wind put the kibosh on lunching at their outdoor bistro, so I skirted the wrought-iron fence and stepped inside the restaurant, a world filled with retro collectibles, musical instruments and mid-century furnishings—including a vintage phone booth. A cozy, casual world that smelled like heaven, where the meat tasted better than backyard smoked.

I hadn't realized how much I'd missed the place.

Jade was nowhere to be found, but owner/friend Lisa Combs, waiting on customers, stopped in her tracks to give me a quick hug. She promised we'd talk once the lunch rush slowed, so I ordered my food and waited for the porcelain princess to arrive.

It occurred to me that this mysterious lunch might be Jade's feeble attempt at a bait and switch, a smoke screen that would allow her to grill me about post-breakup Rico. If so, she'd be sadly disappointed. I was his partner and far too loyal to talk behind his back.

Besides, let's face it, I'm not the coffee klatch type. I'd rather shove a spork through my eye than trade recipes and secrets.

Jade pushed through the door wearing a trench coat and sunglasses, with a scarf wrapped around her head. She glanced out the window, up and down the street, as if she thought she'd been followed. Apparently convinced the coast was clear, she sidled up beside me, leaned in close, and winked over her sunglasses.

I rolled my eyes. "The crow flies at midnight, drama-queen."

"Just grab us a table, please."

I slid into a side booth, facing the front entrance and windows. Occupational training. Never sit with your back to the door. Jade scooted in across from me and got right to business.

"I guess you've heard Rico and I split up."

Dammit. "Yes."

"And?"

I spouted my usual, "No comment."

"Well, don't get huffy."

"Moving on," I said, with a warning stare. "Why all that cloak and dagger shit when you walked in?"

"A girl with a dangerous job can't be too careful."

"Really? I wouldn't know."

She explained that she'd been doing some undercover work on her exposé and was having a hard time dealing with the constant fear of blowing her cover.

Yada, yada, yada. Yammer, yammer, yammer. Yawn.

Our food arrived. Thank God. More chewing, less whining. I bit into my pulled pork sandwich and almost moaned in ecstasy.

"So," I said, sipping my sweet tea. "What's this super-secret intel you couldn't share on the phone?"

Jade answered with an enigmatic smile.

"There *is* intel, isn't there? So help me, if this little soiree was all about—"

She grabbed my arm, leaned across the table, and whispered, "According to one of my sources, someone is manipulating the Z-virus."

"No shit, Nancy Newshound. Tell me something I don't know."

"Ha! You don't know *how* they're manipulating it, do you? Word on the street—"

A hollow thud caught my ear, followed by another, and then another. Someone screamed.

I turned toward the commotion and saw a biter on the sidewalk bang its head against the picture window over and over again, splattering blood across the glass. Customers shrieked and bolted backward toward the cash register, dumping chairs and tables along the way.

Another rotter appeared. And then another, banging their heads in unison against the glass.

I glowered at Jade. "Exactly what kind of hornet's nest did you stir up?"

As if I had time for her explanation.

I sprang from the booth, as more biters gathered on the sidewalk and thrummed their heads against the window. Customers panicked. Things were getting ugly.

After catching Lisa's attention, I nodded toward the kitchen. "Take the customers to the cooler and lock the door. Don't come out until I tell you."

"Freaking rotters," she hissed, hustling the patrons across the floor.

"Hide in there," I said, shoving Jade toward the vintage phone booth in the front corner.

She looked at me like I'd lost my mind. "You're pushing me *toward* them!"

"Get in the damn booth and hide."

"It's got a *glass door!*"

"Crawl under the phone stand and hold the door closed with your foot. Call 911. Call Rico—and call Jimmy at Splatz. We're going to need him."

"He's not in my contacts."

"Google it, nimrod!"

"Breathe," Jade chanted. "Just breathe. Get a grip."

I slapped her twice. Once for me and once for her. "Get your bony ass into that booth, or I'll drench you in barbecue sauce and feed you to the horde myself!"

It's amazing what a little motivation can accomplish.

———

THE ROTTERS THRASHED their heads and carcasses against the window in a never-ending siege. Tiny stress fractures in the bloodied glass expanded and multiplied. I pulled Hawk and checked his load. Ten in the mag, and one in the pipe. Ready to rock. With a quick backwards glance, I spotted Lisa herding the last of the customers toward the cooler.

The loud *crack* of splintering wood echoed from the kitchen, followed by a fresh round of screams. I sprinted past the cash register and stopped short. The rear kitchen door had exploded from its hinges. Pussbags poured through the opening like spoiled salmon surging upstream.

Lisa hovered at the threshold of the walk-in-cooler, one hand grasping its open door, the other covering her mouth in a silent scream.

"Incoming!" I yelled, hip-checking her into the belly of the cooler with the customers. I slammed the door behind her, put my mouth against the thick steel-gauge and hollered, "Block the door."

Lisa's husband Chris, crouched with his back to the smoker, brandished a three-foot meat skewer like a rapier. His eyes scanned from right to left, then left to right, never leaving the horde.

"Take out their brains!" I screamed over the din.

Chris nodded, spearing a puss-bag between the eyes. He pulled out the skewer, swiped it across his apron, and then hunkered back down. "Thanks. But this ain't my first rotter rodeo."

He armed his staff with butcher knives and bread boards, drip pans and boning knives, and any other apparatus that they could use to defend themselves. They'd formed a line, blocking the doorway to the dining area.

We fought shoulder to shoulder, holding that line. Shoot and kill, parry and thrust, wham and bam, lacerate and decapitate. An impressive crew. Chris knew his shit—about smoking meat *and* biter warfare.

The sound of shattering glass burst behind me. *The picture window,* I thought, spinning toward the noise, and leaving my back unprotected.

"Allie!"

I whirled in time to catch Chris impale a corpsicle, its chattering teeth millimeters from my neck. As he pulled back the skewer and hoisted the deadhead through the air, its festering carcass broke in two. He dumped the top half, still stuck on the skewer, into the smoker, slammed down the lid, and wedged it shut with a ginormous barbecue fork. Then he kicked its ass-end beneath the stainless-steel sink, and returned to his post without skipping a beat.

Totally. Freaking. Badass.

"I'll take the front. You hold the back," I yelled, sprinting from the kitchen into the restaurant.

In my defense, I *thought* I would take the front.

But that ship sailed the moment I lay eyes on the swarm of

deadheads streaming though the shattered picture window. Hawk only held eleven shots. Those would barely get me past the cash register.

But that might be far enough.

Police sirens blared in the distance as I blasted my way out the side door, sprinted to the Mustang, stuck the key in the ignition, hit the gas, and aimed for the sidewalk. With a quick spin of the wheel, I sideswiped the building and plowed through the massive mob of meatbags, knocking them down like biter bowling pins.

Booyah, baby!

There was a bit of collateral damage involving Rico's car and the curbside bistro. Small potatoes compared to the big picture, really. Barely worth mentioning.

I leapt from the Mustang, grabbed a couple of pieces of mangled wrought iron and walked through the horizontal horde, skewering their brains, two at a time.

Police cars roared up to the building and screeched to a halt. Gunshots blazed in the rear of the restaurant where Chris and his team were stationed. Seconds later, the shots slowed to an occasional pop, and I breathed a sigh of relief. The siege was over.

I walked through what was left of the front door and surveyed the carnage, whistling long and low.

Jade popped up from the floor of the phone booth and stepped into the dining room, swiveling her head in a 180-degree arc. "Holy shit!"

The news maven snapped pictures and scribbled notes, documenting the scene. I could almost see the little hamster in her brain running in its wheel, drafting her acceptance speech for the Pulitzer Prize.

Shellshocked customers filtered out from the coolers and back into the dining area. Chris, Lisa, and the staff trailed silently behind them, jaws agape, gagging at the stench of decomp. A dazed Lisa picked up a mop and began to scrub the floor, which only spread the zushi further. She snorted in disgust and tossed the mop to Chris, who in turn, whaled it at me.

"Thanks for dropping by, Nighthawk."

The sarcasm was hard to miss.

24

SOME HARD-CORE SHIT

The Middletown Police roped off the crime scene and took statements from all the witnesses, including me. When they were finished, they promised Chris a copy of the report for insurance purposes. I ~~intentionally disappeared~~, ~~wandered off~~, gave them some space during the insurance discussion.

Chris was already peeved. No need to stir the pot.

Liability is a crapshoot when it comes to zombie-related crimes. Deadheads don't have legal standing. They can't be civilly sued or thrown in prison, or even publicly shamed by local news troubleshooters, which means victims are usually left holding the bag.

And victims *never* want to hear that. Who would?

Naturally, they do what any red-blooded American would do. They chase after their pot of gold, or their pile of Benjamins, by suing big fish with deep pockets.

To be clear, I, myself, have no pot (well, that kind anyway), or a single dead president in my wallet. I am a tiny, pocketless minnow in the giant sea of life.

That's my story and I'm sticking to it.

As the police were wrapping up, Jimmy from Splatz, the

crime scene clean-up company, rolled to the curb in his industrial-sized cargo van, a Mercedes Benz Sprinter. He hopped out of the driver's seat, took off his sunglasses, and stared at the melee. His eyes lit up. I knew that look. There were dollar signs in those eyes.

I introduced Jimmy to Chris and Lisa, and since Rico had yet to arrive, I had no excuse to beg off on Jimmy's walk-through. He took a second glance at the exterior damage, made some notes and then stepped inside, calm, cool and collected.

Jimmy had seen it all. He and his crew at Splatz had handled more biter scenes than all the other biohazard remediation services in town put together. He inspected the dining room, took measurements, and jotted notes about the collectibles and their special handling concerns.

When we moved into the kitchen, Jimmy's eyes popped at the sight of Chris's eight-foot smoker. "Dude! That thing's a beast!"

"Yeah. About that," Chris said, opening the lid. The corpsicle inside greeted us with a juicy, undercooked grin. "I'm gonna need a new smoker. And one of these, too." He pulled the drip pan, swirling with liquified rotter, out from beneath it.

Lisa gagged and pointed toward the sink. "The bottom half's under there."

Rico's voice filtered in from out front. Dickhead's too.

The day just kept getting better.

Jimmy finished the walkthrough and scribbled the last of his notes. When he broke out his calculator, I broke out in a sweat. I knew Jimmy like a book. Each note added another digit to the estimate.

"Here's where we are," he said, leaning against the blood-spattered doorway to the dining room. "It's only three o'clock. We'll start today. I'll hire some extra staff and pull in a bunch of industrial fans. We'll board up the window before we leave tonight. I can get replacement glass delivered in the morning. Get you up and running, three days, tops."

Chris held up two fingers, fixing me in a stony glare.

"Two days, Jimmy," I corrected. "Two days, tops."

"That'll cost extra."

My patience had grown thin. "Anything else?"

"What about my smoker?" Chris asked. "No smoker, no sales."

"No problemo," Jimmy said, handing him the estimate. "I'll rent one and have it delivered here tomorrow. You'd probably rather order the replacement smoker yourself, being a professional and all."

Chris dropped his eyes to the bottom of the estimate, and the color drained from his face. He sucked in a long breath and extended his hand to Jimmy. "Thanks for jumping on this, man." He turned and narrowed his eyes at me. "Who gets the bill, Nighthawk?"

Rico and Dickhead popped into view, stepping over the mound of meatbags piled in front of the entrance.

What the hell? I figured. *Horton's here. Let's call this...task-force related...ish.*

I pointed to Horton. "See that tall, balding suit, looks like a giant dickhead? That's William Horton, Assistant Director with the FBI. He gets the bill. I'll text you his address."

Since the walkthrough was complete, I had no excuse to avoid the shellacking that awaited me. I stepped into the dining room to meet my doom, with Jimmy still snapping at my heels.

"Hey! As I recall, you owe me a five-star review on Yelp and a commercial. Remember?"

He'd cut me a price break once, for cleaning my house after a zombie incursion. That had been a while back. I was hoping he'd forgotten.

"I'll get right on that," I said, with an exaggerated yawn. "As soon as I finish this case."

"I've heard that before."

"Really?" I said, shaking my head. "With as much work as I bring you and as many dollars as I drive into your pockets, you're gonna bust my chops over a stinkin' commercial?"

"Damn right I am."

He turned on his heel, and headed out the back door, calling for his crew.

"Fine," I yelled after him. "Call me. We'll set it up."

Why not? I thought. *Just stick a broom up my ass and I'll sweep the floor while I'm at it.*

RICO LOOKED like he was having a blood rush. I couldn't blame him. His Mustang needed a shit-ton of bodywork and a detail job...maybe two. I girded my loins as he and Horton charged across the dining room.

Dickhead took the lead. "What the hell happened here?"

"Isn't that obvious, sir?"

He spun around slowly, ogling the scene. Finally, he raised his hands and asked, "What did you do?"

"I had lunch."

"And a zombie horde just showed up—uninvited?"

"I never invite them, sir. They just seem to find me."

"Why did they attack *here*?"

I nodded to Jade who'd been silently watching from across the room. "Ask Bob Woodward, over there. This lunch date was her idea."

While Dickhead crooked his finger and motioned her to join us, Rico slipped behind me and put his lips to my ear. "In case you're wondering, I'm here courtesy of a beater from the car pool. We'll talk later."

A shiver shot up my spine. Maybe it was the tickle of his hot breath in my ear. Or maybe it was the ice he'd sent coursing through my veins. I never got the chance to find out because a scream burst from the direction of the restrooms. Not a *scared-shitless-please-save-me* shriek. It was more like a battle cry. Rico and I bolted toward the fray, with Dickhead and Jade on our heels.

WE SCREECHED to a halt at the entrance of the women's restroom, where Lisa Combs was straddling a fallen corpsicle and pummeling its head with the business end of a broomstick. Zushi arced across the walls and the floor as the rotter tried to escape by pulling itself down the hallway. Lisa raised the broom over her head and slammed it down like a sledge hammer, snapping it in two.

But the biter wasn't finished.

It jerked its head sideways and went for her ankle.

She leapt away, grabbing the toilet plunger from beside the commode, and resumed her attack. With every blow of the plunger, she screamed, *"Get! Your! Filthy! Stinking! Corpse! Out! Of! My! Restaurant!"*

Breathing like she'd just finished a marathon, Lisa speared the tip of the plunger through the biter's brainstem and watched it twitch, until it twitched no more. Satisfied that she'd finished the job, she jerked the zushi-covered plunger from the puddle of pulp and dumped it into the trashcan.

"Freakin' rotters," she snorted. "Not today. Not in *my* restaurant."

After a quick handwash at the bathroom sink, she strolled past us into the dining room as if she'd done nothing more than tenderize a brisket with a meat mallet.

That was some hard-core shit, right there.

WITH THE LAST of the biters dispatched, Horton circled back to his investigation. "Suppose you tell us what happened here, Ms. Chen."

"Well, I've been investigating Phoenix Innovations—"

"That's the FBI's job," he snapped.

"It's mine too, Director. Do you want the story or not?"

Dickhead's eyes narrowed.

"It wasn't easy," Jade continued. "I had to search domain names, business registrations, court records—even regulatory and licensing agencies. The company's ownership was buried beneath an endless string of shell companies but ultimately, it came back to a legitimate legal entity: Andezo, Inc."

Andezo...Andezo. The name fluttered at the edge of my memory. Had they been one of the sponsors of the Flying Pig?

"And guess what?" Jade smirked. "They're a water purification and bottling company with a location in Camp Washington."

Horton shrugged. "Which helps us how?"

"Put two and two together, Director. You're investigating alternative viral transmission sources and that bottling company is right here in Cincinnati. My guess," she said, leaning in close, "Is that Toussaint is still alive and he's gearing up to spread the virus through bottled water."

25

A BALANCING ACT

A s hard as it was to believe that Jade had actually tripped over a clue, her theory made sense. Horton must have thought so too because he left the scene, saying that he'd schedule a task force meeting at the 51st to get everyone on the same page.

The specter of widespread water contamination was unimaginable, even for Toussaint. If Jade's supposition proved true, Toussaint's dream of world domination, delivered by an army of deadheads, wasn't as far-reaching as it had seemed hours earlier.

Jade was hot on Rico's six as he walked out of the restaurant to ogle his banged-up car. I hung back inside and watched through the missing picture window. Even from a distance, their body language screamed uncomfortable. Jade's animated conversation met Rico's cool, detached shrugs.

Before long, she tossed up her hands and started back inside. I glanced down and pretended to inspect the floor. I didn't like Jade. Not even a little. But witnessing that exchange had made me feel like a voyeur.

"I'm heading back," she called from the doorway. "Need a ride?"

I gave her a crooked smile. "Thanks, but I should ride with Rico. He wants to discuss his car."

"Ha! At least he's talking to you. He's on the phone with the towing company now."

―――――

IT WAS ALREADY past five when we left, and the day had been a suck-fest. After I said goodbye to Chris and Lisa, I climbed into the passenger side of Rico's beater, a rusted, champagne-colored Taurus with a crumpled antenna, trash-covered floor and missing molding strips, and silently swore to keep my sarcastic pie hole shut. Based on past performances, the odds were not in my favor.

I hadn't even buckled in yet when he started on me. "Did you get hurt today?"

"No. I'm fine." I said, rummaging for my seatbelt between the french-fry encrusted cushions.

"Good," he nodded. "That was my Mustang, Allie."

"I know. I'm sorry."

"You promised you'd be careful."

"I was! There isn't a single ding on that car that was accidental. That damage is from when I *intentionally* plowed through the sidewalk bistro and sideswiped the building. You know to...mow down the horde...and save the...people."

Rico blinked. "Did that sound better in your head than when it came out?"

I sighed and clicked my seat belt. "I wouldn't have done it if I'd had any other way. And I truly am sorry."

"But it was my *Mustang*."

"And it was just me against the horde."

"When isn't it, Allie?" After a quick pause, he added, "Where's my half rack and cornbread?"

"Back there in the smoker, cooking with Biter Bob."

Rain began to sprinkle and Rico fell silent. I thought maybe he was finished.

Fat chance.

"Why didn't you tell me you were going to meet Jade?"

Crap.

"Because I figured her intel would be bullshit, like it usually is, and…"

"And what?"

I scrunched down in my seat. "You'd just broken up and I didn't want you to think I was being nosy."

"Did she…talk about me?"

"What is this, second grade? I'll tell you the same thing I told her. Not my circus, not my monkeys. Leave me out of it."

"Good," he said, groping the steering wheel for the wiper control. The blade on the passenger side squealed across the glass, flicking the last of its little rubber squeegee into the wind. Rico grunted and fell silent again.

"What did you think of Jade's theory?" I asked, determined to pull him out of his funk.

"Surprisingly, it makes sense." He tried but failed to stifle a smile. "Don't tell her I said that."

"Never."

"The attack at Combs was no accident," he added. "Obviously, Toussaint's got eyes on you."

A sobering thought, although after everything that had come to pass, not a surprise.

"Great, so we finally agree the bastard is still alive? And Philippe didn't photoshop the picture?"

"Let's just say I'm willing to entertain the notion."

Rico asked if I'd heard from Ferris and I told him no. It hit me that people had begun to inquire about Ferris as an afterthought, and then it was my turn to go silent. Thankfully, Rico let me.

Sometimes, it's okay for partners to disagree or argue, or need headspace. It's a balancing act. The trick is knowing each other well enough to make the right call at the right time. When Rico dropped me off and told me he'd pick me up in the morning, I knew that we were solid.

I WALKED in the back door and found Nonnie and Walter seated at my kitchen table, with Headbutt stretched out on his favorite register vent.

Kulu sat on Nonnie's shoulder while Baby Hyrum cuddled on her wrist. A third African Grey roosted on Walter's shoulder, making cow eyes at Kulu.

"Who's this?" I asked, peering down my nose at it.

"You home so early!" Nonnie said, jumping up from the table. She quickly put Kulu and Hyrum back in their cages. "Walter is babysittings bird for friend. His name Bennu. From mysology."

"Mythology?"

Walter held out his arm, letting Bennu stroll to his wrist. "Bennu is named for the Egyptian version of the Phoenix. He represents the *ba* or the soul of the Sun God, Ra."

"What he represents is one too many birds in my house."

Nonnie clucked. "Is only visiting, Miss Allie."

"Any word from Vinny?"

"No, but is early. Any news on Mr. Ferris?"

I shook my head but couldn't bring myself to answer her out loud.

She pointed to a letter on the table and changed the topic. "Winstels suing you for hundred-dollars for replacement wisteria vine Headbutt pee on."

I eyeballed the dog. Headbutt slunk from his register vent and hid beneath the table. "Coward," I mumbled.

"Miss Allie, I check on internets. Vine costs forty bucks. So, maybe offer forty, problem goes away."

"Not a chance. Twenty and a plate of rugelach. Make it happen, sister. So, Walter," I said, spinning to Nonnie's beau. "When Does Beano fly home?"

"Bennu. Not Beano. Parrots don't pass gas, by the way."

"Fascinating."

Nonnie yanked Walter from his chair and pulled him to the door, with Bennu squawking on his arm. "We just leavings. We visit my house next time. Come, come, Walters."

"Goodnight," I called, as they huddled and crossed the lawn, whispering animatedly.

"Always a pleasure to see you leave, Walter," I mumbled, closing the door behind them.

My life had been simple once. Now, I had three flying feather dusters, a recalcitrant bulldog, a dipstick partner named Vinny, a Nonnie, and a Walter. When had I lost control?

26

RICO SAYS, "I DO"

I awoke to the smell of frying bacon and coffee. It was seven-thirty. Rico would be picking me up in an hour. After a quick shower, I dressed in a fresh pair of black jeans, my *Terminus BBQ* t-shirt, and my zombie-stomping boots. Following my nose to the kitchen, I grabbed a cup of coffee, and noticed a note propped against the salt shaker in front of my place at the table.

"What's this?" I asked.

"Is from Vinny," Nonnie said. "He empty box of dog biscuits and left before I gets here. Or I would have made him eats some peoples food. He working too hard."

"He's cleaning up his own mess," I mumbled. "It's good for him."

After taking my seat, and sipping some coffee, I read his note.

Nighthawk,

Still haven't found Kleinfeld, but neither has CPD. It's

like he's disappeared into thin air. On the bright side, I've taken down four other rotters, so I'm earning my keep. Left the billing details on the counter for Nonnie.

Kleinfeld turned biter six-days ago. That makes him a freshie, bordering on the flesh-eater stage, so his hunger for humans is increasing. I'm going to narrow my search by going undercover in the homeless camps— settling in where he's mostly likely going to feed. Check in when I can. — V

At least the kid was thinking, although I wondered about his ability to pull it off. So much had happened in the last week. That Ira hadn't been spotted in several days was a blessing. Capturing him had fallen from priority number one to the rear of the pack, given the reemergence of Toussaint and yesterday's incursion at Combs BBQ. At least, that's how I viewed the natural order of our issues. But the situation was changing so quickly, I needed a score card to keep up.

Rico arrived in his carpool junker, prompting a round of awkward questions from Nonnie, who wanted to know where his Mustang was. I reminded her to extend my settlement offer to the Winstels, then tossed Rico a piece of rugelach and shoved him out the door, before he could give her too much ammo to use against me. Nonnie the Nose could be wily. No use spilling all my secrets.

"What settlement offer?" Rico asked as he coaxed the Taurus through traffic.

"Nothing. Just another happy neighbor on Pitty Pat Lane."

"You've got a lot of those. Oh, yeah. Horton texted last night. He called a task-force meeting in the conference room this morning at nine. Gird your loins."

"Oh, please," I said, with a yawn. "Not again. Girding gives me hemorrhoids."

———

THE TASK FORCE had taken over the conference room of the 51st. Dickhead and Cap sat at opposite ends of the table. The rest of us filled the seats in between. Rico to my right, and Babs to my left, directly across the table from Eli Stanton and Kelvin Thomas, the cyber-specialist.

Dickhead called the meeting to order in his usual light-hearted way. "Let's get started. Given events of late, this room is the last place any of us should be. But before I ask for your updates, I'd like to provide one of my own."

His eyes drifted toward me. "Although we have not located Agent Ferris, we do have a lead that we are following up on. Since none of you are involved in that investigation, you are not privy to the details. I simply wanted you to know that this is an active, ongoing investigation and we're taking it most seriously."

Finally, a lead! I caught myself smiling and wondering why Horton had provided an update. It surely wasn't because I called him a dickhead the last time I asked about Ferris. And I doubted he'd suddenly grown a heart. But it didn't really matter. A lead was a lead, and I would take the hope that came with it.

Horton cleared his throat and glanced at his legal pad. "We have both old and new business to discuss: the Ira Kleinfeld case, the tox-screen results of the marathon runners, the status of the presumed-dead Toussaint Le Clerc, Dr. Christian's update on potential new transmission sources, the Phoenix Innovations investigation, and last but not least, yesterday's deadhead incursion at Combs BBQ in Middletown."

Horton looked to the far end of the table. "Captain Dorsey, let's start with Ira Kleinfeld, our runaway rotter."

Cap sat forward and rolled his pen between his palms. "Director, Mr. Kleinfeld is flying under the radar...even with our BOLO and the whole force searching for him. As soon as he pops up, he's as good as caught."

Dickhead darted his eyes to me. "You're up, Ms. Nighthawk. Any progress from the private sector with...what's the name of your company?"

"ACME, Inc., sir. And yes, I conferred with my associate Mr. Abruzzi this morning, before I arrived. As Captain Dorsey stated, our bogey seems to have gone underground."

The room was so quiet you could hear a gnat fart.

"However," I continued, "Mr. Abruzzi has gone undercover to infiltrate the homeless camps where Kleinfeld has his best chances of locating fresh meat. We're in communication daily. I hope to have more to report soon."

"Make sure you do," Dickhead said, scribbling notes on his legal pad. "And the tox-screen results from the marathon runners?"

Rico leaned forward. "That would be Miller, Warner and Grant. Two days ago, Doc advised us that the mass spectrometer tests on our first vic, Messmer, came back positive for aconite poisoning. Since, like Messmer, the marathon runners also reanimated within moments of death, Doc requested the same battery of tests for them. We haven't heard back from him yet—"

"But," I interjected, "we did have Doc check his records on Kleinfeld's cause of death—you know, from before he went... AWOL. Messmer, Kleinfeld, Miller, Warner and Grant all died of refractory ventricular arrhythmias."

Horton raised a brow and jotted more notes. "Now, that's interesting. What about Le Clerc?"

I sucked in a breath. "The stinky plant delivery, with my

necklace attached, was as close to proof of life as I had, at that time. But yesterday morning, a dark web contact forwarded me a message and a picture of Toussaint standing in front of this year's Flying Pig Marathon banner. The message said that an old foe of mine was still alive and urged me to be careful."

Horton frowned. "Any possibility the picture was photo-shopped?"

Rico eyed me.

"Maybe," I said. "But after the plant, and the necklace, and yesterday's pack attack on Combs restaurant, I'd say it's highly unlikely. Mass biter attacks are Toussaint's MO, and we have absolutely no physical proof that he's dead. In short," I said, locking eyes with Horton. "I've come to believe Le Clerc is alive and he's an active threat."

The words burned like fire coming out of my mouth.

"I see." Horton eyeballed Kelvin. "Agent Thomas, would you please inspect the image that was forwarded to Ms. Nighthawk? I'd like your opinion as to whether it was manipulated. And while you're at it, verify the sending IP address."

Kelvin nodded. "I'll get right on it."

Horton hesitated, as if he was weighing the prospect of a living Toussaint. I'd already crossed that bridge. Time was a luxury we didn't have, so I pushed on.

"I've not heard back from Dr. Christian regarding his contact tracing results, which could shed light on unknown delivery sources. I'll circle back with him."

The Director jotted a longer flurry of notes, then addressed the group. "It seems that Phoenix Innovations didn't provide their parking lot security tape, as was listed on the warrant. Agent McMillen, I'd like you, Detective De Palma, and Ms. Nighthawk to retrieve that tape. Based on new evidence provided by Ms. Chen, I'd also like you to check out the physical location of Phoenix Innovation's parent company, Andezo, Inc. See if anything feels hinky."

Babs sat tall and squared her portfolio against the edge of the conference table. "Post haste, sir."

"Detective De Palma," Horton fixed Rico in his gaze, "that brings us to yesterday's attack at the restaurant. Miss Nighthawk believes that Toussaint Le Clerc is alive and well and orchestrated the attack. Do you concur?"

Rico glanced at me and answered, "I do."

27

THE 0-2 COUNT

Per Dickhead's direction, I gave Kelvin access to Philippe's message—not because I wanted to but because Horton needed to validate its authenticity. That made sense. It was a way of crossing the T's and dotting the I's in the investigation, but Philippe would be none too pleased that he was on the FBI's radar screen. I turned over his communication because I had to, but he could view that as a betrayal.

I explained to Kelvin that I was sure the image of Toussaint was real, and that because my source was under deep cover, we needed to protect him. Kelvin smiled noncommittally, like he'd heard the same spiel a thousand times.

I walked out of the 51st with Babs and Rico, hoping that Philippe would never find out about my disclosure, and dreading how ugly my next conversation with him could be. He was too valuable a source to lose. And despite his free agency, I instinctively knew that he would never hurt me—*unless* I betrayed him.

Once again, I found myself walking a tightrope stretched between a rock and a hard place.

THE THREE OF us piled into Babs' government-issued SUV and headed down the expressway toward Phoenix Innovations to secure the missing security footage.

I wanted to privately thank Rico for his support during the meeting, but I hadn't gotten the chance. I'd held my breath when Horton asked if Rico believed Toussaint was alive. But I shouldn't have been so apprehensive about his response. As impossible as my partner could be at times, he always had my back.

It occurred to me that I never asked Babs where she stood on the matter either. Of the three of us, she was the only person who'd witnessed those final moments at Congo Square. I wondered if seeing truly was believing. Had she rationalized away recent events because her eyes had told her that Toussaint was dead? I considered asking her there in the car, where she had no escape and would have to answer, but she beat me to the punch.

"I agree, you know," she said, turning onto River Road. "Toussaint's alive. I don't know how that can be, but it is. I feel it in my bones."

It was a relief, knowing we were all on the same page. But underneath that relief, burrowed a tiny seed of doubt that planted in my brain. *All of us but one*, the seed whispered. *All of us but Ferris.*

WHEN WE PULLED into the parking lot at Phoenix Innovations, there wasn't a car in sight.

I craned my neck and looked across the street at the other office buildings. "Today's not a holiday, is it?"

Rico sighed. "There's a For Lease sign by the curb."

"Oh, my," Babs mumbled. "I've got a bad feeling about this." She screeched the SUV to a halt at the front entrance. We clambered out, guns drawn, and burst through the doors.

"It's empty!" I stared in disbelief.

Nothing. Not a desk. Not a filing cabinet. Not a phone. Not even a freaking dust ball.

"Follow protocol," Babs whispered, her weapon still at high ready. "Let's get busy. There are two floors here."

Ten minutes later, we ended up back in the lobby, having found squat. I felt like a fool.

Babs lowered her gun with a huff. "The Director will be most displeased."

"He's not the only one," I said, holstering Hawk.

We left Phoenix Innovations shaking our heads and headed toward the next stop on our agenda, Andezo, Inc., in Camp Washington. I sat in the back of Babs' SUV and placed two calls. The first was to Dr. Christian in Sweden. It was almost four p.m. there and I wanted to catch him before he left for the day. After a few minutes of catch up, he assured me that he had been paying particular attention to contact tracing since our last call, but had yet to find any infections that were unaccounted for, or where the victims were known to have instantly reanimated. The call ended with him pledging to keep his eyes open for any cases that fit our pattern.

Strike one.

The next call went to Jimmy at Splatz, my biohazard cleanup buddy with the memory of an elephant. I went in hot.

"Jimmy, it's Nighthawk. Gimme a time for this commercial."

"Well, I need to grab a cameraman first. But I've written the script."

"The what?"

"Geez, Nighthawk. You think you're gonna...whatchacallit... ad lib the thing? You gotta have a script with the, ah...you know, the details and such. I got it here at the office. Swing by and pick it up, so you can practice. And bring me a copy of the Yelp review you left."

Fuck me.

"Crazy busy this week, Jimmy. How 'bout you e-mail me the script, and I'll send you the Yelp review."

When hell freezes over.

"Sure thing. I'll let you know where to show up to film, to ah, catch me in action, so to speak—show TV-land how the process works. Ha! Been awhile since we did a job at your place. You're overdue."

"Going through a tunnel, Jimmy. Gotta g—" I hung up on the rat-bastard.

Best in the world at what he does, but his mouth runs like a duck's ass.

I'd been yapping so long I hadn't realized that Babs had pulled into an open lot and stopped.

Rico eyeballed me. "Finished organizing your social calendar?"

"Why are we stopped?"

Babs showed me the Waze app on her phone. "We're here."

"This can't be right," I said. "We're supposed to be at Andezo, Inc. This is an open lot."

Rico snorted. "Nothing gets past you, does it?"

"This isn't happening," I screamed, pummeling the back of the driver's seat.

"Do try to keep up, Nighthawk." Babs sighed. "There is clearly no building here."

Perfect. Strike two.

And it was only noon.

28

THINGS GET MAGNIFIED

We piled back into the SUV, dejected, and agreed that returning to the 51st empty-handed would not only be humiliating but masochistic.

Babs' knuckles turned white as she wrapped her hands around the steering wheel. She uttered words I'd never heard from her before. "Damn it."

"Let's backtrack," Rico said. "We suspected Phoenix Innovations was dirty, and it packed up its tents and disappeared. Now, we find its parent company, Andezo Inc., used a fake address on its business registration. Obviously, we're going down the right path."

"Given that Toussaint's still alive," Babs added, "it's reasonable to assume both companies tie back to him. Then Jade's mass contamination theory holds up. Maybe we got too close and Toussaint decided to move his operation."

"To where?" Rico asked.

My stomach growled like a lion at feeding time.

"Copy that loud and clear, Nighthawk," he said, glancing in the review mirror. "Where do we go when we need intel and we're hungry?"

"Oh, man," I groaned. "Not that place!"

Rico directed Babs to the gnarliest mobbed-up joint in the city, while I sulked in the back seat.

Enzo's Bar might have been information central but Ronnie, the bionic bartender, and I had a rocky history. A while back, we'd had a misunderstanding (that was entirely Rico's fault). The big-boned blonde and I had mixed it up. Before the battle was over, she'd pulled me over the bar top and broken a bottle of Fireball over my head. Well, close enough. My hair stank like cinnamon for a week. Believe me, I gave as good as I got. Blondie's jaw looked like a head of purple cabbage.

Rico had separated us before things got totally out of hand, then negotiated a truce. She and I hadn't seen each other since. I was in no mood for a rematch.

We pushed through the front door of Enzo's with Rico in the lead. Babs and I trailed on his six. The joint wasn't as busy as most bars during lunch hour. The place served a mean cheeseburger, but I doubted the bullet-riddled walls and peeling veneer appealed to millennials.

Ronnie thundered around the bar and bear-hugged Rico, lifting him off his feet. If she'd have squeezed him any tighter, his eyes would have popped.

She spotted me behind him and beamed. "Hey, Fireball! Back for round two?"

Bring it on, bimho.

"No thanks," I said, with a jab at Rico's kidney.

Babs' smile was paper-thin as she stared at the tattoo on Ronnie's bicep—a flaming skull with spark plugs blazing from its eye sockets. Inked above the tat were the words: *The Hard Run Fast.*

The three of us opted to sit at the bar. Babs removed her coat and folded it over her stool like a disposable toilet seat cover. Then she pulled an antiseptic wipe from her purse and swabbed down a grimy plastic menu, front and back.

Ronnie leaned in close. "What's her deal?"

"Batshit crazy," I mouthed, circling my ear with a finger.

Rico and I ordered loaded avocado burgers and fountain drinks. Babs ordered bottled ice tea and ten saltine packets. If Blondie had understood that insult, we'd have been squaring off for round two of *Bar Fights Gone Wrong*.

Freaking Babs. She'd either single-handedly save us someday or manage to kill us all. On a good day, I figured she had a fifty-fifty shot. But there, with Ronnie the Hun, all bets were off.

After hollering our orders back to the cook, Ronnie leaned her massive mammaries over the bar toward Rico. He glanced at her cleavage, flashed his thousand-watt smile, and reeled her in like a fish on a hook.

"Hey, girl," he murmured. "I need some intel."

"Come to mama, sugar. I always got what you need."

"Anything big going down in OTR these days? Any new players?"

Ronnie stroked Rico's two-day stubble with her *Fuck Me Red* fingertips. "When you're finished with lunch, give me the high sign. I'll meet you in the hallway by the head. We'll have us a chat."

She blew him a kiss, then sashayed her bodacious booty to the other end of the bar, and disappeared into the kitchen.

I pretended to shove my finger down my throat and retch. "You're disgusting, De Palma."

He flashed his pearly whites and winked. "Works every time."

I scrutinized his smile—the sensual curve of his lips and the bottomless brown of his eyes. The man wasn't wrong.

"Statistically speaking," Babs added. "Seventy-two percent of females are drawn by the smile of potential mates, followed closely by their laugh, physique, and the level of confidence they exude."

Thank God, Ronnie showed up with our food and I didn't have time to tell Babs to fuck off—or wonder why my partner's full-lipped, symmetrical mouth suddenly seemed so compelling.

Rico and I devoured our burgers while Babs put on a show, nibbling her crackers around the edges, working from the outside in, like an OCD-stricken squirrel. When we'd finished eating and Ronnie had bussed our plates, Rico gave her a nod. He strolled away from the bar and disappeared down the hallway to the restrooms, with Ronnie trailing at a distance.

Babs used Rico's absence to dig for some intel of her own. "This may be none of my business, Allie, but early on, after Ferris went missing, Director Horton asked you why Ferris hadn't run the marathon with you. You lashed out and got defensive. Not that that's unusual for you. But it made me wonder if the two of you were having problems."

"You're right. That's none of your business."

"I know you care for Ferris. We all do. It's just that sometimes our feelings for people change. If your feelings for Ferris or...anyone else for that matter...have changed over time, it doesn't diminish your concern for Ferris's well-being. Do you understand what I'm saying?"

Saved by the bell, I thought, watching Rico stroll back to the bar.

"Not even a little," I mumbled. "But thanks for sharing, Master Yoda."

Rico threw money on the bar and waved goodbye to Ronnie. She blew him another kiss and I glanced away, avoiding his smile—a welcome, familiar smile that suddenly and inexplicably made me uneasy.

We pulled on our coats and walked outside. When the door closed behind us, Rico shared our newest bit of intel. "According to Ronnie, the mob's moving some big new op into Over-The-Rhine. She overheard some of the made guys grousing about logistical issues and having to get creative, keeping it under the radar."

Finally, we were getting somewhere.

As we climbed back into the car, I checked my phone and frowned. Three missed calls from Nonnie. One, maybe two, were normal. But three? I called her back.

"You rang?"

"Why?" Nonnie screeched. "Why you never opens your mail, eh? I gives you, but you piles it on table, making big paper mountains."

"Because it's all bills. And creditors don't accept dog biscuits for payment. Whichever bill you're worried about, just put it aside. I'll look at it when I get home."

"Is letter from Hamilton County Auditor's Office. You have tax meeting with auditor at 9:00 a.m. tomorrows!"

Fuuuuuccccckkk.

"It cames three weeks ago!"

Double fuuuuccccckkk.

Nonnie huffed. "Why you never calls them when first letter comes, months ago?"

"Again—the answer is dog biscuits."

"Bah! Funny lady. What you do now?"

"No problem. I got a guy. Talk to you later. Bye-bye."

I hung up before Nonnie could ask who my guy was. Everybody has a guy, right? Everybody except me. I don't have any guys for anything. But I had an attorney who helped me out on a court case once. So I pulled him up in my contacts and gave him a shout.

"Opie? It's Nighthawk. What's shaking, dude?"

"Hey! Good to hear from you. I'm schlepping for the DA's office these days. What about you?"

"I've been summoned to the county auditor's office tomorrow morning at nine."

"What for?"

"A property tax...misunderstanding."

"How big a misunderstanding?"

"Twelve thousand, eight hundred and fifty dollars."

He whistled. "And you called me because..."

"You're my guy, Opie. The one I call when I need legal stuff."

"I represented you once, as a public defender—pro-bono, as a favor to Harry."

"And you won! That makes you my guy."

"But I'm not a *tax* guy, Nighthawk."

"Close enough. Meet me at The Blue Note tonight. We'll have a few drinks...toast Harry. And you can throw me some tips, on how to...you know...stay out of jail."

"They don't have debtor's prison anymore. They'll just garnish your wages."

"Have you ever *seen* me collect wages?"

"You've made money. You're just continuously broke. There's a difference."

Damn it, I thought. *He's going to make me beg.*

"Please, Opie. I really need your help." The 'P'-word had burned coming out.

Opie hesitated. "I'll be at The Blue Note around six, on one condition."

"What's that?"

"You call me by my real name."

Well, that was embarrassing. I had no idea what his name was. I was sure he'd told me once, but the freckle-faced kid would always be Opie to me.

The silence got downright awkward.

"It's Tim," he blurted. "Tim Andrews."

"You got it, Tim. See you at six."

I ended the call and breathed a sigh of relief. When I glanced up, Rico and Babs were staring at me. "What?"

"Nothing," Rico said, raising his hands. "Not a damn thing."

He and Babs opened their doors and climbed out of the SUV. I realized, for the first time, that we were already back at the 51st. The nosey parkers had hung in the car, listening to my entire call before heading inside.

Apparently, they found my life a lot more entertaining than I did.

THE AGENDA for the afternoon was simple. Rico and Babs hung out in the conference room, analyzing the Phoenix Innovations data we secured on our initial visit. I begged off and went to Rico's desk to call Kelvin. His assessment of the image of Toussaint in front of the Flying Pig banner was just a formality, but an important one, evidentiary-wise.

"Kelvin, it's Nighthawk. You done analyzing that photo yet?"

"Yeah. It's the real deal, but there's something more to that image than meets the eye."

"Like what?"

"You tell me. I sent you an e-mail with two attachments."

I pulled up my e-mail and opened the first attachment, containing the picture of Toussaint, standing in front of the banner. After several seconds of squinting, I gave up.

"What am I looking for?"

"See the glass building behind Toussaint, slightly to his right?"

"Yeah?"

"Look at the window panes."

"There's a reflection of a face," I said. "But I can't make it out. It's blurry."

"Okay, now open the other attachment."

I double-clicked on the second attachment and froze. The

original image, magnified ten-fold and cropped to focus on the window pane, revealed the profile of a male. A male I knew.

Kelvin paused. "Who does that look like, Nighthawk?"

"Ferris," I murmured. "It looks like Ferris."

29

A WING AND A PRAYER

My heart ached as I stared at the enhanced image, still hazy due to the refraction of light against the window. The man, neither smiling, nor frowning, showed no hint of distress, as if he were there of his own volition. The man looked like Ferris, but I couldn't swear to it. No one could with the highest resolution of the image still so...imprecise.

We were talking about a man's reputation. His credibility. Whether the man was Ferris or someone else, making sweeping judgments about his state of mind (or guilt or innocence) based on a single blurred image could be dangerous.

I wrestled with showing the image to Rico and Babs. It felt disloyal, as if I believed any involvement Ferris might have had with Toussaint was voluntary. But I needn't have worried. Someone else was more than ready to make that call.

Dickhead beckoned me from the conference room door. The fire in his eyes and the set of his jaw told me Kelvin had already shared the image with him.

I strode toward the room head high, feeling the weight of the officers' stares as I passed by. *Had they seen the image too?* I wondered. It wasn't likely. Not yet, anyway. But they would soon enough. And once they had, another round of stares would begin.

I entered the conference room and the door shut behind me. Horton motioned me to a chair beside Rico and Babs. Once I was seated, he opened his laptop and got straight to the point.

"Agent Thomas has finished his analysis of the Le Clerc photo. The image I'm about to show you has been de-pixelated and enhanced for optimum viewing."

The giant, wall-mounted TV screen lit up, showing an enlarged version of our mysterious male's profile. The room went silent. Blurred and hazy as it was, the image still looked like Ferris.

Dickhead's voice was measured. "Note that at the time of this photo, Agent Ferris was in the immediate proximity of Le Clerc and did not affect an arrest, nor did he request backup to do so. His facial features seem at rest. He exhibits no outward signs of coercion, manipulation or physical discomfort. He's been incommunicado now for three days, despite our attempts to initiate contact. Ugly as it is, we need to consider the possibility that Agent Ferris has gone rogue."

I jumped to my feet, knocking over my chair. "You don't know that! You don't even know for sure that's Ferris! That profile could belong to thousands of people who share his general description."

Babs pointed at the screen. "Was facial recognition software used in identifying the profile as belonging to Ferris?"

"No." Horton frowned. "It wasn't needed. The enhanced image is clear enough."

Babs folded her hands on the conference table. "With all due respect sir, whether we view the image with the naked eye or technical assistance, the details are distorted and blurred. Recognition software identifies eighty nodal points, or facial landmarks, and measures the distances between features. Our subject appears in a shadowed profile view, with less than half his face visible. The available biometric details would likely be insufficient to *definitively* prove that this is Agent Ferris. However, should one of the landmarks not match Agent Ferris, we could eliminate him from consideration."

Dickhead narrowed his eyes. "Are you going to sit here and tell me this isn't Agent Ferris?"

"No. But neither am I one-hundred-percent comfortable saying it is."

Rico nodded. "Me either. And according to investigative journals, even facial recognition software can be fooled."

Horton shook his head. "The goal of the analysis was to validate the authenticity of the Le Clerc photograph. Agent Thomas did that. You can hold out hope that it isn't Agent Ferris in that reflection, but don't let that hope blind you. We need to consider the possibility that he's jumped ship. Failure to do so could cost lives. If any one of you is not willing to accept that possibility, tell me now, and I'll remove you from the case."

Silence reigned.

Horton strolled to the door. "Very well. Finish your review of the evidence from Phoenix Innovations. I want a report on my desk in the morning."

"Yes, sir," Rico said, rising from his chair. "Incidentally, we got a tip today from a C.I. about a mob-owned venture opening in OTR. The timing seems coincidental, what with Phoenix Innovations flying the coop."

"Then you've got your marching orders for tomorrow too," Dickhead said.

We watched quietly as he left the room, cut through the bullpen, and made his way out the door to the parking lot.

Rico whistled. "Damn, that picture looks like Ferris."

"Doesn't it though," Babs said, shaking her head. "It's just so hard to believe."

It was time to put up or shut up. To climb off the fence I'd been riding since the day Ferris had gone missing. Either he'd gone to the dark side or he'd been abducted against his will. On a more basic level, either I believed in Ferris or I didn't. I went with my gut—believing not in what I saw, but what I felt. I knew Ferris better than anyone in that room. The possibility of him going rogue went against everything he stood for—everything we'd fought shoulder-to-shoulder to protect.

God help that man if he proved me wrong.

THE THREE OF us divvied up responsibilities for the remainder of the day. Babs jumped on researching recent OTR property transactions, hoping to either rule in or rule out possible mob involvement, while Rico finished reviewing the confiscated data.

I'd run out of excuses to avoid desk time, so I helped Rico the best way I could. I stayed out of his way, checked my e-mail, and played *Zombie Roadkill* on my phone. Even so, the afternoon dragged.

By five-thirty, I was in the mood to slam Jack Daniel's and drunk text the world—which was convenient, given that I was meeting Opie at The Blue Note. I didn't have any transportation, but that was the least of my problems. Babs and Rico had both offered to take me. Why wouldn't they? Watching me beg, borrow or steal my way out of the poor house would be the highlight of their turd-encrusted day.

I opted to hitch a ride with Babs, mostly because the last time Rico and I had stopped at The Blue Note, the weather had gotten very drunk with the potential for squalls. And the fucker still wouldn't tell me what I said.

I wasn't even sure Babs drank, but if she did, I was willing to bet she'd settle for the occasional glass of white wine. I tried, but failed, to block an unbidden vision of Babs doing Tequila body shots off Dickhead's chest.

You'd think aberrant thoughts like that would worry me. But not so much. I've learned to accept that the degree of my wrongness is matched only by my ability to exceed it. And having accepted that, my life was much simpler.

———

FRECKLE-FACED OPIE WAS ALREADY SEATED at the bar next to Rico, with an untouched boilermaker in front of him. I knew what he was waiting for.

Without prompting, Dallas set us all up with boilermakers. We raised them in unison.

"To Harry," Opie toasted.

"To Harry," I said, smiling at my ghostly partner who raised his glass in return.

I couldn't help but wonder if he was trapped in perpetuity there at The Blue Note, paying off some penance. He didn't seem unhappy, but whatever force had allowed him to return in spirit hadn't given him the power of speech, so it was hard to know for sure.

Opie threw back the boilermaker, slammed down his mug, and then asked how I'd come to owe almost thirteen grand in back taxes. I gave him the *Reader's Digest* version: My father died and left me the house. I lived out of town, so it sat unoccupied until I moved back home in the spring, which prompted a letter stating that I owed three years of back taxes.

"Did you contact the auditor's office?" Opie asked.

"Hell, no, I didn't. Do I look like I have thirteen-grand? I threw the letter in the middle of my kitchen table where I keep my other...pending...bills. A few weeks ago, a second letter arrived."

"And?"

"I tossed the envelope in the pile. Nonnie opened it this morning and called, bitching me out about this meeting I didn't even know I had."

Opie snorted. "Fine. Meet me at the auditor's office in the morning. I'll tell them you just retained me, and ask to have the meeting rescheduled. But don't get your hopes up."

"Whatever," I said, tossing back some cashews. "Just make it go away."

"It isn't going anywhere," Opie huffed. "*You owe the money.* They'll either put a lien on your property or let you pay the balance off in installments. The best we can hope for is that I can buy you some time."

"Fucking perfect." I motioned Dallas for another shot.

Opie glanced up and scanned the faces at the bar. "Where's Ferris?"

I hadn't anticipated that question, but I should have.

"Conspicuously missing," I answered. "And if you value your life, you'll leave it at that."

Vinny wandered through the door and I breathed a sigh of relief. I hadn't seen Vinny in so long, I'd begun to worry about the little pinhead. And, bonus, his arrival would move us past the topic of Ferris.

He bellied up to the bar and sat upwind of me. "Don't yell, Nighthawk. I'm hungry and broke. And I need a beer."

"You need a bath."

Vinny's clothes looked like rejects from a rag bag and smelled like recycled barf. A watchful Dallas slid out from behind the bar and made his way over. The two of them had never met. Judging by Dallas's reaction, Undercover Vinny hadn't made the best first impression.

"Dallas, meet Vinny Abruzzi," I said, slipping in-between them. "Vinny, Dallas. Vinny works with me at ACME. Sorry about the smell. He's doing some cloak-and-dagger work this week."

"Do I stink that bad?" Vinny asked, sniffing his armpit.

"Why don't you sit over here, son," Dallas said, pointing downwind to the last stool. "Give my customers a break."

I ordered Vinny a Bud Light and a couple of burgers, and said to put them on my tab. Dallas raised a brow. Probably because I didn't have a tab. But the barkeep's reaction was all for show. He would never let someone go hungry. I should know. Once upon a time, not that long ago, he'd fed me on the sly.

We ate and drank and caught up between bites. I told Vinny about Jade's widespread contamination theory and recounted the biter attack at Combs BBQ in vivid technicolor. He promised to stay safe and to keep his eyes and ears open.

Rico and Babs chuckled at Vinny's rendition of how a ninety-year-old rotter had continued to give him the slip. By the time Vinny finished the story, another round of drinks had arrived. Gel Boy had cleaned his plate and still looked hungry, so Dallas brought him a double-order of fries.

Time to get back to business, I thought. "What's the latest on Kleinfeld?"

Vinny brought a fry to his mouth, but stopped short of tossing it in. "Something's up. I had two more kills today. Neither one of them was that old fart."

I did the math and frowned. "That's six kills in less than a week."

"Tell me about it. I've been chasing deadheads from one end of town to the other. The bastards lead me down a street and poof, they disappear like socks in a washing machine." He popped the fry into his mouth.

Rico laughed. "They're not going to stand in the street and flag you down, son."

"It's creepy," Vinny said, grabbing a fry and wagging it in Rico face. "Almost like they go to ground."

Babs nodded thoughtfully. "It's possible, you know. Cincinnati is filled with tunnels. Not only do we have the Underground Railroad, we also have the brewery caverns from the 1800s, the prohibition-era hideouts and the abandoned subway system."

"You know it, sister," Dallas said, wiping down the bar. "Once upon a time, there was more going on in the Queen City underground than there was on the streets."

Spectral Harry, hunkered over the bar, nodded in agreement.

I'd heard about the tunnels as a kid but hadn't thought about them in years. Underground hidey-holes for biters. Double the square-footage, double the fun. My job was nothing if not exciting.

As relaxing as the evening had been, Vinny needed to get back to work, chasing bogeys in the projects. He drained the last of his Bud Light and left, promising to check in with Nonnie in the morning to let her know he was still alive.

The rest of us were ready to call it a night too.

"See you at the auditor's—8:45 a.m.," Opie said, slipping on his coat and heading toward the door. "Let me do the talking. And if you even think about calling me Opie, I'll tell them to charge you ten-percent interest."

I waved him out the door, committing the name Timothy Andrews to memory, and hoped that when the urge to call him Opie overcame me, the head-hag would shove a sock in my big fat mouth. But I wasn't counting on it. Some habits die hard.

With a quick nod at Harry, I joined Rico and Babs as they waved to Dallas and filed out the door. Another long, hard day was finished and in the can.

Babs fell silent on the drive to my house, leaving me to my thoughts. Visions of Toussaint and Ferris swirled through my mind, along with underground tunnels, virus-tainted water, the illusive Ira Kleinfeld—and me, an army of one, straddling them all, holding them at bay with a wing and a prayer.

Destiny sucks, I mused.

It didn't matter how many deadheads Toussaint commanded, the war between good and evil would always come down to the two of us.

I settled back in the passenger seat and closed my eyes, wondering what would come of the world if he won.

30

WE'RE DRAWING A CROWD

As much as I loved riding my Harley, I'd gotten spoiled carpooling to work with Rico. My early morning appointment at the auditor's office meant I had to take the lowrider. The November wind was downright brutal. I kept my mind off the cold by pondering the meaning of Philippe's last message, where he wrote that the game was afoot and urged me to be careful. Those words had an ominous ring to them but Philippe was an ominous guy. By the time I parked on Court Street, I'd chalked up his advice to the general paranoia that keeps mercenaries like him alive.

True to his word, Opie was waiting for me on the sidewalk in front of The Hamilton County Auditor's Office. The Muzak version of "Girls Just Want to Have Fun" earwormed its way into my head on the elevator ride to the third floor. When the doors finally opened, we found ourselves in a world of pocket protectors and calculators.

Opie, I mean, Timothy Andrews approached the front desk and announced our arrival. Moments later we were escorted through a fuzzy-walled maze of work stations to a cubicle bearing the nameplate of Dewey Filbert. The office, piled to the ceiling with rows of files and boxes of documents, barely had room for two visitor's chairs. A man popped up from behind a massive fort of manilla folders that bordered the desktop.

"Dewey Filbert," he said, extending his hand. "Please have a seat."

Dewey was a pale, five-foot-nothing pipsqueak who looked a lot like Wally Cox. The smiling auditor put his hands on his hips and gushed, "Gosh, we don't get a lot of celebrities here. Thanks for coming in, Ms. Nighthawk."

Like I had a choice.

"Tim Andrews," Opie said, handing the auditor his card. "Ms. Nighthawk's counsel."

"Make yourself comfortable, Tim. Let's see here," Filbert said, shuffling through a stack of files. "Ah, here it is. Aliya Marie Nighthawk."

I died a little inside.

Filbert shot a coy smile over the top of my case file. "I can't believe it. The Cadaver Diver right here in my cubicle! I'm such a fan of Jade Chen at Channel Ten News."

"Corpse whisperer," I corrected. Of all the monikers Jade had given me, cadaver diver was the worst, and the one that followed me everywhere.

Fuck you very much, you over-processed silicone blob.

"Would you mind?" Filbert asked, sliding out from behind his desk, cell phone in hand. "I'd like to get a selfie with you. Oh, and I'd love your autograph before you leave!"

"I ain't signing shit."

Opie coughed.

"Oh, not to worry," Dewey tittered. "I'll make this visit as painless as possible. Smile and say cheese."

I glared at Opie and snarled. "Cheese."

"Now, to the business at hand." Filbert flipped my file open. "Fairly straight forward. You own the property at 1313 Pitty Pat

Lane, and you're in arrears for three years of back-taxes, amounting to $13,492.50."

Opie frowned. "$12,850.00"

"That was six months ago, compounded by 5% interest equals $13,492.50."

That lying sack of—

"Painless?" I yelled, leaping to my feet. "You call this painless, you pencil-pushing geek?" I reached across the desk and grabbed for Dewey's phone, but he smirked and slid it out of reach.

"A cashier's check will be sufficient."

"Mr. Filbert," Opie said, jerking me back into my seat. "My client just retained me last night. Might we reschedule this meeting, to give me time to review the case?"

"This isn't rocket science, Mr. Andrews. Ms. Nighthawk has known about this debt for six months. I hardly think—"

"I've been busy!" I yelled. "Saving the world from the freakin' horde! So sue me, I missed the damn letter!"

"Don't think we won't." Filbert sneered. "We'll put a lien on your house, if you don't pay up."

"Thirty days," Opie pleaded. "Reschedule in thirty days and we'll work on bringing an acceptable solution to the table."

Filbert tilted his balding head. "Fine. Thirty days. As long as your client comes back with a better attitude and is willing to have an adult conversation about her tax debt. If need be, we can work out a payment plan—assuming she puts down twenty-percent of the new total, which at that time, will include an additional five-percent interest."

My jaw dropped. "Twenty-percent? How am I gonna come up with twenty-percent?"

"Do what other people do," Filbert huffed. "Sell your assets."

"What assets? I have a dog, two birds, and—"

"Thank you, sir," Opie muttered, as he jerked me out of the

pencil-neck's cubicle and dragged me into the hallway. "We'll be in touch."

The pasty-faced attorney had a surprisingly strong grip. He'd nearly dragged me all the way back to the elevator, when I was overcome by the sheer injustice of it all. If I didn't vent soon, I'd implode and the resulting blast would take out half the building.

I cranked Opie's thumb hard to the left and wrenched myself free, then did a spin move toward cubicle-land. "Hey, Dilbert!" I yelled. "I've got your assets, you soul-sucking—"

"Shit, that hurt!" Opie pivoted quickly and launched himself, snagging the bottom of my duster with his fingertips. His voice turned fiery. "I forgot how much I hate representing you."

"Bite me, freckle boy—"

He pulled my duster, reeling me close, and muttered in my ear, "Dial it back. We're drawing a crowd."

Random people, wandering by in the halls of the auditor's office, had stopped in their tracks, mouths agape, to watch the fray. Who could blame them?

I learned a long time ago that my life is the best entertainment value around...unless you're me. In which case, it stinks like a limburger and zushi spring roll.

DARING FATE TO fuck with me twice that morning, I shifted the lowrider into supersonic speed and tore up I-71 to check in with Rico at the precinct. Navigating the ever-present maze of orange construction barrels gave me time to dwell on the salient point of my meeting with Dewey Filbert: I needed money. I always needed money. But the stakes had grown considerably.

In the past, I'd slurped ketchup soup and noshed Milk

Bones to make ends meet. Earning enough money to keep from dying was relatively easy. But the kind of money I needed to appease Dilbert the Relentless couldn't be raised by selling blood, or slinging drinks, or even by raising the dead. I needed a windfall. And don't even think the word inheritance. It was that Cape Cod-shaped inheritance from my father that had created this tax nightmare in the first place. Rest his soul...at least until I get there.

By the time I pulled into the 51st and double-parked behind Rico, I'd realized that winning the lotto was my only shot. Desperation is not a good look on me. I strolled into the precinct around 10:30 a.m., feeling vulnerable. Thankfully, the cops were busy doing cop things and I made it to Rico's desk unscathed.

He glanced up from the computer screen and rubbed his eyes. "How'd it go?"

"Like all my meetings go."

"Sorry."

I plopped into his visitor's chair and stared at the images on his laptop. "Are you still reviewing that security footage?"

"Second time through." He grunted and leaned back in his chair. "I keep expecting something to pop up and grab me. But it's frame after frame of work stations and trash cans and supply closets. Nothing stands out."

He was right. Images of boxed office supplies, reams of paper, pallets of pop, and janitorial supplies. Everything a business needs—even a ghost company that packed up in the middle of the night and disappeared.

The case was getting more complex. I wondered how long it would be before it involved international intrigue and distribution, and if Andezo was the parent company or just one of a dozen layered shell companies. I originally thought Horton had called in the task force too soon. Clearly, I'd been mistaken.

"Where's Babs?" I asked, bellying up to the unoccupied desk behind Rico's.

"Requesting a federal warrant for Andezo. That shouldn't take long. Horton's pissed. He'll fast-track it."

I tried to spout shit about Dickhead but came up empty. Something was distracting me.

Andezo. Andezo. Every time, that name rings a bell. Why?

I had no clue. But my heart told me that Mama Femi would know. I took out my phone, made a mental note to call her later, and pulled up my e-mail. My inbox populated, and the display gave me a start: an encrypted message from Philippe had arrived. I followed the 007 super-secret decoder ring identification protocol, and the message opened:

> **Associates of your old friend Leo Abruzzi are funding an op of interest in OTR. Proceed with caution, Ma Chérie.**

Associates of Leo's would obviously be mob-connected; ergo, the mob was financing Toussaint's latest op. Not surprising, given their history of business partnerships. And Philippe's intel corroborated the scoop we'd gotten from Ronnie, the barmaid at Enzo's.

It was a start.

The pieces of the puzzle had begun to fall into place. But it was a blurry, big-ass 40,000-word puzzle. Breaking this case was going to be a nightmare. That's how this stuff works. Luckily, we had backup.

Vinny, who was already in the area chasing Kleinfeld, could be our eyes and ears on the street. Nonnie the Nose, with her mob connections and goofy way of stumbling into clues, could handle our back door research. And Mama Femi, my guiding light, could help me navigate any Toussaint-related conjuring.

And if all else failed, we always had our B team. Maybe Leo, the mobster accountant, could get a hall pass from heaven and lend a hand. Or Harry the Cop could transcend the walls of The Blue Note, find his voice, and teach me how dinosaur cops solve crimes.

Sometimes, it really does take a village.

As luck would have it, my villagers are a disparate bunch of torch-carrying, pitchfork-wielding wackadoodles. And when the chips are down, I wouldn't have it any other way.

31

IT'S JUST A PIECE OF PAPER

I handed my phone to Rico so he could read Philippe's e-mail. Rico dismissed it with a shrug. "No great surprise. He's only confirming what Ronnie already told us. Your mercenary friend should have better intel."

I wasn't in the best of moods to start with and I didn't have the patience to deal with Rico getting his manties in a bunch. Any other day, I would have called him on that testosterone-fueled bullshit, but I didn't have the energy. Better to redirect the conversation.

"Has Doc sent the tox results on the runners?"

He swiveled back to his PC, pulled up his e-mail, and smiled. "Ask and you shall receive."

Rico's eyes dropped as they scanned the report. "The results for Miller, Warner, and Grant are all consistent with refractory ventricular arrhythmia, secondary to aconite ingestion."

"The popsicle stick?"

Rico grinned. "Coated with aconite."

Well, now. That added some spice to the pot.

Odds were Blake Devlin, the bitchy rep at Phoenix Innovations, had tried to take me out at the Flying Pig with a poisoned popsicle. If I ever got my hands on her, we were going to dance.

Heads turned in unison as Soulja Boy's "Pretty Boy Swag" burst from my phone.

Rico tossed it back to me. "Gotta be Vinny."

"Perfect ringtone or what?" I said, raising the phone to my ear. "Wassup, Pretty Boy?"

"I've got another confirmed kill for billing, but no Kleinfeld. I'm running out of places to look. He moves like the freaking wind."

"He's ninety-two. More like a stale breeze."

"All I know is there's more biters running around out here than we ever knew."

A vaguely disturbing observation.

I gave him the rundown on our new intel and reminded him to keep his eyes and ears open for anything suspicious, like deadheads swarming in a specific area.

"With any luck, you might find Kleinfeld and stumble across a lead on Toussaint's operation. We could kill two birds with one stone."

"Copy that, Nighthawk. Eyes open, staying frosty."

Somebody shoot me. I thought. *He thinks he's in an episode of Justified.*

"Frosty, my ass. Bring that geriatric rotter in *now*, before he liquifies into a pile of zushi on some sidewalk. I mean it, Gel Boy. We'll be the laughingstock of Cincinnati."

"I'm trying! It's just that—"

"Ehhh, wrong answer!" I blew his call into oblivion and phoned Nonnie. She picked up on the first ring, like she always does.

"ACME, Incs. Your one stops shops for puttings down zumbas."

She was quick all right, but her delivery needed work.

"Hey," I said, settling back in my chair. "I need you to do

some research on real estate holdings in town. I'm looking for properties that are mob-owned, either directly, or indirectly. Shell companies, etc. You know the drill."

Nonnie the Nose, widow of a Jewish mobster, knew all the local players. This would be like old home week for her.

"Any calls this morning?" I asked.

"No calls, just empty plate and note on porch from Winstels. They counters your offer."

"They *what*?"

"Agrees to take twenty dollars for vine, and already eats my rugelach, but want film rights to next zumba incursive...incursing...what is big fancy word mean attack?"

"Incursion?"

"Yes, they want film rights for next zumba incursion at your house."

Well, that was slick. How is it they could parlay an ugly, dead-ass vine into a goldmine, while I, who could raise the dead, was going to have to live on dog biscuits? Clearly, I needed to think bigger—and I needed to do it fast.

"New plan," I said. "Tell 'em they can hop the fence the next time the Zumbas break loose and film anything they want—for ten grand. Hell, make it $9,900. Offer them a hundred-dollar discount to cover the replacement of their shitty vine—*if* they pay us in the next two days. Otherwise, it's ten large. Up front. And," I added, feeling froggy, "tell them they have to sign a waiver."

"You have waiver?"

"Of course not."

"But—"

"Just give 'em the message."

My phone dinged. Cap had texted; he wanted to meet in his office.

"I gotta run, Nonnie. If you can manage it, snap a pic of the

Winstel's faces when you chat. I could use a laugh. See you tonight."

I hung up, then texted Cap that Rico and I would be right down.

His response came quick. "Just you."

Danger, danger. Red flag. Repeat. Red flag. One-on-one meetings are never good.

What the hell have I done now? I wondered. The possibilities were endless.

THERE WAS something surreal about sitting in Cap's office without Rico there beside me. And the worst of it was that I had picked the last bit of stuffing out of my chair. Once upon a time, the visitor's chairs had been identical, right down to the cracks in the leather. But mine was flat as a flounder now, while Rico's still had some foam farting out from the cracks. I scooted my chair toward his, then reached over and soothed myself by mining bits of fluff from his seat cushion.

Cap had yet to say a word. He stretched his chair back until it was almost horizontal, then swiped his hands across his bald head, and let out a long, breathy sigh.

"Take a journey with me, Nighthawk. Let's travel back in time to our very first discussion about your desire to be a full-time employee of CPD. We were right here in this office. You were sitting in that very same chair and I was sitting in mine. Do you remember?"

I nodded.

"Speak up, please. Do you remember."

"Yes, Cap."

"Good. Then you should recall that our meeting took place shortly after a biter-education seminar you held for the officers

—so they could learn more about zombies and the world in which you operate."

I didn't like where this was going. Not one little bit. But rather than open my mouth and fall into the abyss that awaited me, I let him continue.

"Yes, yes," he said, leaning forward. "You were on light-duty from a wrist injury, as memory serves me. And you brought in a corpsicle to do a little show and tell."

Fuck me twice on Tuesday.

"Correct me if I'm wrong, Nighthawk, but I think you named that biter Hannibal."

Sweat beads glistened on the tip of my nose. I knew because I could see them. Things had gotten ugly that day. There had been chaos and screaming and zushi. Lots and lots of zushi. Everywhere. Even on Cap. I had to hire Splatz to perform biohazard remediation services.

"But Cap," I said, squirming in my chair, "that situation wasn't my fault. That—"

"Tut." Cap's finger flew to his lips. "Let's not get lost in your creative, yet mind-blowing excuses. The gist of our conversation that day was that you were not hired as an employee of CPD. You were hired as a subcontractor on an as-needed basis. Is any of this coming back to you?"

Oh, fuck. Don't go there.

"Yes, sir."

Cap lowered his voice. "I asked that day if you carried liability coverage. You told me you did. Now, I thought for sure you'd given me a copy of your coverage certificate, but I'll be damned if I can find it. I need it."

Dammit, I told him not to go there.

"I bring this up now, Nighthawk, because I was roasted, once again, at the latest budget meeting over the pending lawsuit filed by Templeman's Funeral Home, as well as anticipated claims for damages at Elysian Fields Cemetery incurred by your numb-nuts partner. Oh, let's not forget the damages to Combs BBQ, which you intentionally rammed with Rico's car. And the damages to Rico's car, of course. These are simply the most recent losses, incurred well after your destruction of both the north wall of Rosehill Cemetery and the Kapinski Mausoleum within it."

"That's not fair," I yelled. "That was a long time ago, on my first case."

"And yet, together, these events establish a pattern. Do you see where I'm going with this, Nighthawk?"

A blind squirrel could have followed that lead.

Cap folded his hands on his desk. "The city's risk management department is closing the purse strings. They have instructed me to give you thirty-days to produce your liability certificate. If you are unable to produce a certificate, the city will withdraw from our employment agreement immediately— and with good cause, I might add. Am I clear?"

"Oh, sure, Cap. No problemo. I'll get you a copy."

Just as soon as I find somebody to forge an original.

Hand to God, folks. At that moment, if I'd had balls, they would have shriveled up inside me and died.

32

IT'S GOOD TO KNOW YOUR LIMITATIONS

I'm good under pressure. I keep my cool, throw out the rule book and act instinctively, using a delicate balance of reflexes and conscious thought—heavy on the reflexes. Thinking too much (or God forbid, planning) gets me into trouble every time.

But that day, as I left Cap's office, the walls were closing in on me.

I wasn't in physical danger. I wasn't hyped-up on adrenaline. I wasn't saving lives. I deal with those stressors all the time and I've learned how to control them. Today's pressure, the overwhelming mound of debt that threatened to drown me, was entirely different and far beyond my control.

Babs would have been proud that I had the self-awareness to realize that. I, on the other hand, thought my state of affairs sucked syphilitic donkey dicks.

What I needed was some wind therapy.

I marched back to Rico's desk and lied out my ass, telling him I had some urgent personal business that needed to be addressed.

He glanced up from his monitor. "You sure you don't want to take a run at the security video?"

The words: "I'd rather stick my head in a wood chipper," tumbled out before I could shove them back in.

I snatched my coat and broke for the door, feeling the weight of his stare. He wanted to know why I was leaving. And he had to be dying to know what my meeting with Cap had been about. But that's the thing about Rico. He's a good partner. He'd hear all about that meeting when I was damned good and ready to tell him. And he knew it.

I hit I-71 North and opened up the throttle, trying to blow a crap-ton of debt-related dung out of my brain: $13,492.50 plus 5% interest for back taxes, the cost of liability insurance I couldn't afford, the lawsuit Templeman had filed (the funeral home was, literally, toast), and the as yet unknown damage total from Combs BBQ, Rico's Mustang, and Vinny's shootout at Elysian Fields Cemetery. The more space the list took up in my brain, the tighter I gripped the throttle.

A siren sounded behind me.

My speedometer read 110 miles per hour.

I pulled over, turned off my bike, and waited for the police officer, hoping maybe I knew him. Or maybe he'd know me. Seriously, after the day I'd been having, I still dared to hope.

What a moron.

The cop sidled up alongside the lowrider, with his ticket book and pen already in hand. "License and registration, please."

I forked them over, praying he'd recognize my name.

Not so much as a blink. He took my documents back to his car to run me through the system. A few minutes later, he came back, looking unimpressed.

"Do you have any idea how fast you were driving, Ms. Nighthawk?"

"Sorry, brother. I'm with CPD too, taking down deadheads in the Paranormal Crimes Unit—with Rico De Palma."

"Yeah." He eyed me over the top of his Ray-Bans. "They made us watch the training video."

I winced. "Any chance you can let this slide, officer? I was on my way to an active biter call."

"No, you weren't. I checked."

"Oh."

The brain bitch snorted.

Apparently, the *shut the fuck up* thought bubble that I believed was floating over my head had accidentally exited my mouth.

The officer stopped scribbling. "Excuse me?"

"Sorry. Shut the front door, you know. Like I can't believe this is happening."

"Don't lie. It only makes it worse." He ripped the ticket off the pad and shoved it at me. "You were driving 110 in a 65—in a construction zone. That's double the fine. Normally, that far over the limit, you'd have to appear in court. I marked *mail in* because De Palma would probably give me shit if I made you appear in court. Have a good day. And slow down."

He climbed into his cruiser, flipped on his turn signal, and eased back into traffic. I sat on the lowrider with the ignition off, staring into space.

Great, I thought. *Let's toss a $300 ticket onto the debt-related dung pile.* I'm not exactly sure when, but somewhere along the line, I'd begun to visualize dollars as monopoly money. Fuck Mr. Monopoly, the son of a bitch. I started my bike and roared back onto the highway, wondering when the old fart would let me land on St. James Place.

Stupid question. I was already bankrupt and out of the game.

The sting of that ticket was still fresh when I pulled into my driveway and walked in the back door. Nonnie bellowed at me from the second floor.

"Come up heres, Miss Allie. Is bad. Very, very bad."

I scritched Headbutt behind his ears, then trudged up the steps to the second-floor, having no idea *what* was very, very bad, but knowing that with my luck, it would indeed be very, very bad. I reached the landing and stopped, staring slack-jawed at the sight of Nonnie straddling a locust tree limb that bisected the width of the dormer.

I gulped. "Tell me that's Winstel's tree."

"No. Is yours."

Damn it.

"Is going to rain soon," she said, peering up through a huge jagged hole on the back side of my roof. She pointed out a line of mare's tails clouds floating by. "Maybe even snow. We should buys some salts."

"Cheese and crackers!" I yelled, spinning in circles, not knowing where to look first. "What the he...What happened?"

"Is not obvious?"

I shot her a withering look.

"Old dead tree falls aparts. Circles of lifes. Walter go to the Depots for tarp and plywoods. He fixes hole when he get back."

"Like hell he will!"

That was all I needed. Grandpa Moses falling off my roof, breaking his everything, and suing me for the last bit of lint he can pick from my pocket. The freeloader.

I pulled out my phone and called for backup. "Vinny, come home, pronto. I need your help with something."

"Sure thing, boss. I could use a break."

There had been a hint of relief in Gel Boy's voice. Little did he know that if any of us were going to fall off the roof, it would be him.

I reeled around and stuck my finger in Nonnie's face. "Don't you dare let Walter set one foot on that roof. Tell Vinny to get his scrawny ass up there and fix this hole now, tonight. I want it finished before I get back—before it rains or snows or spouts a fucking tornado."

I took my finger out of Nonnie's face and pointed it in the air. "You got anything else, God? Go ahead and let 'er rip. You hear me? Just let 'er rip."

I took the steps two at a time, back to the first floor, cursing like the sailor I had surely been in a previous life.

Nonnie's voice trailed behind me. "Where you goings, Miss Allie?"

"To get some spiritual therapy," I yelled, as I pushed outside through the kitchen door.

It wasn't exactly a lie. I was going to The Blue Note Lounge where the bartender likes me and the spirits run free. With any luck, Harry would be there too.

DALLAS GLANCED at his watch as I walked into the bar. "Two o'clock. You're a bit early, aren't you?"

I plopped in my usual stool and a Jack Daniel's slushie magically appeared before me. I must have looked as defeated as I felt. Dallas even added a swizzle stick and sat it on a coaster, like I was a real customer.

"On the house, Allie Cat."

"Thanks. You have no idea how much I need this right now."

"Care to tell your troubles to the oldest bartender in town?"

I gave him the quick and dirty version of my woes. Recounting them out loud made them seem even worse. I hadn't known that was possible.

"You know," Dallas said, taking care not to look me in the eye, "You could really use half of that recovery fee from Elite Trust about now."

"Bullshit. I want the whole 180K."

"Yeah? Well, if wishes came true, I'd live on a remote island with Raquel Welch."

"Your point?"

Dallas wiped down the bar and sighed. "That Marlowe woman stopped in last night. She still wants to partner up with you."

"Ha!" A sip of slushie fizzed in my nose. "That's never gonna happen."

"Why the hell not?"

"Cause the next time I see that ginger bitch, I'm gonna light her up like a bottle rocket."

"Suit yourself, Hard-Case." Dallas grabbed a stack of plastic food baskets and shuffled back to the kitchen.

My old partner had been there the whole time, silently observing my conversation from the relative safety of his stool. The disapproval on his face was hard to miss.

"Oh, what do you know, you ectoplasmic blob?"

Harry dismissed me with a wave.

"If you've got something to say, partner, spit it out."

Harry flinched like I'd jacked his jaw, then turned his shoulder to me.

That was just hurtful on my part, making fun of his mutism. Clearly, he'd thought, given the financial corner I was in, I should revisit the idea of partnering with Marlowe.

That would never happen. Not without an apology from her and the hundred bucks she owed me. Make that $110, with interest. Why the hell not? Everybody else charges interest. Besides, joining forces with her would mean more than just splitting the reward. I'd have to swallow my pride.

Humility isn't one of my 'go to' attributes. According to Babs, I'm narcissistic, inflexible and have no personal insight. It's good to know your limits, even if someone else has to explain them to you. If I gave in now, I might confuse myself.

I crunched my slushie ice and scrolled through my phone, playing *Temple Run* and checking for texts from Nonnie. Hell, who am I kidding. I was still hoping to hear from Ferris. Once again, I came up empty. A smattering of e-mails had come in, but an update from Dr. Christian, another person I'd been hoping to hear from, wasn't among them. The investigation seemed to be stalling.

I finished my second slushie and had moved on to perusing obscure science journals when "Pretty Boy Swag" burst from my phone. I brought it to my ear with a sigh.

"Wassup, Gel Boy."

"Hey, I don't mind tarping your roof, but it's a two-man job. And Walter ain't the man."

"Don't let him on that roof!"

"Fine. But who's going to help me?"

There are only two things in life that spook me: public speaking and heights. Clearly, it wasn't going to be me.

"Relax," I said, "I'll get somebody over there. Is Walter back with the supplies?"

"Yeah. He says you owe him three-hundred-and-fifty bucks."

"Tell him not to worry. He'll be long dead before he sees that money. I'll be home in a bit. Just keep that geezer grounded."

I hit end call and phoned Rico, the friend who never lets me down.

"Nighthawk, where the hell are you?"

"How'd you like to come to my house? Oh, wear gym shoes."

"Why?"

"There's a ginormous hole in my roof and Vinny needs help putting down a tarp."

Rico laughed so hard he snorted. "Remember the time we scaled that warehouse on 14th? And you—"

"Yeah, yeah."

"We were five stories up! I thought you were going to cry. You almost peed your pants."

Jebus. When he wanted to, the guy had the memory of an elephant.

"Are you coming or not?" I snapped.

"What's in it for me?"

"All the rugelach you can eat. Nonnie's been a freaking rugelach-making machine."

"I've got shoes in the car. Be there in thirty."

Rico hung up and my mental health break at The Blue Note came to an end.

I slid off my stool to leave, and a cold wind tore through the room. Menus fluttered, napkins skittered to the floor, and the Historical Cincinnati wall calendar hanging behind the cash register flew across the top of the bar and landed at my feet. A picture of one of the local underground tunnels stared up at me.

I glanced at Harry's stool. It was empty. Mr. Judgy McTurdghost had left without making his goodbyes. Clearly, I had pissed him off—but he hadn't left me hanging. Harry freaking Delk, the dinosaur cop who took down biters with an antique .38 and speed loaders, had left me a clue the only way he could.

I flipped a fiver on the bar, strolled to the door, and whispered, "Thanks for the tip, partner."

33

WHAT IS WRONG WITH YOU?

I heard Rico rumble to the curb in his carpool beater. The clunker had finally lost its crumpled antenna and one of its three remaining hubcaps. He cut the engine, producing a spectacular series of knocks and sputters before the rusted beast belched a cloud of black smoke in the air. Rico climbed out of the death mobile with a disgusted look on his face and trudged through the yard to my porch.

If he didn't get his car back soon, his temporary ride would disintegrate beneath him. As if I hadn't already felt bad enough, a fresh pang of guilt surfaced over what had happened to his car during the attack at Combs BBQ. Worried that I'd be on the receiving end of another tirade, I opened the door before Rico rang the bell and greeted him by shoving a preemptive piece of rugelach in his mouth.

"When do you get the Mustang back?"

"Next week," he mumbled around the pastry. He wiped his mouth with the back of his hand before adding, "The POS is losing oil, so I parked it on the street."

The first thing we saw when we walked into the kitchen was Walter, with a chainsaw at his feet, glued to his usual chair at

my table and playing with his bird Benny, Beaner, Beano...
whatever. He pulled out one of his stogies and lit it.

I continued our game by grabbing it from his mouth and
stubbing it out in the sink. He mumbled something he was
lucky I didn't hear, and then wandered out the door to the back
yard to start the process over again.

Nonnie picked the chainsaw up from the linoleum floor
and made a beeline for the stairs. "I cuts up limb in dormer
now while you fixes roof."

Rico bit back a smile and rescued the saw from her. "I'll get
that Nonnie, after we finish putting the tarp on."

"But whats can I do?"

I sucked in a breath as Rico slipped out of his jacket, loos-
ened his tie, and stripped out of his dress shirt.

He hung them on the back of a chair and flashed Nonnie
one of his irresistible smiles. "Why don't you stay down here
and finish cooking that lasagna I see on the sink? Got any garlic
bread to go with it?"

"Anythings for you, Mr. Rico." Nonnie put her hand to her
mouth and giggled like a school girl as she stared at the six-
pack abs straining against his fitted T-shirt.

That smile of his was stronger than kryptonite, but holy
mamma, those abs!

Vinny had hauled my father's rickety ladders out of the
toolshed before I'd arrived home. He'd carried the extension
ladder around the exterior of the house, leaned it against the
brick wall, and then brought the eight-foot step ladder through
the house to the second floor and positioned it beneath the
hole.

Rico carried the chainsaw upstairs to the dormer, clambered over the tree limb and cut it in two. He shoved the top
half of the limb out onto the roof, and left the lower half inside
to be sawed into pieces after they screwed the tarp down. Then
he and Vinny put on their jackets and went outside, climbed

the extension ladder to the roof, and tossed the limb to the ground.

Operation Jury-Rig the Roof had begun.

I climbed up the step ladder on the second floor and stopped four-feet below the ceiling. So far so good, I thought, holding on for dear life. I heard their feet clomp across the roof as they laid the tarp and fastened it to the two-by-fours, working their way toward the peak. In between spurts from the screw gun, we held a three-way conversation.

"Hey," Vinny's voice drifted down through the hole, "that Marlowe woman's been tailing me. Every time I think I've given her the slip she bounces back like a bad check."

"No kidding," I yelled. "Dallas said she's stalking me at the Blue Note, too."

The stomping grew louder and Vinny peered down through the gap in the roof. "I noticed something today, but I figured she was watching. So instead of checking it out, I thought I'd tell you in person. Remember that day at the Hoffbauer Building, when I cornered that corpsicle?"

Rico's disembodied voice drifted in. "The one you thought was Kleinfeld?"

"Yeah. That one."

"What about it?" I asked.

"I realized today that most of the biters I've bagged have been in a three-mile radius to that place. It's like it's ground zero for snagging deadheads."

Progress. The kid was starting to think like a hunter. We'd checked out that building once, but what better location for Toussaint to use than one that had already been cleared?

"Nice catch, Vinny. We'll head back there tomorrow and have another look."

"You two finished chatting?" Rico called. "It's time to cover the hole."

"Don't worry," Vinny said, as I hopped off the ladder and

laid it alongside what was left of the branch. "I'll get Kleinfeld any day now. I can feel it."

When he backed away from the edge of the hole, a piece of plywood closed off my view of the sky. I heard his feet clomp away and a twinge of guilt prickled inside me. All it had taken to motivate the kid was a little praise, but I'd been so busy busting his chops for stupid shit that I seldom offered him encouragement.

Thankfully, my brain fart passed quickly when I remembered that Vinny excelled at stupid shit. The kid insisted on learning things the hard way.

But at least he was learning.

And despite the mega-dose of crow he'd had to swallow the moment he lost Kleinfeld in the cemetery, he'd stuck with the job and had never given up. Most rookies would have walked away. Vinny would make a good hunter someday—if I didn't kill him first.

RICO AND VINNY finished tarping the roof, and cutting up the tree limb they'd tossed into my yard, just after sunset. Vinny carried the extension ladder back to the toolshed and Rico returned to the dormer to cut up the remnants of the tree branch. He was drenched in sweat, so he took off his jacket, peeled the wet T-shirt off his body, and got to business.

I collected the longer sticks and tied them into bundles, and then gathered the smaller pieces into garbage bags, all the while watching Rico as he worked—watching the flex of his biceps and the sweaty sheen of his tousled black hair. Watching perspiration trickle down his neck and feather across his back, teasing its way around front and settling into the creases of his washboard abs. Despite the frosty air, his face was flushed.

So was mine.

Yikes! What the hell was I doing to myself? And why?

I forced myself to look away, hoping that he hadn't noticed me gawking at him. Mercifully, Vinny broke the spell by plodding up the steps to help me gather the trimmings.

Rico finished sawing and advised me that the tarp might hold a few months, if I was lucky. Unless I stumbled into a windfall, it would have to last a lot longer than that.

The three of us hauled the bundles and bags down from the dormer and out the door, and stacked them alongside the house. Vinny could patch the drywall and paint later, after he brought in Kleinfeld. Nonnie could clean up the dormer whenever the spirit moved her. God knew I wasn't going to do it.

"Wash up!" Nonnie cried, clapping her hands as we trudged through the back door. "Then come sits at table. I have big surprise!"

She ducked out of the kitchen and scurried into the living room.

Dinner wouldn't be much of a surprise, I thought. The heavenly smells had given her secret away. We took our seats and waited for Nonnie to reappear.

She tip-toed back into the kitchen, gingerly carrying an Amazon box like it was filled with vials of nitroglycerin. Something small, white and oval rested at the bottom of the box. A memory surfaced.

I didn't think I was going to like her surprise.

Nonnie gently lowered the box to the table and pulled her hands away to reveal its contents: an unhatched bird egg on a bed of wood shavings and hay.

"Walter and I so prouds," she gushed. "Hyrum having sibling!"

"Ha!" I jumped to my feet, knocking over my chair, and pointed at Nonnie. "You dirty little liar! All that crap about virgin-bird births, and how you had no idea how Hyrum happened. Beano knocked up Kulu, and you knew it the whole time!"

"Bennu," Walter mumbled.

"Whatever." Daggers darted from my eyes and dared him to speak again.

Nonnie puffed out her lip so far that a bird could have landed on it. "I thought you be happys."

"Seriously?" My voice reached an octave I hadn't known I had. "We're outnumbered. We've got a freaking aviary here!"

Rico and Vinny avoided my gaze. They took turns smiling politely at the egg, each giving it a single noncommittal nod. Apparently satisfied, Nonnie whisked the box back into the living room and tucked it away, presumably somewhere safe from me.

"There were two perches in that box," I yelled. "This was no accident. You built them a freaking nesting box!"

"So sues me," she screamed back.

The evening's mood had been set.

Nonnie slammed the lasagna onto the table and hurled the bread basket at me so hard, it bounced off the Formica and nearly hit me in the face. Rico buried his head in his plate and chewed his food like an angry beaver. Vinny scored a new personal best for fastest time inhaling a meal.

Headbutt, Kulu, and Beano swiveled their heads from side to side, eyeing us warily. For once in his short life, Baby Hyrum stopped squawking. Walter, oblivious to the tension, picked his teeth with his fork and slurped his tea.

The din of fast and furious chewing ended when Nonnie snarled, "By the ways, Winstels tolds me you can takes your counter-offer and shove it where is no sunshines. Maybe I say same, eh?"

Nothing to see here, folks. Just everyday dinner conversation at the Nighthawk house.

Vinny finished his meal first. He jumped up from his chair,

gave Nonnie a cautious peck on the cheek, then grabbed some rugelach from a platter on the sink and headed down the hall.

"Taking a shower and hitting the sack," he called from the hallway. "Gotta get back out there bright and early. Night everybody."

Walter disappeared out back to light one of his stinky stogies.

Rico scooted out his chair and rose to his feet, signaling a hasty retreat.

So this is how it's going to be, I thought. Rats deserting the sinking ship.

"Thank you for dinner," Rico said. He scooped up his shirt and tie, then leaned down and bussed Nonnie's cheek. "Best lasagna in town, lady. I love when you cook for me."

She pinched his cheek adoringly while shooting me a wicked side-eye from her chair. "Since Miss Highs and Mighties never say so, thank you for fixing big ugly hole in roof."

"Aw, no problem," Rico said, as he spun and broke for the front door. Nonnie, the pint-sized meatball, flashed me the double-bird salute as I trailed him out of the kitchen.

Once we were out of earshot, Rico turned to me with a twinkle in his eye. "So...that was a pleasant dinner."

"Ha!" I clapped my hand over my mouth, hoping Nonnie hadn't heard me.

"You were a little hard on her, weren't you?"

"Are you kidding! How many birds does she need?"

Rico sighed. "Does she look after them? Feed them, clean their cages?"

"Yes."

"Then what do you care. Don't you want her to be happy?"

Well, big stinking piles of dog shit. I hate when I'm wrong and everyone knows it but me.

"Fine," I said, rolling my eyes. "I'll apologize. She was right about something else, you know. I should have thanked you earlier. You're always there when I need you. Seriously. I, ah... thank you."

His sable eyes grew soft. "That's what partners do. Hold still."

I froze as he brushed his thumb along my cheekbone.

"You had a smudge," he whispered, never taking his eyes from mine.

"Tree dirt," I murmured.

He ran his fingers through my hair and softly kissed my forehead. I tilted my head back, bringing my lips to his. He moved into me, wrapped his arms around my waist, and pulled me close.

"Wait, Mr. Rico!" Nonnie screamed from the kitchen. "I have rugelachs for you."

Damn it anyway.

Rico panicked and launched me through the air like a plague-infested rat. I backpedaled on the landing and caught my balance just as Nonnie trotted into the room. The scarlet blaze on Rico's face was priceless.

A smiling Nonnie patted his arm. "I give you half the pastries. Other half for Vinnys. This one," she said waving in my general direction, "gets nones."

She harrumphed, then turned on her heel and waddled back into the kitchen.

Rico threw on his jacket and mumbled, "Well. I guess...I guess I should go."

"Yeah...I guess."

It took me forever to open the door.

What is wrong with you? Little Allie screamed. *Kiss that man!*

Rico walked out the door and started down the steps, but stopped and held up his bag. "I'll, uh, bring some of these to office tomorrow."

"Thanks."

I didn't know what else to say, but I wanted...more.

"Hey, Rico?"

He spun on his heel, looking hopeful.

I had nothing. At least, nothing I could say out loud. "Just... have a good night."

"Yeah. You too."

I watched him walk into the wintery night, feeling an emptiness inside me. I should have said more. But the only words that had come to mind—the words I had really wanted to say—were stuck so deep inside my heart, that until that moment, I hadn't even known they were there.

34

TOUGH LOVE

Nonnie and I needed space. I hung out in my room after Rico left, listening to her rattle around while she cleaned the kitchen. Eventually, I heard her say goodnight to the menagerie, followed by the sounds of the back door opening and closing. Silence reigned. I was finally alone with my thoughts, and worse, my emotions.

I'm not introspective. I don't ponder the nature of my existence. And I don't navigate feelings well. Anyone's feelings, really, but especially my own. The truth of the matter is that feelings frighten me. It's easier to push people away than to let them get close. It's also easier to shove all that touchy-feely bullshit into a dark corner of my brain and lock the door behind it. But that wasn't cutting it anymore. Like it or not, those feelings and emotions were bursting inside me, screaming to be set free.

I cared for Ferris. A lot. Was it love? Sure...maybe...possibly. But I felt something for Rico, too. Something deeper, more primal. Ferris was fun and sexy and devoted to me. But I couldn't say I felt the same about him. He was my task force partner. And my friend. And he was missing. I'd stop at nothing to find him.

Better I should focus on that, I told myself, lying there in the dark, *than to trot that ridiculous jumble of emotions out into the light of day.*

The best way I could help Ferris was to call Mama Femi. I'd been planning on calling her anyway. My gut had told me she would know the significance of the word Andezo.

It was ten o'clock Cincinnati time, making it nine in New Orleans. Surely, her day's cooking and conjuring duties were finished. I pulled her up in my contacts and tapped her phone number. She was slow to answer. A vague uneasiness crawled up my spine.

"*Ti Kras Zwazo!* I have been expecting to hear from you."

Mama had called me her little bird since I was a child. Her voice sounded weak, but the love it radiated was unmistakable.

"*Manman, mwen te manke ou anpil.* I'm not calling too late, am I?"

"I miss you, too. And it is never too late to hear from you."

"Are you well?"

There was no point in hiding my concern. She would have sensed it anyway.

A sigh reached my ear. "Your *manman* is very old and tired, *sha*. But I am well enough, for now."

My heart tugged. Mama Femi was aging and there was nothing to be done about it. No spells, incantations or offerings could restore her youth. The vibrant Hoodoo queen who had raised me and taught me everything I knew about the mystical world was fading. The apprehension I'd felt while waiting for her to answer my call morphed into sadness.

Mama, an empath who could never tolerate my discomfort, moved the conversation forward. "What can I do to help you, little bird?"

"Does the word Andezo mean anything to you?"

"Of course, it does. And it would to you too, if you had listened to my teachings. Simbi Andezo is the Lord of Two Waters."

Heat rose in my cheeks. "Oh...sure, The Lord of Two Waters. Yeah, that sounds familiar."

"Does it?" Mama's voice betrayed annoyance, hurt or both, none of which boded well for me.

"Let's review," she said, as if I were once again her apprentice. "The two waters can mean many things. Fresh and salt water, or the mangrove swamps where fresh and salt waters merge into one. But it can also refer to the waters of life and death."

All three of those possibilities had potential, but I put my money on the waters of life and death. That was the only kind of game Toussaint played. The easy part of the phone call was finished. Now came the hard part.

"Thanks for the refresher, Mama. I can take it from here. But before I let you go, there's ah...um...something else..."

I was searching for the right words, but they never came.

Mama broke the silence. "Is it about Toussaint?"

"Yes."

"Ah. You've called to say he is back from the dead."

"You *knew*?"

"I had my suspicions. But in magick, the truth is seldom as it seems."

"How... What made you think that?"

"Sometimes, in the dark of night, I imagine I hear his soul flitting between this world and the next...barely there, dark and distant. I tell myself this could not be. That Toussaint is gone, and I am simply a mama who misses her beloved *bway*."

How naïve could I be? Of course, Mama would have sensed Toussaint's energy. She had raised him, just as she'd raised me. Even so, I still felt betrayed and didn't try to hide it.

"Why didn't you tell me?"

"I knew if he was truly alive, he would surface again and make himself known."

"Well, he is back, Mama. And Ferris is missing—just disappeared off the face of the earth and left everything he owned behind. Ferris would never do that."

I dreaded continuing, but Mama deserved the truth. "It's possible Toussaint has him. We discovered a picture during our investigation. It's an image of Toussaint, with Ferris's reflection in the background."

Mama paused. "Did your Ferris appear to be distressed?"

"No. But he would never join Toussaint willingly."

"The Ferris you know would not. But the Ferris Toussaint molds will do his bidding. You can be sure of that. And so," Mama said, matter-of-factly, "you will find them both and learn the truth."

"But what if...if Ferris is under Toussaint's contr—"

"Either way, your struggle between good and evil begins again."

"You mean *our* struggle, Mama. Our struggle begins again."

"This is your battle, *sha*. Not mine."

That sentence—that single sentence was the sum of all my fears. To fight Toussaint without Mama at my side would be the end of me. She couldn't leave me now when I needed her most. I rubbed tears from my eyes and pushed back with everything inside me.

"Toussaint is so strong, Mama." Even to my ears, my voice sounded small and childlike. "He almost killed me at Congo Square. I can't face him again. And I surely can't fight him alone."

"*Sha*, I am too old and too weak to fight."

"I can't beat him without you!"

"You are stronger than you know, child—much stronger than you were at Congo Square. I feel it. Trust yourself. You will feel it too, in time. God put you on dis earth and gave you dis gift for a reason."

"But the spells and the rootwork—"

"Everything you need to know is in your mind and in your heart. I know because I put it there." She laughed ruefully. "I did you no favors making Jade's tonic for you. I should have pushed you to make it yourself. You know the spells. You know the rootwork. You have only to focus and remember them."

"But I *don't* remember th—"

"I cannot live forever, Aliyah Marie! It is time for you to grow up—to take responsibility for your future...your legacy. You must claim it! Own it, so that no one, not even Toussaint, can take it from you."

I'd heard that tone before. Mama Femi had said her final word on the subject. Besides, my thoughts had scattered and my stomach had crawled into my throat. The conversation had come to a close.

"I understand, Mama. It's getting late. Sorry to have—"

"Spit it out, child."

"What?"

"Do not deceive your *manman*. I may be old and weak, but I know you better than you know yourself. There is more calamity in your life than Toussaint. What ails you, little bird?"

And out it came. All of it. I confessed my feelings for Ferris had never equaled his for me. But I told her I wasn't sure if that was because he wasn't the right guy for me, or because I held him at arms-length to keep from being hurt—or maybe even from hurting him. Why wouldn't I think that? People close to me die: my mother, my father, Harry and Dr. Latka.

I told her Rico and Jade had broken up—and I'd found myself strongly attracted to him. And he had feelings for me too. I admitted how guilty all of this made me feel, especially since Ferris was missing. I didn't want to hurt him, but I wanted to be happy, and I had absolutely no idea what that meant, or what it would take to make that happen. I finally ran out of air and ended my jumbled rant by asking her what I should do.

Mama let loose a long sigh. "First, be honest with yourself. Then, be honest with them."

"But—"

"Life is not easy, *sha*. No one can live it for you. Solving your problems falls to you, and you alone."

"But how do I do that?"

"Have you not been listening? You take responsibility for your life and grow up! It is time for my little bird to fly away from the nest. *Bŏn Nwi, ti chĕri.*"

The line went dead.

And for the first time in my life, I felt naked and alone.

My world, a world filled with magick and power, good and evil, came crashing down around me. The prospect of battling Toussaint without Mamma at my side was terrifying.

Numb and shaken, I doubled-checked the locks on my doors, and headed to the kitchen to cover Kulu and Hyrum for the night. The rumble of Vinny's snoring followed me as I shuffled to my room. Headbutt, trotting at my heels, jumped in bed beside me and circled a few times before settling in beneath the blankets. Hawk, snug in his holster, guarded me from my bedpost. I turned off the light and listened. All was well. The house was quiet.

Too quiet, damn it.

Once again, I found myself floundering in the itchy, scratchy world of emotions.

I stared into the dark and contemplated my life. The good times and the bad. Memories of my mother and father, Mama, and even Toussaint, from when we were both young and on the same side of the light.

Snippets of Rico, Ferris and Harry whirred through my head. Times they saved my life, times I saved theirs. Times they made me laugh, and times they made me so furious, I had considered kicking them to the curb, so I could ease back into the life I had before they appeared. A life that, somewhere along the line, had funneled into a solitary existence where I was beholden to nothing and to no one.

Allie Nighthawk, the best of the badass zombie hunters. A cocky, self-professed loner who had never needed or wanted a partner. What a freaking poseur.

35

A GRITTY, FAMILIAR SOUND

I moseyed into the 51st about 9:00 a.m., anticipating a buttload of awkwardness between Rico and me. He barely glanced up from his monitor when I took my usual chair beside his desk, and instantly immersed himself in some report.

Score one for me. I'm always amazed when I call social situations right.

I grabbed some coffee, then scouted out Cap's office to harass any new receptionist that might have arrived, but was sadly disappointed. By the time I circled back to Rico's desk, he was standing with his coat on, waiting for me.

"Let's go," he said, avoiding eye contact. "We need to hit the Hoffbauer Building."

I fell in step beside him as we left the precinct, silently swearing that if he ever tried to kiss me again, I'd smack the living shit out of him. No man was worth this amount of torture. I ducked into the passenger side of the death mobile and sighed as the seat springs groaned beneath me. The side-view mirror fell off when I closed the door. It thudded to the parking lot and shattered into pieces. I opened the door, mumbled a quiet curse, scooped up the mirror frame and tossed it onto the backseat floor.

"Onward, James," I said, with a grand sweep of my hand.

Rico bit back a smile. "I hate this fucking car."

He drove us to OTR and pulled to the curb around the corner from the Hoffbauer Building. He cut the power and the behemoth heaved and shimmied several times before giving up the ghost.

"Huh," he said, pointing to a biter disappearing around the corner of the building. "Vinny might be on to something. Let's wait a few minutes and see if we get any other rotters."

Rico reached around to the backseat, grabbed a plastic bag, and handed it to me. Nonnie's rugelach. At least we'd have something to eat during our stakeout.

I dunked a piece in my coffee and stole a glance at Rico. "Friends?"

He fidgeted. "Yeah, about last night…"

Oh, sweet Jebus.

"I…we…I shouldn't have—"

"No, seriously." I waved him off. "No sweat."

"It's just, we're partners, and I don't want to…"

"Absolutely. I get it. Partners it is."

I bit into my rugelach and tried to send him a telepathic message to drop the whole thing before I melted into the floorboards.

Rico frowned. "Did that deadhead ever come back around?"

"No," I mumbled, twisting around to take in a wider view. "Wonder where it went."

"Only one way to find out. Should we let Horton know?"

"No. It could be nothing."

Or something, I thought. *In either case, Rico and I should be able to handle it.*

A flashback hit me from last night, when Mama rocked my world by telling me I was on my own. I shrugged off an uneasy feeling and resolved that she would never have turned me loose if I hadn't been ready. From my very first day in her care, Mama had been my safety net, protecting and guiding me at every turn. Never once had she failed me. Yet, even with all that I'd learned, if she hadn't distracted Toussaint during our battle at Congo Square, I'd be dead.

Clearly, the lack of her safety net had left me with a confidence problem. And if I wasn't careful, it could cost me dearly.

Rico radioed into dispatch that we were leaving the car for a walkaround.

"We're going to need some flashlights," he said, as we climbed out of the death mobile.

He walked around back and tried to open the trunk, but the lid stuck. Not much of a surprise. The rusty beast finally surrendered when he punched it a few times. Mission accomplished.

Flashlights in hand and ready to rock, we headed for the rear of the Hoffbauer Building.

———

GAINING entry wouldn't be easy. After our last visit, all the openings had been boarded shut. The grounds were littered with overgrown weeds, broken bottles, used syringes and enough biohazardous material to produce a new species.

We picked through the brush, slowly and carefully, inspecting the foundation for gaps and other potential points of entry. A root cellar on the far side of the house caught my eye. The rotted double doors were layered with trash, like the rest of the grounds. It looked like the cellar hadn't been used in decades.

Expecting to be disappointed, I tugged on one of the doors. It creaked open and swung all the way back to the ground. The rubbish on top of the door remained in place. It had been fastened to the wood.

"Slick." Rico eyed the doors with admiration. "The perfect urban camouflage."

"Isn't it, though? Right up Toussaint's alley." Still, something struck me as odd, something I couldn't shake. "When we were here before—when Vinny called us and said he had Kleinfeld cornered—we checked out the whole building, right?"

"Affirmative."

"We checked behind every single door?"

"Checked and double checked."

"There wasn't any interior door to this cellar."

I flicked off the trigger guard on my holster and Rico followed suit.

"After you, *madame*."

Since the cellar was on the far side of the house (away from the prying eyes of the street) we opted to leave the doors open. We'd need all the light we could find. Moving quickly and quietly, we descended the three flights of steps before us. The right side of the steps looked newer than the left, like they had been widened recently.

"Should we wave?" Rico asked when we got to the bottom, nodding at a surveillance camera mounted by the stairs.

"Eh, fuck 'em." I flipped Toussaint a set of double birds, hoping he was watching through some closed-circuit TV.

"It's freaking November. Why is it so warm in here?' I asked, unbuttoning my duster. My words echoed through the large open space ahead of us.

Rico wandered into the cellar and shined his light at the limestone walls. "This has to be an old brewery tunnel. This far below ground, they're naturally climate controlled."

We were deep underground. The air was dank and smelled of mold. We lost the sunlight quickly as we ventured deeper into the tunnel. My foot brushed against something soft that skittered across the floor. In a sketchy environment like this, it was dangerous to wander around in the dark. No matter who might see us, or what might be drawn to us, we needed to use our flashlights.

I shined my light to the left and frowned. Other than cobwebs, a few critter corpses, some broken pallets, shredded shrink wrap, and randomly scattered plastic bottles, the place appeared to be empty.

I put my hands on my hips and sighed. "Just a bunch of crap. You find anything?"

Something bounced across the floor when Rico moved beside me. I snapped my head toward the sound and reached for Hawk.

"Sorry, just me" he said. "I kicked a plastic bottle."

He bent over the bottle and centered its label in his flash-light beam.

"Crescent City Spring Water, bottled by..." Rico turned to me with eyes the size of golf balls. "Andezo, Inc."

I almost peed my pants.

"Holy shit, dude! Look at the logo—those 3 wavy lines? That's the sigil of Simbi Andezo!"

"The what of who?"

I filled him in on my conversation with Mama. "A sigil is a symbol that holds power. I called Mama Femi last night and asked if she'd heard of the word Andezo. She reminded me that Simbi Andezo is a Vodoun Loa known as Simbi in Two Waters. The waters of life and death."

"Well, doesn't that fit like a fucking glove?" Rico booted the bottle across the floor.

It was easy to forget that Rico had his own score to settle with Toussaint. The bastard had kidnapped both Rico and Jade in New Orleans. And Rico had nearly lost his mind when Tous-saint injected Jade with the Z-Virus.

For a while, Rico had blamed me for not helping Jade with

her biter exposé to begin with, so she wouldn't have followed us to New Orleans. I hadn't been sure he'd ever forgive me, and I'd worried that we might never partner again, let alone be friends.

"Nighthawk." Rico's voice had grown oddly quiet.

I turned and followed his gaze to the end of his flashlight beam, focusing on an object roughly fifteen-feet away.

I don't remember walking to the object or bending down to examine it. I only remember my despair when I realized what it was—a broken pair of Oakley sunglasses, Radar EV Path style for runners. Like the pair I'd given Ferris for his birthday. To the right of the broken glasses were a pair of iron-cuffed chains anchored into the stone floor. They were covered in dried blood.

I wanted to puke.

A sound broke in the distance. A gritty, familiar sound that set my jaw and churned my blood. The sound of shambling feet as they scraped against stone, just as they had at Congo Square.

Rico and I locked eyes. We drew our guns and aimed our flashlights out into the darkness. The shuffling grew louder. And closer.

"Four David Twenty-Six," Rico barked into his mic. "Backup requested. Officers in need of immediate assistance. Repeat: urgent request for backup. We're surrounded by biters."

36

FAMILIARITY BREEDS CONTEMPT

A whiff of decay hit my nose. The rotters were closing in. Rico and I moved back-to-back, semi-autos drawn, holding our flashlights alongside our gun barrels, punching tiny pinholes of light in the darkness.

One by one, and two by two, a stream of rotters shambled into the light beams, moaning and groaning and gnashing their teeth. Freshies, flesh-eaters, and judging by the air quality, a shit ton of corpsicles. The whiff of decay from seconds before had grown to an all-out stench.

Rico fired his Glock, sending a hail of 9mms into the horde. The sound of gunfire bounced off the limestone walls and nearly shattered my eardrums. I let Hawk fly until his mag was empty. An anxious moment of silence followed when we'd both run out of bullets.

"How many more mags you got?" Rico yelled, as he slammed in a fresh magazine.

"Two." I jammed a new mag into place. "You?"

"Same."

We resumed firing in 180-degree arc, targeting the front line first. The next wave of deadheads slowed as they stumbled over the growing mound of corpses, giving us time to aim and increase our odds of making kill shots. That was a solid plan— assuming we had more bullets than biters. By the time we'd reloaded a second time, and the rotters were still coming, I'd begun having doubts.

It wasn't like we had a lot of options, but I'd shit kittens if we had to resort to hand-to-hand combat. Rule Number 9: Never resort to fists in a biter brawl.

I held Hawk high, squeezed his trigger and counted down the shots.

When I got to zero and slammed in my last mag, the swell of biters was just as deep as when we'd begun shooting.

I was starting to get miffed. "Where the hell's that backup?"

"Beats me."

"This sucks. If I get bit, just shoot me."

"You bet."

Rico fired again. "Hey, Nighthawk?"

"Yeah?"

"Don't get bit."

Fluids oozed from the bloated corpses and pooled around us. Footing got dicey. The stench of decomp-related methane gas was so extreme, I wondered if a stray bullet might spark and we'd all go up in a blaze of glory.

Nearing the end of my last mag, I flashed back to a similar situation I'd shared with Harry, when Toussaint had set us up at the Crosley Building. We'd gotten lucky back then. I wondered if I still had that much luck left inside me. By the time I'd fired my last bullet, the biters were still coming, and I had my answer.

Rico called over his shoulder. "I've got five shots left. Allie... I... I...if we don't ma—"

Oh no, he is not!

"Focus," I yelled, holstering Hawk and retracting my hands

into the sleeves of my leather duster. "See that stack of pallets to the right?"

"Yeah?

"Just keep firing and when you run out of bullets, join me."

Rico resumed shooting, while I hurdled the mound of bodies, and pushed through the surge of rotters, blocking with my arms. I slipped once and almost face-planted in a free-flowing river of zushi. Catching my balance, I hit the stack of pallets on a dead run, grabbed one from the top of the stack and slammed it to the floor, breaking it into pieces.

I held on to a long, jagged splinter and flipped another one to Rico. Scraps of wood that could be used as stakes weren't much protection, but other than our knives, they were all we had. My Ka-Bar blade was seven-inches long. The boards were close to two-feet in length. Bigger was better.

Knives would be our weapon of last resort.

When the echo of gunfire ended, Rico bounded over the corpses like a linebacker and barreled to my side. The dead-heads closed ranks and shifted course straight for us. We resumed our back-to-back formation and waited. There wasn't anything left to do but pray—for rescue or a quick and final death, whichever came first.

A dim light pierced the darkness. Then another. And another. Lights popped randomly throughout the tunnel and then multiplied, growing brighter. The welcome sound of a multitude of feet pounding against the limestone floor drowned out the groans of the rotters.

Shouts rang out, but I had no idea what was being shouted because the words were distorted by the continuous echo. Gunfire blazed from every direction. Rico and I took cover behind the stack of pallets while the cavalry mowed down rest of the horde.

"Are you okay?" I screamed over the din, pawing at Rico's arms and neck. "Did they get you?"

"No. I'm fine. You?"

"Not a scratch."

A group of CPD officers made a beeline for our location. The gunfire slowed, and eventually faded to a series of sporadic pops.

Moments later, the shooting ceased and another group arrived on the scene. Director Dickhead, with his task force in tow, strolled through the sea of decommissioned deadheads and threw up his hands as if the entire scene was beneath him.

Isn't that just like him? I thought. *To let CPD handle the call before he wades in, rolling his eyes at a supernatural war he doesn't understand.*

It didn't take long for the bastard to spot me. Once he did, things went south quickly.

"Nighthawk, what the hell happened here?"

He'd have crucified me if I told him we were following up on a lead from Vinny "Numbnuts" Abruzzi.

"It's my fault, Director," Rico said. "We were following up on a lead—"

"A *task force* lead, De Palma. Not CPD business. A matter of national fucking security. What gave you the right—"

"Enough!" I shoved my finger in Dickhead's face. "We're all working this case together, Director. We're a team. Rico and I didn't bring you the lead because we didn't know if it was credible, and we didn't want to divert resources if it turned out to be a dead end."

Horton's voice rose an octave. "That wasn't your call to make. You have no—"

"Perhaps," Babs said gently, "We can agree now that the lead was, in fact, credible and move on."

Go, Babs!

I stifled a grin. Even though she had been diplomatic, Babs had never before openly questioned Dickhead's lead. Judging by his reddening cheeks and narrowed eyes, he wasn't happy about it.

Horton pursed his lips, then took a deep breath and glanced at his watch. "We'll pick this up today at two o'clock at the FBI office in Kenwood. The entire task force is to be present. No exceptions."

He spun on his heel and navigated back through the corpses toward the entrance of the storm cellar.

Babs, wearing a sheepish smile, lingered until he was out of earshot. "I'm sure, I'll pay—"

"Agent McMillen!" Horton hollered to her, as he reached the exterior steps. "Join me, please. A word."

"Don't worry. He'll be back shitting on me in no time."

"Verily," Babs said, with a sigh as she left. "The shit shall raineth upon me as he speaks his piece."

Whatever that meant. After a while, with Babs, I'd just stopped asking about things like that. It was the only way to avoid a lengthy explanation that left me with more questions than answers, on subjects I didn't give two shits about.

Horton's team might have been leaving, but the small matter of a massive biohazard cleanup in the cellar remained. Not that I would be dealing with it. I gave the officer in charge of the scene Splatz's phone number and begged Rico to take me home so I could shower and change. I reminded him that we had to be in Kenwood for the task force meeting at two.

His eyes twinkled. "Where's your go bag?"

"Bite me, Boy Scout."

"Mine's in my trunk, where it belongs."

"Mine's at home, filled with dirty clothes. Surprised?"

"Nope. I'd have bet my pay check on it."

Without another word, he headed back down the highway toward my house and I thought to myself: *See? It's nice when partners know each other as well as we do.*

Little Allie caught me by surprise, asking me if I'd heard that old saying: *familiarity breeds contempt.*

Freaking head hag. Clearly, she'd been listening to Babs.

37

THE BLIND SQUIRREL AND THE ACORN

The clock was ticking. I-75 (aka Orange-Barrel Heaven) was backed up due to an accident at the Norwood Lateral interchange. When Rico finally parked at the curb in front of my house, I told him to bring his clothes in from the car and shower at my place to save time.

He winced. "Are you sure? I mean, has Birdgate been resolved?"

"There's an unhatched egg in an Amazon box, shoved under my dining room table. What's to resolve?"

"Have you and Nonnie ironed things out, yet? You were pretty intense the other night."

"We haven't killed each other, if that's what you mean."

Rico pulled his go bag out of the trunk and shoved the lid closed. The driver's side mirror fell off and slammed to the ground, spraying the street with silvery shrapnel. Wow. Both mirrors in one day. Rico rolled his eyes and mumbled something, then bent over and picked up the frame.

"I've got the rest," I said, racing around to his side of the car and gathering up the shards. Once I had them stacked in a neat little pile in the palm of my hand, I hurled them as far as I could into the Winstel's yard.

"Things still going well with the neighbors, I see," Rico said, with a nod.

Headbutt greeted us at the back door, squiggling and wiggling. He panted and slobbered and wound himself around Rico's legs, before settling into the perfect scritching position and demanding his toll for admission into the house.

"Mr. Rico!" Nonnie wrapped him in a big Italian hug and kissed both of his cheeks. "I fixes you some lunch, eh?"

Neither Headbutt nor Nonnie had yet to acknowledge my presence. Walter was the only one who made eye contact with me. He rose from the table and squeezed past us to finish his stink stick outside.

I eyeballed him as he made his exit. "A quick lunch would be great, Nonnie. Rico and I are going to take a shower. We have a meeting in Kenwood in an hour or so."

Nonnie raised her brow. Rico bit back a laugh.

"I mean, Rico and I both need to shower. Separately. For our meeting. In Kenwood. In an hour."

'You first," I said, pulling a towel from the hall closet and tossing it to Rico.

Nonnie hip checked me out of the way. "Hand dirty clothes out door, Mr. Rico. I wash with Ms. Allie's. I makes special detergents for zumba messes."

Once he handed his clothes out to Nonnie, closed the bathroom door and started the shower, Nonnie was all over me like a cheap suit.

"I saws what you two was doing the other night by the front door. You was canoodling. I knows canoodling. And that was canoodling. And today, you come here to shower together!"

"I explained that, Nonnie. That was just a slip of the tongue."

"No, no, no! No tongues! No tongues!"

Kulu and Hyrum let loose, mimicking Nonnie's hysterics perfectly. I hadn't been there five minutes and already had a headache.

"Nonnie, just go make some lunch. Please?"

I gathered up some clean clothes that matched (more or less) and then let Headbutt out the back door for his midday poop.

"What's that?" I asked, pointing to the Winstel's second-floor balcony.

Nonnie squinted. "I think is camera."

"A camera on a tripod. Oh, and look! They installed a floodlight."

The nerve.

After those nosy bastards had shot down my counter-offer, they were going to try to make a buck filming me in action anyway. Someday. Maybe. If I ever had a biter incursion at my house again. The odds of that were better than you might think.

Strangely, I had a hard time getting worked up over the whole thing. While Babs might have called that personal growth, my money was on exhaustion.

When it came to personal battles and vendettas, I was like a one-armed paperhanger, spinning plates on a stick, with a hand grenade stuck between my teeth and a Bouncing Betty tucked beneath my feet. No use looking for trouble. It always found me anyway.

Rico popped out of the bathroom and slipped down the hallway, taking his time putting on the clean shirt from his go bag. I heard Nonnie suck in a breath. Well, it could have been me. I was a little distracted.

Showered, blow-dried, and dressed in less than fifteen, I made it out of the bathroom in time to grab a pastrami on rye to go.

Rico stopped on his way to the door and bussed Nonnie's

cheek. "Sorry, gotta run. Thanks for lunch. It was great, as usual."

I stepped out of the house behind him, eyeballing Walter's ever-present stogie as he moseyed past us to go back inside. He mumbled something I couldn't hear but stubbed the nasty thing out on the ground without me having to snatch it from his mouth. A small victory, for sure. But I'd take what I could get—even if he would relight it five minutes after I left.

Rico ducked into the driver's side of the Taurus and settled into his seat, wearing the hang dog look of a kid who'd gotten busted for smoking in the boy's room.

"What's wrong?" I asked.

"I'm not sure. While you were in the shower, Nonnie accused me of canoodling. What does that even mean?"

I HAD a habit of showing up to Dickhead's task force meetings fashionably late. But this time, Rico and I were the first to arrive. The receptionist had us sign in and gave us visitor badges. I closed my eyes while we waited in the sterile conference room, listening to some torturous Muzak version of Pink Floyd's "Run Like Hell."

Rico chuckled. "You ever watch *Stranger Things*?"

I cracked an eyelid. "Huh?"

"It's like we're stuck in some spiffy, upside-down version of Cap's office, waiting to get chewed out."

"Ha! I miss those crappy red chairs." I instinctively began mining for foam from the bottom of my plastic stack-chair. A totally unsatisfying experience.

Cap joined us, and moments later, the entire task force filed in with Dickhead riding herd. *The gang's all here,* I thought, remembering the intensity of those meetings at the NOLA FBI office nearly six months earlier, when Toussaint had kidnapped both Jade and Rico. Emotions ran high—mine especially. This time Ferris was missing. And if Dickhead expected me to be any less pit bull, he'd be sadly mistaken.

Babs sat directly across from me. Kelvin Thomas and Eli Stanton took seats across from Rico. Horton waited for everyone to settle in before ascending to the podium and adjusting his mic.

The self-important douche-waffle. There were six of us at the table. What the hell did he need a mic for?

He cleared his voice, then took a breath and slowly let it out. "It's been a while since we've had a group update. If we're going to function like a team, we all need access to the same information, ideally as close to real-time as possible."

I felt his eyes on me and bristled.

"Let's start with a recap. Agent Stanton, do you have any updates as to where the corpse flower might have come from?"

"They are quite rare," he said, staring at his hands folded on the conference table, "but they are not impossible to find."

"Yes or no, Agent Stanton. It's a simple question."

"No, sir. Not really. The card was plain stock, no finger prints other than Ms. Nighthawk's. We checked with known commercial growers. None of them showed any recent sales to individuals. So we spread our search to the private sector. We found one grower who remembered a cash sale of a specimen to a person who may have resembled Agent Ferris. The seller couldn't provide much by way of description other than gener-alities: height, weight and hair color. No security cameras in the area to help us out. The trail stopped there. If I had to guess, it came from that private grower."

I frowned. "That reminds me, Director. Is the lab finished processing my stolen necklace, the one that was attached to that big stinky dick? I'd like it back."

"I have no idea. You can check at the ECR after our meeting."

"The what?"

"The Evidence Control Room. Shall we continue, please?"

"Certainly." I waved him on, which thoroughly pissed him off.

"Agent Thomas, after our last meeting, did you run the photo, presumed to be that of Agent Ferris, through facial recognition software? And if so, what were your findings?"

Carrot-topped Kelvin pushed his glasses up his nose. "I did run the software. The facial recognition landmarks were sufficiently obscured to prohibit excluding the subject in question from consideration."

Horton sighed. "English, please."

"Due to the refraction of the light, the landmarks weren't clear enough to allow us to either include or exclude Agent Ferris as the subject of the photograph."

"And there are no further avenues to pursue that would allow us to make that determination?"

"No, sir."

"Very well." Dickhead swung his eyes to Babs. "Have you been successful in obtaining a federal warrant for Andezo, Inc?"

Babs clasped her hands and nodded. "Yes, sir. Although we had a bit of a problem executing the warrant, given that the address of record proved to be an empty lot."

"Were you eventually able to serve the warrant?"

"No, sir. We're continuing to research Andezo's true location. We're also checking out some leads that suggest possible mob-related involvement—their property holdings in OTR and nearby Camp Washington."

"I see." Horton took a deep breath, then slowly eyeballed each of his agents. "So, in fact, collectively, you are zero for three." He shook his head, then turned to me with a chilling smile. "Ms. Nighthawk, perhaps we should revisit our earlier conversation about the Hoffbauer Building. Correct me if I'm wrong, but hadn't you and Officer De Palma previously investigated that property?"

How the hell had he known that?

"In case you're wondering, Captain Dorsey filled me in on that little snafu."

Cap's eyes were glued to the table.

"Yes, sir," I said. "Vinny thought—"

"I don't care why. My point is, *how* did you miss the cellar *full of biters*?"

That same stinking question had been gnawing at me, so I gave him the line I'd fed myself.

"We went through every room in that house. None of the doors led to the cellar. The exterior storm cellar door was the only means of entry or exit. We investigated Vinny's call concerning him having a rotter cornered inside the house, and then we left. We had no reason to search the outer grounds."

"Fair enough. Perhaps you'd like to explain why today you chose to run with a lead, rather than report back to me, so I could provide you with proper direction. Or, God forbid, a warrant."

"I'd rather not, sir."

I'd rather dig my intestines out with a spork.

"This isn't a democracy, Nighthawk. You don't get a vote."

"I had no idea what we'd find in that tunnel. Reporting the lead seemed...premature."

"Until it wasn't. And then, you needed to be rescued, wasting time and valuable resources."

Rico pushed back from the table. "With all due respect, sir, I stand by our decision to enter that cellar without a warrant. The building wasn't a residence or a place of business. It was abandoned and Agent Ferris is still missing. We found evidence that someone had likely been held captive there. We also found what we believe to be Agent Ferris's sunglasses. If we'd have waited for a warrant to enter, those glasses and the Andezo bottling remnants might have disappeared."

Dickhead shook his head. "How could you possibly know those glasses belonged to Ferris?"

I shot from my seat like a rocket. "Because I gave them to him for his birthday! And if you analyze the blood on those metal chains we found, I'd bet my paycheck it belongs to Ferris. But don't let me tell you what to do."

Judging by Dickhead's magenta-colored face, my mouth had just shifted into overdrive. Hell, who was I kidding? When it came to dealing with flat earth stupid, that's the only gear I had.

I started pacing behind the table. "Fuck procedure, Director. We need to ask ourselves why we found evidence of a deserted bottling facility in that cellar. Then we need to ask why it's now filled with a metric ton of decommissioned meatbags."

I continued, without waiting for an answer. "I think Toussaint's operation was based at the Hoffbauer Building, but he moved to a new location after we unknowingly stumbled into it the first time. And what better place to warehouse a bunch of biters than an underground storage facility?"

"All well and good, but we need to find Toussaint's *current* operation."

"But we're on the right trail! Let us work the case our way."

"Last I checked, Nighthawk, this is my op. I want every one of you to go back through your work, through your videos and photos, your warrants and city plots, searching for clues you might have missed." He skewered me with his eyes. "Like a basement full of fucking biters!"

Judas Priest, I'd never live that down.

"So, Director," Cap said, wearing his best poker face. "What's your plan of attack—once we find Toussaint's operation? How do we bring it down? How do we bring *him* down?"

Dickhead leaned forward and planted his hands on the conference table, shoulder-width apart. "Phase One: Shock and Awe. We breach black-op-stealth mode, with a dual-contingency of SWAT and HRT teams, using flash bangs and pepper balls. Le Clerc will never know what hit him. We'll take him and his deadheads down—using extreme prejudice on Le Clerc if needed, and then clear the site. Phase Two: Agent Stanton, you and your team will enter after the property is secured, to analyze and dismantle the laboratory, and gather samples for reverse engineering."

I freaking hate plans. They always go sideways. But, at least at first blush, this plan showed promise, proving that even a blind squirrel can stumble into acorns.

"Fine," I said. "Eli's a great choice to lead the science team but, and no offense, Eli, you're way out of your depth when it comes to carovescology."

Eli nodded. "None taken. Ms. Nighthawk is correct."

"I want Dr. Christian on the team. He's the world's foremost expert on the disease. He'll know what he's looking at, and he'll be a heck of a lot faster when it comes to reverse engineering."

Horton pursed his lips. "Stockholm to Cincinnati? That's a twelve-hour flight. When it's go- time, I'm not waiting on him to arrive."

"The European CDPC has a designated jet housed in Stockholm. I'll let Dr. Christian know to be expecting our call, and that he should be ready to roll on a minute's notice."

Horton scanned the room, locking eyes with each of us. "What are you waiting for? Go—find the missing link. The sooner we locate Le Clerc, the sooner we take him out. Agent Ferris's life may, or may not, depend on it. Either way, I want him back."

38

NONNIE AND HEADBUTT FOR
THE SAVE

Thanks to Horton's hissy fit, Rico would have to go back through that stinking security video from Phoenix Industries again. So far, I'd wrangled out of that snooze fest twice, but short of bleaching my eyeballs or throwing myself in front of a train, this time, I was doomed. The best I could do was postpone the agony.

"Hi, there," I said to the receptionist as we were about to turn in our security badges, "Can you point me to the Evidence Control Room?"

She peered over the top of her glasses. "Excuse me?"

"I need to get my necklace back, if you're finished processing it."

"You've never done this before, have you?" She pulled a form from a tray on her desk, snapped it onto a clipboard, and handed it to me. "Fill out this FD597 and have it signed by the agent in charge. Bring it back to me completed and I'll have the evidence brought out. You'll have to sign for it."

I was dealing with the FBI. Whatever had made me think this process would be simple?

"You got a pen?" I asked. "Or do I have to sign for that too?"

She scowled and handed me a Bic, then nodded toward a set of visitor's chairs.

Rico followed me over and plopped down on a seat across from me. "You know, I'd be pissed about sitting here waiting on you, if I didn't have endless videos to review for the third time."

"You surely do."

"We. We have endless hours of video to review. You're not getting out of it this time."

"Worth a shot," I mumbled, scanning the form. I knew some of the necessary information, but most of it would have to come from the case file.

Horton strolled out of the conference room, deep in discussion with Babs. I bolted across the lobby, clipboard in hand, and stopped them both midstride.

"Director Horton, is Bab—Agent McMillen in charge of this case?"

"She is, indeed." He glanced at the clipboard, then nodded at Babs. "Would you please handle this, Agent McMillen?"

"Certainly, sir."

Babs placed her laptop on the receptionist's desk, then opened the case file, filled out an electronic version of the form, and e-mailed it to the evidence control room.

"Done is done," she said, snapping her laptop closed. "I've asked them to expedite this for you. Assuming they're finished processing your necklace, it should be out front in a few minutes. If not, they'll notify Gloria." Babs smiled at the receptionist. "Otherwise, Gloria will have you sign for it, and you can be on your way. I, on the other hand, will be knee-deep in case notes and researching mob-related property purchases in OTR and the surrounding area."

I didn't tell her I had asked Nonnie to check out the mob angle as well. Two heads were always better than one and we needed all the help we could get. Babs left us to return to cubicle land, and within fifteen minutes, an agent approached with my property. Gloria thrust a release at me and made sure I signed it before the agent deposited the obsidian necklace in my hand.

Mama's necklace. The necklace of a nighthawk that she had given me years ago, on the day I'd left New Orleans to make my way in the world. Toussaint had taken it from me when we tangled at Congo Square.

I rolled the finely-carved gem between my fingers, feeling its warmth—a warmth that came from Mama, not from the stone itself. I slipped the necklace over my neck and shivered as that warmth spread through my chest. Mama may have left me to my own devices to solve this case, but this necklace and the energy it contained was proof that part of her would always be with me.

AFTER A QUICK TRIP TO Skyline for an early bird dinner, Rico and I headed back to the 51st for a few soul-sucking hours of video analysis. I called Nonnie to let her know I'd be later than usual. She told me the computer system had gone down briefly, but she'd gotten it back up and running. She said she'd feed the pack for me, and that she wanted to stick around to finish some invoicing.

Rico and I settled in to scour the security footage: corridor videos, cubicle videos, cafeteria videos, supply videos. All benign looking, all slices of the everyday Americana workplace. Neither of us had expected this third viewing would yield anything of importance. But neither had we stopped to consider that the attack at the Hoffbauer Building had given us a better understanding of *exactly* what we were looking for.

A couple of hours in, we both caught an innocuous clue during a replay of a sweeping, panoramic view of cubicle land. Row upon row of fuzzy, grey cubicles filled with chairs, sweaters and folders, office supplies, personal photos and water bottles—bottles of Crescent City Spring Water, to be exact. Some were empty, some half-finished, and some unopened. We took screen prints of the bottles in situ, marked the time on the video, and continued searching.

Pallets of the same brand of water showed up in footage taken of the supply closet, as well. Rico zoomed in on the packing list affixed to the bottles just below the shrink wrap binding. Bingo. Crescent City Spring Water, bottled by none other than Andezo, Inc.

I leaned in to the monitor and squinted at the fine print below the corporate name. "What's that address?"

Rico enlarged the image. "230 Hopple Street."

We issued a collective sigh. That was the address of record, the one Babs had used on the federal warrant. The same address that turned out to be an empty lot.

The remainder of the footage didn't reveal anything useful. By the time eight o'clock rolled around, our eyes were toast. It was Friday night, so we decided to pack it in. A light snow had blanketed the ground during our evening stint at the 51st. While Rico wound the Taurus through the shimmering streets on bald tires, I began to ponder the production and distribution of Crescent City Water.

"Help me think this through," I said. "Your internet search didn't find this brand of water retailing anywhere, right?"

"Affirmative."

"Obviously, Toussaint's still gearing up for production. So why were there cases of Crescent City Water at Phoenix Industries?"

Rico shifted in his seat. "Maybe they're market samples that hadn't been tampered with. Otherwise, lots of their employees would have contracted the virus and turned, right?"

"Right."

"Maybe Kleinfeld and the dead marathon runners all ingested some of the tainted water."

That made sense. The pieces of the puzzle were starting to come together, but there were some outlying fragments that didn't seem to fit.

I stared out the passenger window for a few moments, thinking. "Bottled water is clearly the intended means of transmission. So why was Messmer poisoned with a popsicle? And why did we only find one popsicle at Phoenix, as opposed to boxes of market samples...like the water?"

Rico frowned. "Maybe Messmer was an experiment, to see if the virus would keep its properties when frozen. You have to admit, his heart condition made him the perfect guinea pig."

"Maybe. Or maybe they already knew the virus could handle the cold and dosed him with the popsicle to throw suspicion away from the pallets of tainted bottles."

"Well...both theories do hold water."

I rolled my eyes. "How long have you been waiting to use that joke?"

"Since the day Jade spouted her contaminated water theory. She sure hit the nail on the head this time. Scary, isn't it?"

I left his comment hanging. Jade figuring anything out was fair game for a laugh in my book, but there was too much at stake to make light of it now.

The snow was coming down hard and fast. Rico slid up my driveway on the Taurus's worn tires and delivered me to the back door. "I need to work on the other twenty case files on my desk tomorrow. If anything comes up, I'll give you a call."

"I need to check in on Vinny anyway," I said, as I climbed out of the death mobile. "Careful driving home." I pointed at the skid marks that lined my driveway.

Rico waited to make sure I got the door open, then left me with a beep and a wave.

Nonnie, hunched over stacks of bills and invoices at the

kitchen table, barely looked up when I walked in the house. "Is left overs chicken parmesan in fridge. Eats. You skinny."

Not the slightest bit hungry, I sat on the floor and wrapped Headbutt in a hug. Kulu fluttered down from her perch, landed on my shoulder, and nuzzled my cheek. Baby Hyrum squealed nonstop until I ruffled the feathers around his ears. When the menagerie calmed down, I moseyed into the dining room and checked on the egg in the Amazon box. Still there, unhatched.

Nonnie called from the kitchen, "I finds some informations for you today. Two houses next to each other on Hopple Street solds to same buyer, Alfonso Reina. Owns transportations company. Reina old Sicilian name."

"Meaning mob connected?"

Nonnie nodded, then poked her index finger below her eye, and mumbled, "*Stai attento!*"

I shrugged. "You told me once there are two hundred and fifty Italian hand gestures. Give me a hint."

She hushed me with a finger to her lips. "*Stai attento!* Watch out. Not so loud." She repeated the gesture, then crossed herself for good measure.

"You mean in case the mob bugged my kitchen?"

"*Basta!* Enough!"

I was having too much fun and Nonnie was about to implode. Time to get back to the subject. "Did you find anything else?"

"My contacts says large shipments coming into town."

"Shipments of what?"

"No one knows. Trucks usings big tarps. Very suspicious," she mumbled, thumbing through her invoices.

Headbutt craned his neck toward the door and pricked his ears.

I focused on the background noise but didn't hear anything unusual.

Probably the wind, I told myself. I got up from the floor and wandered to the window above the sink and looked outside. The wind was howling and the snow was coming down in huge wet flakes.

First snowfall of the year, I thought. *Rico'd better get those tires looked a—*

Headbutt growled, soft enough that Nonnie hadn't appeared to notice it. But I had. My bully baby slung his tail low and flexed his knees. He was ready for battle.

I flicked off Hawk's trigger guard and put my ear to the door. The gate outside clanged against the fence post.

Nonnie's head popped up. "What dat?"

"The gate," I said, nonchalantly, switching on the porch light. "Must have blown open in the wind. I'll check on it."

I told myself it was probably nothing. No use upsetting Nonnie over a little wind. But no one knew Headbutt better than me. There was only one thing that sent the bulldog into overdrive.

When I turned to tell Nonnie to lock the door behind me, she was already at my back, cast-iron skillet in hand. The blue-haired fossil had fought zumbas before. God knew she swung a mean skillet, but I worried about her losing her footing in the snow. One slip in Biterville could be her last.

"Stay put," I told her. "I'll yell if I need you."

Headbutt had attached himself to my hip and was awaiting my command. I pulled Hawk and nudged off his safety.

"C'mon, boy," I whispered, easing us out the door, into the swirling winter squall.

The floodlight on the Winstel's balcony blazed like the noonday sun.

Well, shit, I thought. *They might get their million-dollar footage, after all.*

I waited motionless on the porch, letting my eyes adjust and listening for the click of the deadbolt as Nonnie slid it into place. Despite his excitement, Headbutt followed my lead without question.

Multiple sets of footprints were visible in the snow, marching up my driveway from the street, and merging into single file order at the gate. The prints were fresh, showing signs of both living and undead trespassers—obvious by their sliding, shuffling indents in the snow.

The motion light on the front of Nonnie's garage burst on and illuminated my side yard. I caught a quick glimpse of a man, dressed in black, scaling the rear fence and running off in the storm.

A chorus of moans, groans and growls reached my ear. Headbutt twitched and scratched the ground with his hind legs, waiting for my signal. A trio of biters rounded the corner, thirty-feet away and made straight for us.

"Headbutt, *stay*." I focused on the horde and raised Hawk. "Wait...just a little closer," I whispered. A little—"

I took aim and fired, slamming the closest deadhead to the ground. The second biter closed in quickly. A freshie, for sure. I squeezed the trigger and blew it to smithereens, a little too close for comfort. Zushi blowback drenched my face.

The third rotter, a stinkin' corpsicle, teetered toward me Frankenstein-style, until one of its legs sloughed off at the hip about eight-feet away. It toppled over sideways, chittered its teeth, and crawled at me.

I stepped back to avoid another zushi bath and pumped a 9mm in its brain.

Three up, three down, and I still had all my fingers and toes. Not bad. *I'd only shot three times*, I thought. *Not too much commotion.*

Normally, a nighttime skirmish like this could be cleaned up before dawn, but beneath the halogen glow of my neighbor's flood light aliens could see this mess from Mars. My side yard looked like a giant bloody snow cone, with a chunky topping of biter bits.

Rotting corpses and the severed leg aside, at least no one got hurt. It could have been wor...

Headbutt growled.

Ah, shit. Really?

Deadhead-shaped shadows on the back lawn grew taller and closer as a pack of rotters converged at the back corner of my house.

How many are there? I wondered, hoping my ammo would hold. *Seven left in the mag, one in the pipe. Make 'em count.*

The air exploded in a symphony of chitters, hisses and groans. I opened fire and grabbed the screen door to take cover inside, but saw another horde approaching from the driveway. The bastards had flanked me! Sirens wailed in the distance. I hoped they were for me, but I doubted they would make it in time.

Headbutt snarled, flexed his muscles, and lunged.

"Headbutt, *no!*"

The best zombie-hunting dog on earth tore across the snow-covered ground and launched himself at the knees of a biter, knocking it on its ass.

He was going to get himself killed, but I would never leave him behind.

I let go of the screen door, brought Hawk to bear, and put a 9mm slug between the eyes of the rotter Headbutt had downed. Nonnie flew out of the house, swinging the skillet like a Louisville slugger and took out two more deadheads with a single 360-degree arc.

I put my back to the house, opened fire and prayed. Headbutt raced in and out between the biters' legs, causing them to stumble and fall into a writhing jumble of arms and legs.

Berries and cherries lit up the front of the house. Footsteps thundered up the driveway. The cavalry had arrived. Muzzle flashes peppered my yard like fireflies in summer. All I had to do was stay out of the way. The battle didn't last long. Within moments, the firing ceased.

"Watch out!" Nonnie screamed.

I whirled around to find a straggler that had managed to elude the bullet barrage. It lunged at my neck and snapped its snaggle-toothed grill at my jugular. Headbutt raced to my side and clipped the bastard, bringing it to its knees.

I felt a whoosh of air as Nonnie swung her skillet and knocked off its head. It flew like a meat missile over the fence, bounced a few times, then bowled over her garden gnome.

Booyah, baby.

"That was a little too close, Nonnie," I said, touching my face to make sure it was still there. "You almost decapitated me."

She snarled and wiped the brain-encrusted skillet across her dress a few times. "I hate *fottuti zumbas.*"

"Yo, Nighthawk!"

I glanced over my shoulder and was surprised to find Jimmy from Splatz standing in my driveway. "What the...? What're you doing here?"

"I was listening to the police scanner. Got here in time to get some of the attack on tape." He nodded to some yutz with a camera, rolling footage of my yard from the Winstel's side yard.

"How'd you get past the police?"

"I'm crime-scene clean up, for God's sake. I know better than to trample evidence. I'm what you'd call their... ah...whatchamacallit, their colleague...professional courtesy and such."

"You catch any footage of somebody hopping my back fence?"

"Naw. Must have happened before I got here. But I got some awesome deadhead film."

I sucked in a breath, and exhaled for a ten-count. "For the commercial? You filmed this shit...for your commercial?"

"Yeah." He motioned to the yutz to zoom in on me and handed me an index card. "Just look at the camera and read this."

"Seriously? After the—"

"You're always: *I'm busy. Maybe next week. My grandmother died.*"

"Sorry, guy. Grandmas die."

"Not three times!"

Freaking turd. I shot him the Italian umbrella arm, scanned the index card, and deadpanned into the camera:

"I'm Allie Nighthawk, the best of the badass zombie hunters. And when it comes to zapping zushi, I only use the best: Splatz Biohazard Remediation Services. Tell 'em Nighthawk sent you."

"And cut." The cameraman gave Jimmy a thumbs up.

"See? Easy-peasy, Nighthawk. We're all square now."

"Bite me, Jimmy."

He blew me a kiss and waved, then started toward his van.

"You said we're even now," I screamed after him. "That means this job too. You'd better get this mess cleaned up before sunrise, or I'm leaving a new Yelp review!"

"You never left the old one."

"Yeah? Well, you...you..."

Ah, what the hell.

I watched him disappear into his van and noticed a CPD officer trotting toward me up the driveway. Once he reached the glow of Nonnie's spotlight, I knew exactly who he was.

"Donald, buddy! Thanks for saving my ass!" I glanced at the gaggle of cops huddled at the bottom of my driveway. "How did you get elected to talk to me?"

Donald was the rookie cop I'd humiliated in my training session at City Hall a while back. I had hurt my wrist, falling into an open grave while chasing a pedo meatbag named Cephus McCoy and I needed light duty work. So Cap asked me to review zombie combat with the guys in the 51st.

"Nobody else wanted to." Donald's grin stretched from ear to ear. "What the hell are you doing? Wrangling another rotter for a training class?"

I'd brought Hannibal the Corpsicle to the training session for use in a demo. Long story short, things went sideways—lots of drama, lots of screams, and way, way too much zushi. Not my finest hour, but if nothing else, my boy Donald had learned how to drop a biter in hand-to-hand combat.

"Listen," I said, pulling him aside. "This is my house. Can you have the guys turn off the lightbars, take their pics, and scoot? Maybe write up your reports back at the precinct? Splatz has gotta get this cleaned up before dawn. HOA rules and all. You understand."

Donald winked, "Heard ya, sister. We'll be on our way as soon as we can."

I harbored no illusions that this wouldn't be in the papers in the morning, or that Director Horton McFuckface wouldn't catch wind of it. But I had an idea. As soon as Donald and the rest of the CPD crew got the hell out of Dodge, I'd launch a little investigation of my own. And I knew just where to start.

39

THE POWER OF LITTLE WHITE LIES

The cops asked Nonnie and me their questions, took a million pics, and vacated the house around eleven. Jimmy and his crew started hoovering up zushi the minute CPD left. The Winstels turned out their flood light about the time the last cruiser pulled away and headed down Pitty Pat Lane.

Freaking Winstels. I didn't care how late it was, they were going to have a visitor.

After I put Headbutt back inside and walked Nonnie home for the night, I trudged through the grass and pounded on the Winstel's door. They didn't answer. I pounded a few more times.

Nada. Nothing but silence.

One by one, the lights on the first floor flicked off.

Nice try.

"Yo! Winstels! *Open up.*" I put my ear to the door and laughed. Sid and Evelyn were bickering on the other side.

"You get it," Evelyn hissed.

"No, you."

"Tell her to go away."

"No. She's...scary."

"If we ignore her, she'll leave."

"No. I won't!" I yelled, smacking the door.

I leaned into their Ring doorbell for a thirty-second count, paused, then did it again. "Seriously, guys. I can do this all night."

Sid's voice drifted through the door. "What do you want?"

"I just want to talk."

The door creaked opened a few inches and Sid peered out. "About what?"

"The video."

"What video?"

"The video you shot of my back yard tonight."

Evelyn gasped in the background.

Beads of sweat dotted Sid's brow. "I don't know what you're talking about."

"Sure you do. The video I wouldn't agree to let you shoot, but you did anyway, on account of my dog pissing on your ugly-ass vine and killing it."

"Oh...that video."

"Look, you can keep it. All I want to do is watch it. Just play it for me."

Sid's eyes narrowed. "How do I know you won't steal it?"

"With what? I don't even have my phone on me."

Evelyn's eyes peeped out below Sid's head. "Maybe you'll come back later tonight and kill us for it."

"Guys, my family and I have lived next to you for thirty years. If I was going to kill you, I'd have done it a long time ago. And believe me, there were times..."

Their eyes widened.

Apparently, my comment hadn't come across as reassuringly as I'd hoped.

"It's late," I said, holding up my empty hands and stepping

back from the door. "Why don't I wait on your porch, and you go get your laptop and play the video for me. *Please*."

The "P" word had hurt coming out. I smiled anyway. "Just let me watch it. And then I'll go home, and we can all get some sleep."

"Hold on a minute." Sid slammed the door. The solid clack of a deadbolt followed.

I'd always known that the HOA, and my neighbors in particular, had never been fans of mine. But accusing me of wanting to murder them, slamming the door in my face, and locking it with a deadbolt seemed downright hurtful.

Moments later, Sid emerged with his laptop. He ran his eyes over me and scrunched his nose. "You're ah...you're covered in..."

"Zushi. I'm covered in zushi and blood and brains, and all sorts of bio-hazardous material. Maybe we should make this quick. You don't want to catch my cooties. Play the video from the beginning, please."

Sid pulled up the footage and clicked *play*. The date and time appeared in the lower left-hand corner. The footage opened at 8:45 p.m., when the man in black that I'd seen from my porch moved close enough to the Winstel's house to trigger their million-watt flood light. The intruder snapped his eyes toward the camera.

"Freeze it!" I yelled.

Sid clicked *pause*.

"Now, enlarge it."

Seconds later, a close-up shot populated, and my heart sank. It was Ferris. The same piercing blue eyes, the same rugged jaw. The same sandy blonde hair, wisping out from beneath his jet-black hoodie. I'd know his face anywhere. My heart ached.

Why? How could he... What would make him...

Stop it! Little Allie scolded. *You need to focus.*

I breathed in deep and collected myself. "Okay, Mr. Winstel. Press *play* again."

I watched the rest of the video, including Ferris's hasty exit over my back fence, and the entire attack as it unfolded. The bird's-eye balcony view captured the full extent of the carnage. One thing instantly stood out: Ferris was not infected with the virus. He was moving as fluidly and as gracefully as he always had. A wave of relief washed through me.

Ferris was no traitor. No way in hell he would do this on his own. That meant he was acting under Toussaint's influence, the influence of the most powerful necromancer, next to Mama, I had ever known. I'd have my work cut out for me.

"Mr. Winstel, would you send me that screenshot?"

"You said you only wanted to watch it. Now, you want a copy?"

"Just a copy of the screenshot."

"I don't want it leaking out before..."

"Before you sell it to the highest bidder? I want to catch the person who set up this shitshow. Don't you?"

Winstel hesitated, like he was weighing his options.

I pointed to my bloody snow cone of a yard. "Do you want more deadheads dropping by for a visit?"

"No, but they seem to anyway—"

Everyone's a critic.

"Focus, Mr. Winstel. Help me, help you—help our HOA—help America. Help the world."

"Fine," he said, wearily. "But I'd better not see that face on TV."

"I promise. I will not put it on TV."

Of course, I wouldn't. Why the hell would I? That's not the kind of thing that endears you to your neighbors. But neither did I tell Winstel about Jimmy's competing commercial video. Mostly, because one way or the other, flesh-eater footage would fly, and I didn't give a rat's ass which one of them made the most money. None of it was going to me.

My scheming neighbor closed his computer, then turned around to step back inside.

"Mr. Winstel, if it's all the same to you, could you e-mail it to me now, from your laptop?"

Because I wouldn't trust you to help your own mother across the street, you greedy huckster.

He snorted disdainfully, but opened his laptop and pulled up his e-mail. I told him my e-mail address, then watched him type it in and click *send*. Mission accomplished.

"Goodnight, Mr. Wins—"

For the second time that night, that bastard slammed his door in my face. It's not true what they say about good fences making good neighbors. I had a perfectly fine fence, but the shittiest neighbor on earth.

———

THE FEW DOZEN steps back to my house seemed like a mile. I had so many questions and so much to think about. Should I tell Dickhead or Rico about the video, or the screenshot? And if I did, what would they do? Would they arrest Ferris on sight... or worse?

I needed to get to Ferris first and counteract whatever spell Toussaint had used to control him. The prospect of that made me nauseous—because when it came to rootwork, I had no idea what I was doing. My knowledge of hoodoo was light-years behind Toussaint's.

And what about Ferris himself? What if he fought me? What if it came down to me killing him? Could I pull the trigger? Could I end his life? My nausea morphed into agony when I remembered that, once upon a time, I'd had to put my own father down. Absolutely, without question, I could take out Ferris. But what did that say about me?

Was there even a trace of humanity left inside me?

I walked back into my house feeling small and lost. Head-butt flanked me as I wandered down the hallway, stripped off my clothes, and tossed them into the special plastic bag for my work clothes. (a pleading request from Nonnie who does my laundry.)

I slipped my gris-gris bag over my head and hung it on the edge of the bathroom mirror, then turned on the shower and let the water wash my sins away. At least, that's what I hoped— and on a good night, even believed.

But not that night.

After a bit of rummaging, I found the only nightshirt that would do, a well-worn black cotton Tee, size XXL, that had once belonged to Harry. On its front was the picture of a smoking .38, along with the words *Ballistic Therapy.* The shirt was oversized and warm, just like Harry. And just what I needed.

Headbutt and I plodded out to the kitchen where I poured myself a double-shot of Jack, then reconsidered and added a bit more. *To hell with slushies,* I thought. Tonight, I would drink it straight.

Happy Friday night, I whispered, taking a sip and feeling the welcome burn as it slid down my throat. *Friday night.* The evening had been so crazy, I'd almost forgotten something. Something important. Something that would continue to grow in importance before this case was through.

I retrieved my gris-gris bag from the bathroom mirror, and placed it in a shot glass. Covering it with a generous pour of Jack, I refreshed the protective magick Mama had blessed it with on the day she had given it to me.

Thank you, Mama, I whispered. *I love you.*

And I, you, Ti Kras Zwazo. Forever and always.

Had that been Mama's voice? Or had I been so tired and so utterly lost that I simply wanted it to be?

I settled back on the couch, closed my eyes, and started a mental checklist of everything I needed to do the next day. Headbutt's ears pricked. Someone was fiddling with the lock on the back door. The door creaked open and then quietly closed. I knew without looking, Vinny had come home. He had a distinct way of struggling with the key that broadcast his entries.

He walked into the living room and plopped beside me on the couch. "It's too cold for deadheads. They're tucked in their hidey holes for the night, so I figured I'd come home and get some shuteye."

"Sure." The word came out flat. I didn't have the strength or the interest to argue.

Vinny swiveled sideways and looked me in the eye. "Nighthawk, I...I'm so sorry this job is taking me so long. You'd have caught Kleinfeld on day one. No, you never would have lost him in the first place. This is all on me."

"Vinny, it's—"

"No. Hear me out. I know you think I act like some stupid kid with my head up my ass...and okay, sometimes I do. But right hand to God, I'm bringing Kleinfeld in. No matter what it takes. I'm going to prove myself. You'll see."

Damn it, I thought. *He's so much like his dad. Obnoxious and arrogant one minute, disarmingly humble the next.*

The kid needed some confidence, someone who believed in him. Hell, he needed to believe in himself. And he wasn't the only one who needed help in that area. The irony wasn't lost on me.

"I believe you, Vinny. Get some sleep and pick up where you left off tomorrow. I got a feeling you're going to catch that crusty old bastard sooner than you think."

A little white lie never hurt, especially when it helped

someone else. I found myself wishing that someone were there to lie to me.

Vinny rose from the couch, gave my shoulder a gentle squeeze, and padded toward the hallway.

"Hey," I called. "Would you mind covering the birds for me?"

"No problem. Good night," he said softly, as he reversed course to do as I'd asked.

"Good night," I muttered, closing my eyes, and snuggling under an afghan Nonnie had crocheted for me. It smelled of lavender, oregano and Headbutt. It smelled like home.

Let's see, I thought wearily. *Tomorrow, I have to decide whether or not to tell Dickhead about the video. I have to get in touch with Dr. Christian to tell him he needs to be on stand-by. I have to...*

The last thing I remember is feeling Headbutt's warmth as he curled up alongside me and settled in for a good night's sleep. Sometimes, a snuggle from a dog can do the job of a little white lie.

40

THERE MUST BE AN EASIER WAY TO DO THIS

The phone woke me up at nine o'clock Saturday morning. Headbutt and I were still sacked out on the couch. Normally, my bully boy would have been doing the pee-pee dance by the back door no later than eight. I shook the cobwebs from my brain and checked the call display. It was Rico.

"Good morning." The words slurred off my not-quite-awake tongue.

"You guys all right? I didn't catch the call going out over dispatch last night, or I would have come back."

I stumbled to the kitchen window, uncovered the birds, and peeked through the curtains. "We're fine. Nothing that Nonnie, Headbutt and I couldn't handle, with help from CPD."

"Wow. Nonnie got into the act. Did she use her skillet?"

"Technically, my skillet, but yes. God knows, I'd never hand her a gun."

Rico laughed. "I'm at the 51st, working on my backlog. Just wanted to check in on you guys."

Part of me wanted to tell Rico about the video. But most of me didn't. At least, not yet.

I multi-tasked, making coffee while we chatted. "I'll give

you a call later, after I talk to Nonnie. If I can schmooze her into making some Pizza Margherita, you down for dinner?"

"Like you even need to ask."

It struck me as we ended the call that he and I were entering a new phase in our partnership. A phase that seemed much more natural and fluid than when Jade was an immoveable obstacle between us.

I sat at the kitchen table for a long time, sipping my coffee and thinking about the case. Obviously, the biter attacks at the Hoffbauer Building, and later again at my house, meant we were getting close to finding Toussaint. But it seemed like he was baiting me, drawing me out on purpose. He'd even sent Ferris to my house.

I was smart enough to realize Toussaint was taunting me, which fit perfectly with his MO. I'd always been able to handle his games, and for the most part, even handle him. But handling him, without the safety net of Mama's magick, raised the bar on my battle with Toussaint to a new level. Brushing up on conjuring and rootwork would be my only salvation.

I needed to scour my old textbooks for two very different kinds of alchemy: First, I needed to find a way to break Toussaint's hold on Ferris. And second, I needed to convey upon Ferris a lasting protection against the powers of the left hand—the powers of black magick. As if the situation weren't difficult enough, the conjurations I came up with would have to be applied on the run. Between Toussaint and an influx of federal agents who, for all I knew, would shoot Ferris on sight, I'd have little time to act once we located him.

Mama had shipped my old text books (a collection of her hand-written conjuring manuals) to Pitty Pat Lane shortly after I moved in. They were packed away in my basement. I trudged down the cellar steps, thinking it would take a miracle to find them. But after moving a few more recent boxes (containing some of my father's belongings that Nonnie had packed up), I recognized Mama's handwriting on a shipping label.

The wrinkled manuals were a bit frayed around the edges, but even as I glanced at them, some of the spells and incantations came back to me. I carried the box to the living room and carefully turned it upside down on the coffee table. The manuals came to rest in a neatly stacked vertical pile. The physical labor was finished. The more taxing mental labor was just beginning.

I flipped through the manuals, scanning their contents page by page. Four manuals in, I came across the Vodoun God Damballah Wedo. *An excellent choice*, I thought, if memory served me correctly.

Damballah Wedo, the serpent god, also known as *Li Grande Zombi*, is the father of all Gods, or Loas. When he manifests in rituals, he never speaks. He hisses like a snake. His coils are said to shape the heavens and earth. In Catholic Church doctrine, parts of which are assimilated into Vodou, his counterpart is St. Patrick. He is never viewed as evil, but as the holder of intuitive knowledge, wisdom, and healing.

What better God to lift Toussaint's curse and restore Ferris's health?

I skimmed through that section of Mama's manual and wrinkled my nose when I read that Damballah Wedo's favorite offering is two egg whites plopped on a mound of white flour. But in for a penny, in for an egg white. Thick gelatinous albumin might not suit my taste, but I'd learned long ago to never mock the Loa.

Protecting Ferris from future attacks should prove easier. I could make him a gris-gris bag, similar to the one Mama made for me. According to the manual, I needed a two-by-three-inch scrap of red flannel sewn into a drawstring bag.

I'd have to draft Nonnie for that. My domestic talents were nil.

The instructions stated that the bag should contain an odd number of items, no less than three, nor more than thirteen. These included a personal effect of great significance, and any of a number of items specific to the desired purpose: combinations of herbs, stones, roots, bones, coins, charms, crystals and sigils written in magical ink on parchment paper were all acceptable ingredients.

The next provision proved slightly problematic:

Preparation of the gris-gris bag should take place at an altar and the bag should be consecrated to the four elements: earth, fire, water and air. I had no altar—yet. But (*heavy sigh*) once upon a time, I had been taught how to make my own. Exact instructions were buried somewhere in these manuals.

The other tiny wrinkle associated with creating the gris-gris bag was the personal effect of great significance to Ferris. There was nothing earth-shattering at my place. That meant I'd have to make a return trip to his condo.

If not exactly simple, everything in the text books was at least doable.

Once I found Mama's notes on how to create an altar, I called Nonnie and asked her to fix Pizza Margherita for dinner, and find a two-by-three-inch scrap of red flannel and sew it into a drawstring pouch. By the time I had gotten that far, it was already noon.

I threw Headbutt and the birds some biscuits, pulled on three layers of clothes plus my duster, hopped on my Harley and headed for Ferris's condo in search of...

I had no idea what, but I was hoping I'd know when I found it.

INSTEAD OF FOCUSING on how the wind bit through my multi-layered clothing, I gave thought to which items might be suitable for use in Ferris's gris-gris bag. Awards? Family photos? His FBI graduation pin? I left my options open.

Twenty-minutes later, after traveling across town at the speed of light, I let myself into his condo with my key and scanned the place, hoping something would jump out at me. Eventually, something did. Something that, knowing Ferris, held some real estate in his heart.

I wrapped it up tightly to protect it, and headed back to my place.

Even bundled up, it was freezing outside. I spent the ride conjuring warm, happy images of me lying on a tropical beach, soaking up the rays of a blazing sun that suddenly explodes in a brilliant flash and goes supernova, swallowing the earth like a black hole.

That's just how my brain works, folks. Never a happy ending in sight.

BACK AT MY HOUSE, I was happy to find Nonnie had finished the hand-sewn red flannel drawstring bag. I was slightly less happy to find that the cloth had come from my favorite plaid shirt. Soft as brushed cotton and two sizes too big, it was my go-to on cold winter nights while I vegged out on the couch, watching *Dancing With The Stars* and inhaling Doritos.

"*Oy gevalt!*" Nonnie crossed herself, then threw her hands in the air. "Is more holes than shirt and has no buttons. Look!" she cried, holding up the remnants of my shirt. "Has big oily cheese stains on front and stinks like hooches."

"Yes! And you cut it up anyway, damn it. Why?"

Knowing that Nonnie would never understand the lure of my favorite shirt, I pulled out a particular textbook of Mama's and studied it closely. Wow. Creating an altar was harder than I remembered.

"Nonnie, do we have a white sheet, parchment paper, a couple of religious relics, three white tapered candles, some holy water, fresh cut flowers, incense and an incense burner?"

She answered with a long, silent stink-eye.

"I need it to save Ferris."

That was the short answer. The longer explanation that included veneration of a pagan god would've sent Nonnie into apoplexy.

"We gots everythings but incense. Will stinky Glade candle work? Is Bubbly Berry Splash."

I was tempted to give it a go, but with Ferris's life hanging in the balance, it was better to stick to the script.

I threw my duster back on, headed to the door, and stopped. "Can I borrow your car? It's too cold for my Harley."

"Vinny using it."

Damn it.

"Fine," I said, marching to the closet and adding a scarf, hat and gloves to my ensemble. "Gather all that crap and meet me back here in an hour."

"Where you goings?"

"To buy High John the Conqueror root, powdered jelly fish, dried toadstool, graveyard dirt, snake shed, camphor and dragon's blood incense."

Seriously. What else would you add to a Vodoun altar and a gris-gris bag?

THERE WAS ONLY one place in Cincinnati to get what I needed, a mystic shop on Cooper Road named Earth and Fire. I stopped in there every once in a while to refresh the ingredients in my own gris-gris bag. As I braved the frigid ride, I made a mental laundry list of the other 'special' items I would need to reverse Toussaint's curse, once I located Ferris.

The store manager, Thad, was a fan. He had me in and out of the store in fifteen minutes flat, loaded for bear, if a few hundred dollars poorer. Credit cards are both my friend and my enemy.

During the trip home, I thought of all the work ahead of me. These ingredients, as well as the items Nonnie was collecting, would need to be blessed before I got to work creating both my means to banish Toussaint and to protect Ferris.

I arrived back at the house forty-five-minutes after I'd left. Nonnie had yet to return. I cleaned off the coffee table, then grabbed my bag of flour, the salt shaker, two plates, a pair of scissors, an egg, a mug and a monkey bowl from the cabinet above my refrigerator.

Nonnie walked through the door, carrying a plastic bag filled with the objects I'd requested in one hand and her Christmas cactus in the other. Its brilliant red blooms were magnificent. She wouldn't like what I was going to do to them.

I nodded toward the living room. "Perfect. Now, put that stuff down by the coffee table."

She plunked her bags down at the designated spot, then took a seat at the end of the couch. "What you do with all this stuffs?"

I pulled the white sheet from the bag and draped it over the table. "I'm making an altar to pray and make offerings to the serpent god."

Nonnie gasped, then crossed herself, and spewed a guttural barrage of consonants in my direction. Apparently unsure I had understood her meaning, she shot me the double-barrel Italian horned hand and scurried back into the kitchen.

Ha! I knew that would get her out of my hair. If she didn't appreciate my pagan altar, the rest of the process would send her into orbit. Before adding objects to the altar, they had to be consecrated. The candles had to be blessed and dressed, which entailed a slightly more involved ritual.

I rubbed my hands with juju oil, a combination of myrrh, mimosa, jasmine, patchouli, and galangal.

"As above," I whispered, coating the candles at their centers and working toward the top. Then, dressing the candles downward, I murmured, "So below," while reciting Psalm 23:

"The Lord is my Shepherd; I shall not want. He maketh me to lie down in green pastures: He leadeth me beside still waters. He restoreth my soul: He leadeth me in the paths of righteousness for His name's sake."

So far, so good. Next, I washed the bowl, mug and plates with salt water to purify them.

Now, I was ready to build an altar.

I consulted Mama's textbook to verify the placement of the various objects, and set the altar up accordingly: the three white candles formed a triangle, two placed at the rear of the table on each end, and one close to the front. Between the two rear candles, was a crucifix and a photo of Our Lady of Sorrows. Centered between, and slightly in front of them, went the incense burner. To the right of the burner, I placed my monkey bowl and poured in the holy water.

I glanced around to make sure Nonnie was still in the kitchen. Then I snipped the blooms off her Christmas cactus, crammed them into the coffee mug, and placed it to the left of the incense burner. Last, but not least, I shook a thick blob of salt onto a dessert plate and centered it at the front edge of the altar.

Voilà! Creating the altar had been the easy part, now came the hard part—the magick.

41

DOING THAT VOODOO

I hate when I'm about to summon supernatural powers and mere mortals interrupt.

Nonnie stuck her head out of the kitchen, covered the phone with her hand and mouthed, "Director Horton."

Crap.

I hadn't notified him about the skirmish at my house. Seeing the video of Ferris participating in the attack had thrown me off my game. At the time, I'd made a split-second decision to keep the video to myself. And nothing had changed. I hadn't told anyone about the footage, except Nonnie, and only because she'd known about the Winstel's camera.

Had that been a lapse in judgement? Maybe. Probably.

But once the Winstel's footage comes to light, my ass will end up in a wringer. Horton won't care why Ferris went rogue —only that he *had* gone rogue. Ferris would be open game. He'd need protection, and the best way I knew to protect him was to keep that video under wraps as long as possible.

"Tell him I'm not here," I said, casually sliding to my left to hide the deflowered cactus.

Nonnie held up a finger, motioning me to wait. Then she

nodded a few times and finally frowned. "He say he hears you, and comes take the phone before he fires you."

I inhaled deeply and took the phone from Nonnie. "Director. What a surprise."

"Did you really think you could keep me from finding out about the attack?"

"Why would I hide that?"

"I hoped you could tell me."

"Just an oversight, sir. CPD helped get the situation under control. Their reports should be on file, or will be shortly. I'll have copies sent to you."

"I don't suppose you gained any intel from the attack? No prints? No forensics?"

Don't say it—

"No video?"

"No fingerprints, sir. Deadheads and all, their skin bloats—even sloughs off sometimes. Biter foot prints are useless too. You know, with their irregular gaits."

"What about video?"

Oh, hang up already, damn it.

"Jimmy Readon, the owner of Splatz, heard the call on the scanner. He arrived during the attack and took a short video for use in one of his commercials. Nothing that will help us."

"You're not paid to make those decisions, Nighthawk. I want a copy of that film."

"No problem, sir. Anything else?"

"You in a hurry?"

Actually, I was about to summon an ancient god.

"Not, really."

"I want that video on my desk Monday morning, along with the police reports."

"You bet, sir. Bye now."

Wow. The little white lies were mounting.

I pitched the phone back to Nonnie, scared that it might

explode in my hand. "Would you call Rico for me? Ask him to come eat pizza with us. Whatever time it's ready is fine."

She pursed her lips and studied me through slit-shaped eyes. I'd seen that look before. It was her *'I know you're up to something. I just haven't figured out what'* look.

I busied myself smoothing the sheet on the coffee table and pretended not to notice. Eventually, she gave up and wandered back into the kitchen.

It was time to create a talisman.

TALISMANS ARE SMALL, inconspicuous objects that can be made of almost anything: stones, jewelry or ornaments. The talisman I was making for Ferris would be drawn on a scrap of parchment paper in dragon's blood. It would include a sigil that held meaning for Toussaint. What better sigil could I choose than that of Simbi Andezo—the wavy three-lined logo of Toussaint's Crescent City Spring Water.

I anointed the four corners of the parchment paper with Juju oil in order to 'cross' Toussaint, and then folded the corners forward to draw his negativity away from Ferris.

Before the talisman could be placed in the gris-gris bag, it needed to be blessed by Damballah Wedo.

I lit the incense on the altar as an offering, as well as the triangle of candles, and centered the talisman between them. Sprinkling the talisman with salt, I whispered, "I consecrate you with the element of earth, that you will provide an aura of protection to the person who holds you. Special protection is requested against the powers of Toussaint Le Clerc, a servant of the left hand, who binds the person who holds you."

I repeated that incantation three more times, passing the talisman through the remaining elements: incense smoke for air, over a candle flame for fire, and sprinkling it with holy water for...water.

When I finished, I laid the talisman back on the altar, placed my hands over it, and visualized a white light beaming down from above, infusing it with power.

A surge of current flowed through my hands and into the talisman. "I charge this talisman to serve Sean Patrick Ferris, for I, Aliyah Marie Nighthawk, am servant of the Divine Damballah Wedo. So be it!"

I extinguished the candles by pinching out their flames. The talisman was now considered blessed and ready to become part of Ferris's special gris-gris bag.

Preparation of the gris-gris required that the altar be reset, with the four elements placed in a cross-shaped pattern representing the crossroad, the division between the spiritual and earthly planes. I placed a bowl of graveyard dirt at the southern point of the cross. To the east, I placed a single purple candle for protection; to the north, the incense, and to the west, a bowl of water.

I laid the red flannel bag in the center of the cross, open and ready to accept my chosen components.

I cracked off a small piece of High John the Conqueror root, blessed it with holy water, and dropped it into the bag. Next followed bits of snake shed, powdered jelly fish, camphor and the talisman I'd made, each blessed with holy water before entering the bag. Only one addition remained. I shoved my hand into my pocket and pulled out the object I had retrieved from Ferris's condo—the object I believed he would treasure above all else: the engagement ring he had purchased for me.

I anointed the ring and slipped it into the red flannel bag, then brought the bag to my lips, and breathed life into it. After a sprinkle of holy water, both the bag and its contents were consecrated.

In one final act of supplication, I filled a plate with flour, cracked an egg on top, and offered it to *Li Grande Zombi*, Damballah Wedo.

The ritual was now complete, and a supreme offering had been made in appreciation for the favors of the serpent god.

All my efforts that day had gone into manufacturing this one tiny, but incredibly powerful, trinket. I studied it closely and felt a pride I'd never felt before.

I'd made this trinket *myself*. A trinket that, through *my* actions, held the power to save the life and soul of one of the dearest people I had ever known.

The magick was ready. I was ready. The only thing missing was Ferris.

42

HARRY PLAYS CHARADES

Nonnie stuck her head out of the kitchen and announced, "Mr. Rico be here at five o'clock for pizzas."

She froze, mouth agape, staring at my altar. Her eyes appeared to be fixated on the mug filled with cactus blooms. When she recovered the power of speech, she gave me the evil eye and asked, "What you do to my cactus?"

"I needed the blooms for the, ah..." I swept my hand to the altar. "I'll buy you another one."

She mumbled something, then bit her hand at me, and popped her head back into the kitchen. That was one of the Italian hand gestures I understood. It meant that when she caught me, she would kill me. Not literally. At least, I didn't think so.

Rico would be on his way soon. Having played with dirt and oils all afternoon, I ducked into the shower and changed clothes. Almost ready for company. But there was still one more chore I needed to take care of—calling Dr. Christian.

Much to my surprise, he answered the phone himself. "Allie, my friend! So good to hear from you. How may I be of assistance?"

"Hi, Doc. Where's Ilse? She usually puts me through to you."

"I'm in New York for a conference this weekend, so I had the line forwarded to my cell."

"Sorry to bother you, but I need a favor. We think we're closing in on Toussaint. He's here in Cincinnati. When we make our move, we'd like you to head the sweep on his laboratory. No one knows the Z-virus better than you."

"Of course, anything I can do to help. Will you need my team?"

"No, the FBI's epidemiology team is on call. They'll be at your disposal. The real issue here will be timing. Once we get the green light, you'll need to be here, pronto."

"As it happens, I'll be lecturing at Columbia this week. And I have the jet on call. I can be there within a few hours. If the raid occurs after I've returned home, we'll find a way to make it work."

A few hours was faster than I'd hoped and it would have to be good enough.

We chatted for several minutes. After I ended the call, I turned to find Rico eyeballing the bird egg in the dining room. "When's this thing going to hatch?"

"Hell if I know."

Nonnie popped her head in from the kitchen and glowered at me, placing her index finger under her eye.

"Ha! I know that one. It means you're watching me."

She ignored me and smiled sweetly at Rico. "Pizzas ready *un momento*."

"The silent treatment," Rico said. "What'd you do now?"

"I cut the blooms off her Christmas cactus."

Rico nodded toward my makeshift altar. "So I see."

Once upon a time, he'd have called the scene on my coffee table some *crazy voodoo shit*. But over time, he's seen and experienced enough hoodoo to know better than to mock what he doesn't understand.

The aroma of garlic-infused basil lured us into the kitchen. Rico and I grew quiet as we stuffed our faces, but Nonnie chatted up a storm. She loved having people to cook for—especially Mr. Rico.

"Ah!" Nonnie waved her hands excitedly. "Did Miss Allie shows you the picture of Mr. Ferris from zumba attack other night?"

Rico froze mid-bite and locked eyes with me. "No. No, she did not."

Freakin' blue-haired blabbermouth.

I excused myself from the table and moved to the couch, where I pulled up the shot of Ferris on my laptop.

Rico looked over my shoulder and shook his head. "That's... hard to believe."

"He's under Toussaint's control. That's the only way he could be involved."

"Did you show this to Horton?"

"No! If he thinks Ferris jumped ship, he'll go in shooting and ask questions later."

Rico sat on the couch and heaved a sigh. "Well, that's the fucking cherry on a long, shitty day. I'm ready for a drink."

He got no argument from me.

Rico thanked Nonnie for dinner, then kissed her on the cheek, while I threw on my coat and flew out the door without saying goodbye.

Call me petty, but part of me thought Nonnie intentionally spilled the beans about the screenshot, because she was pissed about the pruning I'd given her cactus. I know, because if I'd been in her shoes, I would have done the same thing. The more time Nonnie and I spent together, the more alike we became. That was a scary thought.

A little time apart sounded like a great idea.

It was Saturday night and the Blue Note was hopping, but most of the action was at the tables and dart boards. Rico and I snagged stools at the bar and resumed our discussion about the case.

"So," Rico said, a little awkwardly. "I couldn't help but over-hear some of your conversation with Dr. Christian. Do you really think we're close to Toussaint?"

"Yeah. The closer we get, the nastier he plays."

Harry suddenly materialized. Someone had taken his favorite stool, so he hovered over Rico's shoulder like a party balloon. Harry must have wanted in on the conversation because he rolled his finger over and over as if to say 'keep talking, don't let me interrupt.'

"Andezo has to be the key," I said, flagging down Dallas and motioning him for a round. "Simbi Andezo, the Lord of Two Waters, Crescent City Spring Water, it's all part of Toussaint's game plan."

Harry gave me a thumbs up. Obviously, he thought I was on the right track.

"The bastard toys with us, dropping random clues," Rico said. "Then he gets his jollies watching us jump through hoops to figure them out. That's his MO."

Harry nodded enthusiastically and put his finger on the tip his nose. We were getting warmer.

Dallas set down our drinks and glanced at Rico. "Johnny Walker, neat, right?

"Good memory."

Customers bellied up to the bar and Dallas quickly moved on.

I resumed my conversation with Rico. "Toussaint's all about gamesmanship. Like during Leo's case, when he used an anagram of his name to create his fake company, Stanous Electric, to throw us off track."

Rico sipped his scotch. "You think Andezo is an anagram?"

"No. But he gave us the wrong address for Andezo, right? So maybe the clue is connected to that address."

Harry waved to get my attention, then craned his neck forward as far as he could, and peered over the top of the bar. Three times. He was obviously trying to tell me something, but I had no idea what.

I shot Harry a discreet nod. "We'll have to take the investigation back to ground zero with Andezo and start over. We're missing something."

Harry held up his arms to signal a touchdown.

You never know, I figured. Harry had never steered me wrong while he was alive. Maybe dead, he had access to information I didn't.

Rico swirled his scotch and lapsed into silence.

"You okay?" I asked.

"Yeah. Sure. It's just…"

"Just?"

"I haven't seen Jade lately."

"You say that like it's a bad thing."

He chuckled softly. "No. She was upset about the breakup. I hope she's okay."

Come to think of it, I hadn't seen her in a while myself. It was almost like when Rico broke up with her, she stopped hounding me. Talk about a win-win.

I glanced up at the TV and bit back a smile. "Somehow, I think she's moved on."

Rico looked up in time to catch the end of Jade's interview with a handsome, young sheriff's deputy who had rescued a toddler from a pond. Jade was on him like a second layer of skin, batting her demi-lashes and tossing her product-infused hair—flirting with the deputy, the way she used to flirt with

Rico. The poor schmuck's face was frozen in a goofy, love-struck smile.

"God," Rico moaned. "Tell me I didn't look like that."

"Pretty Boy Swag" blared from my phone. I snatched it from my back pocket, glad that I didn't have to tell Rico the truth. "Yo, Vinny. What's the good news."

"I've got him, Nighthawk!"

"Kleinfeld?"

"Got him cornered in the old church on Freeman Ave—where I found him last time."

"Is that ginger-bitch on your six?"

"Not any more. I spotted her tailing me a couple of hours ago, so I pulled into McDonalds and ran inside. Then I doubled back out the side entrance, snuck up on her car, and slashed her tires in the parking lot. That should fix her."

Maybe, I thought. But that jolly green ho-bag had been stuck to Vinny like gum on his shoe. She was relentless.

"Good thinking, kid. Whatever you do, keep Kleinfeld cornered. Just don't kill him. I'm on my way."

Harry smiled and raised his boilermaker in salute.

Dallas slid our tab in front of Rico. "I'm giving this to you. Otherwise, I'll never get paid."

Rico threw on his coat, tossed a twenty on the bar, and told Dallas to keep the change.

"We've got him this time," I squealed, tossing back the last of my Jack Daniel's. "I can feel it. Just imagine—180,000 green-backs. All mine. First thing I'm gonna do is roll around in it, naked."

Rico grew quiet as we walked out the door toward what was left of the Taurus. I thought maybe he was picturing me naked, rolling around on all that money. But seconds later, he shot that fantasy to shit.

"What's my take?"

"Huh?"

"My take—what's in it for me?"

"Are you freaking kid... I've sweat blood on this case. Well, Vinny has and—"

"But I'm your wheelman," he said, with a twinkle in his eye. "That should be worth something."

"Vinny's ten minutes away, tops. What do you want? Gas money?"

"It was a joke, Nighthawk. Just get in the car."

43

WHO THE HELL IS EDGAR?

R ico parked on Freeman in front of the crumbling, moss-covered church. We climbed out of the Taurus, into the cold November night, grabbed some flashlights from the trunk, and took a beat to acclimate ourselves to the surroundings.

The air was still as death. Under the moonlight, the massive gothic-styled building, with its weathered brick and stone exterior, looked empty and desolate; an ignored, forgotten husk. The perfect biter hole.

Where's Vinny? I wondered.

Kleinfeld had been dead a little over a week. He'd graduated from a freshie into a flesh-eater—with seventy-five percent of his reflexes and an appetite restricted to flesh and brains. I wished I had reminded Vinny of that while we were on the phone. Too late now. He would either sink or swim.

The large graffiti-laced door at the top of the steps hung ajar. Rico and I stepped into the nave, with our guns at condition one: locked, cocked and ready to rock. We swept our flashlight beams over the interior, up and down and side to side.

"Nighthawk?" Vinny's voice drifted out from deep within the church.

"It's me and Rico," I yelled. "We're coming in."

A series of thumps, groans and growls followed.

"Yo, Vinny. Any bogeys here besides Kleinfeld?" Rico asked.

"Naw. Just him."

I zeroed in on the sound of Vinny's voice and noticed a blood trail leading up the center aisle. A few yards later, we ran into a severed arm, and then another, followed closely by two legs. "You okay, kid?"

"Yeah. Those are Kleinfeld's."

The blood trail led to the front of the church where we found Vinny sitting cross-legged on top a worn wooden pulpit. Kleinfeld's torso squirmed on the floor below.

"Sorry, Nighthawk. I had to shoot off his arms and legs to keep him...contained."

Kleinfeld flipped and flopped beneath the pulpit, lunging up at Vinny. If there hadn't been all that money on the line, I'd have snapped a pic of Vinny perched on top of that lectern. But the prospect of all that money had me salivating. Business first. I needed to ask the $180,000 question. And the best part was that he'd be incapable of lying to me. Lying requires deliberation and intent. Biters function on instinct.

I squatted on my haunches and got eye to eye with Kleinfeld's corpse. "You've caused me a lot of grief, Mr. K. And God only knows what the damage total's going to be from Vinny chasing your wrinkled ass through Elysian Fields Cemetery. But you tell me where your stolen money is, the money you embezzled from Elite Trust Bank, and we'll call it even."

Kleinfeld chattered his teeth at me.

"Now, that wasn't nice. Just answer the question. Where's the money?"

"Edgar's. Got. It."

"Edgar?" Vinny uncrossed his legs on the pulpit and slowly slid to the floor. "Who the hell's Edgar?"

Kleinfeld jerked his torso and rolled into Vinny's legs hard enough to bring him down. That sausage-shaped rotter was on the kid faster than flies on stink. Vinny's high-pitched squeal pealed though the air as Kleinfeld's teeth gnashed millimeters from his neck. Rico and I fired at the same time, blowing the geezer's brains, and my $180,000 wet dream, to smithereens.

We hadn't had a choice. But that didn't keep me from wanting to hurl.

"Gunshots already? Tell me I'm not too late."

The voice, slightly muffled, had come from the back of the church. But its timbre and pitch were unmistakable.

A low growl hummed in my throat. "Marlowe."

The biggest thorn in the history of thorns strutted up the center aisle on her giant, stork-like legs. "Sorry I'm late. I'd have been here earlier, but the kid put the kibosh on my car. Nicely played, by the way."

Vinny grinned. "I thought so."

Marlowe batted her eyes at Rico. "I'll bet pretty boy here will tell me what I missed."

"Nothing much," Rico said. "Kleinfeld went into attack mode and we had to put him down. All he gave us was a name."

"Really? What name?"

"Slow your roll, Red." I waggled my finger at her. "I beat you to the punch. That money's mine, fair and square."

Little Allie screamed, *"It would be if you knew who Edgar was. But you don't, moron. Maybe she does."*

I didn't think Marlowe knew her ass from a hole in the ground, but I'd give her a shot. "Why should I tell you the name?"

"There isn't one damn thing about that man I don't know. Try me! I researched him and his family. I knew what he ate and when he shit. I've been in his house, for chrissake. Hell, I even went to visit him in the old folks' home."

What did I have to lose? I couldn't collect the reward with the information I had. If she knew who Edgar was, I'd get my hands on a lot of dough. If she didn't know, the entire discussion was irrelevant.

"Fine," I said. "We'll give you the name, you tell us what you know. Since we did all the leg work, it's an eighty-twenty split."

"Fifty-fifty, or I walk out of here and that 180K's nothing but a memory."

"For a freaking name? That's ridiculous. Seventy-thirty. Take it or leave it."

"Did I stutter? Fifty-fifty."

"Pound salt, you overgrown woodpecker. And stop staring at me like that."

"Like what?"

"Like you're trying to suck my thoughts out of my brain."

"Is it working?" Rico asked.

"No!" I glared at both of them.

"Can't blame me for trying." Marlowe turned on her heel, then stopped and blew a kiss over her shoulder at Rico. "Bye, sugar. We could have had us some fun."

The visual of all that money floating away made me nauseous.

"Damn it!" I screamed. "Fine! Fifty-fifty you skanky—"

"Ah-ah-ah. Be nice."

"Fine. Fifty-fifty—plus the hundred you screwed me out of."

Marlowe rolled her eyes. "Agreed. We'll shake on it. But I don't trust you, so pretty boy can video it on his phone."

I've been gut-punched, knifed, shot and beaten. Shaking hands with that wench hurt worse than all of that put together.

"The name was Edgar," I muttered, wiping my cootie-stricken hand on my jeans.

"Edgar! Of course! Edgar is..." Marlowe paused, for dramatic effect. "The name of the taxidermied bear that stands beside the fireplace in Kleinfeld's winter home in Bessemer, Michigan."

"Liar!' I yelled. "Nobody that rich winters in Michigan!"

"What can I say? The guy used to ski, before he ended up in the old folks' home. He was pretty spry for ninety."

"Tell me about it," I said, glaring at Vinny.

Rico frowned. "How could you possibly know that, lady?"

"I wanted to check out his place, thinking maybe he'd hidden the money there. So, one night, I arranged to run into him accidentally on purpose. One thing led to another, and he invited me home with him. I got the grand tour. That's when he introduced me to Edgar."

"If you're lying," I said, sticking my finger in her face. "It will be the last lie you ever tell."

Marlowe held out her phone. "Let's call the insurance investigators at Elite Trust right now. Together. That way, we're both on record as having found the stolen money. They'll get the warrant to rip the stuffing out of Edgar and we'll get 90K each."

"Vinny, clean up your mess," I said, waving at what was left of Kleinfeld. "Call Doc Blanchard and tell him he can pick up Ira's remains to test for aconite poisoning. And update Cap so he doesn't find out about this on TV. Well, shit. That reminds me. Call Jade and give her that exclusive I promised her at the cemetery."

Vinny fidgeted. "I thought...well, you told Jade..."

"What?"

"That you handle the PR for ACME."

"This was your case, from start to finish. You earned it."

"Thanks, Nighthawk. I won't say anything stupid. I promise."

A flurry of smart cracks sprang to mind. But fruit that low's no fun to pick.

Sooner or later, Vinny would have to learn how to open his mouth without tripping over his tongue. If he could master that, I could foist Jade and rest of the paparazzi on him any time I wanted. Now was as good a time as any to get started.

Besides, Big Red and I had a phone call to make.

I DON'T REMEMBER MUCH about the call and the ride back to my house. My head was in the clouds. Hell, I'd never had two nickels to rub together, and now I was going to have...twenty nickels in a dollar, $90,000 times 20...slide the bead, bundle the tens, well, a shit ton of nickels. Sure, I didn't have the money in my hand yet, but even the hope of money, the very idea of it, filled me with shallow, materialistic joy.

I could pay off my tax debt and afford E&O coverage (if anyone would underwrite me.) And I'd still have money left over for incidentals, like settling with Templeman and covering Vinny's damages at Elysian Fields Cemetery.

Problem solved. But we still had to nail Toussaint and rescue Ferris.

Rico dropped me off and promised to pick me up at ten the next morning, so we could review everything we knew about Andezo, Inc. When I opened the passenger door, the handle came off in my hand.

"It's okay," I said, giggling. "I can buy you a new one!"

"It's a POS pool car, don't bother. I get the Mustang back next week."

Oh, yeah, I thought. *Add the Mustang to your list of incidentals. Shit, and the roof.*

My windfall was disappearing quickly, but even that couldn't ruin my mood. I started up the driveway, then reconsidered and trotted back to the car.

Rico rolled down his window. "Forget something?"

"Just...thanks. For everything. I don't want to get all sappy, but I like working with you. You and me, we make a good team."

"Surprising, isn't it?"

Our eyes connected and we had a moment. A special nothing-else-in-the-world-matters kind of moment. Rico's gaze was soft and warm. A half-smile played at the corner of his lip.

I'd seen him wearing that expression before, but I had trouble placing it. Suddenly it came to me. He was looking at me the way he used to look at Jade.

"Sweet dreams, Nighthawk," he murmured. His eyes held mine for another beat, before I forced myself to turn and walk inside.

The house was quiet as a tomb, and my critters were down for the count. So I triple-checked the locks, turned out the lights, and went to bed.

Like that was going to work.

Who could possibly fall asleep after having a day like I'd had?

44

THE ELEPHANT IN THE ROOM

Nonnie woke me up at nine, when she trundled through the back door carrying empty laundry baskets. Sunday, Funday. My laundry from hell day. I showered and dressed, then slipped my necklace and gris-gris bag on over my head, and wandered into the kitchen to find Rico holding a box of hot, fresh Duck Donuts and coffee. He handed me a coffee, then gave the donuts to Nonnie with a kiss on the cheek, and thanked her for feeding him more often than his own mother.

She set them on the sink, beaming, and motioned us to help ourselves. Vinny stumbled into the kitchen, still half asleep, claiming that the smell of donuts had awakened him. We sat around the table and held our own mini-task force meeting to congratulate Vinny on his capture of Kleinfeld, the runaway rotter.

"You should've seen me, Mrs. N." Vinny leaned back in his chair and stretched his legs out in front of him. "I was fu...I was awesome. Nighthawk got the location of the stolen money out of him, so now she can collect half the reward money."

"Only halfs?"

"Yeah, that P.I. lady from Mystic County helped...sort of. So they're splitting it."

"Ah, Rowing Merlot! Imagines that, Miss Allie." Nonnie didn't even try to hide her smile. "Maybe she not your enemies after all."

My ass. I cocked an eyebrow. "Rico and I have to leave now. We have work to do."

THE RIDE to Camp Washington was quiet. Neither one of us mentioned our moment from the night before, but without a doubt, it was the elephant in the room. Freaking feelings. That's what they do. They make situations awkward. They complicate things that are already complicated enough. Rico had just broken up with Jade. And Ferris, the man who loved me enough to buy me an engagement ring, was missing.

I knew how to drop a deadhead and I could hold my own fighting just about anyone. Hell, I could even raise the dead. But feelings are like a freaking virus you don't even know is there, until it sucks the life out of you.

"Here we are," Rico said, pulling into the familiar-looking empty lot that was supposed to house Andezo, Inc. He turned off the car and shrugged. "Now what?"

I stared out the window and mentally catalogued the surroundings. A large, empty gravel lot, riddled with at least fifty years of dirt and potholes. Hopple Street bordered the front of the lot. Its back edge was bordered by a stone wall. The side edges were a tangle of overgrown weeds and trees. A rusted, overturned dumpster dotted the northeast corner of the lot. And that was it.

"What are we missing?" I asked. "This location, with its proximity to the subway and brewing tunnels, makes absolute sense. Toussaint could set up his lab underground—even connect it to other abandoned tunnels for storage and transportation purposes. His operation would be completely hidden. Think about it. His lab techs could come and go unnoticed. He could get deliveries and ship his tainted water without anyone ever knowing what he was doing."

"Aren't you forgetting something?"

"Like what?"

"There's nothing here!"

"Humor me," I said. "Walk the lot with me."

We climbed out of the Taurus and checked the entire perimeter. It was clean. I even got Rico to help me shove the crappy dumpster across the ground to see if there was a secret door hidden beneath it. No dice.

"It has to be here!" I stomped my foot. "This whole underground plant theory screams Toussaint."

The image of Harry looking over the bar popped into my brain. He had been so insistent that I pay attention. He'd made this exaggerated effort, craning his neck, to look over. To look over...what?

What the hell am I supposed to look over, Harry?

I gazed across Hopple Street and noticed a crumbling concrete railing that bordered a ravine about twenty feet beyond the berm.

"C'mon," I said, pulling Rico across the road.

When we reached the railing, I looked down and saw a concrete abutment in the hillside. In its center was a rusted, iron gate.

I smacked Rico's arm. "That's a subway station, baby!"

"Look," he said, pointing to a tall oak across from the gate, with a trail cam strapped to its trunk.

"We've got to get in there. Ferris might—"

"There could be an army in there for all we know. Horton's going to want proof before he sends in the troops."

"Proof? Like a trail cam watching the entrance of an abandoned tunnel? Everything about this fits and you know it!"

"Hold on." Rico trotted to the end of the railing and scrambled down into the ravine. The slope was steep, but a copse of young trees provided him with handholds along the way.

I yelled over the railing, "What the hell are you doing?"

"Getting Horton some proof." He grabbed a tree with one hand, then reached down with the other, and snagged what appeared to be a piece of trash. When he climbed out of the ravine, he wiped mud from it, and handed it to me with a grin. "This oughta do it."

He'd found a crumpled Crescent City Spring Water bottle.

I pulled out my phone and made two calls. The first was to Director Horton, advising him that we'd located Toussaint's lab in an underground tunnel, but that we had no idea how many bogeys, including deadheads, were onsite. Horton scheduled a STAT meeting for four o'clock and agreed to call in the Hostage Rescue and Epidemiology teams.

My second call was to Dr Christian, asking him to report at 1600 hours to the FBI's Kenwood office in Cincinnati. The raid on Toussaint's laboratory was imminent. All systems go.

Anticipation, fear, joy and dread swirled through me at the same time. I'd been in this situation before. I'd had Toussaint dead to rights too many times, yet somehow, he always managed to get away. And every time we tangled, I paid a price. But not anymore.

It had to end here, and it had to end now.

45

SOUL SEARCHING AND GRIT

I asked Rico to drop me at home because there were a few things I needed to take care of before the meeting. That was true. But there were also things I wanted to do. Things I over-looked on most days. On that particular day, those things weighed on me. We take for granted that there will always be a tomorrow. What a load of shit. I'm never more aware of that lie than when I'm about to face Toussaint.

The first thing on my agenda was a long, welcomed nap. I'd need all the energy I could muster. Next, I took Headbutt outside and threw his ball so he could watch me fetch it. He seemed to get a kick out of that. I gave him extra scritches and a handful of chicken-flavored dog treats—the ones we all fought over. He waddled to his favorite vent, spent and happy, and closed his eyes.

Kulu fluttered onto my shoulder and nuzzled my neck, waiting for her share of the treats. I scritched behind her ears, then kissed her beak, and told her she was good girl, for a smart-mouthed pterodactyl. She cuddled closer and purred like a cat.

Baby Hyrum, perched on my opposite hand, fluttered like a drunken feather-duster and screeched, "Oy vey," in my ear.

I gave him the last of the treats, thinking that some things never change.

Nonnie, reading spreadsheets at the kitchen table, peered at me over the top of her wire-rims. "Whys you at home this hour?"

"Just taking some time."

To get my affairs in order.

"Nonnie," I said, gazing out the kitchen window. "You've done a lot for me and for ACME and Rico and Ferris. I never say it, so thank you."

"Wassa matter? You sick?"

"No."

"Am I sick?"

Why is she making this so hard? "No! Just...thank you."

Her reflection in the window turned and stared at me in silence. God, this was going to be so hard.

"Nonnie, if something ever happens to me, will you take care of Vinny and the critters?"

"Why you ask su—"

"I'll leave you the house."

"I have house."

I heard the Taurus pull into the driveway. "Then give it to Vinny."

"Miss Allie—"

"I can't do this right now."

I darted down the hallway to my bedroom, grabbed the gris-gris bag I made for Ferris, then loaded my jacket pockets with extra mags and a few magickal provisions that would come in handy once I found Ferris.

Nonnie leaned against my doorway, fighting back tears. "You come home tonight, Miss Allie. You hears me? You come home."

I pushed past her. "Promise me you'll take care of Vinny and Headbutt and the birds. Promise me!"

"I always do," she murmured, clasping her hand to her heart.

I wrapped her in what I intended to be a quick hug. It lasted longer.

"I love you, too," I whispered, then turned and ran to the Taurus, wondering if she'd heard me.

RICO and I stepped into the packed conference room. Dr. Christian had arrived on schedule and was already seated to the right of Horton. The doctor smiled broadly and rounded the table to shake my hand. As many times as we'd spoken, we'd never met in person.

"Let's get started," Dickhead said, leaning into his table mic. "Although most of you know each other, for the sake of this operation, we have two additional members: Captain Jason Ressick, the leader of the HRT team, and Doctor Ingmar Christian of the European Center for Disease Prevention and Control. Doctor Christian is the world's foremost authority on the study of the Z-virus. By way of introduction, gentlemen, the established members of our task-force, from left to right, are: Agent Doctor Barbara McMillen, our profiler. Agent Kelvin Thomas, our cyber-terror specialist. Agent Doctor Eli Stanton, our bio-terrorism specialist. Detective Rico De Palma, CPD's Paranormal Crimes Unit Liaison. And Allie Nighthawk, our... corpse-whispering zombie hunter."

Damn, he made that sound cheap.

"Captain Ressick and his men will lead the breach into the tunnel. Captain, I believe you may have some recon data on our attack site already?"

"That's correct, sir." Ressick reminded me of a young, buzz-cut Arnold Schwarzenegger. "We flew an arial drone over the location of the tunnel and tried some thermal imaging, to get an estimate on the number of bogeys. We came up empty, which suggests that either the tunnel itself runs too deep, or Le Clerc may have lined it with mylar. We located and tagged three trail cams for destruction at the start of the breach."

Dickhead frowned. "Any other options for intel?"

"No, sir. We're going to have to go in blind."

The hair on the back of my neck stood up.

Eli Stanton raised his hand. "I recommend the breach team wear CM-7M masks. You have no idea what he's got in that lab."

"Way ahead of you," Ressick said. "I'd breach with a fifteen-man team, with backup in the wings, in case resistance is greater than anticipated. We use a flash bang, plow the road, then let the bio-team do its thing."

Horton nodded. "That's where Dr. Christian comes in. What's your plan, doc?"

"Agent Stanton and I will isolate the various known viral strains and search for any as yet unidentified synthetic variants. It's also conceivable that Le Clerc might have created an antidote."

Horton steepled his fingers under his chin. "Nighthawk, is there any evidence that LeClerc is being backed by the mob? That could play into the amount of resistance we find in the tunnels."

"Speculative evidence only," I said. "There are two nearby properties on Hopple that were recently purchased by a known mob-affiliate. It's possible the tunnels and the basements could connect and provide transportation or warehousing of some kind. Le Clerc has partnered with the mob before and there's no reason he wouldn't this time. You may already know this," I said, turning my attention to Captain Ressick. "With biters it's head shots only. Center mass won't get the job done."

Ressick grinned. "We know the drill."

Dickhead turned to Babs. "Agent McMillen, you will be the senior agent on this mission. Agent Thomas, I need you to intercept all electronic site transmissions, both incoming and outgoing. Starting now."

"On it, sir." Thomas scribbled notes in his portfolio. "What's go-time?"

Dickhead looked at his watch. "It's five now. By the time you gear up and coordinate onsite, it will be six and dark. So, six it is. Keep your eyes out for Agent Ferris. We don't want any friendly fire incidents. Any questions?"

Not a single hand raised. We knew our mission. We knew the risks. And we were going in anyway. The only unknown was which of us would live and which would die.

46

THE MYTH OF ROCK BOTTOM

A t 1800 hours, a drone took out the trail-cams surrounding the tunnel. And at 1801, the raid began.

Ressick and his team advanced through the dark, wearing bio-masks integrated with Bluetooth and night vision. Rico and I were right beside them. The headgear was hot, heavy and uncomfortable, but necessary. It would have been easier to approach the tunnel from the ground beside I-75 North, but at that hour, we'd have drawn too much attention.

"How you hanging?" Ressick murmured, as we scrambled down the ravine.

"I'm fine," I said, licking sweat off my lips. "You realize Toussaint knows we're here?"

"I've done this before, Nighthawk."

"So have I."

Ressick smashed his index finger on the mouthpiece of his mask—the universal shut the hell up sign.

Copy that.

When we reached the mouth of the tunnel, Ressick motioned for Rico and me to hold. Our participation in the raid was contingent on letting the HRT team advance first. We would follow on their heels.

Ressick chucked a flashbang through the iron bars of the gate. An earsplitting roar followed, bringing me to my knees. Smoke billowed through the tunnel, providing cover for Ressick, as he set the charge and blew the gate.

The team breached the channel in single file, splashing through stagnant water puddled on the floor. A flurry of unseen claws skittered across the concrete. Our night vision goggles painted the smoke-filled tunnel an eerie green hue. The air smelled musty and dank. A century's worth of graffiti coated the walls. Forgotten and neglected, the tunnel made the perfect camouflage for Toussaint's laboratory.

Fifty yards later, we were still walking. The tunnel widened into what appeared to be a warehouse. We were surrounded by multiple rows of steel shelving, twenty-feet-tall, that held double-stacked pallets of Crescent City Water. Forklifts, work-benches and safety equipment randomly dotted the aisles.

This tunnel was massive in comparison to the others in the city. Clearly, it had been enlarged. Bright yellow traffic lanes marked the floor. Iron handrails had been bolted to the walls.

How long has Toussaint been planning this? I wondered. *And where are all his people?*

The hair on the back of my neck stood up.

Shouts, chatter and static flooded my Bluetooth. Hisses and groans bled through. The odor of decomp followed. Shadows of biters danced in my peripheral vision.

"Condition one," I yelled, bringing Hawk to bear. "Remember, head shots only."

The team plowed through the tunnel, taking out the dead-heads, one by one. Ressick began systematically opening the doors that lined the walls of the tunnel and clearing the spaces behind them.

My gut told me Ferris was in one of those rooms. I snapped

in a fresh mag, grabbed Rico and sprinted toward the front of the team.

Ressick tried a door that wouldn't budge. He shot the lock, then reared back and kicked it open. Rico and I pushed our way to his shoulder and peered through the doorway. The ten-by-twelve room was empty, except for Ferris, zip-tied to a chair in the center of the floor.

"Keep going," I yelled. "Find Toussaint and get Dr. Christian to the lab. I've got this."

The glare in Ressick's eye told me we wouldn't escape a butt-reaming later about having disobeyed his orders, but at that moment, he had bigger fish to fry. He and his team moved deeper into the tunnel. Rico slammed the door shut behind us, then leaned against it.

"Ferris!" I bolted to his chair and knelt beside him. "Are you hurt?"

He didn't answer, so I pinched his hand hard. Still nothing.

He was non-responsive, his eyes half-closed. I checked his pulse and breathed a sigh of relief. Good steady beat, normal respirations, no needle tracks or bite wounds that I could find. Based on the video of him during the attack at my house, and the way he looked there in the tunnel, he hadn't been infected. But his trance-like state and inability to communicate were clear signs that he was under Toussaint's control.

"Rico, hold that door."

I grabbed a baggie of salt from my jacket pocket and poured it in a circle around Ferris's chair, forming a protective barrier against evil and its minions. Next, I pulled out a small bottle of holy water, a black taper, a Bic lighter, a page from my Vodoun Rites book and the gris-gris bag I'd made.

Rico's jaw dropped. "How much shit did you bring?"

"Only what I need."

The gunfire that had been raging only moments before had

faded to a few shots here, and a few shots there, until finally, there was silence. The horde had been neutralized.

I poured the holy water in a line from Ferris toward the door, signifying the path toward the power that bound him. Then I lit the candle. "Toussaint Le Clerc, through the power of Damballah Wedo, I bind you from harming Sean Ferris. May this flame repel your evil and provide him with protection."

I placed the gris-gris bag around his neck. "I charge the talisman within this bag to serve as protection to Sean Ferris, for I, Aliyah Marie Nighthawk, am servant to the Divine Damballah Wedo. So be it!"

Ferris blinked, then blinked again. His gazed traveled slowly across the room until it came to rest on me. A smile crept across his face. "Allie, what—where the hell are we?"

The rituals had worked!

Ferris struggled against his zip ties, trying to reach out to me.

"Rico, would you cut Ferris loose, please." I held Ferris's face in my hands. "I'm sorry it took so long to find you."

Ferris chattered while Rico cut his ties. "I got called in to work the environmental sweep at Messmer's house. I didn't tell you, because I was still angry about our fight. But I changed my mind and stopped by the race on my way to the sweep, because I realized I was being an ass. Toussaint's men drugged me, shoved me in a car and..." His voice trailed off.

After Rico snipped the last of the ties, Ferris rose slowly from his chair, wrapped me in his arms and kissed me. The door creaked inward so quietly I almost missed it. Ferris and I broke from the kiss, opened our eyes and turned toward the door in unison. A red laser dot was centered on the back of Rico's head.

Ferris threw me aside and dove for Rico.

A single shot pierced the air.

All three of us hit the floor.

The gunfire fire stopped as quickly as it had started. Rico scrambled on all fours back to the door, slammed it shut and blocked it.

"Thanks, buddy." Rico huffed, trying to catch his breath. "That was close. You okay, Nighthawk?"

"Yeah. How 'bout you, Ferris?"

A heavy stillness hung in the air.

I spun to find Ferris lying a puddle of his own blood. Half his skull was missing.

An unbearable ache, the sheer agony of loss, burned in my heart. Tears welled in my eyes, and slipped down my cheeks—tears I couldn't afford. Because there's no crying in corpse whispering, and Toussaint Le Clerc was still on the loose. I was absolutely certain, in that moment, that my world had hit rock bottom.

I couldn't have been more wrong.

RESSICK and his team returned within moments. After taking a quick look at Ferris, Ressick pulled Rico and me out into the main channel of the tunnel and asked us to provide as much detail as we could on the shooting. There wasn't much to share.

The team swept the tunnel twice, ensuring all the dead-heads had been decommissioned, and that Ferris's shooter had either died from our return fire or had vacated. The only bodies found were those of biters. The shooter was long gone.

Ressick declared the tunnel secure.

"No, it's not," I said, shaking my head. "Toussaint's still here."

Ressick put his hands on his hips and measured his words. "Look, I'm sorry about Ferris. Once the bio-team's finished, we'll take him topside. But we turned this place inside out, twice. It's clean."

"You're wrong." I continued to argue with him, until he tuned me out and walked away.

A contingent of HRT officers escorted Dr. Christian and Agent Stanton to the laboratory, while Ressick and the others settled in, waiting for the bio-team to complete its investigation.

Rico returned with me to Ferris's side for a moment, while I processed his death—at least enough to pull myself together to do what needed to be done.

As far as I was concerned, Ressick could sweep that tunnel a thousand times. Toussaint was there. I felt him in the air, a whir in my ear, a cool rush that touched my skin. He'd shot Ferris. I knew that in my heart. I wanted to stay in that room, holding Ferris's hand forever, but the longer I lingered, the more time that bastard had to escape.

Mourning would have to wait.

I laid Ferris's hand across his chest, then pulled off my mask and swiped my sleeve across my face. Rico squatted down and squeezed Ferris's shoulder, then laid his coat over the top of Ferris's corpse. We walked out of the room together and closed the door behind us.

"Where are you going?" Ressick called, as Rico and I trudged deeper into the tunnel.

"To find Le Clerc," I hollered back. "Feel free to join us."

I knew better than that. Ressick would never second-guess himself.

Rico and I traversed the channel on our own, searching for clues the team might have missed. We moved forward to the lab, where the doctors were deep in their investigation. With white-tiled walls, pharmaceutical-grade refrigerators and stainless-steel sinks, this could have been any lab in the world. But a rack of pressure positive suits with HEPA-filtered hoods, elastic cuffs and sleeve protectors revealed the hazardous nature of the research taking place within its walls.

The doctors glanced up briefly, then carried on, without

acknowledging our presence. Their research was as important as finding Toussaint, so after Rico and I performed our search and found nothing, we left them to their work and finished walking the rest of the tunnel. Not thirty yards later, the modified channel gradually tapered to its original size.

A low, rhythmic *whoop, whoop, whoop* filled the air. Rico and I stared in wonder at a huge industrial ventilation fan inset at the end of the tunnel.

"Excuse, me," Dr. Christian said, trotting toward us. "We're working with some particularly nasty viruses in the lab, Allie. For your own safety, please put your mask on."

I'd forgotten that I'd taken it off. When I slipped it back over my head, the doctor pointed toward the fan and smiled. "It's magnificent, is it not? At times like this, when the ambient air quality is satisfactory, it runs on low, providing a constant flow. But in the event of accidental contamination, with a flip of this switch, the blades rotate faster and increase the air flow. Fans like this have saved many a scientist's life. You'll excuse me, won't you? I must get back to work. Stay safe, my friends."

Rico chuckled while Christian jogged back to the lab. "Everything you ever wanted to know about fans but were afraid to ask."

Searching every nook and every cranny, every closet and every supply room, from one end to the other had taken time. But the bio-team was still working, so we trekked back to the warehouse and started over again.

"Look at this." Rico lifted a piece of paper from the top of a desk and handed it to me. "It's a purchase order for —"

Gunshots rang out, followed quickly by more. Muzzle flash peppered the tunnel. *Are those our guns?* I wondered.

My Bluetooth crackled. "Bogeys! Due north. Weaponized. The bogeys are weaponized."

"Biters don't use weapons," I said. "It's got to be Toussaint's mob buddies."

Rico grabbed my arm. "They're headed north. That's the lab!"

We slipped in fresh mags and sprinted back to the laboratory. Chatter flooded the Bluetooth. Shouts and words bled together in jumble of noise.

Suddenly my name burst through. "Nighthawk! Christian is down! Repeat! Dr. Christian is down!"

47

HEROES NEVER DIE

R essick's men held the lab from the doorway and provided us with cover fire. I tucked and rolled through the opening, then scrambled out of the line of fire, coming face to face with Eli Stanton. He'd had been shot in the leg and was losing a lot of blood. One the team members pressed a cotton pad into the wound to staunch the bleeding. Stanton thrashed and moaned.

Dr. Christian's body lay where it fell, directly in the line of fire. He'd been hit center mass with what might have been a hollow point, judging by the damage to his chest cavity.

Guilt consumed me. I should have made Ressick listen, made him understand. He'd never dealt with Toussaint before. But I had. And I'd known better than to believe that bastard would run away from the fight. Ours would be a battle to the death—his or mine. I wasn't sure that made a difference to Toussaint anymore.

Stanton reached out to me. "Nighthawk, we finished identifying and cataloging all the specimens. We were packing them for transport, when Christian made one more sweep and came across a bottle of the antidote tucked beneath the false bottom of a drawer. He told me to keep packing while he analyzed it under the scope. I was nearly finished, when he said that he'd isolated it—the formula for the antidote. That's when the gunfire broke out and we both got hit."

"An antidote for Toussaint's synthetic virus or for the organic virus?"

"I don't know. We were attacked before he could say."

"Where's the antidote now?"

Stanton gulped. "After the shooting, Le Clerc showed up and ripped the vial from Christian's hand. He said to tell you he'll never stop."

Damn it to hell and back.

I burned a hole through Ressick for having doubted me, then turned back to Stanton. "Did he write down the formula? Where are his notes?"

"He didn't have time. It was all...all in his...head." His voice trailed off, and he began to cry.

I felt numb.

Within a matter of moments, we had found and lost the antidote to carovescitis—the cure that could end the plague of the undead—the weapon that could be the undoing of Toussaint. This antidote, or its formula, was of unparalleled importance to the scientific community. I couldn't let it slip away. But there was only one way to obtain that formula now. I'd have to raise Dr. Christian.

That was a dark and ugly fact—one that posed a dilemma: Should I raise Dr. Christian first, which would require peace and quiet after the firing stopped? Or pursue Toussaint now, while he was here in striking distance, and then raise the doctor?

Toussaint knew that my first instinct would be to go after him. But I knew how much he craved that chase. I asked myself: *What if I confront him now and die in the process?* The cure would be lost. The responsible thing to do was raise Dr. Christian first, before facing down Toussaint one last time.

ONCE THE HRT team drove Toussaint's thugs from the tunnel and took the battle outside, the quiet I needed for a raising returned. Ressick ran back in to check on Stanton, called him a chopper, and returned to the fray. I didn't have much time. I'd need Stanton's help to make this happen.

I grabbed his notepad and pen from the counter and handed them to him. "I have no idea how to write a formula or even what to ask. Get ready to write."

Then I knelt beside Dr. Christian and centered myself, placing my hands over his chest. When the familiar tingle blazed in my palms, I whispered, "Ingmar Christian, in the name of God, I command you to rise."

Tendrils of light-infused energy arced from my body into his. He pitched off the floor, flailing his limbs and clenching his teeth. He was resisting and needed another push.

"Awaken, Ingmar."

His body settled quietly on the floor. He batted his eyes a few times, then slowly opened them. He seemed calm, but puzzled. The dead always looked confused when I raised them.

Stanton, wide-eyed and slack jawed, stared at me in disbelief.

"Dr. Christian, this is Allie Nighthawk. You remember me, right?"

He nodded but didn't answer.

"Can you talk to me? Maybe tell me who that is across the room?" I pointed to Stanton.

"Eli. Stanton."

"That's great Dr. Christian."

His eyes grew large. "Am. I. Dead?"

"Yes, sir," I said, feeling my throat tighten.

Confusion and fear are the two most common responses to raising. It's difficult to watch and even harder to cause.

"Do you remember what you were doing when you were shot?"

"Found. Antidote. Formula. Important."

"Yes, it is. Do you think you could tell Dr. Stanton that formula?"

"I. will. tell."

I nodded to Stanton who raised his pen. "I'm ready when you are, Dr. Christian."

Stanton scribbled furiously and asked for clarification on a few points. Christian complied, slowly and carefully, stressing that the antidote formula he was relaying was for the synthetic virus. When they were finished, Stanton gave me a nod.

I took the dead man's hand and held it tight. "The information you've given us is invaluable, Dr. Christian. You'll be remembered as a hero. Thank you, sir. Close your eyes and rest now."

The chopper arrived within minutes. I thanked Stanton for his help as the medevac team carried him away. He handed me the formula with a weary smile. "Maybe you should hang on to this."

I tucked the formula back into his hand and lay it on his chest. "With what I've got coming up, Doc, the formula is safer with you."

After Stanton and the medevac team disappeared down the tunnel and I heard the chopper fly away, I placed my Ka-Bar against Dr. Christian's brain stem and pictured the face of every person I'd known who had been tortured or killed by Toussaint. My father, Rico, Jade, Ferris, a couple of CPD officers, Dr. Latka, and now, Dr. Christian.

"I'm so sorry," I whispered, knowing that I was the common thread to their suffering.

With a quick turn of the blade, I laid Ingmar Christian to rest. *God have mercy on him*, I prayed. *And God have mercy on me.*

It was time to kill Toussaint.

Ressick and a handful of men returned from the battle outside. He said the skirmish was over and they'd kicked ass.

He and his men wanted to hunt Toussaint, but I told him Le Clerc was mine. He didn't take that kindly.

"Nobody tells me to stand down."

"I'm not. I'm asking you to leave him to me. I owe this to Ferris."

"And what if he kills your ass?"

I laughed in spite of myself. "Then, by all means, have at him."

48

ONLY THE DEAD HAVE SEEN THE END OF WAR

— PLATO

I left the lab and entered the tunnel feeling a charge in the air. Toussaint was close, so close I could smell him. My breaths were deep; my focus, sharp. Rico was at my six, a few yards back. I turned and motioned him forward. He flashed me a thumbs up.

The hunt was on.

We fanned out, twenty-feet apart, our guns at high ready, and pushed deeper into the tunnel. I hugged the right wall; Rico, the left. We advanced quickly, but quietly.

My senses heightened. Darkness grew darker. Sound intensified. The patter of our footsteps echoed off the tile walls and surrounded us.

Within moments, the fading sounds of Ressick's team had been replaced by an almost cosmic nothingness.

My skin began to crawl.

A metallic *click* broke dead ahead, followed closely by another. Angry hissing erupted. Two small cylinders rolled out from the darkness and bounced across the concrete floor, before coming to rest in the center of my flashlight beam.

Orange smoke exploded through the air.

Thanks to Dr. Christian, I'd put my mask back on. Tearing and coughing wouldn't be an issue, but visibility, which had been challenging before, would be worse.

I closed my eyes, took a long, slow breath, then used my other senses to identify what lurked inside the swirling smoke.

The air felt cool and moist against my skin. A subtle hint of decay wafted by. The quiet hum of a low moan rose from Rico's direction. I snapped my eyes open in time to catch a fleeting glimpse of rotten flesh, slipping in and out of the churning fog.

Rico fired once. Twice. The flash from his Glock marked his position.

I stared into the smoke, waiting. Waiting for them to attack me. But nothing came. Not a single biter. *Why?*

A flurry of shadows pushed through the orange haze toward Rico. Too many bogeys for him to handle. He opened fire. I joined in, keeping the tunnel wall at my back. Every couple of rounds, I darted my eyes front and center, wondering when the horde would come for me.

Focus, Little Allie shouted. *Rico needs you.*

I swung to my left, leveled Hawk at the pack and let him fly until he ran out of ammo.

I ejected the empty mag, jammed my hand into my pocket, and wrapped my fingers around a new magazine. Pain seared my right bicep as I pulled my hand from my pocket.

A hot breath whirred in my ear. "You should have eaten the popsicle."

I leaped away, then spun to find Blake Devlin, wielding a fillet knife. The skank had sliced through my jacket sleeve. Warm, sticky blood trickled down my right arm and over my hand. Red droplets dripped from my fingertips, painting small, random patterns on the ground.

Damn it. Enough was enough.

"That was a leather jacket, you bitch."

"A bit boxy for my taste. Suits you well enough."

I nodded at the knife in her hand. "Got to admire a woman who does her own wet work."

"Only the best for you, Nighthawk." Devlin circled me, lunging here and there, testing my reflexes.

I matched her stride for stride, never taking my eyes from hers.

Rico sent another hail of bullets into his horde. Devlin flinched, instinctively whirling toward the gunfire.

I swung Hawk low across my body and coaxed the mag into place with a grunt. I raised him shoulder high and fired.

She spun sideways. The bullet grazed her flank.

In the blink of an eye, she raised her knee and snap-kicked Hawk from my hand. He went airborne, landing behind me with a clatter, and skittered out of sight.

Devlin glanced at her wound and forced a smile. "Wasn't expecting that."

She stepped closer, brandishing the knife slowly from side to side like a katana. "I'm disappointed. You aren't nearly as tough as Toussaint said you were."

I pulled my seven-inch Ka-Bar. "Let's see what you got, bitch."

She lunged. I sidestepped and spun full circle, swinging my blade. It sliced the back of her shoulder. Nothing deep, but the contact gave me a moment to breathe.

The blood that had been trickling down my arm was starting to flow. She'd gotten me good. *This was going to be like chum for biters.*

Devlin grunted and rubbed her shoulder. Then she gave me a look that had crazy bitch written all over it, lowered her head, and charged me like a bull.

I backpedaled, slipping in a puddle of my own blood and landed flat on my back.

Devlin raised her knife high over her head as she launched herself at me. She had the angle. She'd skewer me before I could slip my knife between her ribs.

I drove my foot into her gut and hurled her over my head.

Devlin tumbled ass-over-teakettle, before landing face-down a few yards behind me. She struggled to her feet, shook herself off, then came at me again.

I saw my gun out of the corner of my eye, less than three feet away. I rolled to my stomach, grabbed it, then whirled onto my back and squeezed the trigger.

Nailed her right between the eyes. Popsicle Bitch didn't have as much game as she thought. Hallelujah. One round was enough.

I collapsed, sucking air like a Hoover. Even corpse whisperers can run out of energy—not to mention blood.

I suddenly realized Rico was no longer shooting. I raised my head a few inches and saw him running my way. No biters on his ass, thank God.

Rico grimaced at the river of blood that surrounded me. "Let's take a look at that arm."

"That's not all mine," I said, struggling to sit upright.

"So I see."

"Take this mask off me, will you? It's freaking hot in here."

He slipped the mask over my head and peeled off my jacket. The laceration was deep, but nothing was spurting. Devlin had laid open the entire width of my upper arm, but she'd missed the artery.

Stars burst before my eyes as Rico stripped off his belt and fastened a tourniquet just below my shoulder.

"Good as new," I gasped, climbing to my feet. A wave of wooziness washed over me, but I didn't tell Rico. No need to worry him. Now that the blood flow was staunched, I figured the feeling would pass. And it did, for a while.

We continued down the tunnel, guns at the ready.

Several yards in, my mind began to drift. I tried to refocus, but something or someone was blocking me.

A soft chuckle filled my ears. *Another toady, I see. You have too many men in your life, Ti Kras Zwazo.*

I spun around, almost falling on my face.

"You okay, Nighthawk?" Rico asked.

"Not really."

Where is Mama this time, eh? Too old and frail to help? Such a shame.

I did a slow 360, eyeing every nook and cranny. "Show yourself, you fucking weasel! Get out of my head and fight like a man."

"As you wish." Toussaint materialized behind us, holding a 9mm aimed at Rico's head.

"No!" I rolled to my right for a clean shot, but Toussaint lunged.

He let his gun-hand drop and squeezed the trigger, sending a slug into Rico's leg. Rico crumpled to the floor, but didn't cry out.

I centered Hawk between Toussaint's eyes. "You're a better shot than that. You missed on purpose."

"So I did." The bastard instantly disappeared, but his words still carried in the air. "I've already taken one of your men. I waited until you were here to finish him off, so you could watch."

"You freaking coward!"

"Might want to tighten that belt around your arm, Little Bird. You're bleeding harder now."

Toussaint's voice faded as Ressick and his men charged back up the tunnel. Bunch of assholes. They never should have left us in the first place.

I fixed Ressick in a stony glare. "Where the hell have you been? We could have used your guns when the rotters attacked."

"We were already topside and had to work our way back down. Where's Toussaint?"

"He's around," I said, waving Ressick off with my gun. "Rico's wounded. Take him with you when you leave."

"I'm not going anywhere," Rico snapped.

"Neither one of you is in any shape to finish this."

"We had a deal." I growled. "Toussaint's mine."

Ressick glared at me, but ordered his team to stand down. He propped Rico up against a tow motor parked along the wall, and wrapped a makeshift tourniquet around his leg to stop the bleeding. "If this goes south, Nighthawk, I'll shoot you myself."

It wasn't a threat. It was a promise. Hell, if this went south, I'd already be dead.

As Ressick's team withdrew, Toussaint's disembodied voice returned. "Awfully brave of you. Now that your friends are gone, what say we put the firearms aside and fight *mano a mano*. Use of powers acceptable, of course."

"Let's do this."

"Don't!" Rico yelled. "Don't let him goad you, Allie."

Toussaint snickered. "Oh, you too, little man. No guns today."

Rico's Glock flew out of his hands, turned red hot in midair, and smelted into a heap on the tunnel floor.

I raised my 9mm but had no idea where to shoot. Hawk instantly sailed from my hand and joined Rico's in a twisted mass on the floor.

"Your back-up pieces as well," Toussaint added. "Or you'll share the same messy fate."

We tossed out our guns and watched them dissolve before our eyes.

"So, tell me," I said, raising my hands in mock surrender. "How'd you do it? How did you come back to life at Congo Square after I shot you? Ferris checked your pulse and said you were dead."

Toussaint reappeared, wearing a sly smile. "Smoke and mirrors, my love. A bit of yogic breathing. Lucky for me, your man was in hurry to leave and get you to the hospital."

Ferris had been telling the truth. How could I have doubted him?

Toussaint reached toward the gris-gris bag that hung around my neck and waggled his fingers. Nothing happened. He tried again and scowled.

"Look at that." I grinned. "Guess I'm stronger than I used to be."

Toussaint summoned his power and pushed me with his mind.

My knees strained, but didn't buckle.

A bead of sweat trickled down his forehead. Not used to having to work so hard, he balled his fist, then let it fly, smashing my nose.

Fireworks exploded behind my eyes and tears flooded my cheeks.

Stay Focused.

I circled to his left, swiping away the tears. "Why'd you kill him?"

"Which him, dear." Toussaint paced me to his right. "Be specific."

"Ferris. You didn't have to kill him."

"Of course, I did. You loved him."

I charged, plunging my good fist into his diaphragm. "That's for Ferris."

He doubled over, gasping for air.

"And this is for me," I said, driving my boot into his kidney.

Toussaint fell to the floor and curled into a ball with a moan. But he sucked in a breath and staggered back to his feet with a roar.

His eyes turned black as he stretched out his right hand and thrust his palm at me.

My legs wobbled, but held.

He thrust at me a second time, and my knees gave way.

I stumbled back, but recovered, and planted my feet shoulder width apart.

He pushed again. My footing held. Blood dripped from his nose.

He was weakening. But so was I.

Fight smarter, not harder, Little Allie scolded.

I moved to his left. He followed suit and lashed out, kicking my feet out from under me.

I slammed on to my back, bashing my head against the concrete floor. Air whooshed from my lungs.

Thoughts and images ricocheted through my brain like shrapnel. Nausea bubbled in my gut. Breathless, muddled and in pain. I felt so...helpless. So alone.

Just like New Orleans, I thought. *He's too damn strong.*

"Enough!" Mama's voice flooded my mind. "*Did you not hear me, child? You have all that you need. Your body is wounded, but your powers are strong. Use them!*"

Toussaint lunged at me. I rolled to my good side, and for the second time, pummeled his kidney with a side kick.

He howled and grabbed at his flank, gulping air.

I scrambled to my feet, woozy, then stumbled to the wall, grabbing the metal railing for support.

Now, more than ever, I needed to center myself—to be aware of my surroundings and to 'see' three steps ahead. I cleared my mind and scanned the tunnel, searching for my next move. The move that would end Toussaint.

Clarity came, and with it, my answer.

I stepped left, away from the wall, and inched closer to Toussaint. He struggled to stand upright and catch his breath.

That was a good sign. He wasn't ready to fight again—yet. But he would be, soon.

He shuffled to his right, maintaining our distance.

Just a bit more, I thought, staring into his eyes. I made a quick feint left; he staggered right.

For the first time that day, I felt hope. Toussaint was exactly where I wanted him.

I darted my eyes toward the tunnel wall and stared at it, willing a tiny switch to move. Nothing happened. I pushed harder. Capillaries began to break. The coppery taste of blood filled my mouth. The switch refused to budge.

Mama's words replayed in my mind. I'd followed her advice. I'd used my powers. This was my play—the only play that would give me a shot at walking out of here alive.

Either the switch would move or it wouldn't.

Fuck it. I pushed again.

The switch flipped—quietly and inconspicuously. But it flipped.

The industrial fan behind Toussaint, that had been cycling at a slow, constant speed, began to churn. The *whoop, whoop, whoop* of its blades grew louder with each revolution.

Toussaint glanced over his shoulder at the fan, then turned back with a laugh. "Nicely played. But we both know anything you can do, I can do better."

He darted his eyes around the tunnel, as if he were probing, seeking.

He's searching for the switch, I thought, moving to my left to block his line of sight.

He grimaced and spat blood on the floor. "Where's the switch, Little Bird?"

I sucked in a breath as he burst into my head, scouring my thoughts. *Mind Scavenger.* A game we'd played countless times when we were kids.

I flooded my brain with images of Mama's instruction manuals. Page upon page of spells and psalms and rootwork. Memories of my mother and father and Harry. Anything but the location of that switch.

The fan churned faster. Airflow increased, drawing everything in the tunnel toward the whirling blades.

I pressed against the wall, crying out in pain as I wrapped my arms through the railing to keep from being sucked into the blades. I glanced back at Rico. He was wedged beneath the tow motor he'd been leaning against, clinging to one of its forks.

"You bitch!" Toussaint screamed, whirling in circles, combing the tunnel for the switch. He stopped suddenly and fixed the fan rotor in an unrelenting stare.

Shit, since he couldn't find the switch, he was going to try to kill the motor.

The huge fan blades shimmied, screeched and groaned as he willed them to stop. But his target was too large. The strain was too much.

Blood burst from his nose and eyes. His hold weakened. The fan started spinning faster.

Toussaint's feet slid backward, bringing him closer to the blades. He struggled against the airflow, trudging forward one step, then sliding back two.

Once more, he fought against the air current, leaning against the pressure to take another step forward. But the suction was too strong. He lifted off the floor with an incredulous look in his eyes, screaming as he sailed into the spinning blades, head first.

The gruesome shriek of bone on metal will stay with me forever.

Digging deep, I summoned my power one last time and flipped the fan switch to off. As the blades gradually slowed and spun to a halt, I tried to wrap my head around the fact that the war between us—the war between good and evil—had finally ended.

And I had won.

So many times, I had imagined this moment, wondering if it would it bring me peace. Or righteousness? Or maybe joy?

But I felt none of those things. In that moment, memories of our shared childhood, filled with pain and loss, love and laughter, simply ceased to exist. All that remained was emptiness.

Toussaint, Mama's *bway,* whom she had lovingly called her dark angel, was gone forever.

And I was the reason why.

.

49

AN ANGEL GETS HIS WINGS

Ferris would have appreciated the turn out for his funeral. FBI agents from all over the country came in droves, some I'm sure he'd known, others who simply wanted to honor a fallen comrade.

The church was standing room only.

The front rows were reserved for what little real family Ferris had. Those of us who had loved and worked with him considered ourselves family of another sort. We sat together further back, surrounded by his brethren agents. Nonnie, Rico (still on crutches), Vinny and I slid across our pew to make room for Cap, Babs and Director Horton. Dickhead had never struck me as the emotional type, but that day, he wore his heart on his sleeve.

I don't remember much about the homily, and I shut out all the pious platitudes about God taking those He loves first. My heart couldn't handle them.

The graveside service, with its flag-draped coffin and twenty-one-gun salute, released the tears I'd been holding back. For once, I let them fall without swiping them away. Ferris deserved every single one of those tears.

We filed past the open grave, one by one, and tossed a handful of dirt on his steel-gray coffin as it was lowered. A piece of my heart went with it.

Dickhead left the cemetery quickly, something about having to catch a flight. The rest of us weren't finished honoring Ferris, so we held a wake at The Blue Note.

DALLAS GOT things started by pouring us a round, on the house, and offering his own toast to Ferris. Rico and Babs followed suit. But the words I had for Ferris would stay locked in my heart. There were many rounds and many toasts that followed. Not all of them sad.

Vinny raised his glass. "To Agent Ferris, who threatened to kick my ass daily while we were in New Orleans. And look at me now. I brought in a $180,000 bounty."

"$90,000," I corrected.

"It's not my fault you agreed to split it."

"To Vinny," I said, holding my glass high. "For digging me out of the poor house. Or at least, out of its basement."

That reward money wasn't in my hand yet, and with my arm still in a sling, I'd need a bit more time off work. Thankfully, Dallas offered to float me an interest-free loan until it appeared, so I could fix my roof, pay off my taxes, and buy E&O insurance.

As for Templeman's lawsuit and the Combs Restaurant debacle, I'd do my best to schmooze them. Fuck the Winstels and their stinking vine. They're making a mint off that zombie invasion video they shot in my yard.

"To Vinny," came a shout from the crowd.

I knew that voice. *Damn it.*

"Go away, Red." I snarled at Marlowe's reflection in the mirror over the bar. "I got nothing to say to you."

"Well, I got something to say to you." She sauntered up beside me and cleared her throat. "Sorry about your friend. I heard about it in the news. And congrats on snuffing that bastard, Toussy, or whatever his name was. Anyways, like I said, to Vinny! For making me 90K richer."

I don't care what anyone says. I will never like that broad.

Dallas handed me a daffodil arrangement from behind the bar. "This came for you this morning."

The card read:

Well done, ma chérie. Until we meet again. P.

Daffodils signified a new beginning—a world without Toussaint. But how had Philippe even known about The Blue Note? Perhaps he would tell me one day, over another dinner.

Harry popped in and shot me two-thumbs up, for taking down the most dangerous necromancer on earth and living to tell the tale. I nodded and tipped my Jack to him. He and his mimed clues had helped put an end to that chapter of my life. Maybe now I could move on.

Jade stopped by with her new boy toy. She said her ratings had soared after the raid on the old subway tunnel and thanked me for letting Vinny give her the exclusive on Kleinfeld.

"There's something else," she said, leaning into my ear. "Thank you for...killing Toussaint...and for the medicine that keeps me from turning into, you know, a deadhead. Any chance you can make more when I run out?"

I smiled, thinking about the last batch, the one I'd taken credit for that Mama had made.

"Sure," I said. "Just give me a couple weeks' notice to buy more snake shed."

Oh, why the hell not? I figured. She wouldn't need the medicine much longer. Now that we had the formula, big pharma would start producing the antidote she needed.

I was feeling pretty good about the whole conjuring thing, thanks to Mama's kicking me to the curb and making me fend for myself.

Dallas and Nonnie huddled over their drinks at the end of the bar, laughing and smiling into each other's eyes. If I hadn't known better, I'd have said they were canoodling. They looked cute together, in an age-spotted, wrinkly kind of way.

Why shouldn't my two favorite oldsters hook up? Especially since Nonnie had told me that morning she'd broken up with Walter.

Thank you, God!

Walter, the 180-pound cigar-smoking albatross, had nested in my house like one of those swallows from San Juan Capistrano. Nonnie called him an ungrateful yutz and said she didn't like the way that Beano bird was eyeing Gertie—the chick from the egg in the Amazon box. It had finally hatched on the night of the raid.

Mama-drama geezer-style that left me with yet another mouth to feed.

Rico checked his email while we hung out at the bar, then smiled, and handed me his phone. "Look at this. Doc's autopsy report found no trace of aconite in Kleinfeld's system. But he did find the Z-virus and a small peri-mortem human bite wound, etiology unknown."

"So Kleinfeld wasn't poisoned?" I asked, scanning the email.

"Nope. He died of refractory ventricular arrhythmia, caused by his pre-existing heart failure—likely aggravated by the shock of the biter attack."

"How about that. Ira blasted out of his cardboard box because he'd been infected with the Z-virus the good old-fashioned way. Once the investigation started, I was sure Doc would find aconite."

"Don't beat yourself up. I was right there with you," he said, winking.

Rico, the world's best partner, who had seen me at my best and had tolerated my worst, was always by my side. He was a good man. A man who would give me space and time to grieve. But the look in his eyes told me he would be ready to take our partnership down new roads, if or when I decided the time was right.

Babs sidled up beside us and delivered some news of her own. "I thought you'd like to know that Horton raided the mob-owned properties on Hopple Street. Both buildings had subterranean passages that connected to the tunnel. Toussaint was able to transport people and supplies with complete discretion."

I paused for a sip of my Jack. "That explains how Devlin and the biters accessed the tunnel after Ressick and his team cleared it."

Vinny pushed through the crowd and threw his arm around my good shoulder. "Maybe this isn't the time to ask, boss, but with you killing Toussaint and delivering the antidote for the latest Z-virus, did you just hero us out of a job?"

I wanted to answer yes, but there would always be another greedy necromancer waiting in the wings—another virus, organic or synthetic, that would rear its ugly head. Like it or not, saving mankind from the horde was my destiny.

I threw back my Jack and elbowed him in the ribs. "Relax, kid. Give it a week. Something'll pop up."

Cap and Babs needed to get back to work. So did Rico. He offered me a ride home and I gladly accepted.

I'd had enough emotion for one day, so I said my goodbyes and started for the door. But something made me turn back.

I saw a golden shaft of light appear before Harry. He smiled, blew me a kiss, then walked into the light and disappeared.

Apparently, I was the only person Harry had haunted. Maybe helping me save the world one last time was the price he had to pay to earn his wings.

With Toussaint dead and in his grave, Harry could rest. In fact, we all could rest...at least, until the next time.

THE MYSTIC COUNTY JEZEBEL SOCIETY

Our membership consists of two paranormally-gifted divorcees and a gin-soaked pocket-bitch named Alimony. We opened our own private detective agency in Mystic County, a haven for every supernatural species known to man—and maybe a few that aren't.

Relax, already. We're just a couple of chicks solving mysteries and sipping Mai Tais from hundred-proof incendiary pineapples.

What could possibly go wrong?

Stay tuned for H.R. Boldwood's spinoff series: *The Mystic County Jezebel Society,* featuring Rowan Marlowe (introduced in *Corpse Whisperer Torn*).

ACKNOWLEDGMENTS

I WOULD LIKE TO EXPRESS MY GRATITUDE to the many people who helped bring this book to life:

Christiana Miller, your drive and focus have given *The Corpse Whisperer* series wings. Thanks for believing in me and Allie Nighthawk.

Robert M. Burdick, who reviewed, suggested, and corrected this manuscript—thanks for giving *Corpse Whisperer Torn* copious amounts of your time, your literary expertise, and your devotion.

Ms. Jane Ludlow, CFSP and Adjunct Professor Mortuary Science for sharing her knowledge of embalming and other funerary processes.

Ms. Logan Ashley, lifelong resident of New Orleans, who served as my local flavor and Creole consultant. I couldn't have written this without you!

Officer Scott Burdick who has stepped into his father's shoes as my police/weapons expert. Thank heavens you answer my every question, no matter how many times I have asked it!

Ms. Jenni Roosa Lindgren, multi-year participant in the Flying

Pig Marathon, for sharing the details, ecstasies and agonies of Cincinnati's world-famous marathon.

Kristin Bryant for the great cover designs.

Last, but not least, Chris and Lisa Combs of Combs BBQ Central, in Middletown, Ohio, for being such good sports and kickass zombie hunters.

ABOUT THE AUTHOR

 H.R. BOLDWOOD, author of the *Corpse Whisperer* series, countless short stories, and Imadjinn Award finalist, is a writer of horror and speculative fiction. In another incarnation, Boldwood was a Pushcart Prize nominee and winner of the Thomas More College 2009 Bilbo Award for creative writing.

Boldwood's characters are often disreputable and not to be trusted. They are kicked to the curb at every conceivable opportunity when some poor unsuspecting publisher welcomes them with open arms. No responsibility is taken by this author for the dastardly and sometimes criminal acts committed by this ragtag group of miscreants.

You can send H.R. Boldwood a message at hrboldwood@gmail.com. To learn more about H.R. Boldwood, visit her website at: www.hrboldwood.com.

f facebook.com/hrboldwood
X x.com/BoldwoodH
BB bookbub.com/authors/h-r-boldwood

ALSO BY H.R. BOLDWOOD

www.ingramcontent.com/pod-product-compliance
Lightning Source LLC
Chambersburg PA
CBHW050514110726
47899CB00005B/1453